WILD S...

DELORES FOSSEN

AND

UNFORGETTABLE
BY
CASSIE MILES

MILLS & BOON

First published in Great Britain 2012
by Mills & Boon, an imprint of Harlequin (UK) Limited,
Eton House, 18-24 Paradise Road, Richmond, Surrey TW9 1SR

© Delores Fossen 2010

ISBN: 978 0 263 89501 8

46-0212

Harlequin (UK) policy is to use papers that are natural, renewable and
recyclable products and made from wood grown in sustainable forests. The
logging and manufacturing processes conform to the legal environmental
regulations of the country of origin.

Printed and bound in Spain
by Blackprint CPI, Barcelona

WILD STALLION

BY
DELORES FOSSEN

Imagine a family tree that includes Texas cowboys, Choctaw and Cherokee Indians, a Louisiana pirate and a Scottish rebel who battled side by side with William Wallace. With ancestors like that, it's easy to understand why Texas author and former air force captain **Delores Fossen** feels as if she were genetically predisposed to writing romances. Along the way to fulfilling her DNA destiny, Delores married an air force top gun who just happens to be of Viking descent. With all those romantic bases covered, she doesn't have to look too far for inspiration.

Prologue

"Shhh," Bailey Hodges heard someone say. "If they find you, they'll kill you."

Bailey tried to open her eyes to see who had just spoken that warning, but her eyes didn't cooperate. Neither did the rest of her. Everything felt thick and sludgy.

"Who are you?" Bailey managed to mumble. But someone quickly clamped a hand over her mouth.

"Don't let them hear you," the person whispered. It was a woman. But why had she said that? "If they find you, they'll kill you."

Bailey heard someone else call out her name. Not a woman this time, and the person sounded angry. Or something.

What was going on?

She was in the San Antonio Maternity Hospital. There shouldn't be anyone shouting for her. She shouldn't be in danger.

Bailey forced herself to think. It wasn't easy. She'd just come from surgery where she'd had a C-section because her baby had been breech. The doctor had tried to give her an epidural, but when it hadn't taken effect, she'd been given a general anesthetic instead. It had knocked her out completely.

"My baby!" Bailey tried to say, but the hand stayed clamped over her mouth.

Bailey struggled as much as she could, but her arms and legs wouldn't cooperate.

"Your son is safe," the woman said.

"Son," Bailey mumbled. She had a boy.

"Stay quiet," the woman warned. "They're close to us now."

Bailey didn't know who "they" were, but the man calling out her name was indeed nearby. He sounded right outside the door. Oh, God. Was he really going to try to kill her? If so, she couldn't fight back. But she had to do something to protect her baby.

"I have to leave," the woman said. "It's the only way I can keep your baby safe. Do you understand?"

"No." Bailey didn't understand. "What's happening?"

"Gunmen have taken the entire ward hostage. If I don't get out now, they'll find the baby. They might hurt him to get to you. Hush, or you'll get us all killed."

Bailey shook her head and managed to force her eyes open. She still couldn't see clearly. Everything was swimming in and out of focus, and she could barely make out the woman, or rather, her outline. But Bailey couldn't see her face.

She heard the sound then. Not the man yelling for her. Not the woman. It was a kitten-like cry, and she instinctively knew it belonged to her baby.

"My son," Bailey mumbled.

The woman slid her hand away from Bailey's mouth

and hurried toward the door. She didn't tell Bailey where she was going, but Bailey could see that the woman had something in her arms.

A baby wrapped in a blue blanket.

The woman ducked into the hall and disappeared.

Bailey tried to scream, to tell her to bring back her son. But she remembered the warning.

"Hush, or you'll get us all killed."

That robbed her of what little breath she had, and she felt the tears burn as they slid down her cheeks. She was helpless. Too weak to move. Too drugged to do anything to stop this nightmare.

Bailey had no choice. Her eyelids drifted down, and the darkness took over.

Chapter One

Four Months Later:
The Malone Estate, Copper Creek, Texas

Jackson Malone watched the woman from the surveillance monitor on his desk. She was either the most inept Christmas tree decorator in the state, or else…

Jackson didn't want to go there yet.

By nature, he wasn't a trusting man, and now that he had become a father his distrust was stronger than ever. That probably had something to do with the threat he'd received just that morning.

He glanced at the letter, the warning spelled out in letters cut from magazines.

"Jackson Malone, I won't forgive and forget. Watch your back."

It was the third one he'd received in the past month. No name. No postmark. The others had been placed on his car windshield, but not this one. This particular letter had been left on the sidewalk outside his downtown San Antonio office building. It'd been a blind spot for security cameras, so there was no footage of the person who had left it for the night watchman to find, but Jackson had some ideas. After Christmas, he'd deal with it.

Or maybe sooner.

His attention went back to the surveillance monitor and the inept tree decorator. The leggy brunette was still trying to untangle some Christmas lights, a task she'd been at for the better part of an hour. She was perched on the lower rung of a ladder next to the ten-foot-tall blue spruce. She had a wad of lights in her hands, but her attention was everywhere but on the task she'd been hired to do. Unlike the others who had accompanied her.

On the split screen, Jackson could see there was a crew on the grounds, decorating the trees and shrubs of his country estate. Another woman was in the great room arranging greenery and crystal angels around the massive stone fireplace. Another pair was on the porch dealing with the door and white marble columns.

So who was this woman on the ladder?

And was she doing surveillance for a robbery, or God knows what else?

He looked through the names of the work crew that his groundskeeper had provided. Her name was either Marita Hernandez or Ann Reeves. Since she wasn't Hispanic, he was betting she was the latter.

Jackson grabbed the phone from his desk and called Evan Young, his business manager. It was three days before Christmas, and Malone Investments was closed for a two-week holiday break, but as Jackson expected, Evan was in his office because he gave new meaning to the word workaholic.

Jackson had once given Evan a run for his money in the hours-at-work department, but since his son, Caden, had come into his life, Jackson had cut way back, not just on the hours, but on his commitment to the job. These days no one could accuse him of being married to his company.

"Evan," Jackson greeted, and even though he was eager to get down to business, he paused and waited for Evan, just in case the man wanted to mention the significance of this particular date.

"No need to call and check up on me," Evan stated. His voice was void of any emotion. "I'm doing fine."

Jackson doubted that was anywhere near the truth. It was the six-month anniversary of Sybil Barnwell's death. She was Evan's fiancée. Evan might be cold-blooded in business, but Jackson knew that the couple had been in love, and even though Evan had refused to take much time off, he'd been devastated by Sybil's death.

And Jackson suspected that, deep down, Evan blamed him for what had happened. Hell, Jackson blamed himself.

"I have a possible problem," Jackson explained. Best to get right onto the business at hand, rather than dive back into those memories of Sybil's death. "Tap into the security feed here at the estate and zoom in on the Christmas tree decorator in the foyer. That's camera eight. Have security run the facial recognition program. I want to know who she really is."

"You think she's connected to the threatening letter left for you this morning?" Evan asked.

"Could be." And that's what he intended to find out.

Jackson ended the call, got up from his desk and headed to the foyer. It was nearly two p.m., which meant

Caden would be up from his nap in a half hour or so. Waking time was Jackson's favorite part of the day, and he wanted this possible situation with the decorator resolved by then.

He went through the maze of corridors and smiled when he thought of Caden again. In another two years or so, his little boy would no doubt be riding a kiddy tricycle around the mansion on these now pristine hardwood floors. He'd be laughing, making noise, and Jackson couldn't wait.

There'd been a dark cloud over this place for too long.

Jackson kept his footsteps light, and paused at the top of the stairs so he could look down at the decorator and observe her in the flesh. She had finally made it to the point where she was actually stringing lights, but her gaze was still firing all around.

She wore jeans and a gray turtleneck sweater. Both nondescript. She definitely wouldn't stand out in those clothes. He could say the same for her short, light-brown hair and her lack of makeup.

"Looking for something?" he asked, his voice echoing through the foyer.

She gasped, obviously startled, and nearly fell off the ladder. Jackson started down the stairs in case he had to pick her up off the floor, but she managed to keep her balance, even though she dropped the lights. Some of the bulbs shattered when they smacked against the glossy marble, and bits of colored glass scattered everywhere.

"I'm, uh, decorating, of course," she said, sparing him a glance. She got off the ladder and onto her hands and knees to gather up the glass bits. "You scared me. I thought you'd be at work."

"I'm working at home today," he volunteered. In fact, he'd been in a business meeting with a client when the decorating crew arrived. It was the reason he was still wearing a suit.

Jackson walked across the foyer toward her, and glanced up at the security camera tucked in the corner behind a sconce. Evan was no doubt watching them, and probably trying to get a good shot of the woman's face so he could process it through the facial recognition program.

"Leave the glass," Jackson instructed, so she would stand. It'd give Evan a better angle of her face. "The housekeeper will take care of it."

But the woman shook her head and stayed down, and she didn't look at him when she spoke. "My boss would fire me if I didn't clean up after myself. Besides, we wouldn't want to have the floor messy when you bring your baby boy in to see the tree for the first time."

Everything inside Jackson went still.

Maybe it was the latest threatening letter, or maybe this was just his paternal instincts yelling out for him to keep Caden safe. Either way, he wanted to know who the hell this woman was.

"Who said I'd be bringing down my son to see the tree?" he challenged.

Her hand froze over a bit of broken glass, and Jackson saw her fingers trembling. That was his cue to reach down, catch onto her arm and haul her to her feet. Her expression froze, caught somewhere between shock and fear.

"I asked you a question," he reminded her.

He put his fingers beneath her chin and lifted it to force eye contact. Finally, here was something that wasn't nondescript. Her eyes were a cool ocean blue. Definitely memorable.

And disturbing.

Jackson didn't exactly step back, but he didn't approve of the way she or her eyes made him feel. There was that hit of attraction, something he didn't intend to feel when it came to her or any other woman he distrusted.

She tried to shrug. "It's in all the newspapers that you're in the final stages of adopting a baby."

"I am." And he left it at that.

"He's four months old, I heard. The right age for really noticing the lights and decorations. Since this is his first Christmas, I just figured you'd bring him down to see the tree as soon as we were done."

That was the plan. But it wouldn't happen with this woman around.

She stepped out of his grip, turned away from him and discarded the bits of glass into a trash bag hung alongside a box of ornaments. "I hope this doesn't sound too personal, but what made you choose adoption?"

Oh, this conversation seemed well beyond personal. "Let's just say I recently had a life-altering experience, and it put things in perspective."

"Yes," she agreed, as if she knew exactly what he meant. "You survived a plane crash about six months ago. I read about that, too."

"You read a lot about me." Though he knew his survival had been a front page story in all the state's newspapers.

He'd been the only survivor among the eight people

who'd been on his private jet when it had to make a crash landing. Evan's own fiancée, Sybil, who was one of Jackson's attorneys, had been killed. So had two of his department CEOs and other employees. They were all on that plane because he had insisted they accompany him to a hostile takeover meeting in Dallas. Jackson, on the other hand, had literally walked away, but he'd walked away a changed man.

A lot of lives had changed that day.

"I need to get something out of the work van," the woman mumbled.

Jackson didn't intend to let her get away that easily. He caught onto her arm again. "Who are you?"

"Ann Reeves," she quickly supplied. Again, she broke his grip.

He stepped in front of her and blocked her path. "Ann Reeves?" he repeated. "Why were you looking around the place as if you planned to steal something?"

Her eyes widened. She shook her head. A thin breath left her mouth. "I would never take anything that wasn't mine. Never."

Jackson expected her to break the eye contact, to try to move away from him again, but she didn't. She held her ground and stared at him. "Can you say the same?" she asked.

Now that was a question he hadn't expected. "Would I take something that wasn't mine?" he clarified. "It depends."

She blinked, her memorable blue eyes narrowing. "You know what I'm talking about."

No. He didn't. Nor was he sure why he'd given her that "it depends" answer. The old Jackson would have said that. And in the past he would have meant it. There'd been a time in his life when he would have acquired property, or whatever he wanted, not through illegal means exactly, but he hadn't been above stooping to down-and-dirty business tactics.

That was before Caden.

Before he'd held his son and had his world and his heart turned upside down.

Jackson was about to ask her to explain her last comment when his phone rang. While still blocking her path, he took the cell from his pocket and answered it.

"Evan," he responded. "What do we have?"

"Well, she's not Ann Reeves," Evan quickly provided. "Her driver's license photo is a match to a woman named Bailey Hodges. She's thirty-four, and her address is on the north side of San Antonio."

Bailey Hodges. The name sounded familiar, but Jackson couldn't put his finger on where he'd heard it before.

"I'll have her background in a few minutes," Evan added, and he hung up.

Jackson put away his phone and got right in her face. "All right, why are you here in my home, Bailey Hodges? Did you leave that threatening letter for me?"

She opened her mouth to say something but seemed to change her mind. "What threatening letter?" And she was too surprised and concerned for that not to be a real question.

He continued to study her. "The one I sent a copy of to the San Antonio Police Department so they could investigate it." That was all Jackson intended to tell her about that matter. "Why are you here?" he repeated.

She didn't answer him. Instead, she took out a folded

piece of paper from her jeans pocket. For a moment, he thought it was another threatening letter, but it was a pair of photographs that looked as if they'd been copied from the computer. She thrust the paper at him.

"Do you know either of these women?" she demanded.

He glanced at the two photographs. They were both strangers. "What does this have to do with you being here at the estate?"

"Everything," she whispered. A moment later, she repeated it.

Tired of this confusing conversation and whatever game she was playing, Jackson stepped out of her way. "It's time for you to leave."

"No."

"No?" It wasn't often anyone said that to him. In fact, he couldn't remember the last time. The woman was gutsy. Or maybe not very bright.

"Look at the pictures again, *please*. Perhaps the hair color isn't the same. They could have done something to alter their appearances when or if you met them. So look hard and tell me if you know one or both of them."

Jackson didn't bother looking at the photos again, and he handed the paper back at her. "I don't know them. Or you. But I do know you're lying about who you are, and I know I want you out of my house now."

She hesitated and then turned as if she might just do as he'd ordered. But she stopped. "What kind of letter did you receive?"

He mentally groaned. "I don't intend to discuss that with you."

More hesitation. "Was the threatening letter a warning about me?"

"What?" This conversation had just taken a more confusing turn. "Why would it be?"

She seemed relieved. Or something. And she waved him off. "I'll go, for now. But I can't stay away. I have to know the truth about him."

Jackson couldn't remember the last time he'd been dumbfounded, but he sure as hell was now. He watched her walk to the double entry doors and wondered if he should stop her and demand an explanation. But his phone rang again.

"Evan," he said, answering the call.

"I found out some things about Bailey Hodges," Evan started. "She's single. A graphic artist who designs promotion brochures and such. She's actually done some work for us. She was engaged, and her ex-fiancé was her business partner, but things must have soured, because he moved to Europe nearly a year ago, and she removed him from her business records."

"She did work for us," Jackson mumbled. "Maybe that's why her name sounds familiar."

"Maybe. But it's probably because she was one of the San Antonio maternity hostages."

Now that did more than just ring bells. Four months ago, a group of pregnant women, new mothers, medical staff and even some babies had been taken hostage by two masked gunmen. They'd been held for hours.

Several people had died that day, including a cop's wife.

That instantly gave Jackson a connection with her. They'd both survived something that others hadn't. It'd been the top news story for weeks, even after the two gunmen and their boss had been captured.

But then Jackson remembered something else about that hostage situation.

One of the newborns had gone missing.

He remembered the Amber Alert that had been issued, mainly because he had been involved with the preliminary adoption process at the time. Even though he'd yet to hold Caden or even know of his existence, Jackson was now fully aware of how heart-crushing it would be to lose a child.

A child that had come into his life just two weeks after the hostage situation and the Amber Alert.

"Yes," Evan said, as if he knew exactly what Jackson was thinking. "Bailey Hodges's baby is the one the cops couldn't find after they rescued the hostages."

Jackson's stomach twisted into a cold, hard knot.

"A coincidence," Jackson mumbled.

"Could be. Caden's four months old. The age is right, but the adoption lawyer you're using is reputable."

Still, it was a private adoption, and there'd been room for some loopholes. None that he knew about.

But that didn't mean there hadn't been some.

That's the reason he'd been checking and double-checking the paperwork. In fact, he'd had a conversation with Ryan Cassaine, the attorney, just the day before. Jackson hadn't wanted to have a problem arise down the road. He wanted to confront any possible issues now, and work them out before the adoption became final in less than a week.

"The lawyer wouldn't have dealt in stolen babies," Evan added. "Ryan Cassaine went to law school with Sybil, and she had nothing but high praise for him."

"Make sure everyone else feels the same about him," Jackson insisted. And he cursed. This couldn't be happening. Caden was his son in every way that mattered.

Bailey Hodges's lost child had nothing to do with them.

Jackson replayed the look in her eyes. The cryptic warnings. The strange conversation. And he prayed he was right—that this was all just some bizarre coincidence that could be explained away.

"There's more," Evan continued. "The cops are concerned about Miss Hodges. She's apparently been conducting her own investigation into her son's disappearance. She's hired someone to hack into files. She's been following the suspects, so much so that one of them got a restraining order."

Jackson shrugged. "Her behavior is understandable. She wants to find her son."

"I agree. But there's more. Not long after the hostage incident ended, someone tried to kill her. The cops think it was the gunmen or their boss."

This wasn't helping his decision to go after her. It was only creating more sympathy for the woman. "But the threat is over, now that the gunmen and their boss are dead, right?"

"Maybe." And Evan paused, the moments crawling by. "The last time she spoke to the cops, she said someone was still following her."

Hell.

"Was the threatening letter a warning about me?" she'd asked.

Now, he understood why she wanted to know. But she'd also told Jackson that she couldn't stay away, that she had to know the truth about him.

Him.

Had she meant Caden?

Cursing even more, Jackson headed for the door so he could try to figure out what was going on. But he got there just in time to see Bailey Hodges driving away in the work van she'd ridden into the estate.

Jackson clicked off the call with Evan so he could phone Steven Perez, his estate manager, and have someone shut the front gates. Bailey Hodges probably wasn't headed to the address on her driver's license, and with her suspicions about someone following her, she likely wouldn't be an easy woman to find. Jackson didn't want to lose her.

But he was damn concerned about who she might really be.

His house manager answered, but Jackson didn't get a chance to issue the order to shut the gate.

"We have a problem, sir," Steven said. "An exterior sensor was tripped, so I checked the security feed. We have an intruder."

That didn't ease the knot in his stomach. "You don't mean the decorator in the van, do you?"

"No, sir. I mean the person who just scaled the west fence on the back side of the property. He's armed, and he's making a beeline for the estate."

Chapter Two

Bailey blinked back the tears. She couldn't cry. She'd save those tears for later. For now, she needed to get off the Malone estate and away from whoever had been alerted because of Jackson Malone's suspicions about her.

Her face had no doubt been caught on a security camera. She'd anticipated cameras of course, but she hadn't anticipated that she would alarm the estate owner to the point where he would have her investigated.

It'd been a huge mistake to come here today.

She wanted to kick herself for not being able to resist the chance to see the baby that Jackson Malone was adopting. Now, her weakness had put her in a position where she had to regroup. Heaven knows how long it would be before she got another opportunity to get back on the grounds and see the baby.

The estate road leading to the highway was a series of deep curves, and she had to ease up on the accelerator. She certainly couldn't risk crashing into one of the massive pecan trees that were on each side of her.

An injury could delay her search.

Bailey spotted the wrought iron gates just ahead. In only a few seconds she'd be on the highway where she could turn onto one of the side roads and get out of sight of anyone that Jackson would send to follow her.

But the gates started to slide shut.

Her heart went to her knees, and despite the danger from the trees, she hit the accelerator. She had to make it through them before they closed. If not, Jackson might have her arrested for trespassing.

Bailey took the last curve, the tires squealing in protest at the excessive speed, and for just a moment she lost sight of the gates. When she came out of the other side of the turn, her heart did more than drop.

The gates closed right in front of her.

Bailey slammed on the brakes. She smelled the rubber burning against the asphalt. Her body lurched forward, the seatbelt digging into her stomach and chest. And then there was the sound. Metal slamming into metal when the front of the van collided with the wrought iron.

The airbag deployed, smacking into her and pinning her against the seat. Bailey didn't take the time to determine if she was hurt. She had to get out of there now. There was a footpath gate next to the wrought iron ones, and she might be able to leave that way.

She fought with the airbag and managed to shove it aside. Maybe because her hands were shaking, getting out of the seatbelt was no easy feat either. She finally got her fingers to cooperate and she disengaged the lock. Ready to run, Bailey threw open the door.

But she didn't get far.

A rail-thin young Hispanic man came bursting through the shrubs and trees. She recognized him. He was with the estate gardening crew who had told them where to put some exterior lights.

He was dressed in work clothes, jeans and a dirt-splattered denim shirt, and with his breath gusting, he caught onto her arm. "Mr. Malone says you're to come with me," he told her. "A man just climbed over the security wall. An intruder."

Oh, God. "Where is he?"

He started to run with her in tow. "He's headed to the main house."

Bailey didn't know how she managed to hold on to her breath after hearing that. Was the intruder after the baby? Was that what Jackson's threatening letter was all about? He was a very wealthy man, and someone might be attempting to kidnap the little boy for ransom.

She had to help keep the baby safe, even if he wasn't hers. And even if it meant putting herself in danger.

Bailey didn't ask where the man was taking her, but she did make sure he wasn't armed. There was no visible weapon, and he wasn't big or strong enough to be hired muscle. If she had to, and she might, she was fairly certain she could fight him off if he turned out to be someone who wasn't concerned about the baby's safety.

They cut through a garden on the east side of the property. The man didn't stop running. Neither did Bailey, though the icy December air was knifing through her lungs and making it hard to breathe. She hadn't put on a coat for her escape, and the chill was slowing her down.

She finally spotted the estate, but the man stopped next to some thick shrubs and checked around them before they ran the last hundred yards across the lawn to an east entrance. It was a sunroom decorated with plenty of lush green plants and pristine white furniture.

"Miss Hodges," someone said the moment they entered.

Jackson Malone was standing there in the opening that divided the sunroom from the main house. Unlike when she'd seen him earlier in the foyer, he'd ditched his perfectly tailored midnight blue business coat and loosened his tie. His storm black hair was rumpled. His eyes were troubled.

And he had a gun pointed at her.

Bailey wanted to scream at herself. How could she have been so stupid? She'd bought the gardener's story about an intruder, and in doing so, she'd come right back to the lion's den.

Jackson looked at the gardener who'd *rescued* her. "Thank you, José. Now go back to your quarters and lock the door. I don't want anyone out on the grounds until we know what we're up against."

The man gave a shaky nod, mumbled something in Spanish and hurried away, leaving Bailey alone with an armed man.

"I would have gone after you myself," Jackson said, as a threat, "but I didn't want to leave my son." He motioned for Bailey to follow him.

She didn't. Bailey stayed put. "Is there really an intruder?"

"There is." His tone left no room for doubt. He held up the sleek, multifunction cell phone he had in his left hand, and on the tiny screen she saw what appeared to be video feed from security cameras. The man was dressed in camouflaged clothing and a ski mask.

And he was carrying an assault rifle.

"My advice?" Jackson added. "Bullets can go through glass, so if I were you I'd move."

She glanced at the sunroom, three sides of which were indeed glass. Still, Bailey didn't budge. Going inside could be just as dangerous as staying put. Jackson didn't have his gun aimed at her exactly, but it was angled so that aiming it would take just a split second.

"Is this some kind of trick?" she asked. "Do you want me dead and out of the way?"

Jackson just stared at her. "Funny. I was about to ask you the same thing."

Bailey shook her head. "The last thing I want is you dead." And she meant it.

He stared her, those ice-gray eyes seemingly going right through her. "Get inside," he ordered. "You might not value your life, but I'd prefer you stay alive so I can figure out who the hell you are."

She debated it, but in the end she couldn't dismiss the part about bullets going through glass. Yes, despite his comment that he preferred her alive, Jackson Malone might indeed have murder on his mind, but right now Bailey felt safer with him than she did with the ski-masked intruder. She only hoped she didn't regret trusting her instincts. She certainly didn't have a good track record in that department.

Bailey stepped out of the sunroom and into the main part of the house, and Jackson immediately closed the double doors and locked them. He pressed some numbers on a security system keypad, and then stepped in front of her to prevent her from going any farther.

"We'll wait here," he insisted.

Here was a casual living room with a butter-colored sofa. Floral chairs. A fireplace. There were toys in a basket on the hardwood floors.

That caused her breath to catch.

"Who's the intruder?" Jackson asked her, checking the phone again.

Bailey pulled her attention from the toys and that phone so she could shake her head. "I don't know, but maybe he came here to kidnap the baby."

"Funny, I was thinking the same thing about you," Jackson mumbled, making it sound like profanity. He shoved the gun into the back waist of his pants, crossed the room, pressed some buttons, and a bar opened from the wall. He poured himself a glass of something from a cut crystal decanter, tilted back his head and took the shot in one gulp.

"You have someone after the intruder?" she asked. "Someone who can stop him from getting inside?"

"I do. And my son has been taken to a panic room where no one can get to him. We've called the sheriff, and he's on the way. Now, what does the intruder want?"

Because her legs felt shaky, Bailey stepped to the side so she could lean against the wall. "I don't know."

"Then guess," he demanded. "And while you're guessing, try to figure out how this intruder could be linked to you."

"To *me?*"

"You," he verified.

He walked back to her and got close. Probably to violate her personal space and make her feel uncomfortable.

It worked.

Everything about him, from his clothes to his scent, to the liquor on his breath, screamed expensive, but that look he was giving her was from a powerful man who knew how to play down-and-dirty.

An attractive man, she reluctantly admitted to herself.

That's the first thing Bailey had noticed about him when she saw his photo in the newspapers. With his perfectly cut, but a little too-long hair, Jackson Malone looked like a bad boy rocker turned billionaire. He was drop-dead handsome, and despite the lousy circumstances and her personal feelings about him, her opinion about his looks didn't change. He was the kind of man women noticed, and she apparently wasn't exempt from that.

He glanced at her jeans pocket. "Why did you ask me about the two women in the photos?"

It was a simple question; and unlike many questions, Bailey actually knew the answer to this one, but she had to debate how much to tell him. She could just come clean about everything. That could cause him to gather up his soon-to-be adopted son and go deep into hiding, where he could keep the baby away from her.

Bailey wouldn't blame him for that.

But she couldn't risk Jackson leaving with the baby. She had to know the truth.

"Four months ago, when those men stormed into the hospital and took everyone hostage, I was in recovery. I'd just had a C-section." Bailey had to take a deep breath. She didn't remember much about that afternoon, and what she did remember wasn't good. Just blips on her mental radar. "I didn't know at the time, but the gunmen wanted to kill me."

"Because they thought you could identify them," he supplied. "I read about that."

She nodded. She'd read all about it, too—after the fact. "Apparently, the two gunmen tried to break into the hospital lab the day before, and they thought I'd seen them without their masks. I might have," she admitted.

"You don't remember?" he questioned.

"No. I was there for some pre-op tests, and my mind was on the baby I was going to have. But they didn't know that. They thought I was a threat. So they found out who I was and made a bogus call for me to come to the hospital for a bogus appointment. But I was already at the hospital because my labor started early."

He checked the phone monitor again. "Why didn't the gunmen just go into the recovery room after you?"

Bailey heard the question, but she had to know what was going on. Jackson kept looking at the phone, but he was giving her no clues as to what was happening. "Where's the intruder?"

"Still at the rear of the property. My men are closing in on him. Now, back to the question. Why didn't the gunmen go into recovery after you?"

"Because someone hid me, and my baby. I don't know the person who did that, but I think it might be one of the two women in those photos. Both of them worked at the hospital at the time of the hostage incident."

He made an impatient circling motion with his finger when she stopped. "Keep going."

"The woman told me she had to take my son because the gunmen might hurt him." Bailey had to pause again when she relived those last moments with her baby. "She took him and disappeared. I've been looking for him ever since, but I think someone doesn't want me to find him. There have been three attempts on my life."

Jackson made a sound of mild interest. "I read the gunmen are dead now, and the person who hired them is in prison."

She nodded. "But I'm pretty sure someone has continued to follow me. I don't know if it has anything to do with my missing son, or if it's just someone who wants to do a news story. Some of the former hostages have been hounded by reporters."

No sound of mild interest this time. He groaned, a deep rumbling in his throat, and cursed. "Still, someone tried to kill you, but you decided to come here anyway?"

"Those attempts on my life have nothing to do with this visit." She couldn't say it fast enough. "It's been days, weeks even, since anyone has followed me. That's why it was time for this visit. I thought I should come here today...."

"Say it," Jackson demanded when she stopped.

Bailey wasn't sure she could. She'd searched for so long, and it was bittersweet to think she might be this close and still be so far away from having the life she'd planned.

"I thought if I could see the child you're adopting," she whispered, "that I would know if he was— well—*mine.*"

There it was. She'd just let him know that Caden James Malone could be the child who had been stolen from her.

And in Jackson's mind that meant she was the enemy.

She'd read all about him. The ruthless business practices, the endless string of properties and businesses he'd acquired, often through hostile takeovers. His failed marriage in his early twenties to a woman who'd turned out to be a gold-digging opportunist. Rumors were, the sour relationship had embarrassed him and his family and had cost him millions. And it had also caused him to vow to stay single for the rest of his life.

Obviously, that vow hadn't extended to fatherhood.

Bailey had poured over every article she could find, and it seemed as if, more than the money and his billion-dollar portfolio, the one thing Jackson Malone wanted most was children.

Now he had one.

And God knows what he would do to hang on to the baby.

"Do you have any proof?" he asked. There was pure skepticism in his tone.

"Some. I've researched all the adopted baby boys who were born in Texas on his birthday, and Caden is the only one I haven't been able to exclude."

He gave her a flat look. "Who says your son was adopted? He could have been taken to another state, or across the border. His adoption could have been illegal. Or maybe there was no adoption at all."

Yes. And that possibility had caused her many sleepless nights. Not knowing what had happened was the worst.

"I have my son's DNA," she continued. "I got it from the umbilical cord that had been saved after his delivery. The police kept that quiet so no one in the media would report it. They wanted to be able to use it when and if they found a baby matching my son's description. But the police also gave me a copy of those test results, and I was hoping you'd let me compare that DNA to the baby you're about to adopt."

His right eyebrow lifted, and he gave her a cold, hard stare to let her know that wasn't going to happen anytime soon.

"It's best for all of us if we know the truth," Bailey said, still trying.

"Really?" he challenged. "Here's what I do know." But a sound cut off whatever he'd been about to say.

It was a loud bang.

A gunshot.

Jackson's attention went straight to the phone, but he turned the screen so that she couldn't see.

"Because you came here today, you might have endangered my son," he continued, with his gaze fastened to the screen. "If what you've told me is true, someone could still be trying to kill you. So why the hell would you want to involve an innocent child in all of this?"

Her eyes burned, and Bailey tried to blink back the tears. She wasn't quite successful. "Because I don't think anyone is still trying to kill me. Besides, I had to know if he's my son."

"And then what?" Jackson snapped. He glared at her.

That was the hardest question of all, because she couldn't just walk away until she'd learned the truth.

She swallowed hard. Even if Caden was indeed her son, Jackson Malone wasn't just going to let her claim him. He no doubt approached fatherhood like he did his business, and that meant she was in another fight for her life.

"Caden's adoption is legal," Jackson concluded. "No one stole him from you. His birth mother is an unmarried college student from Austin who couldn't raise him, so she contacted a private adoption agency after he was born."

That was info that Bailey hadn't been able to uncover. But it didn't mean it was true. Maybe it was a story concocted by the woman who'd stolen Bailey's newborn.

His phone buzzed, and Jackson glanced down at the screen. He pulled in a deep breath and used the device to make a call. "Well?" he said to the person who answered.

Since this was likely about the intruder, Bailey tried to listen, but she couldn't hear the explanation that Jackson was getting. She held her breath, waiting.

"My men have the intruder," Jackson relayed to her when he hung up.

Relief flooded through her. "He's alive?"

"For the moment. He was wounded when he tried to run. That was the shot we heard."

But he was still alive. Bailey went to Jackson and caught onto his arm. "Have your men question him. Find out why he was here. You'll learn that he didn't come here because of me. He's probably a would-be kidnapper after the baby."

"The sheriff just arrived," Jackson said, not addressing anything she said. He stared at the grip she had on his arm, and didn't continue until Bailey drew back her hand. "And here's what I'm offering. You have two choices. You can leave now and look elsewhere for your missing baby. That includes you never attempting to contact me or my son again."

Her relief over the intruder's capture was short-lived. Bailey shook her head. "But don't you want to know the truth?"

Jackson shrugged. "I already know the truth, and

Caden is not yours. He's mine. Leave now, and someone on my staff will drive you back to San Antonio."

She couldn't leave. She might be just a room away from her baby.

"And if I refuse to leave?" Bailey challenged.

Another shrug. "Simple. The sheriff will arrest you for trespassing and take you to jail. Your choice, Miss Hodges. Which will it be?"

Chapter Three

Jackson rarely bluffed, but that's exactly what he was doing now.

Part of him, the paternal part, wanted this woman as far away from Caden as possible. He didn't want to believe a word she was saying. He wanted to dismiss those photos she carried around like emotional baggage.

But he couldn't.

He wasn't the type of man to live in denial.

"Okay," Bailey said. She nodded, drew in a long breath. "Have me arrested, but I'll pay the fine, or whatever, and keep coming back. I'm not going away. I *will* learn the truth."

So his bluff had failed. She hadn't backed down on her story. Still, that didn't mean she was Caden's birth mother. It didn't mean anything other than she was a woman who didn't give up easily.

Well, she'd met her match, because he didn't give up at all. *Ever.*

He checked the phone to see the progress going on outside. His men still had the intruder pinned down, and he could see the sheriff and his deputies approaching the ski-masked man.

Jackson wanted to be out there. He wanted to be the

one who got answers from this SOB who had dared to break in to the estate. But he had to stay put. He certainly didn't want to leave Bailey in the house with Caden. The first thing she would do is go look for the baby. She wouldn't find him, but he didn't want his staff to have to deal with containing her.

In the distance, he could hear the siren of an approaching ambulance. It wouldn't be long before the sheriff came inside to give him an update. By then, Jackson had to decide what to do about the brunette in front of him.

"If this is some kind of scam," he said to her, "I'll destroy you." Best to put that out there right up front. He might have toned down his ruthlessness, but he'd resort to a few old habits if this woman was out for money.

"It's no scam. I just want to know if he's my son."

Jackson moved closer to her again, because he knew it made her nervous. The last time he'd gotten in her face, her bottom lip had trembled. He didn't get any satisfaction at the idea of frightening her, but it might be the fastest way to get to the so-called truth that she claimed she wanted.

He slid his gaze over her. All over her. And he mentally pulled back a little when he felt that punch of attraction again. Hell. Hadn't his past taught him anything? He couldn't live his life thinking below the belt.

"Caden doesn't look like you," he pointed out.

She touched her hand to her short, spiky hair. Yep, she was trembling all right. "This isn't my natural color. I dyed it after the attempts on my life. I have black hair, like yours."

Like Caden's.

But he kept that to himself.

"What color are his eyes?" she asked. Despite the trembling, she no longer seemed afraid. She seemed— well—*hopeful*.

"Blue."

Similar to Bailey's.

But many people had blue eyes, he reminded himself. Not that shade though. When he'd first seen her eyes, he'd thought they were memorable. And they were. Because they were a close match to Caden's.

"Blue," she repeated, smiling. The smile quickly faded though. "You said he was safe? Are you sure?"

"Positive." To prove it to himself, he used his phone to scan through the security cameras, and he zoomed in on the panic room. Caden was there, still asleep. His nanny, Tracy Collier, was holding him.

"May I see him?" Bailey's voice had so much breath in it that it hardly had any sound. Also, there was that hopefulness in it again.

But Jackson didn't show her the images on his screen, and he wouldn't. Not until he'd done some investigating, and even then it might not happen.

He used the phone to call Evan again, and, as expected, his business manager answered on the first ring.

"Is everyone okay?" Evan immediately asked.

Jackson settled for saying, "They caught the intruder."

"Yes. I was watching the security feed, but I'm on my way out to the estate now. I figured you might need some help."

"I do, as a matter of fact." His gaze met Bailey's, and he didn't think it was his imagination that she was holding her breath. "I need you to get the contact info for Caden's birth mother."

Evan didn't answer for several moments. "Are you sure?"

"Positive."

A lot of money had gone into that private adoption. Well over a million dollars. The attorney had said it was to expedite the process and to pay the birth mother's expenses, both medical and the cost of her return to college. Jackson hoped that was all the money had been used for, and that it wasn't part of some illegal process.

"Anything else?" Evan asked.

Jackson looked at Bailey again. "Yes. Get me a detailed report of the hostage incident at the maternity hospital. I want everything the cops have, including info on employees they might have suspected in the disappearance of Bailey Hodges's newborn."

Evan made a sound of disapproval. "That sounds like a messy can of worms you're opening, Jackson."

Yes, it was, but this particular can was already open, and the proof was standing in front of him.

"I have the women's names," Bailey volunteered the moment he ended the call with Evan. "And I've ruled out everyone else who was on the maternity ward that afternoon. Well, hopefully. There's always the possibility that the woman who took my son wasn't on any official records. She could have come in with the gunmen."

And if that were true, then there'd be no way to trace her. That would mean no definitive answer for Bailey. That, in turn, meant she wouldn't make a hasty exit out of his life. The fastest way to end this was to figure out what had happened to her son.

"Give me the photos," he instructed.

She pulled the folded sheet of paper from her jeans and handed it to him. But not without touching him. Her fingers brushed his. She was still trembling.

Hell.

He didn't want her fear and emotions—or his reaction to them—to have any part in this. He wanted a cool detachment between Bailey and himself while he helped her, and himself. But that zing of heat didn't equal anything cool. Jackson was betting the detachment wouldn't go far, either. And that meant he had to do something about it.

Bailey jerked back her hand as if he'd scalded her, and she dodged his gaze when she spoke. "The first woman is Shannon Wright, an RN who was on the fourth floor of the hospital that day, but no one remembers seeing her after the gunmen arrived. She claims she hid."

It was possible Shannon Wright was telling the truth—hiding would be the logical thing to do—but Bailey was right to suspect her.

"The second one is Robin Russo. She works in records in the administration section. The other floors of the hospital were evacuated after the gunmen arrived in the maternity ward, and someone saw Robin leave her office, but no one, including the police, actually saw her leave the building."

Jackson gave that some thought. "You have a motive for either of these women?"

She shook her head. "Well, unless they got money from selling my baby to someone."

And that was something Jackson couldn't rule out—yet—but he would.

"What about your son's father?" Jackson asked. "Maybe he's the one who had your son taken?"

Another headshake. "My baby's father broke off things with me when I told him I was pregnant. He took a job in Europe, and I haven't heard from him, other than an email to remind me that he wanted nothing to do with the child."

Jackson tried not to have any visible reaction to that, but her story only made him feel more sympathy for her. And empathy, because of his own bad relationship. He had to keep his distance from her, because empathy and attraction were a lethal combination.

"If I find out you're lying about any of this..." he reiterated.

"I know. You'll destroy me. And if I find out you knowingly stole my son, all your money and power won't stop me from coming after you."

He almost smiled. Almost. Considering her predicament, she still had some fight in her.

That wouldn't mix well with the attraction, either.

"The sheriff will come inside any minute," he reminded her and himself. "If you're here, he'll want to know why. Are you prepared to answer his questions?"

Jackson didn't want her out of his sight, but he also didn't want to risk her being underfoot. He would have her followed when she left, so he could keep tabs on her until he had more information about her and her missing child.

"I'm prepared. Well, as prepared as I can be. The last time I was in protective custody, I was nearly killed." She paused. "I suppose it could happen again. That's the reason I've avoided the cops, but I'm too close to turn back now."

It was what he expected her to say. So he had to do whatever was necessary to speed up this process and get her out of his and Caden's lives.

"May I see Caden?" she asked.

"No." Jackson didn't even have to think about it.

She nodded, and paused as if she might challenge that. But she didn't.

The intercom system made a slight buzzing sound. A moment later, his household manager, Steven Perez, spoke through the tiny speaker built into the wall. "Sheriff Gentry is out front waiting for the ambulance. He says once he has the man on the way to the hospital, he wants to speak to Bailey Hodges if she's still on the grounds."

The color drained from Bailey's face. "How did the sheriff know I was here? And how did he know my name? Did you tell him?" She still didn't look ready to bolt, but it was possible she might faint. Or hyperventilate.

"No. I didn't tell him your name, but you can trust the sheriff," Jackson told her. "I've known Alden Gentry my whole life, and he wouldn't do anything illegal."

Still, Bailey shook her head…and then she tried to grab his gun. He snagged her wrist, but she tried to get the weapon with her left hand.

Jackson finally just caught onto her shoulders and put her against the wall. Body-to-body. Not the brightest idea he'd ever had, but it stopped her.

"Please," she said, her warm breath brushing against his mouth at the same time her breasts pressed against his chest.

That "please" wouldn't work, but Jackson knew it wasn't a good idea to keep touching her like this.

"Why does Sheriff Gentry want to see Miss Hodges?" Jackson asked, directing his question to the intercom so that Steven would hear him.

"Because she might be involved with the intruder," Steven answered at the same moment that Bailey issued a denial.

"I had nothing to do with this," she insisted.

"Not according to the sheriff," Steven contradicted. "When Sheriff Gentry approached the man, he said Bailey Hodges brought him to the estate with her."

Her breath was gusting even harder now, and she frantically shook her head. She also struggled to break free of his grip. But Jackson held on.

"Did the intruder say why she brought him here?" Jackson asked.

"He did." Steven paused again. "He claims Bailey Hodges paid him to kill you."

Chapter Four

Bailey made a sound of outrage, but she wasn't able to speak. She could only grab onto Jackson and shake her head, denying the intruder's accusation.

He claims Bailey Hodges paid him to kill you.

"I didn't," she finally managed to say. "I swear, I didn't hire anyone to do anything."

But she didn't even wait for Jackson's response. Why should he believe her? She'd lied her way into his home and had then tried to escape when he confronted her.

Mercy.

She was so desperate to find her son that all her desperation must have made her seem insane. And maybe she was. She certainly hadn't slept through the night since this entire nightmare had started four months ago. Jackson might have her arrested or hauled off to the loony bin.

This visit could cost her everything. And that cut through her heart.

The pain and the frustration slammed through her, and Bailey felt her legs turn boneless. Much to her disgust, she even started to cry. She would have no doubt fallen to the floor if Jackson still hadn't had her in his grip.

"I didn't," she pled, though the words barely had any sound. Her throat had clamped shut, and the tears were streaming down her cheeks.

With Jackson's body still holding her in place against the wall, steadying her, he used his left hand to lift her chin. Bailey didn't want to make eye contact, because she figured she knew what she would see there on his face: his determination to have her arrested.

But his ice-gray eyes combed over her for what seemed an eternity.

And then he cursed.

He kept on cursing when he let go of her and stepped back.

"Leave us," Jackson told the man who had rushed in and relayed what the sheriff had said. "Tell Sheriff Gentry the intruder is lying. Miss Hodges is a guest in my home and didn't hire anyone to kill me."

The man looked suspiciously at Bailey. "You're sure, sir?"

Jackson hesitated. "I'm sure." But he sounded far from convinced of her innocence. "I want to speak to the intruder before the ambulance takes him to the hospital. Let the sheriff know that."

When the man hurried out, Bailey shook her head again, not understanding. And Jackson didn't explain. He latched on to her arm and practically dragged her to the sofa, where he had her sit. He rummaged through his pocket, extracted a handkerchief and thrust it into her hand.

"Wipe your eyes," he snarled.

She did, but the tears continued to come. Bailey stared up at him, blinking back more tears. And waiting. Jackson scrubbed his hand over his face, groaned and paced.

"Convince me," he finally said. "Tell me why I should believe that you didn't hire someone to come here and kill me."

Bailey certainly hadn't expected this gift. And it was definitely a gift. It was possible Jackson had called off the sheriff simply because he didn't want the authorities questioning him about Caden or the adoption. If the sheriff took her into custody, there would certainly be questions.

Did that mean Jackson had something to hide about the adoption?

Possibly. Or it could be a simple matter of his wanting to get to the bottom of this himself. That was certainly what she wanted. Bailey had been hiding in fear for her life for four months, unable to trust anyone, and seemingly not getting any closer to finding her baby. Maybe, just maybe, this was her first positive step in the right direction.

Or it could be a fatal mistake.

"My medical records prove I had a child," she said, not really knowing where to start. Jackson continued to pace. "And you know from police reports that my newborn went missing. A woman took him."

He stopped, and that icy gaze snapped onto her. "One of the women in those photos? Shannon Wright or Robin Russo?"

She nodded, surprised that he could recall the names. He'd barely glanced at the photos when she had shown them to him earlier. "Was one of them involved in your son's adoption?"

"No." And he didn't hesitate. "I've never seen either of them before."

Bailey believed him. Maybe because he believed that she hadn't hired that intruder. Of course, this could all be an act, but the truth was, she could be under the same roof as her son. That was worth any risk.

"Those photos aren't proof that Caden is your missing baby," Jackson pointed out.

"No." Bailey wiped away the last of the tears and gathered her resolve. "But I could have DNA proof."

His stare narrowed, and she could have sworn it took on a lethal edge. Now here was the Jackson Malone she'd read about.

Ruthless. Dangerous. Intimidating.

"Remember, I told you my son's umbilical cord was stored right after he was born," Bailey explained. "It's there at the San Antonio Maternity Hospital storage facility. The police worked up a DNA profile from it, and you could compare it to Caden's."

He blinked. That was his only change of expression, but Bailey thought he was both shocked and terrified about the possible outcome.

She understood completely.

If the DNA didn't match, then this would be a painful dead end for her to accept. She wouldn't stop looking for her baby. She would *never* stop. But as long as she didn't feel safe trusting the police, that would slow down her search. Eventually, she would run out of money. And resources. God knows what she would do then.

But a DNA match could at least let her know that her baby was alive and safe. Later, she could deal with getting him back. Right now, the "alive and safe" part was the most critical.

"The police have the DNA profile," she continued after trying to clear her throat. "I also have a copy in a safe deposit box."

"A profile that could have been doctored," Jackson snapped.

Bailey nodded, readily accepting his doubts about that. "But then, of course, there's me. My own DNA. You can do what's called a maternity study and see if Caden's DNA matches mine."

Jackson squeezed his eyes shut a moment and then started to pace again. At least that's what she thought he was doing, but then he headed out of the room.

"I want to talk to the intruder," he let her know.

Bailey jumped from the sofa and hurried after him. "So do I. But I also want to know the truth about Caden."

He stopped and whirled around so fast that she plowed right into him. Suddenly, his arms were all around her, embracing her. Well, almost. Just as quickly, he pushed her away, but not before she caught his scent. Yet something else about him that smelled expensive.

"No more talk about Caden, especially not to an armed man who trespassed onto the grounds of my estate," Jackson warned. "Something is happening, something dangerous, and I want to keep my son out of it."

Bailey opened her mouth to try to change his mind, but she couldn't. He was right. Something dangerous was indeed happening, and she had to try to stop the immediate danger first. That had to be her priority. Then she could press Jackson for the DNA test.

"We're not on opposites sides of this," she tried to

tell him. "We both want Caden safe. And we both want the truth about what's going on."

"Oh, we're on opposite sides all right," he snarled.

Jackson didn't wait for her to respond to that. He went through the foyer and to the front door. He shot her a warning glance before he stepped onto the porch. That warning was no doubt a reminder for her to stay quiet about the adoption.

The front lawn was nothing short of chaos. The decorators were still there, all standing away from the sheriff, two deputies and several men that she suspected were Jackson's employees. There were at least a dozen of them milling around, shouting out orders, talking on their phones. In the distance, Bailey could hear the sound of the ambulance siren.

Lying facedown on the ground in the center was a man wearing military-style camouflaged clothing. There was a bloody gash on his sleeve where he had no doubt been shot, and next to him was a black ski mask.

He lifted his head and looked up at her. And despite the look of pain on his face, his mouth bent into an oily smile.

"You recognize him?" Jackson asked.

"No." In her four-month-long ordeal, she'd never seen him.

Bailey wanted to demand to know why he had accused her of trying to kill Jackson, or why he had aimed that smile at her, but she decided to heed Jackson's warning and approach all of this with caution. She certainly didn't want to give the injured man any more information.

"What's his name?" Bailey asked, hoping that someone would be able to answer.

The tall, lanky sheriff looked at her. "He hasn't volunteered that yet." Then he raised an eyebrow when he turned his attention to Jackson. "You're sure I don't need to take her into custody?" the sheriff asked.

But Jackson didn't answer the question. He stared at the wounded intruder. "Has he said anything else about why he's here at the estate?"

The sheriff shook his head, but his eyebrow stayed cocked. "You do know I'll need answers—about her, about this guy on the ground and about any- and everything else that might be going on around here," the sheriff said, volleying his cop's gaze between Jackson and her.

"Yes," was all Jackson had time to say before someone shouted his name.

Bailey spotted the sandy-haired man making his way across the lawn toward them, and this time it was someone she did recognize. From his photos, that is. She'd seen articles about him in the newspaper archives that she'd researched when she had checked Jackson out. This was Evan Young, Jackson's business manager, and in fact, he'd been in the photo that had started her suspicions about Caden being her missing baby.

The San Antonio paper had printed a photo of Jackson coming out of family court after filing the successful adoption petition. He'd held a blanket-wrapped Caden in his arms, and behind him in that photo was Evan. All she had been able to see of the baby was his dark hair, and that had planted the seed that he could be hers.

"You should be inside," Evan said, and he tried to catch on to Jackson's arm.

Jackson threw off his grip. "In a minute." He went closer to the intruder and stooped down.

Because of the approaching siren from the ambulance, Bailey couldn't hear what Jackson said to the man, but it erased any trace of that slimy smile he'd given her. She walked toward them, hoping to hear the truth about why he was there, but Evan stopped her.

"I wouldn't advise that," he shouted over the howl of the siren. "The man is obviously dangerous."

Their gazes connected, and while Evan's tone seemed to indicate that he was concerned about her safety, she saw no such concern in his eyes. However, she did keep her distance because the ambulance pulled to a stop between Jackson and her. Since Evan was already tugging her in that direction, she stepped onto the porch with him.

The siren stopped and the medics jumped from the ambulance.

"Are you responsible for any of this?" Evan asked her.

"No. I have no reason to want Jackson harmed."

"Right," he mumbled.

She wasn't surprised he was suspicious. After all, Jackson had asked Evan to run some kind of background check on her so the man knew his boss had suspicions of his own. Plus, the intruder had lied about her hiring him.

"Jackson's going through a difficult time right now," Evan continued. "Did he tell you that someone sent him a threatening letter this morning?"

"He mentioned it," Bailey said, recalling Jackson's

question to her in the foyer. "He said he faxed a copy to SAPD."

"Really?" Evan pulled back his shoulders. "Jackson doesn't usually involve the police in his personal matters."

But this was more than personal—it was a safety issue that might spill over to Caden. "Just what kind of threat was it?"

Evan hesitated so long, she wasn't sure he was going to answer her. "It said 'Jackson Malone, I won't forgive and forget. Watch your back.' Someone left it outside his San Antonio office, but two others were left on his car when it was parked in the underground garage at work."

Bailey shook her head. "Maybe it's related to his business?"

He made a sound deep within his throat that hinted it might be related to her. But how could it be? If the person or persons who wanted her dead also wanted to silence her for something connected to the hostage situation, then why go after Jackson?

"The bottom line is that it isn't a good time for you to be here," Evan warned.

"Maybe not," Jackson interrupted. He had obviously overheard what his business manager had said. "But she's staying until I clear up some things."

Bailey was thankful that he might actually believe she was innocent, but she didn't think Jackson was extending any invitations for her to see Caden. "What did you say to the intruder?"

"I told him I would bury him if he didn't tell me the truth." Jackson said it calmly, but there was nothing calm about his demeanor.

"Did he tell you who he is?" Bailey pressed.

"No. But I suspect he's some kind of hired gun. He doesn't seem smart enough to pull a stunt like this on his own. When the sheriff runs his prints, I'm betting we'll know a lot more about him." He turned to Evan. "Why are you here?"

Evan shrugged, as if the answer were obvious. "First the threatening letter. Then Bailey's arrival. I thought you could use a little backup."

The muscles in Jackson's jaw stirred, but he kept his attention fastened to the injured man the medics were loading into the ambulance.

"In addition to getting me the info on Caden's birth mother, there is something you can do," he said to Evan as the ambulance drove away. The sheriff and one of the deputies followed along right behind it. "There are two women who were at the hospital during the hostage situation. Shannon Wright and Robin Russo. I need you to dig deep and see if one of them possibly took Bailey's son."

"Considering they were connected to the hostages and investigation that followed, I'm sure the cops have already done this," Evan quickly pointed out.

"Do it again." And it was definitely an order. "While you're at it, I want another thorough background check on Ryan Cassaine." Now Jackson looked at her. "He's the adoption attorney I used."

That sent her heart racing again. Did that mean Jackson was at least allowing for the possibility that Caden was her son?

"Why are you doing this?" she heard herself whisper. "Why are you willing to help me?"

"I'm not," Jackson quickly clarified. "I want the truth

so I can get you out of my life. I don't believe Caden
is yours. I think you're so desperate to find your child
that you're willing to latch on to mine."

That stung more than she thought. Probably because
she had started to feel this weird camaraderie between
them. And the equally weird attraction. But Bailey just
realized that Jackson had put her in her place.

"You're not going to have her taken into custody for
questioning?" Evan demanded.

Again, Jackson hesitated. "No. Not until I have the
answers I want."

Answers the intruder might provide. But there was
another way to settle one aspect of this baby issue once
and for all. "You can do the test to compare Caden's
DNA to mine," she reminded Jackson in a whisper.
However, her lowered voice failed because Evan obviously heard her anyway.

"A DNA test is a bad idea," Evan instantly responded.
Again, he tried to take Jackson aside, but Jackson held
his ground. "Consult your legal department. I doubt one
of those highly paid lawyers will tell you to consent to
anything this woman wants."

Jackson stayed quiet a moment. "Probably not." Another pause. "But arrange for the test anyway." He went
inside with Evan right on his heels.

Had she just heard Jackson correctly? Was he really
going to allow the test, or was this some kind of trick
to placate her?

"You can't do this," Evan insisted. "She could be a
scam artist."

"Then the test will prove that."

Still stunned about Jackson's possible cooperation, Bailey continued to follow the men so she could listen.

"But it could prove...*other* things," Evan said, lowering his voice to a near whisper. Bailey heard him anyway.

Yes, it could prove the adoption was illegal. Jackson could lose custody of the baby he was trying to adopt.

Jackson had been practically iron-jawed during this conversation, and for that matter, the crazy events of the day, but she saw the flash of pain on his face. Pain she understood. He wasn't just Caden's soon-to-be adoptive father, he obviously loved the child, and ironically, if Caden was her son, Jackson had spent more time with the baby than she had.

Bailey hadn't even gotten to hold him.

"Do the background checks on the adoption attorney and the two women from the hospital," Jackson continued, talking to Evan. The pain was gone, and the iron-dragon persona was back in place. "Get that DNA test here today."

Evan's chin came up, and there was fire in his eyes. "And if I object?"

"You won't," Jackson simply answered, and he walked away.

Obviously fuming now, Evan started to leave, but then he turned to her. He pointed his finger in her face. "So help me, if you do anything to hurt Jackson or the baby, I'll make sure you're locked up for the rest of your life."

That was yet another surprise. Here, Jackson had just butted heads with the man, and yet Evan was protecting his boss. And his boss's son. Part of her appreciated that, because Bailey was worried that all of them might need protection before this was over.

"Your business manager obviously doesn't want me here," Bailey mumbled as Evan walked away.

"Neither do I," Jackson mumbled back. He looked over his shoulder at her, his gaze searing right into her.

That seemed to be her cue to leave. But Bailey didn't want to do that until she had tried one more time. "May I see Caden?"

Jackson turned so quickly that it startled her. Bailey jumped back, overbalancing herself, just as he caught her. Unlike before though when he had stopped her from falling, the grip he had on her arms felt punishing.

"No," he answered, though she had no idea how he could speak with his jaw clench that tight.

It seemed as if he wanted to say something else, but he shook his head and tightened his grip even more.

She winced, made a small sound of pain, and just like that, he jerked back. He stared at his hands a moment and then gently pushed up her sleeve.

"I'm sorry," he whispered.

Bailey looked down at her forearm. "You didn't bruise me," she let him know.

"But I came damn close." He groaned and rolled his eyes toward the ornate ceiling. "There was a time in my life when I would have intimidated you into leaving."

She nodded. "There was a time in my life when I would have been intimidated. Not now, though. Not with the possibility of finding my baby at stake."

Bailey inched closer and reached out. Mercy, she was afraid to touch him. Not because she didn't want to do exactly that, but because she knew that touching was the last thing they needed. Their minds were both racing with the possibilities of her and Caden's DNA.

And racing with other things, too.

For some reason, being around Jackson reminded her that it had been well over a year since a man had touched her in any kind of way. Over a year since she had been in a man's arms. A year since she'd felt that trickle of heat in her body.

Jackson was the wrong man to make her feel any kind of trickle. But she couldn't seem to convince herself of that.

She put her hand on his arm, in about the same spot where he had gripped her. But instead of pouring her frustration and anger into that grip, she traced her finger slightly down his arm. Hopefully, a gesture to soothe him.

He probably thought she was sucking up to him, but Bailey didn't care. She didn't want to make an enemy of this man.

Even if they felt like enemies.

After all, he could have her son, and he could be keeping the baby from her.

"So what do we do?" she asked.

He blew out a long breath and checked his watch. "I need to bring Caden out of the panic room. He's probably up from his nap now, and I don't want him frightened by the strange surroundings."

Again, her heart latched right on to that as a possible opening. Even though it didn't make sense, Bailey thought if she saw the baby that she would immediately know if he was hers or not.

"No," Jackson said, and he realized he was staring

at her. "I can't let you see him because, quite frankly, I don't trust you."

She nodded, accepting that. Bailey didn't fully trust him, either. "You won't try to hide Caden so I can't get to him?"

Jackson's hesitation didn't help the tightness in her chest. "I agreed to the DNA test, and I'll have it done. But that's only because I don't believe he's yours. Think this through," he said, pulling away from her. "Someone stole your child. So why would that person risk placing the baby up for adoption?"

Bailey had an answer, only because this had constantly been on her mind. "Two possible reasons—as long as the woman has the baby with her, he, and therefore she, could be linked to the hostage situation. Plus, she kidnapped my son. Her intentions might have been good at the time. She might truly have wanted to save my baby's life. But when she didn't return him, she became a kidnapper and therefore a felon."

He continued to study her. "And the second reason?"

"Money. I read this was a private adoption. Money no doubt changed hands."

"It did. But I paid it through an attorney to Caden's birth mother, who was a college student."

Bailey gave that some thought. It could have been the college student in that hospital room with her. Bailey had no idea who had walked out with her baby that day. "Does this student have any DNA proof that the child is hers?"

"No. But then neither do you." Jackson tossed his comment right back at her.

"Not yet anyway."

She instantly regretted that snap, because it put some fire in his eyes. Fire that she didn't want there.

"You can wait in the guesthouse until Evan returns with the DNA kit." His voice was cool now. Detached. With just that arrogance and suspicion she'd encountered when he first walked down the stairs and confronted her. "I'll have one of the servants show you the way."

Jackson reached for the phone on an end table, but he didn't get a chance to pick it up. His own cell rang, and after glancing at the caller ID screen, he answered it right away.

"Sheriff," he greeted. "Please tell me you learned the identity of the intruder."

Bailey moved closer, hoping to hear the sheriff's response. This could be big. If she knew the man's name, then maybe she could learn who had hired him.

"What?" Jackson asked. Not exactly the tone of a question. More like stunned anger. "How the hell did that happen?"

Alarmed, Bailey went even closer, but she still couldn't hear what the lawman was saying. *My God, what had gone wrong now?* Had the man managed to escape? If so, he might double back and try to break into the estate again.

He might endanger Caden.

Even if the baby wasn't hers, she didn't want him in danger. It had been a horrible mistake coming here, she admitted to herself, again.

Jackson slapped his phone shut, but he didn't say anything right away, despite the fact he obviously knew

Bailey was anxious to hear what the sheriff had just told him.

"Well?" she prompted. "The intruder got away?"

Jackson shook his head. "Worse."

Chapter Five

Jackson listened to Sheriff Gentry's latest account of his investigation, but it was hard to concentrate with Caden staring up at him with those big blue eyes.

It was morning. Caden's favorite time of the day, when he seemed to be full of energy and new discoveries. His son had just squealed with delight—though Jackson didn't know why—and now Caden seemed to be waiting for him to respond to that baby outburst. Jackson did. He gave the boy an exaggerated grin that caused Caden to grin back.

"You do know what this means?" the sheriff asked, his somber voice pouring through the speakerphone on Jackson's desk.

Jackson did know. The day before, he'd listened to every word of Sheriff Gentry's account of what had happened when the ambulance arrived at the hospital with the intruder. The minute the medics had taken the man out to usher him into the ER, someone fired shots.

Now Jackson was listening to the latest update: the shots had been fired from a long-range high-powered rifle. The intruder had been killed instantly. There were no signs of the killer or the weapon he used.

"This means it was probably a professional hit," the sheriff continued.

Yeah. Jackson had come to the same conclusion. "And still no ID on the intruder?"

"No, because the man had no fingerprints. I don't mean none were on file. The man had no prints, period. They'd been burnt off with acid or something. It looked like a sloppy job, but an amateur isn't likely to go that far to conceal his identity. Of course, we'll still try to do a DNA match from our database."

They might get lucky. *Might.* But Jackson had to accept that the intruder was a dead end, literally. Besides, those missing prints were the sign of yet another pro. A hired gun in his own right.

So why had he trespassed onto the estate?

"You want me to send a deputy out to your place?" the sheriff asked.

"No. I have enough security." He hoped. And while he was hoping, Jackson added that he hoped he could get all of this cleared up fast. The situation with the latest threatening letter. With the intruder.

And especially with Bailey.

He wanted to enjoy every moment of Caden's first Christmas; but here he was, worried to the bone that instead of a celebration, his son could be in danger.

"What about your houseguest?" the sheriff asked, as if reading Jackson's mind.

Of course, it wasn't anything as miraculous as mind-reading. In a small town like Copper Creek, secrets didn't stay secrets very long, and the sheriff or his deputies had interviewed some of Jackson's staff. Sheriff Gentry knew that Bailey had spent the night at the estate.

"I'm not sure about Bailey Hodges yet," Jackson settled for saying. "Have you made any connection between the intruder and her?"

"Zero. The dead man had a prepaid cell in his pocket, with only one number called, and it wasn't to Miss Hodges. It was to a woman, Shannon Wright."

Jackson froze for a moment. "Shannon Wright? The nurse who was at the San Antonio Maternity Hospital during the hostage situation?"

"Yeah. How'd you know that?" the sheriff asked.

"It wasn't a lucky guess. Bailey thinks this Shannon Wright is a possible suspect in her baby's disappearance."

"Interesting. I'll look into it." The sheriff paused. "Where exactly is Miss Hodges right now?"

"In the guest quarters, away from the main house." Jackson paused to reach for the stuffed toy horse that Caden was offering him. Of course, the moment he took it Caden wanted it back. This was a game that Jackson knew all too well, and it made him smile.

"Good," the sheriff concluded.

That grabbed Jackson's attention. "Good? Why?" Because he certainly didn't consider it a good thing. He wanted her away from the estate, and that would happen as soon as he got the results of the DNA swabs he'd taken from her the day before. Then he would get Bailey on her way, if the results were what he wanted.

And what Jackson wanted was proof that she wasn't Caden's biological mother.

If she was, well, that was a kettle of fish he'd deal with later. One thing was for certain, no matter what the results were, he wasn't just going to hand over the baby to her—or anyone else.

Caden was *his*.

"San Antonio PD wants to question Bailey again," Sheriff Gentry explained. "You do know she hasn't been cooperative with them since shortly after the hostage incident four months ago?"

"Yes. Because she claims someone tried to kill her while she was in protective custody."

"Someone did try, just a day after the hostage situation ended. SAPD thinks the attempts were made by the now-dead gunmen, but they aren't sure. No proof. Personally, it sounds as if she should be back in San Antonio, trying to work with the cops who are running that investigation. She doesn't need to be out here in Copper Creek."

The sheriff obviously didn't know that Bailey was looking into the matter of Caden's DNA. Of course, that left Jackson with something he couldn't explain.

Knowing what Bailey thought about Caden, why had he let her stay?

He mentally cursed. It was this damn camaraderie over the near-death experience they'd survived. Plus, the baby angle. He now understood all about a parent's love for a child, and he could see that Bailey was desperate for answers about her lost baby.

There was also the damn attraction. Jackson only hoped that it wasn't playing into this. On most days he didn't think below the belt, but for reasons he didn't want to explore, that seemed to be happening with Bailey. But his camaraderie and stupid testosterone weren't going to run wild here.

"My plan is to have her gone as soon as possible," Jackson assured Sheriff Gentry. As soon as he had those test results. "Let me know if you get anything else on the intruder or his killer."

The sheriff assured him that he would, and Jackson ended the call.

Despite everything that was now weighing heavily on his mind, Jackson pushed it all aside and got down on the thick quilt that he kept on his office floor. It was Caden's favorite spot, and when he placed the baby on his stomach, Caden immediately began to move his arms and legs, causing his denim overalls to slide against the quilt. Caden couldn't crawl, but he seemed to love attempting it.

The phone rang, but when he glanced at the caller ID he saw it was a client. A client who could wait. Jackson let it go to voicemail and continued his daddy time with Caden.

It was amazing how much he loved his son. Amazing even more that he was already thinking of adding another addition to his family. Maybe a daughter. Heck, he might even give up his investment company and adopt a whole houseful of kids. His thirst to add more and more millions to his billion dollar portfolio just wasn't there anymore.

There was a knock at the door and Jackson decided to ignore it as well. But then it opened, and he had no choice but to look up from Caden.

It was Bailey.

Jackson silently cursed. He'd instructed his staff to tell him if Bailey left the guest quarters.

He got to his feet, leaving Caden to play on the floor, and he did that not just because his son was having fun. Jackson also did it because his desk blocked Bailey from seeing the baby. *That wasn't being petty,* he assured himself. *It was simply sheltering Caden from a woman who could potentially be a threat.*

The intercom on his desk buzzed, and a moment later he heard his house manager's voice. "I'm sorry, sir," Steven Perez told him. "I just got the word that Miss Hodges is on the way to your office."

"She's here," Jackson let him know. "Instruct the staff to give me a faster heads-up if this happens again. I know we're not accustomed to these security measures, but I want everyone to do a better job."

"Of course, sir. Do you need me there?" In other words, did Jackson want Perez to have Bailey removed?

"I'll take care of it," Jackson insisted, and he pressed the button to end the transmission. He put his hands on his hips and stared at her, waiting.

Bailey certainly didn't look like a threat, standing there. She looked lost and scared. Hell. Jackson felt that need to console her again, but he resisted.

What he couldn't resist was noticing what she was wearing. The loose, casual red dress skimmed over her body and created an interesting contrast with her milky-white skin. It was a loaner dress no doubt, and probably belonged to someone on his staff, since Bailey hadn't arrived with a change of clothes, or even any toiletries.

"I'm sorry," Bailey said. "I just thought maybe you had an update on the dead intruder."

He did, but he didn't intend to discuss anything with her while Caden was in the room. Jackson hit the button on the intercom that would no doubt send the nanny hurrying to his office.

Caden squealed, the sound of happiness amplifying through the room.

Bailey gasped and put her hand to her heart. She

hurried toward his desk, toward the sound, but Jackson blocked her from racing behind it. Still, she came up on her toes and looked over his shoulder.

The sound she made would have melted a heart of stone. It was a painful mix of shock, joy and loss all rolled into one. Jackson looked deep into her eyes, to see if all that emotional mix would give him clues as to what she thinking. But she was only staring in awe at Caden.

"He's beautiful," she muttered, her voice as filled with emotion as her eyes suddenly were.

Did that mean she believed this was her son?

Jackson didn't ask her, and she didn't have time to volunteer. Tracy Collier, the nanny, came into the room. She stopped just in the doorway, probably trying to figure out what the heck was going on, but Jackson gave her a nod. That nod sent Tracy behind his desk, where she scooped up Caden into her arms.

"Tell Daddy bye-bye," Tracy prompted, kissing Caden on the cheek.

"D-d-d-d," Caden echoed.

It was Caden's new sound, something he'd been saying for several days, but each time Jackson heard it, he was reminded of just how much he loved his little boy.

"He's already trying to say 'daddy,'" Bailey mumbled. "That's early. All the books I read said that normally happens at six months, or sometimes even later." She kept her attention fastened to Caden until the nanny and he were out of sight. She likely would have followed them if Jackson hadn't caught hold of her.

"No," was all Jackson could manage to say. He

didn't want his son part of what would no doubt be an emotional encounter unless he had no other choice.

She blinked back tears and finally nodded. "He looks like me."

"He looks like a four-month-old baby," Jackson countered. But he couldn't dismiss that there might be a resemblance. With that added to the fact that someone had indeed stolen Bailey's son, he knew he had to start accepting that a DNA match was a possibility.

How much money would it take to make her go away?

Just the thought of it sounded ruthless and made him sick to his stomach. Like the old Jackson. But he rationalized that if Bailey could indeed be paid off, then she wasn't much of a mother anyway. So he would make the offer, and maybe, just maybe, it would be an offer she couldn't turn down.

He poured her a cup of coffee from the silver carafe on his desk and motioned for her to sit. She took the coffee, the cup rattling because of her shaky hands, but she didn't sit.

"When will Evan have the test results from the DNA swabs?" she asked.

"Maybe as early as this afternoon." For those results anyway.

Jackson had arranged for others that he wouldn't mention to Bailey or Evan. Old habits died hard, and Jackson had wanted some kind of backup for the tests.

She nodded again and took a sip of the coffee. At least she tried, but the shaking sloshed it out of the cup and onto her hand. Jackson took the cup from her and put it back on his desk.

"The sheriff just called," he told her. Best to use this

time to give her an update, rather than go back to the subject of Caden. He also checked her hand to make sure the hot coffee hadn't burnt her. "No identity yet on the dead intruder."

Bailey didn't do a good job of hiding her disappointment. "And the person who killed him?"

"Nothing yet on that, either. But the intruder did call Nurse Shannon Wright."

She took a deep breath and slowly drew back her hand. "Shannon," she repeated. "And does she have an explanation why a possible killer would have called her?"

"Not yet. The sheriff will look into it. But don't get your hopes up that Shannon is guilty of anything. The intruder accused you of hiring him, so he could have also made a call to Shannon to implicate her."

"Of course. I hadn't thought of that." She paused. "Thank you for letting me stay last night. I was a wreck. Still am," she added in a mumble.

He didn't doubt that. He wasn't feeling at ease either. "Who knew you were coming here to the estate?"

Bailey shook her head. "No one should have known. I used an alias when I applied for a temp job with the decorating crew. And I only applied two days ago."

"Maybe someone had been watching you, following you," Jackson suggested.

"That's possible. Maybe the woman who took my son has been keeping an eye on me. Maybe she wants to make sure I can't ID her."

"Can you?"

She made a slight sound of frustration and closed her eyes a moment. "I wish. But the only thing I can remember is that it was a woman. She warned me to be quiet or the gunmen would kill me. She also said they might take the baby to get me to cooperate."

Jackson tried not to let that get to him, but it had to have been terrifying. "Maybe this woman is the one who hired the intruder. She could have sent him here, not for me or Caden, but for you. She could have done that to cover up the fact that she stole your child. Maybe she wants you dead."

Not a sound of frustration this time, but her eyes widened with surprise. No. Make that shock. "But why kill *me?* I don't know who she is."

"She might not realize that. If she believes you could identify her, then she would want to keep you on the run, away from the police. And if she thought she could no longer do that, then she might hire someone to kill you."

"Oh, God." And Bailey kept repeating it. With each repeat, she grew paler and her breath started to race. "I can't believe I didn't make the connection. I thought the intruder was here after you or even Caden—maybe a kidnapping for ransom. How could I have been so stupid?"

Jackson was about to point out that the intruder could indeed have been there for a kidnapping attempt. Of course, that still left the question of why the man had implicated Bailey?

"I've considered the possibility that the intruder somehow eavesdropped on my conversation with Evan," Jackson explained. "When I talked to Evan in the foyer, I said your name and asked him to run a background check on you. If the intruder heard that, using some kind of long-range eavesdropping device, he might have latched on to it because he would have known I was already suspicious of you."

She frantically shook her head. "Or he already knew my name before he arrived."

That was his number-one theory. "But if this woman who stole your baby wants you dead, why try to have you killed here at the estate? Why not wait until after you left? There's a long stretch of country road between here and San Antonio, and if the intruder had attacked there, fewer witnesses would have been around."

Bailey shuddered. "I don't know why it happened the way it did. But I can't pretend that man didn't come here looking for me. That means I brought the danger here with me. I'm sorry for that. I was so desperate to find out the truth about Caden that I failed to remember it might not be safe for me to come here."

Jackson couldn't argue with any of that. Except he, too, had been threatened by those mysterious letters. Now, the question was, were the threats connected? He couldn't immediately see how, but then he didn't like the timing of the latest letter and Bailey's arrival at his estate.

"I'm sorry," she repeated. She turned quickly and headed for the door.

Jackson hurried after her. "Wait. Where are you going?" He caught up with her just outside his office and stepped in front of her.

"Far away from here. I'll call you about the test results." She swallowed hard. "I swear, I didn't mean to put Caden or you in danger."

"The danger was here before you arrived," he conceded. Part of him wanted to step aside and let her leave, but he wasn't stupid. This particular Pandora's Box had already been opened, and whether Bailey left or not, he didn't think the danger would go with her.

When she tried to dart around him, Jackson put her against the wall again. Hell. He'd been manhandling Bailey a lot lately, but he wasn't going to let her leave until she saw the whole picture.

Even if it was a picture he wasn't sure he wanted her to see.

"This is a theory," he started, "with a lot of *if*'s. But it's a theory that kept me up most of the night. If this mystery woman did indeed hire the intruder to kill you, and if she also arranged Caden's adoption, then she might want to cover that up as well. That might be the reason she sent the hired gun here to the estate."

Bailey uttered another, "Oh, God."

Yeah. Oh, God *summed it up.*

She grabbed on to handfuls of his shirt. "You have to beef up security—"

"I already have. And my house manager is in the process of getting even more guards out here. Trust me, Caden will be safe."

The breath swooshed out of her, and she dropped her head onto his shoulder. Even though he couldn't see her face, he had no doubt that she was crying. Jackson could feel her knotted muscles, and he heard the sob she was trying to hold back in her throat. He hadn't needed anything else to convince him that Bailey was on the up-and-up, that she truly was just trying to find her missing baby, but her reaction was definitely more proof that she was the victim here.

She lifted her head, met his gaze. "Why aren't you throwing me out?"

Jackson was asking himself the same thing. He was

good at coming up with the angles, and one angle was that he should keep her close, just in case that payoff would become necessary. But his usual heart of stone didn't feel so stone-cold all of a sudden.

He wanted to help her. Even if that meant facing a truth he didn't want to face.

Jackson cursed, and that caused her forehead to bunch up. No doubt she was wondering what he was cursing about. But this profanity was for *her*—for those needs she stirred deep inside him.

She stood there, her breath hitting against his mouth. Her incredible blue eyes wide with concern.

And with her body pressed against his.

Jackson especially noticed that body-to-body part.

He was responsible for it. After all, it had been his manhandling that had resulted in her being against the wall again.

There was a moment, just a split second, when his body started to think below the belt again. A moment where he wondered what it be like to kiss her.

How did she taste?

And were those lips as soft as they looked?

Jackson felt himself moving in closer. His body revved up, everything inside him preparing for something that damn sure shouldn't happen.

He breathed in her scent, some kind of floral shampoo maybe. But beneath the bottled stuff was something that was all woman. Something warm and silky. Something that triggered his asinine male brain into thinking that kissing her was a good idea after all.

Her eyelids fluttered down. A velvety feminine sound left her mouth. Her body moved slightly closer, brushing against his.

Everything about her was soft. Her skin. Her scent. Even that clingy cotton dress that was now pressed against his jeans and shirt.

"This shouldn't happen," she whispered.

Even though her voice was soft as well, it was the hard mental slap that Jackson needed. He jerked back and tried to rein in that stupid urge to haul her to him and kiss her until neither one of them had any breath left.

"Sorry," he mumbled.

He was ready to fumble with an explanation about the danger creating the heat between them, but thankfully the house phone on his desk rang. He felt thankful for a moment before he remembered this was the line his staff would use if there were any other problems with security.

Jackson hurried into his office to grab the phone.

"It's me," Steven Perez said. With just those two words, Jackson could hear the concern in his house manager's voice.

"A problem?" Jackson asked.

"Could be. Ryan Cassaine is at the front gate."

The adoption attorney. "Why is he here?"

"He won't say. He claims it's important, but I checked your calendar, and you don't have any appointments."

No. But he did want to see Ryan so he could clarify that everything had been aboveboard with the adoption. "Let him in," Jackson instructed.

"He's not alone," Steven interjected. "He has a woman with him. Shannon Wright."

Jackson thought he might have misheard. "Shannon Wright?"

"Yes, sir. She's one of the two women you asked me to investigate."

He had indeed. Jackson had asked Evan and the sheriff to do the same. After all, Shannon Wright was a suspect in the disappearance of Bailey's son. The hired gun had also used his cell to call her. "What does she want? And better yet, why is she here with my adoption attorney?"

"Neither one of them is volunteering much to me, but Shannon is insisting that she talk to you. She says she has to tell you something important about your son."

Chapter Six

Everything seemed to be happening so fast that Bailey had trouble catching her breath. In the past twenty-four hours, she'd encountered an armed intruder, saw the precious child that might be her own and had flirted with danger by nearly kissing Jackson.

And now a suspect she'd been trying to question for four months had shown up on Jackson's doorstep.

What the heck was going on?

That was something she didn't get a chance to ask Jackson, because the moment he gave his house manager permission to escort Shannon Wright and Ryan Cassaine onto the estate, Jackson began a flurry of calls.

Some of those calls involved background requests on Shannon, but most were about security and moving Caden to the panic room. However, he also phoned Evan, his business manager, to see if he knew anything about this visit. Judging from what she could hear, Evan didn't have a clue, but he was on his way back out to the estate as well.

Maybe with the DNA results.

As critical as those results were, however, Bailey had to put the thought of them aside so she could focus on this meeting. Was it possible Shannon had come to confess that she had indeed taken Caden? If so, that could be as critical as the DNA results.

"Come with me," Jackson told Bailey when he ended the call. "I don't want this meeting to take place in the house while Caden is here."

Bailey agreed. She had no idea what the attorney's role in any of this was, but Shannon was a suspect in a newborn's kidnapping. Plus, the intruder had called Shannon. Her number was on his cell phone, and Bailey wanted an explanation for that, along with the rest.

"Shannon could be armed," Bailey pointed out as she followed Jackson down the stairs.

"Steven, the estate manager, will search them both."

Good. But Bailey wouldn't breathe easier until Shannon said what she had apparently come to say and then was off the estate and far away from Caden. Or arrested. If the woman confessed to kidnapping the baby, then Bailey would make sure Shannon was hauled off to jail.

Jackson led Bailey through the house and to the sunroom. It faced an elaborate garden that still had spots of green despite the winter weather.

Bailey looked out the glass at the approaching car and the three people who exited when it came to a stop. She recognized Steven immediately, but it took her a moment to realize the stocky woman in the billowy gray dress was indeed Shannon Wright. In the picture Bailey had, and the last time she'd spotted her, the woman had been a brunette, but now Shannon was sporting auburn hair that was cut short and choppy.

The tall, dark-haired man walking next to Shannon

was no doubt the adoption attorney. He spared Bailey a glance.

Shannon didn't spare anything. When she caught sight of Bailey, her mouth dropped open, and she came to a dead stop. Either Bailey's presence was a genuine surprise, or Shannon was faking it so she would appear innocent of having any dealings with the intruder.

"Strange bedfellows," Jackson mumbled. He glanced at her. "You okay?"

"Yes," Bailey lied.

Jackson must have known that, because he gave her arm a gentle squeeze. It seemed so…intimate. But Bailey accepted it as a gesture of comfort. Too bad Jackson was the last person from whom she should be seeking anything except information, but she kept finding herself drawn to him.

Steven ushered the visitors inside the sunroom, but he didn't come in. He stayed on the other side of the glass as if standing guard. Good. Because Bailey had no idea what could happen during this so-called meeting. It could simply be an attempt to set her up for another attack.

"Ryan," Jackson greeted. He shook hands with the attorney. "This is Bailey Hodges."

Everything about the man seemed uncomfortable. His shoulders were pulled back. His facial muscles, tight. His mud-brown eyes were narrowed and filled with suspicion.

"First thing this morning, I got a call from Evan, several calls in fact," Ryan said, without bothering to introduce Shannon. "He said you have some questions about the adoption. Not a good time for this, Jackson, considering the adoption will be final two days after

Christmas. If you had questions, you should have called me directly when we started this process."

"I didn't have questions *then*." In contrast, Jackson kept his voice calm. He looked laid-back and casual in his jeans and white shirt with rolled up sleeves. However, Bailey sensed the storm brewing beneath the cool facade. "Obviously, I have them now. Questions for you, too," he said, turning that lethal gaze on Shannon.

With that, Jackson sat on the wicker sofa and waited. Because Bailey's legs weren't feeling very steady, she sat as well. Eventually, so did Shannon. Ryan continued to stand and hover over them.

"I know who you are," Shannon volunteered, staring at Bailey. "You followed me. Hounded me," she amended. "And all for no reason. I didn't take your baby."

Bailey listened to each word, replaying them in her head. Even though she had wanted to meet and talk with Shannon for months, this was Bailey's first chance to hear the woman speak. Shannon had obviously been avoiding her, just as Bailey had been avoiding the cops.

Was this the same woman's voice she'd heard in the hospital?

"I'm innocent," Shannon persisted. "Though I'm guessing you don't believe that, because I got a call that SAPD was looking for me again."

Bailey wasn't sure she bought the woman's denial, and judging from the rumbling sound that Jackson made deep within his chest, he was skeptical as well.

"You could have told us this with a phone call," Jackson pointed out. "Instead you opted for a face-to-face meeting, with my adoption attorney no less. How do you two know each other?"

"She called me out of the blue last night," Ryan jumped to explain.

"I'd read he was your attorney," Shannon continued when Ryan didn't add anything else, "and when I realized that SAPD still considered me a suspect, I called Ryan." She huffed and looked at Bailey. "SAPD has questioned me more than a dozen times. The same questions over and over again. And I still have the same answers. I didn't take your baby. I didn't even see you during the hostage standoff. The first chance I could, I got out of there and haven't been back since."

Bailey lifted her shoulder. "Then if you're innocent, why call Ryan?"

"Because I learned from a cop friend that SAPD was questioning Ryan, too. At first I thought that was good, that I was no longer a suspect. But then I realized they were trying to connect *me* to Ryan and some moron who tried to break into your estate yesterday."

"An armed moron," Jackson supplied. "Who had called you just hours before he came here."

"So the police said." Shannon moved to the edge of her seat so she was closer and eye-to-eye with Bailey. "I don't know the man who came here. I never spoke to him, and I have no idea why he called me."

Bailey was about to suggest a reason—because Shannon might be neck-deep in all of this—but Jackson spoke before she could say anything.

"You didn't know the gunman, and you didn't know my adoption attorney. Am I supposed to believe that? After all, you're here together."

Shannon mumbled something under her breath, then

said, "I'd never met or spoken to Ryan Cassaine before last night. I said I needed to clear up some things with you and asked him to drive me out here. I wasn't sure you'd let me in if I came alone."

"I wouldn't have," Jackson assured her.

Shannon snapped back her shoulders and stared at him.

"Shannon didn't give me a stolen child," Ryan explained, sounding more frustrated with each word. "No one did. And everything about that adoption was perfectly legal." He paused, then shook his head. "Jackson, I can't believe you'd think I would do something like that. You asked me to find a baby. A private adoption. And that's exactly what I did."

Bailey didn't blindly accept that. "You don't think there's any chance, even a slight one, that Jackson's adopted son is my missing baby?"

"No." But Ryan had no sooner said that when he dodged her gaze.

Mercy, was the man hiding something?

"You were with Caden's so-called birth mother when she delivered him?" Bailey pressed Ryan.

"Of course not. Jackson asked me to find a baby, so I did some checking. I put out a lot of feelers, and soon I got the call from the birth mother. And she's not 'so-called.' She is his birth mother."

"Go over the details of that again," Jackson insisted.

Ryan huffed, louder this time. "She called me hours after she gave birth and told me that she wanted to give up her baby for adoption. A healthy baby boy. But she had no insurance and a lot of medical and credit card bills. She also wanted to go back to college. So, as you know, I contacted you, and together we came up with a sum to compensate her."

"How much compensation?" Bailey wanted to know. And she looked at Jackson for the answer.

He shrugged. "A million to the birth mother, and then there were Ryan's legal fees."

A million dollars. That was probably a drop in the bucket for Jackson, but Bailey figured there were many people who would have sold a baby for that amount or less.

Her baby.

She turned to Ryan. "What proof do you have that this woman actually gave birth to Caden?"

"The usual documents. Hospital records. The application for a birth certificate. A statement from the midwife who assisted with the delivery."

"They could have been faked." Bailey slid her gaze to Shannon. "And someone who works in a hospital would have known how to fake them."

That brought Shannon to her feet for another round of denial. Ryan got in on it as well.

"Quiet!" Jackson ordered. It wasn't a shout. It didn't have to be. Jackson had a way of commanding attention. "I want to talk to the birth mother."

Ryan was shaking his head before Jackson even finished. "Impossible. Evan has already tried and failed. She demanded a closed adoption, and you agreed. That was all part of the deal."

"Renegotiate the deal," Jackson insisted. "Offer her more *compensation*. All I want is a simple conversation."

Ryan glared at Bailey as if she were the cause of this demand. And she was. But Jackson seemed to be on a quest for the truth as well. Was that because he believed Caden wasn't her son and therefore she wasn't a threat to the adoption?

"I'll make some calls," Ryan finally conceded. "I'll see what I can do."

Jackson didn't thank the man, but instead looked at Shannon. "And as for you, I'd like you to take a lie-detector test."

Shannon looked at him as if he'd lost his mind. "SAPD gave me one and I passed."

"Then you shouldn't mind taking another. I have a friend who teaches at the FBI Academy in Quantico. He's a truth analyst, and he uses some cutting-edge technology that's several steps beyond the normal lie detector."

Bailey examined Shannon's expression. The woman seemed even more uncomfortable than she had when she first arrived, but then maybe anyone would be in her position. Bailey so wanted it to be Shannon who had taken the child, because Shannon was here, right in front of them, and if she confessed, then it could all be over. She would know what had happened when the mystery woman walked out of the hospital with her newborn son.

But Shannon didn't appear to be on the verge of confessing anything.

"All right," Shannon told Jackson. "Schedule the lie-detector test and I'll take it."

Bailey was both surprised and relieved, though agreeing to the test was one thing. Taking it was something else.

"Will you help me clear my name?" Shannon said,

and it took Bailey a moment to realize that the woman was talking to her and not Jackson.

"I'm doing everything to find my son," Bailey told her. "And if finding him helps clear your name, then of course I'll help. But if you're guilty, if you are the one who took him, I want you to tell me now."

"I didn't take him." Tears sprang to the woman's eyes. "I swear I didn't."

Ryan couldn't have looked more disinterested about Shannon's emotional response. He checked his watch and glanced impatiently at his car. "I need to get back to my office and contact the birth mother."

"Or you could give me her number and I'll contact her myself," Jackson offered.

"I don't have her number, only her attorney's. Since it's the holidays, it might take me a while to reach her. She's likely on break from her college classes."

"You'll find her," Jackson said with complete certainty, and in such a way that it sounded like a threat.

Ryan didn't miss the undertone. The attorney's jaw tightened again, and he motioned for Shannon to follow him.

"I'm innocent," Shannon insisted one more time before she left with Ryan.

Jackson and Bailey stood there and watched them drive away. Steven followed behind them in his truck, probably to make sure they left the grounds.

"Well?" Jackson asked. "Did you believe everything they said?"

"I'm not sure. You?"

"I never believe anyone until I have proof."

"You believed me," she reminded him.

That brought his gaze to hers. And he nodded. "I

believe your son is missing. I believe someone wants to harm you. I believe you're searching for the truth."

"And if I find the truth?" she asked cautiously.

"The truth doesn't change, even if it's hard to accept." He stared at her. "I've had Caden for nearly four months now, since he was a week old."

She knew what he was saying. She hadn't even held her son, but Jackson had been Caden's father. And even though she might indeed be the little boy's mother, she was a stranger to him.

Yes, the truth was often hard to accept.

And in this case it was heartbreaking.

Jackson turned, eased his arm around her and pulled her to him. This didn't feel like a veiled threat. It didn't feel intimidating.

Unfortunately, it felt right.

It would be so easy just to take what he was offering her. But Bailey pulled back.

"Does this chemistry between us have something to do with Caden?" she asked.

Those dangerous gray eyes narrowed slightly. "Do you mean am I pretending to be attracted to you? No," he answered before she could respond.

He pulled her to him again. "Trust me, if I could feel differently about you, I would. You're a threat, plain and simple, and yes, I have been thinking about how to neutralize the threat." He stayed quiet a moment. "But then I've also been thinking about kissing you."

That both frightened and excited her, because she'd been thinking about kissing him, too. "I'm not faking the attraction either," she confessed. "That means we have a problem."

Jackson was so close now, practically right in her

face, looking down at her. The corner of his mouth lifted, causing a dimple to flash in his cheek. A dimple. On any other man, that might have added a touch of wholesomeness to dark, rugged looks, but his looks were nowhere in the realm of being wholesome.

In a fantasy, Jackson would have been the pirate. A Wild West outlaw. Or the vampire who had his deadly desire barely under control. A face and body perfect for seducing and drawing women in.

But she suspected he'd never had to seduce a woman in his life.

"Are you as bad as I think you are?" she asked.

Mercy. There was too much breath in her voice, and she sounded as if she were under his spell. Heck, she was. Maybe that vampire fantasy wasn't so far off the mark.

He nodded. "Once, I was attracted to a business rival, and I slept with her. The next week I did a hostile take-over of her company."

For some stupid reason, that made Bailey smile. What was wrong with her? She should be pulling away, but the sound of his voice and that half smile made her feel all warm and golden.

"I'm not a nice guy," he added. And he lowered his head and touched his mouth to hers.

Bailey felt as if she were melting.

She'd expected his mouth to be slightly rough and warm. It was. She'd expected him to know how to kiss.

He did.

But even with all those expectations in place, she was still shocked at what he was doing to her. It was as if he knew just the right pressure, just the right angle to draw as much from the kiss as was humanly possible. This was the reason people kissed and fantasized about kissing, she decided. So they could feel this slow hunger slide right through them.

The moment was perfect: the sun-washed room, the devil in the great-fitting jeans who had her in his arms, her body yielding to the pressure and heat that his mouth had created.

Bailey lifted her hand to slip it around the back of his neck and draw him closer, but she stopped at the last second. What she didn't do was stop the kiss. She couldn't. She began to tingle, the sensation starting at her mouth and gliding through the rest of her. Everything inside her suddenly wanted this.

And more.

It had been so long since she'd had *more,* and she'd never had the likes of Jackson Malone. Kissing him was playing with fire, and that still didn't make her pull away.

Jackson was the one who stopped. He blinked and stared down into her eyes. "That was better than I thought it would be," he complained. "And my expectation had been pretty high."

Yes. She knew exactly what he meant.

Thankfully, Bailey didn't have to voice that, because his cell rang. And just like that, the moment was lost. Good thing, too. One kiss shouldn't feel like hours of foreplay. It shouldn't leave her body with a dull ache that only one thing would cure. And that one thing was someone she couldn't have or kiss again.

Jackson answered the call, but continued to study her. "Evan," he greeted, after glancing at the screen.

That was it. All he said. But it snapped her back to

reality and out of the land of kissing foreplay and wild fantasies. A good thing, too, because this call could be critical. Again, Bailey couldn't hear the conversation, but she prayed Evan had the DNA test results and that the results would prove that Caden was hers.

Jackson didn't exactly put on a poker face. As he listened, his jaw muscles went to war with each other. His mouth bent into a snarl.

"Find out what happened and get someone down to that lab immediately. If there's been any kind of breach in privacy, I want to know about it."

That finished sobering her up. *Sweet heaven. This certainly didn't seem like good news.*

"What happened?" she asked, the moment he hung up.

"The lab misplaced the DNA test results."

"What?" Her mind began to race. Had the woman who'd stolen her baby somehow got the results so that Jackson and she couldn't learn the truth?

"Don't go there yet," Jackson mumbled. "It's the holidays. The lab is working with just a skeleton crew, so the tests could still be there, but maybe misfiled."

She shook her head. He seemed so calm about this. Maybe too calm. "But someone might have tampered with them."

"Evan's taking a second set to another lab."

And that brought her to yet another concern.

"Can I trust Evan?" she asked. "Would he doctor the results to get me out of the way?"

"No," Jackson said with complete confidence. "He might insist that I lie to you. He might even try to handle getting you out of the picture on his own. But he would tell me the truth."

Hopefully, Jackson would do the same for her, but Bailey had to be realistic. She needed to figure out how to get her own sample of Caden's DNA so she could compare it to the stored umbilical cord.

"Don't borrow trouble," Jackson murmured. He put his hand on the small of her back to get her moving inside.

But Bailey didn't move a single step when she heard the loud noise.

A blast of some kind.

Everything happened fast. Too fast for her to figure out what was going on. One second she was standing, and the next moment she was on the floor of the sunroom where Jackson had pushed her.

She looked back at Jackson, ready to ask what was going on, but the next sound clarified things for her.

Something slammed into one of the sunroom panels and sent glass spraying over them.

My God.

Someone was shooting at them.

Chapter Seven

Jackson pulled Bailey to the side of the sofa.

It wasn't a second too soon.

Another bullet came tearing through the sunroom, shattering the glass and sending the dangerous spray of jagged pieces right at them.

"Caden!" Bailey shouted, covering her head.

"He's in the panic room." Jackson was beyond thankful for that. The panic room was bulletproof and impossible for anyone to penetrate, unless they knew the security codes. His son was safe.

Jackson couldn't say the same for Bailey and him. Their lives were on the line.

Whoever the hell was doing this would pay and pay hard. Of course, the question was, who was firing those shots? And with all his safeguards in place, how the devil had anyone gotten onto the grounds?

"Not again," Bailey mumbled. "Please God, this can't be happening again."

She couldn't keep from remembering the hostage situation at the maternity hospital and reliving the nightmares that came with that fateful day. Jackson couldn't stop the flashbacks, not for her or himself. Images of the bodies from the plane crash came back at him like lethal bullets. But he wouldn't let that old trauma immobilize him and stop him from figuring a way out of this life-and-death situation.

"Stay down," he warned Bailey, and he pushed her all the way to the floor.

Jackson tried to shelter her as best he could, but it was next to impossible. They were literally in a glass room, and the delicate wicker furniture didn't provide much protection. Added to that, he didn't have any weapons he could use to defend them.

More shots came, each of them eating through what was left of the glass and tearing into the furniture. Jackson made sure Bailey stayed flat on the floor so it would minimize the shooter's kill zone, but he figured this measure wouldn't save them for long.

He had to get Bailey out of there.

But how?

Jackson glanced back at the entry into the main house. The door was wide open, but it was a good twenty feet away. They could crawl to reach it, but that was twenty feet wide out in the open. A lot of bullets could come at them during that short space.

In between the din of the bullet barrage, Jackson could hear the shouts from inside the house. No doubt his staff was trying to figure out what to do. Someone had already called 9-1-1. Steven had almost certainly been alerted. Help was on the way.

But help might come too late.

The next round of bullets came directly at the sofa. And that told Jackson a lot about the shooter. He was probably using a rifle with a high-powered scope. In other words, the gunman knew exactly where Bailey and he were. It also told him something else.

The shooter might not even be on the estate.

It was possible their attacker was positioned in one of the tall trees that grew along the estate walls. As long as the walls themselves weren't touched, it wouldn't have triggered the security system and therefore wouldn't have alerted anyone on his staff. Of course, Jackson had considered something like that would be possible, but since he'd spent his entire life without being shot at, he had never considered it to be a real threat.

But it was real now.

"What do we do?" Bailey asked.

She was shaking, but her voice was surprisingly strong and determined. Good. Because she would need every ounce of strength and determination to get out of this alive.

"We have to move," Jackson told her, knowing that this might not be the right thing to do.

Hell, it was possible they didn't have any right moves. But he couldn't blindly accept that they were going to die today. Somehow, he had to figure out a way to stay alive for the sake of his son. He intended to raise his little boy, to love him, and Jackson wouldn't let some SOB take away Caden's father.

He glanced back at the entry that seemed to be getting farther away, and he spotted José, one of the gardeners. The terrified-looking man was holding a rifle, and he lifted it, no doubt questioning Jackson about what he should do.

Jackson wanted him to return fire, hoping it would give him an opportunity to get Bailey into the house.

"Can you get the rifle to me?" Jackson shouted.

The young man gave a shaky nod, and he got down

into a crouching position so he could inch toward the entry.

More bullets slammed into the sofa. But not just there. A spray of shots went into the entryway where José was making his way toward them.

"Stop!" Jackson told José. "The shooter must be able to see you."

Probably through a long-range scope on his rifle. And that meant, if the gunman could see José, he wouldn't have any trouble homing in on Jackson and Bailey if they tried to dive through the entryway.

But what choice did he have?

They couldn't just lie there and wait.

"Where's Steven?" Jackson called out.

"On his way," José relayed. "He was at the gate."

No doubt ushering out their guests. Hopefully, Steven was armed and was already trying to pinpoint the shooter so he could try to take him out. Or at least create a diversion. And that gave Jackson an idea.

He could create his own diversion.

"Everyone inside, get down," he instructed. Jackson had to yell over the sounds of the gunfire. "José, crawl toward the window and lift the rifle so it can be seen. Stay down though. Don't get anywhere near the window."

Because, if the shooter took the bait, it wouldn't be long before the bullets went that way.

"Get ready to move," Jackson told Bailey, and he got her into a crouching position so she could scramble to the entryway, a move that would happen only if the diversion worked.

The seconds crawled by, and with each one, Jackson had to fight to stay calm. Timing and a clear head were everything right now, and he had to focus solely on getting Bailey out of there.

"I'm lifting the rifle now," José called out.

Jackson could no longer see the young man, or for that matter, the window where he had positioned himself. But he had immediate proof that José was there.

The shooter shifted his aim, and the bullets blasted through the window.

"Stay down!" Jackson reminded everyone. But as he was shouting out that order, he grabbed onto Bailey's arm.

They had one chance at this. Just one. Because once they were out in the open, the shooter would no doubt turn those bullets back on them.

"Now!" Jackson shouted, making sure that Bailey heard him.

He turned, placing himself behind her and began to shove her toward the entry.

Bailey didn't have time to think. She scrambled forward, with Jackson pushing her toward what she prayed would be safety. Somehow, they had to get out of this nightmare.

In the back of her mind, she realized that Jackson was protecting her. He had taken the most dangerous position, placing himself behind her like a human shield. Bailey didn't want him to take that kind of risk, but it was too late to reverse things. The only thing that counted now was speed, because the sooner they got inside, the safer they would both be.

She hoped.

Bailey prayed this wasn't some full-scale attack. If so, Caden could be in danger.

Each step seemed to take a lifetime. Probably because

she had no breath and her entire body was a tangle of nerves and adrenaline. They were just a few feet away when the bullets shifted again. Away from the window, and back to Jackson and her.

Several shots slammed into the jamb around the entryway and tore through the wood. Still, Jackson didn't stop. He made a feral sound of outrage and rammed into her, shoving her through the entry.

Bailey landed hard on the floor, knocking what little breath she had right out of her, but she still managed to latch onto Jackson and haul him inside with her.

Jackson looped his arms around her and rolled to the side, away from the gaping entry. Some of the bullets ricocheted off the marble floor and careened into the walls and furnishings.

"Everybody get out!" Jackson shouted, and his staff began to scramble.

Jackson dragged her behind a large stone coffee table and pulled her back to the floor.

"José, I need that rifle. And I need you to take Bailey to the panic room. When you get there, give Tracy the code word, 'silver rose,' and she'll let you in." Then he turned to Bailey.

Somehow, she managed to shake her head. Bailey wasn't objecting to the panic room order. She wanted to go there. She wanted to be as far away from those bullets as possible. But she wanted Jackson, José and anyone else in the house to go with her.

"What are you going to do?" she asked Jackson.

Every muscle in his body was rock-hard and primed for a fight. His face was misted with sweat despite the cold air gushing in through the broken glass.

"I'm going after this SOB," Jackson insisted.

"No!" But she might as well have been talking to herself because Jackson motioned for José to switch places with him.

They did, and the moment José had hold of her arm, Jackson signaled for them to get moving.

"No!" Bailey repeated. "Think of Caden. He needs you."

"I *am* thinking of Caden." Jackson took the rifle and checked to make sure it was loaded. "José, get her out of here."

Bailey wanted to argue. She wanted to convince Jackson not to do this, but another round of bullets sent José and her running for their lives. The shooter might not be able to see them inside the house, but with the bullets bouncing off all the marble and stone, it wasn't safe to be anywhere near a window or exterior door.

Of course, that meant Jackson was right in the line of fire.

José had a death grip on her arm and sprinted with her toward the center of the house. She could still hear the gunfire. Heavy, thick blasts. Each of them potentially lethal. And she prayed Jackson would have backup soon.

"This way," José told her, and he led her into a library that was on the same floor as the sunroom.

There were floor-to-ceiling shelves lined perfectly with books, but there was also a floor-to-ceiling window on the far center wall. José didn't take her anywhere near that. He pressed a button beneath one of the shelves, and a small book-size monitor dropped down. Bailey immediately saw the nanny, Tracy Collier. She looked as terrified as Bailey was.

"Mr. Malone says I'm to tell you 'silver rose,'" José said to the woman.

Tracy nodded and turned from the screen while she pressed in some numbers on a keypad behind her. A moment later, the shelf slid back to reveal a metal door. Bailey heard the locks disengage, and José opened it. Tracy was there, just on the other side, and the nanny was armed.

"Stay here," José insisted. "I'm going to see if I can help Mr. Malone."

Good. She wanted Jackson to have all the help he could get, but she had second and third thoughts about going into hiding while Jackson and José were taking all the risks.

"Mr. Malone's orders," José reminded her, and he pushed her inside and shut the door.

Bailey was ready to pound on the door, but then she looked around the room. Tracy and she weren't alone. Two of the housekeepers were there as well, and they were standing against the far wall, apparently waiting for the nightmare to end.

The room wasn't that large compared to the rest of the house. Probably twenty by thirty feet. There was a sofa, several chairs, a fridge, desk and a storage cabinet.

And then she saw Caden.

He was sleeping on a thick quilt stretched out on the carpeted floor.

Oh, mercy.

Again, she was hit with all the feelings of mother-hood. All the things she had missed in the past four months. Bailey didn't know if this baby was hers, but she felt the love pour through her heart.

"The sheriff just arrived," Tracy whispered.

Bailey tore her gaze from the baby to look at the monitor set into the wall. Actually, it was a series of monitors, six of them in all, and they showed various parts of the estate.

"There," Tracy said, pointing to the monitor that displayed the front gate. The sheriff's vehicle was indeed there, along with two other cars, and they were making their way to the estate.

"What about Jackson?" Bailey asked. She frantically searched the screens but didn't see him. She didn't see the shooter either, and since the panic room was apparently soundproof, she couldn't hear if there were shots still being fired.

It seemed to take forever, but Bailey finally spotted him. Jackson was out of the now-shredded sunroom and was in the rose garden. He had the rifle and had taken cover behind a marble statue.

"He shouldn't be out there," Bailey mumbled, and she put her fingers to her mouth to stop her lips from trembling.

Here, she barely knew Jackson, but he had risked his life for her. He had saved her from those bullets. And now he was outside, continuing to risk his life so he could make sure Caden would stay safe.

She glanced at Caden again and understood his need to protect that precious little baby. The gunman, whoever he was, had to be stopped. Killed, even. Bailey didn't want a repeat attack.

Volleying glances between the baby and the monitors, Bailey watched as Jackson leaned out from the statue. He took aim.

And fired.

The recoil snapped his shoulder back, but he quickly

re-aimed and fired again before taking cover. For a moment she thought he was going to repeat the process all over again, but he stopped and looked in the opposite direction.

Where the sheriff was approaching.

Two deputies got out of their vehicles and fanned out over the garden. She saw Steven, the estate manager. He was armed, and he followed behind one of the deputies. Along with the sheriff, they all began to walk toward the west fence, partly concealed by clusters of trees and shrubs.

The sheriff said something to Jackson and then motioned toward the estate. It was clear from Jackson's expression that he was arguing, but he soon turned and began to race back into the house.

Bailey's heart dropped.

My God. What was happening now? Had the gunman managed to get into the house?

"No one can break in here," Tracy reminded her. "There's another panic room where most of the household staff went, and even they can't get into this one without the password and then me punching in the code to the locks."

That made Bailey breathe a little easier, but Jackson was still out there, possibly under the same roof with a would-be killer.

Tracy adjusted one of the monitors, switching to a camera inside the house. Jackson was running through the foyer and toward the library.

Behind them, Caden made a sound, and Bailey saw his eyes open. It wasn't a happy sound, either. He immediately started to cry.

"Pick him up," Tracy said to no one in particular. She

hurried to the door, probably to wait for Jackson so she could let him in.

Bailey glanced at the two housekeepers. They were still huddled in the corner with their arms wrapped around each other. One of them moved, as if to go to the baby, but Bailey got there first.

Her heart was pounding out of her chest by the time she leaned down and picked up Caden from the quilt. He didn't stop crying, and it actually got worse when he looked at her. No surprise there. She was a stranger to him, and he had just woken up in a strange room. He was scared.

"Shhh," Bailey whispered. She brought him closer to her, snuggling him against her chest, and she started to rock, hoping it would soothe him.

It worked.

The sobs turned to a whimper, and he stared at her as if trying to figure out who she was. Bailey was sure she was staring at him the same way. He felt like hers, but she couldn't dismiss that serious emotions were playing into this.

Tracy punched in the codes, and the door slid open. It was Jackson of course. His gaze fired all around the room until his attention landed on her.

Part of her was so relieved to see him, to know that he was safe, but he put the rifle aside and immediately went to take Caden from her arms.

Bailey thought her heart might have literally broken at that moment.

Jackson didn't ask why she was holding his baby, and he didn't have to voice his disapproval. She saw it there, all over his face.

"Where's the gunman?" she managed to ask.

Jackson kissed the top of Caden's head and hugged him, maybe a little too tightly, because Caden protested.

"I don't know," Jackson answered. He kept a firm hold on Caden while he checked the monitors.

Bailey checked them, too, and saw the sheriff and the others converge near the west fence. She held her breath, waiting and praying.

Jackson's phone rang, and Tracy put aside her weapon so he could hand her the baby. Bailey didn't have time to be hurt that he hadn't offered Caden to her. That's because she was on pins and needles waiting for an update.

But Jackson didn't say anything. He just listened to the caller.

"Where?" Jackson asked. But it was more like a bark than a question.

Sweet heaven, whatever he was hearing, it obviously wasn't good news.

"No," Jackson said a moment later. "I'll make the arrangements."

Jackson ended the call, snared her gaze and then took a deep breath. "The gunman wasn't on the estate," he told her. "He launched the attack from one of the trees just behind the fence. The sheriff just found what appears to be his vehicle, dozens of spent cartridges…and some other things."

Bailey took a step closer, almost afraid to hear the answer to the question she had to ask. "And the gunman?"

Jackson shook his head. "He got away on foot. But the deputies are in pursuit."

Oh, God. Jackson didn't have to spell out what that meant. There could be another attack. Maybe soon.

"What should we do?" But Bailey was already considering the possibilities. This danger was linked to her. She was the one the gunman was after.

"I should leave," she said before Jackson could speak. "If I go, the gunman won't come back to the estate."

Jackson went to her and slipped his arm around her waist. "You're wrong. Yes, it appears the gunman was trying to kill us. But a rifle wasn't the only thing he had with him. In the vehicle, he had an infant seat and baby supplies."

She shook her head, not understanding. "Why?"

"Because he didn't just come here to kill us, Bailey. He came here to kidnap Caden."

Chapter Eight

Jackson sank down in the chair behind his desk and drained the shot of whiskey he'd just poured. He swore to himself.

It was the first time he'd had a few minutes to himself since the attack in the sunroom, and even though he was well aware of how close Bailey and he had come to dying, the alone time allowed everything to sink in.

He cursed again.

Someone wanted him dead. And worse, that someone wanted his son.

Who the hell was doing this? And better yet, why? If he knew the *why,* he would probably know the *who.*

He glanced at the threatening letter again: "Jackson Malone, I won't forgive and forget. Watch your back."

It was pretty generic for a threat. There were plenty of people he'd crossed while taking his company to the billion-dollar level. But why would someone he'd trampled over in the business world want to go after Caden?

They wouldn't, he decided.

A person out for that kind of revenge would go after the company. Since the company was no longer Jackson's top priority, it would be easier to try to worm into the investments and create some havoc. But there had been no such attempts on Malone Investments.

So that brought him back to Bailey. Now, this is where the pieces fit.

Someone, a woman, had taken Bailey's newborn, and maybe this woman was afraid of being caught. Of course, that theory worked only if Caden was indeed Bailey's missing son.

Or if someone believed he was.

Jackson glanced at his laptop, which showed split screens of the estate and grounds. There were people and law enforcement officers milling around both inside and out, most either working on the investigation or putting the new security measures in place. Jackson had hired new guards—as many as he could get on such short notice—and a new security system was being installed.

On another monitor, he saw Bailey in the nursery with Tracy and Caden, who was taking his afternoon nap. Tracy was reading a paperback, but Bailey was sitting, staring at Caden.

Keeping watch.

While Jackson didn't care much for the idea of Bailey spending time bonding with Caden, he welcomed the extra set of eyes and ears. Especially Bailey's. If someone tried to get to Caden, she would die protecting the baby. He had no doubt about that, and right now he wanted to do any- and everything to protect his little boy.

That included learning the truth.

Jackson took out his phone and called Evan.

"Are you okay?" Evan asked, the moment he answered.

"No," Jackson answered honestly. He was dealing with the adrenaline crash from hell, and he still wasn't completely confident of his security measures.

"I've been looking into places where you could take Caden," Evan went on. "How about your ski lodge in Colorado? It's at the top of the mountain, and it might be easier to control security."

Jackson had already considered it. He'd also considered his other properties. Or maybe his parents' villa in France.

"The problem is, that no matter where I go I have to set up security." And not just any ordinary security. It had to be all-encompassing. "At least here at the estate, I already have people and equipment in place."

"Yes, but is it a good idea to stay here?" Evan pressed.

"It will be, if we can get to the bottom of what's happening." Jackson looked at the security screens again and saw Bailey leaving the nursery. He watched as she stepped into the hall and headed toward his office. No doubt she wanted an update, and Jackson hoped he was about to get one.

"What about the DNA test?" he asked Evan.

"The lab found the samples and they're running them now. We might have results by the end of the day."

Well, that was…progress at least.

"I do have some information on the background checks I ran on the two women from the maternity hospital. Shannon Wright and Robin Russo. I just emailed you an interesting financial report on Shannon. And as for Robin, well, she's actually in the waiting room right outside my office."

That grabbed Jackson's attention. "Why?" He

continued to watch Bailey. She was looking around, as if she expected someone to jump out and attack her.

"Robin wants to see Bailey and you. Apparently, the renewed interest from SAPD has unnerved her, and she wants to try to convince you that she's innocent."

"Is she?"

There was a soft knock at his door, and Jackson got up to let Bailey in. She was leaning so close to the door that she practically spilled into his arms. Jackson put his hand on her waist, to steady her.

And to touch her, too.

She seemed to need some kind of reassurance, and Jackson suddenly felt more than willing to give it to her.

"I'm not sure if Robin is innocent or not," Evan answered. "Do you want to talk to her and ask her yourself?"

Jackson caught Bailey's gaze. "You think it's a good idea if we have a meeting with Robin Russo?"

Bailey's eyes widened and she nodded. "Yes, especially if Robin can give us any information about who launched this attack."

Jackson wasn't sure they would get that from the woman, but since the danger could very well be linked to what happened at the maternity hospital four months ago, he didn't think it would hurt to hear what Robin had to say.

"Bring her out to the estate. To the guesthouse," Jackson corrected.

"But isn't the guesthouse where Bailey is staying?" Evan questioned.

Not any more. But since Bailey didn't know that yet, Jackson kept it to himself. "Just bring Robin and get me those DNA test results," Jackson insisted, and he ended the call.

"Robin is coming here?" Bailey asked.

"Yes. Evan is leaving his office with her now, but I won't bring her inside the house itself." Of course, last time that hadn't worked very well, since their attacker hadn't even gotten on the grounds, and yet he'd managed to do some serious damage to both to the estate and Bailey's and his peace of mind.

Bailey scrubbed her hands down the sides of her dress. "Well, at least the sheriff and his deputies are here in case something goes wrong."

True. The timing was in their favor anyway. "I'll have her searched for any weapons before she'll be allowed through the gate," he explained. Though again, would that be enough?

"Tracy said you're installing a new perimeter security system," Bailey commented.

Man, her nerves were right there at the surface. Her mind was probably still firing on all cylinders as well, but he was betting the adrenaline crash had left her beyond exhausted. It certainly had for him.

"I am. There are sensors that will detect anyone or anything that gets near the fence. I'm having the fence reinforced as well."

More hand rubbing. "Must have been hard to get all the workers here, with Christmas just two days away."

It was. But money spoke loud and clear, even if the workers would rather be spending this time with their families.

"Evan said he emailed me some updates on Shannon Wright and Robin Russo," Jackson told her, hoping it would get her mind off all the security details he was already obsessing over.

One obsession at a time, he reminded himself.

But then he made the mistake of looking at Bailey.

There it was. That punch below the belt. She looked so feminine and soft, the exact opposite of how she made him feel. And those eyes… Her eyes always seemed to be giving him some kind of invitation unintentionally.

Still, she was attracted to him, too. He could feel that as well.

But feeling it and acting on it were two different things. He couldn't control his body's response to her, but he sure as hell could control what he did about that response.

Jackson hoped.

Mentally groaning, he opened the email Evan had sent him and read through the reports. Bailey moved behind him, her hand gripping the back of his chair. Her fingers brushed against his shoulder.

So much for hoping. She might as well have kissed him.

He was toast.

"Both women seem to have some financial issues," Bailey said, obviously reading the email and hopefully not noticing his reaction to her touch.

"Yeah," Jackson agreed, forcing himself to concentrate on the reports. This was damn serious stuff, and he shouldn't be thinking about her softness, her eyes, or any other part of her.

"Evan thinks Shannon is living beyond her means," she concluded. Bailey moved closer, dipping down so that her head was right next to his. "She certainly has a lot of debt for her income."

She did. About fifty thousand dollars in credit card bills and loans. But that made her appear to be a poor money manager, not necessarily a baby snatcher.

"If she'd sold your son, then Shannon would have gotten a chunk of that one million dollars. So why hasn't she used the money to pay off her bills?"

"Maybe she knew if she used the cash right away, it would draw attention to her," Bailey pointed out. "After all, the police are still investigating her."

True. And that meant Shannon could have the money stashed offshore somewhere. Or maybe she had used it to a pay for a hired gun or two.

Bailey's warm breath hit his neck, and she slid her hand around the outside of his arm so she could touch the screen.

Great.

Now, he could feel her and take in her scent, too. Added to that, she was close enough to kiss. He couldn't think about kissing her, because that last session nearly had him dragging her off to bed. Not the way to keep the distance between them.

But maybe there was no need for distance.

Maybe he could take her and still be objective about this investigation.

He rolled his eyes. *Sheez.* An aroused man could come up with all kinds of stupid justifications for kissing an attractive woman.

"Look at this." Bailey tapped the report on Robin Russo. "Robin Russo recently bought a house and paid cash."

Now that was a massive red flag, and he wondered if SAPD knew about it. Of course, there were a lot of reasons why someone might pay cash, but paired with

Robin's presence at the hospital the day of the hostage crisis, it made the transaction suspicious.

"I'll have Evan dig deeper into her financials," Jackson added. "And we can ask her about it when she's here."

Bailey pulled back slightly, but still stayed close. "Why do you think she wants to see us?"

"Probably to get us to back off any investigation. Even if she's innocent, it can't be fun to have the cops examining her every move."

At least he hoped that's what the cops were doing. He also hoped SAPD still had both Shannon and Robin under surveillance, because if either of the women had hired the gunmen, there might have been some kind of contact or face-to-face meeting to make the payment.

"What are you thinking?" Bailey asked, still staring at the screen.

He could have given her a good answer. Nothing sexual. Nothing to do with kissing. One that proved to her that he was pouring over every detail of Evan's report. But he had already absorbed the details. He was good at that—taking huge chunks of information and processing them quickly.

Still, there were things to be done.

Jackson would have to contact SAPD about that surveillance question. He would need more financial info on both women. He wanted to check for offshore accounts. And he'd do all those things and more. But for now, he had to get something off his chest.

Or rather *on* it.

Hell. He was going with his gut here, and not his business brain, because he was reasonably sure his brain would get outvoted by the rest of him.

Bailey was still so close to him that he didn't have to move far. Jackson simply reached out, slid his hand around the back of her neck and eased her down to him. He took his time. Kept the motion slow and easy so she would have a chance to back away.

But she didn't.

Bailey moved closer as well, and their mouths met.

Her lips were soft. There was that word again. *Soft.* But he couldn't remember soft ever feeling so damn good. However, it was more than just pleasurable. Jackson felt that jolt deep inside him. Familiar but different. This felt like something more than just a reaction to a really good kiss.

It couldn't be more.

Kissing Bailey was a bad enough complication, but making more out of it than it really was could be a huge mistake. They weren't friends. Or lovers. Even though it suddenly felt as if they were.

"Oh," she muttered, stretching out the syllable so that it sounded dreamy. "You're a really good kisser."

That was information he didn't need to hear. Though it made him smile.

Toast.

Yes, that's exactly what he was.

"You're not so bad yourself," he let her know.

"Really? Because I think this is all your doing. I think I'm under your spell."

Good. Because he didn't care why she was melting into him, only that she was. He wanted Bailey hot, wanting and ready. And she was getting there fast.

She made a feminine sound when the tip of his tongue touched hers. That sound created another jolt of heat and need. The jolt got stronger when she slipped her arm around him, turning her body so that she was directly in front of him.

Finally, she was against his chest.

He could feel her breasts. Small but firm. He dropped his hand from the back of her neck to her waist, and he pulled her onto his lap.

Jackson figured he'd lost his mind. But he no longer cared. The only thing that he could think of right now was taking Bailey.

Chapter Nine

Bailey couldn't breathe. She couldn't stop her heart from racing. And she definitely couldn't stop herself from touching Jackson.

But what she could do was feel.

Oh, yes. She could do that all right.

She was suddenly aware of every inch of her body. And Jackson's. That probably had something to do with the fact she was now on his lap. Her hands were on his chest and on all those toned muscles that she had fantasized about. Now she didn't have to fantasize. He was hers for the touching.

So she touched.

Bailey slid her hand down to this stomach and had the pleasure of feeling those muscles respond. Jackson responded, too. There was a deep rumble in his throat, and he snapped her even closer.

The kiss deepened and got even hotter. She couldn't remember the last time she'd been swept away like this. And all with just kisses. If he could set these kind of white-hot fires inside her with just his mouth, it left her breathless to think of what it would be like to make love with him. He wouldn't be gentle. Not Jackson. She was betting he was as take-charge and thorough in bed as he was in business.

And Bailey was burning to find out if that was true.

She felt his hand on her leg. On her bare skin. And while he kept up the intensity of the kiss, he slid his palm up, pushing up her dress along with it.

In the back of her mind, she realized this was too much too soon. She hardly knew him. They had a ton of other things they should be doing. But in the front of her mind, Bailey could only feel the electric sensations he was creating.

His hand stopped midway up her thigh.

She wanted him to move higher. She wanted him to take this to the next level, even if that meant having sex on his desk. The thought of that shocked her.

And made her even hotter.

She'd never had sex on a desk. Never had sex with a man like Jackson. But she was betting it would be an experience she'd never forget.

He brought everything to a standstill, pulling back just slightly so they could make eye contact.

"You aren't going to stop me, are you?" he asked.

Bailey felt herself blush, but she wasn't actually embarrassed. The fire was too hot for that, and she was still trying to figure out if she wanted to keep pressing. It wouldn't take much. After all, she was on his lap and she could feel the proof of his arousal.

He was ready to do what she was fantasizing about.

Well, physically ready anyway.

She saw the doubt in his eyes, doubt that mirrored in hers.

"I was just…" But she didn't know how to finish the

statement. *I was just going to let you do whatever you wanted to me? I was just too hot to stop?*

No.

Best not to pour out her raunchy thoughts like that. Besides, Jackson already knew that she wanted him. It wouldn't help this situation to spell it out.

"Should I apologize?" he asked.

Bailey got up from his lap, not easily, and smoothed down her dress. "Don't you dare."

Jackson smiled, causing that killer dimple to wink in his right cheek. But the smile quickly faded. "So what should I do?"

His words dripped with carnal undertones. "Not that," she murmured, giving him a quick kiss. "You were right to stop."

"Really? Because it doesn't feel right."

Oh, the man was a charmer, and coupled with those incredible hot looks, he was charming her right into his bed—or his desktop.

The phone on his desk buzzed, but it was several long moments before Jackson tore his gaze from hers to answer it.

Sweet heaven.

What was she going to do about this untimely attraction?

"Let them in," she heard Jackson say, and then he hung up the phone. "Evan is on his way with Robin Russo."

That required Bailey to take a deep breath.

"You don't want to see her?" Jackson questioned, obviously not missing her reaction.

"No. I do. I've met her before. Actually, she's the one who filed the restraining order against me because I was following her. I thought she might have answers about my missing son."

"She never volunteered anything or let anything slip?"

Bailey shook her head. "But then I wasn't very subtle. I was desperate. Still am." She paused. "Which is probably why you should handle the questions. When I see Robin Russo and Shannon Wright, my instincts are to shake them senseless until they tell me what I want to hear—that one of them took my son, that he's safe and that he'll be returned to me immediately."

Jackson slid his hand over hers. "Maybe that'll happen today."

She didn't miss the slight catch in his voice, perhaps because if that miracle did happen, it could mean they would learn that her missing son was Caden. And that would create even more of a firestorm than this insane attraction between Jackson and her.

He patted her hand and stood. "I've changed my mind about meeting them in the guesthouse," he let her know. "I don't want you outside just yet. So I'll have them brought into the sitting area just off the foyer. Fewer windows in there."

And not too far from the front door. Bailey approved of that, even though she doubted they were going to have to toss Robin or Evan out of the house.

Jackson typed in some keys on his laptop and tapped into the video feed from the nursery. She saw Tracy in the rocking chair next to the crib. Caden was still sleeping. Maybe he would continue napping through this meeting, and then Bailey could sneak back up to the nursery. Jackson hadn't exactly issued an invitation for her to visit with Caden, but he hadn't objected to her presence there after the shooting.

He touched the screen, running his fingers along Caden's sleeping face. Then he huffed and opened his desk drawer. He took out a small handgun and slipped it into the back waist of his pants.

"It's just a precaution," he assured her, probably because she didn't completely choke off a gasp.

Good. Despite the surprised gasp, Bailey wanted to take all possible precautions. She didn't want another attack like the last one.

While they walked toward the stairs, Jackson made a call. "Tracy," he said. "It's time to move Caden into the panic room."

Yet another precaution Bailey approved of, even though it would probably wake him. The baby had already had too much of his routine disrupted, and that riled her. This needed to end so that Caden could have some normalcy.

Jackson led her down the stairs and into the foyer. They walked past the tree and Bailey made a mental note to finish decorating it if the danger—and—life settled down long enough for that to happen. It seemed a little trivial in the grand scheme of things, but she wanted Caden to have as much of a Christmas experience as possible.

Even if she wouldn't be there to share it.

Bailey had to accept that, despite the hot kisses they'd just experienced, Jackson could at any moment demand that she leave.

They'd just made it into the sitting room when the front door opened, and Steven ushered both Evan and Robin inside. Robin gave her a cool glance, followed by a huff. Evan's reaction was more of an eye roll. He obviously didn't want Bailey there at the estate, encroaching on his boss's territory.

Robin had a different reason for that huff.

It had been only a month since Bailey had last seen Robin. Or rather, since she'd last watched the woman. Bailey had sat in her car across from the medical clinic where Robin now worked, and waited for her to come out. Bailey had followed her, praying that Robin would lead her to any clues about the baby. But nothing came of it. Robin had merely done some grocery shopping and had then returned to her apartment. Hardly incriminating.

Like now.

Robin was the picture of propriety, with her sleek shoulder-length brunette hair, perfectly styled. Her makeup was perfect as well. And she looked holiday festive in her emerald-green business suit that was almost an exact match with her eyes. Which were narrowed.

"You wanted to speak to us," Jackson prompted.

"To *you*," Robin clarified, turning her entire body in Jackson's direction. "I haven't had much luck convincing Miss Hodges that I didn't take her son."

Jackson shrugged and sat on the sofa with Bailey. "Why do you think that is? Have you done something to make Bailey suspicious?"

That didn't improve Robin's narrowed eyes. "I was at the wrong place at the wrong time. The San Antonio Maternity Hospital should have provided better security. They didn't. And because they didn't, those gunmen were allowed to storm in and take the hostages. I was nearly taken myself, but I managed to duck into a supply closet."

"Lucky you," Jackson commented, taking the sarcasm right out of Bailey's mouth.

Bailey had also been at the wrong place at the wrong time, and she'd had her child stolen. Possibly by this woman.

God, she wished she could remember the face and the voice of the person who'd walked out of that room with her child. Ironically, this person had saved Bailey, but Bailey would have traded her own life to know that her son was safe.

"I understand Shannon was already here," Robin said a moment later.

Both Jackson and Bailey looked at Evan who confirmed that with a nod. "I told her. She also knows there was a gunman. She wanted to come anyway."

"To tell you to back off," Robin said to Bailey. She sank down onto the love seat across from Bailey and Jackson. "I don't have time for more investigations. I'm trying to get on with my life. So should you."

"Not without my son," Bailey fired right back. "And not until I find him and the person responsible for taking him."

"Robin insists she had no part in that," Evan volunteered, causing all three of them to turn in his direction.

"I can speak for myself," Robin snapped. "But he's right. I didn't take your son." Instead of a huff, she gave a heavy sigh, and her expression softened. "I'm sorry for your loss, Bailey. I truly am. But I can't go through another round of this investigation."

"You sound stressed," Jackson commented. "Does that have something to do with moving? I understand you recently bought a house."

Robin blinked and gave an accusing glare at Evan. "I suppose you're the one who told him that."

Evan paused but finally nodded. "Jackson and I would like to know where you got the money."

"None of your business," she barked and got to her feet. Robin pointed her perfectly manicured index finger at Evan. "You said this would be a fair meeting. No ambush. You said they would listen to what I had to say."

"We listened," Jackson assured her. "But I'm not so sure we believe you. I'm certainly not going to ask SAPD to call off the investigation."

Robin gave an indignant nod. "Then don't expect me to cooperate. I'm leaving here and going to the police. I'll file charges against Bailey for harassment."

Bailey started to get up and tell the woman to take a hike, but Jackson caught on to her arm and kept her anchored to the sofa.

"I don't think you want to take on Bailey," Jackson warned Robin. "Because if you do, you'll be taking on me. You think you can handle that?"

Her chin stayed high, but Robin dropped back a step. "No. But I won't be bullied. Don't think I won't play dirty, too. I'll announce to anyone who'll listen that Bailey is hiding out here with you." She turned that venomous gaze on Bailey. "It's my guess you don't want certain people to know where you are."

Mercy. Robin must have known about the attempts on Bailey's life, because that had been all over the news, but did the woman also know that Bailey had been followed? And that the two gunmen who'd come to the estate could be linked to her as well?

Robin didn't wait for Bailey or Jackson to respond.

She stormed out of the room and toward the front door. Jackson sprang from the sofa and hurried to watch her. Probably to make sure she did indeed leave.

"My advice?" Evan said. He went to Jackson's side but waited until Robin had closed the door behind her before he continued. "Don't put any more heat on Shannon Wright or Robin Russo. Just let me quietly handle this."

"Quietly?" Bailey wanted to scream. "My son is missing, and I don't want to stay quiet. Besides, you're the one who brought her here."

"Only because I thought it would smooth things over."

"Nothing will be smoothed over until I find my son." Bailey had to fight hard to hang on to her temper. She was sick and tired of being stonewalled and placated. She only wanted her baby back.

"Antagonizing Robin won't help," Evan tossed at her.

"Maybe not. But those DNA results will. Where are they, by the way?" She glanced at Jackson to see what his reaction was to her grilling his business manager, but he only looked at Evan, apparently waiting for him to answer her question.

"I'm working on it," Evan snapped. He aimed a why-aren't-you-defending-me glare at Jackson.

Jackson only shrugged. "I want those results, too."

Evan mumbled something and headed out, keeping the same rapid pace that Robin had when she made her exit. He slammed the front door behind him.

"Sorry about that." Jackson quickly went to the front door, locked it and reengaged the security system, using a keypad on the wall. Then he went to the window and watched Robin and Evan drive away.

"What are you thinking?" Bailey asked, unable to read his expression.

"I'm thinking I need to do some digging on Evan."

"I agree." She was glad they were on the same page. She also wanted the DNA tests repeated. "Do you think Evan might hold a grudge against you for his fiancée's death?"

"Maybe." He didn't say anything else for several moments. "Before today, I looked for any signs of that. Any subtle clues that Evan blamed me for that crash. No clues, subtle or otherwise. But then, Evan's a smart man. It's the reason I hired him to help manage my company."

Bailey thought about that a moment. "It doesn't make sense though. That plane crash was six months ago. If Evan had wanted revenge, he would have taken it then."

"Maybe. And maybe he's upset now because I'm truly happy for the first time in my life. Caden's adoption is just a few days away from being finalized. Plus, I've been thinking about selling my company."

"What?" This was the first she'd heard of that, and it certainly hadn't been mentioned in the papers.

Jackson lifted his shoulder. "I want to adopt another child, and I don't want to put in long hours at work. If I sell Malone Investments I can start a small consulting business. Evan suspects what I'm about to do, and I'm pretty sure he doesn't approve."

No, he wouldn't, because it would essentially mean he was out of a job.

Jackson checked his watch then looked at her. "I'm

moving both Caden and you into my suite. For security reasons," he quickly added.

Her heart gave a little leap. His suite? "You're sure? I figured you'd want me gone, not underfoot."

"Part of me does want you gone," he admitted. Then he shook his head. "But I can't send you away with someone trying to kill you."

Her heart leaped for a different reason. "Maybe that's exactly the reason I should go. As long as I'm here—"

He pressed his fingers to her mouth. "The last gunman came to kidnap Caden. This is no longer just about you. We're all in the middle of it."

True. But she was surprised Jackson had been able to accept that. She certainly hadn't come to terms with it yet.

He checked his watch again and took out his phone. "I'll call Tracy and tell her it's okay to come out of the panic room. Why don't you go on up and check on Caden for me?"

Bailey was thrilled to do that, but she didn't budge. "Why? Is anything wrong?"

"No." Jackson's answer was fast and sharp. "Just go on up and meet them as they come out of the panic room. I won't be long."

Bailey studied him a moment longer and finally nodded. There was no way she would give up a chance to spend some time with Caden, even if she suspected that Jackson might be up to something.

She went up the steps, glancing back at Jackson. He glanced at her, too, and motioned for her to go. She did. But because she couldn't shake the feeling that something just wasn't right, she stopped in the hall.

And waited.

She watched as Jackson did indeed make a call. From her position, she could even hear the beeps as he pressed in the numbers.

"It's Jackson Malone," he said to whomever answered. "Do you have those DNA test results for me?"

Bailey shook her head. She didn't think he was talking to Evan, so what was this about? Why would he be calling anyone but Evan about DNA results?

"I see," Jackson said a moment later. His back was to her, but she watched as he pressed his fingers to his forehead. "No. I'm still here," he continued.

Bailey inched even closer because she didn't want to miss any part of this. What was Jackson doing?

"Repeat the tests," Jackson said to the caller. "When you get back the second test results, call me. Then destroy the samples. I don't want anyone else to know what you just told me."

Chapter Ten

Jackson eased off the sofa in his suite and tiptoed to the crib so he could check on Caden. His son was still asleep, thank God, because he'd had a restless night. Probably because of the change of rooms. But Jackson had had no choice. He'd wanted both Caden and Bailey nearby, in case there was another attack.

It was the reason Jackson had kept not one gun but two by his side throughout the night. That was a first for him. He'd never woken up to guns on Christmas Eve day.

He leaned down and brushed a kiss on top of Caden's head. The baby stirred a little but didn't open his eyes.

"My son," Jackson mumbled.

That was certainly how he felt about the baby; but soon, very soon, he was going to have to come to terms with the fact that Bailey felt the same way about the little boy. Jackson had been wrong to think he could offer her money. Wrong to think he could intimidate her into leaving. Besides, he didn't want to intimidate her. And that was a problem in itself.

He wanted her in other ways.

Thankfully, they hadn't had time to act on those

"other ways." Jackson had been tied up with security arrangements and calls about updates in the investigation. All of that had lasted well into the night, and by the time he'd returned to his suite, both Bailey and Caden were asleep. He'd considered waking Bailey because there was something important he had to tell her.

He had to tell her about the call he'd made after Robin and Evan left.

That call had been critical. Life-changing, even. But when Jackson gave her the news, he wanted her to be alert so they could talk it out. He decided that talk could wait until morning.

Well, it was morning now, and even though he was dreading what he had to tell Bailey, he couldn't put it off much longer. The day was likely to get hectic fast. Hopefully, that wouldn't include any new dangers. They had enough of those as it was.

Jackson gave Caden another kiss and made his way to the adjoining bedroom. His bedroom, normally. But this morning Bailey was sleeping in his bed. She was co-cooned there in the center of the massive bed, snuggled beneath the white, goose down comforter.

Completely covered except for her bare leg.

And her thigh.

All that bare skin revved up his body. Not that he needed much to rev him. All through the night, his body kept reminding him that Bailey was close enough to touch. Close enough to kiss. And even close enough for him to get off the sofa in the sitting room and climb into the bed with her. Then they could continue what they'd started the day before in his office.

Jackson was still staring at her thigh when he heard a slight sound. His gaze slid up higher, and he saw that Bailey was not only awake, she was staring at him with sleepy eyes. She was obviously aware that he was gawking at her.

She smiled. It was sleepy and slow as well. She clearly wasn't fully awake.

"I dreamed about you," she whispered. And from the sound of it, it had been a hot dream.

"Oh, yeah?" Jackson came closer and sank down on the bed next to her. "Because I dreamed about you, too."

He leaned over, working his fingers into her hair, which was fanned against the stark white pillow. In fact, Bailey was the only spot of color amid all that white. And she looked better than any dream he'd ever had.

So Jackson kissed her.

She made a wistful sound of pleasure, rolled toward him and slipped her arm around him. Bailey might have still been half asleep, but she did a darn good job of kissing him right back. And more. She drew him closer—and closer—until she pulled him on top of her. Since his shirt was unbuttoned, his bare chest landed against her flimsy gown and her breasts.

Jackson glanced back into the sitting room. He couldn't see Caden's crib from this angle, but the suite door was locked and secured with the new security system, and he figured he would hear Caden if he awoke.

Bailey lifted her leg, sliding it around his, pulling him even closer to her. Jackson responded all right. He got rock hard, and he deepened the kiss. Yeah, it was probably a stupid idea to do this, but Jackson figured there was no way he was going to talk his body, or hers, out of a quick round of morning sex.

But then she stopped.

Bailey just froze.

Jackson pulled back and stared down at her, trying to figure out what was wrong. For one thing, she no longer looked sleepy or aroused. Her eyes were wide, alert and somewhat accusing.

He pulled back farther. "What's wrong?" Because he didn't think he had misinterpreted the sexual signals she'd been sending him. Not just now either, but those signals and the attraction that had been there from the moment they met.

She sat up and adjusted the comforter so that it was completely covering her body. "We need to talk."

A talk that would no doubt include the reminder that they were in danger.

"I heard you on the phone last night," she said, the tone of her voice as accusing as the look in her eyes.

Jackson shook his head. "When? I was on the phone at lot—"

"The call you made in the foyer."

Oh. That one. The call. The one that could change their lives forever.

"'I don't want anyone else to know what you just told me,'" Bailey said, repeating him verbatim. "What are you keeping from me?"

But Jackson didn't get a chance to answer. The phone next to his bed buzzed. He considered ignoring it so he could finish this conversation, but it might be important. Plus, the sound apparently alerted Caden, because he started to cry.

"We'll finish this talk later," Bailey insisted, and she got up from the bed so she could pick up Caden.

Jackson cursed under his breath and took the call.

"It's Ryan Cassaine. I'm here at the estate."

"Really?" Jackson didn't bother trying to sound civil. "At this time of morning?"

"It's important, and it couldn't wait. I have Shannon Wright with me, and we need to see you immediately."

"Shannon?" Jackson didn't sound civil about that, either.

"The last time you two were here, Bailey and I were attacked. And Shannon is one of our suspects."

"She wouldn't have orchestrated that attack," Ryan countered without hesitation. "Just let us in and listen to what Shannon has to say. I can promise you, when she's done you'll be convinced that she has no desire to harm Caden or you."

Jackson still wanted to say no, but he couldn't. Did Shannon have some kind of proof that she hadn't offered during her last visit? It certainly sounded like it.

"I'll meet you in the downstairs sitting room in ten minutes," Jackson told Ryan. And he hoped like hell this was worth the worry that it would no doubt put Bailey through.

"You're meeting them again?" she asked, the moment he hung up. Yes, there was the worry in her voice. She probably hadn't forgotten the talk they needed to have, but the possibility of renewed danger overshadowed it.

Jackson nodded, then phoned Steven so he could let the pair in. "Search them both," Jackson reminded Steven.

Then he went to Bailey. She had a fussy Caden in her arms and was rocking him.

"I just need to hear what Shannon has to say," Jackson

insisted, and he left it at that. He headed to his closet so he could get ready.

"I'm going with you," Bailey said from the other room. He heard her use the phone to call for the nanny.

Jackson wished he could do this alone, just in case this was some kind of ruse to launch another round of gunfire. But he also figured he stood zero chance of talking Bailey into staying put. So that meant he needed to find out what Shannon had to say so he could end this meeting as soon as possible.

When he came out of his dressing room, Bailey wasn't there. Tracy now had Caden in her arms.

"He's hungry," Tracy let Jackson know. "I'll be in the nursery with him."

"Keep your phone close," Jackson warned her, and he placed his gun in the back of his jeans. "I might have to move the two of you and Bailey back to the panic room."

Tracy's eyes widened. "Not more trouble?"

Jackson wanted to assure her that wasn't the case, but lately, trouble seemed to have an easy way of finding him.

They went into the hall, but Jackson didn't head for the stairs until he made sure that Tracy and Caden were indeed in the nursery. And then he waited for Bailey. He didn't have to wait long. Within seconds she came out of the room next to his where her clothes and toiletries were now stashed. She'd changed and was now wearing another loaner dress. This one was a dark green.

"You could stay with Caden and Tracy," Jackson reminded her.

But as expected, Bailey just shook her head and

headed down the stairs. Yes, she was as anxious for the truth as he was, but she was also no doubt equally anxious for that private conversation the two of them needed to finish.

By the time they made it to the bottom of the stairs, Steven had opened the front door, disengaged the security system and was ushering in their guests.

"This better be worth our time," Jackson warned both Shannon and Ryan.

"It is," Shannon assured him, but she didn't say anything else until they were all in the room just off the foyer. Even then, it took several moments for her to continue. "You might want to sit down for this."

Bailey and Jackson exchanged glances, and Jackson decided it was a good time to show both Ryan and Shannon that he was armed. He did sit, but he took out his gun and placed it on the table next to him. Bailey sat next to him, so that either of them would be able to reach the weapon if necessary.

Shannon already looked ready to jump out of her skin, but this upped her anxiety significantly. Jackson could see sweat popping out above her upper lip, and she had a death grip on her purse.

"I lied to you," Shannon finally said, aiming that remark at Jackson. "Well, at least I lied by omission. What I didn't tell you…" She took a deep breath and blinked back tears. "What I didn't tell you was that I'm Caden's birth mother."

The room went deadly silent.

Jackson's gaze flew to Bailey, and she'd gone ash pale. She was holding her breath and staring in disbelief at the woman who'd just dropped a bombshell.

"You're Caden's mother?" Bailey challenged.

Shannon started to sob now, and Ryan sat beside her and put his arm around her.

"I didn't know until this morning," Ryan explained.

"This doesn't make sense." Bailey shook her head. "You were working in the hospital the day that Caden was born. There's no way you could have given birth on that day, and there was no mention in the investigation of your being pregnant."

"Because I hid the pregnancy." She plucked at her oversized caftan dress. "People just thought I was gaining weight, and I didn't tell them any differently."

"Why would you do that?" Jackson pressed.

Shannon swiped at the tears that spilled down her cheeks. "My family is very conservative, and they would have disowned me for having a child out of wedlock. So I hid it from them, too."

The tears were genuine, but Jackson figured that was the only thing about this story that was. "And what about Bailey's question? Caden was born on the day of the hostage situation."

"The day after," Shannon corrected. "I gave birth to him in my apartment. Delivered him myself. I had arranged for a private adoption, but it fell through. So when I heard you were looking to adopt a child, I had a friend call Ryan Cassaine. I had the friend lie and say she was a college student who needed compensation for her medical bills and tuition."

"Oh, God," Jackson heard Bailey say, and he also heard the enormous pain in her voice.

Bailey clamped her teeth over her bottom lip, but it was too late. It was already trembling. So was she.

"He's not my son," Bailey mumbled. "Caden's not

mine." She got up from the chair and would have no doubt raced from the room, but Jackson caught onto her.

"I can't do this," Bailey insisted, and she broke free of his grip.

This time, when she tried to run Jackson didn't stop her. She hurried up the stairs. Jackson wanted nothing more than to go to her, but first he had to settle some business with Shannon.

"You have proof that you're Caden's mother?" Jackson asked.

She nodded and took an envelope from her purse. "That's a maternity test I had done right before I handed Caden over to Ryan. It proves he's my son."

Jackson took the envelope but didn't open it. "So what do you want? Why are you really here?"

"Not to claim my son. I want you to raise him, that's why I put him up for adoption."

"But you want more money," Jackson concluded.

Shannon dried her tears again. "I have debts, and if those were paid, then I could leave Texas. I could go live with my cousins in Seattle. I swear that you'd never hear from me again. The only thing I need other than the money, is for you to stop this investigation. If you press for the truth, my family will learn about Caden and they'll make my life a living hell."

Jackson's hands fisted, and he felt the envelope crush under the pressure.

"No," Jackson told her.

"No?" Shannon question. "No to what?"

"To the money and to stopping the investigation." Jackson didn't know who was more surprised by his refusal—Ryan or Shannon.

Ryan held up his hands in defense when Jackson aimed a glare at him. "I had no idea she was going to ask for payment. She came to me with the maternity test results and said she wanted to show you the proof, so that you'd have some peace of mind."

"I didn't want Bailey Hodges trying to scam you," Shannon piped in. She jumped to her feet. "I don't want much money," she concluded. "A hundred thousand is all, and that's chump change to a man like you."

"It's extortion," Ryan grumbled. "I'm sorry, Jackson. I really had no idea this is what she wanted to do." Ryan grabbed on to Shannon's arm and started to move her toward the door.

But Shannon dug in her heels and wouldn't budge. "A hundred thousand or whatever you happen to have in your safe right now. And for that, I go away. There'll never be any questions about me trying to regain custody of my son."

It took every ounce of his willpower not to throw her out the door. "Get her out of here," he told Ryan. "Now."

Shannon continued to resist, but Ryan shoved her out of the sitting room. "I'm sorry," he repeated to Jackson.

"You're the one who'll be sorry," Shannon insisted, looking back at Jackson. "A hundred thousand dollars is a small price to pay to keep my baby." And she repeated that threat all the way out the door.

"I'll make sure they leave the estate," Steven said, following them.

Jackson shut the door, rearmed the security system and glanced down at the envelope Shannon had given him. Hell. This was yet another issue that he would have to deal with. But first things first.

He had to check on Bailey.

Jackson retrieved his gun from the sitting room and headed up the stairs. He had no trouble finding her. All he had to do was follow the sound of her sobs. She was on his bed, her face buried in the pillows.

"I'm so sorry," she said without looking up at him. "I only wanted to find my baby. And by coming here, I've placed your son in danger."

Jackson drew in a long breath and went to her. He eased down on the bed and touched her shoulder, turning her so that he could see her face. Or rather, so she could see his.

"I'm the one who needs to apologize," he told her.

She stiffened slightly and swiped her hand over her eyes. Bailey studied his expression. "What do you mean?"

This wasn't a blow he could soften, so Jackson just decided to say what he had been keeping secret from her for the past twelve hours.

"Remember that call you overhead in the foyer?" he asked.

Bailey nodded. She pressed her hand to her chest as if to steady her heart.

"I had another DNA test done from the same samples I gave Evan. I wanted to verify the results with a second lab. Last night I got the results."

Her breath was uneven now, and she grabbed his shirt. "And?"

Jackson looked her straight in the eyes. "The DNA was a match. Caden is your son."

Chapter Eleven

"Wh-what?" Bailey managed to say. She scrambled to get to a sitting position, and she blinked back the rest of her tears so she could clearly see Jackson's face.

"According to the DNA, you're Caden's biological mother," Jackson repeated.

She heard the words, but it still took several seconds for them to sink in. She hadn't been wrong. Caden was her missing baby.

"Oh, God." Because she had no choice, she dropped her head onto Jackson's shoulder.

The relief flooded through her, and so did the other dozens of emotions. She'd searched so long, four months, and now she'd finally found her son. Not only was he alive, he was under the same roof, just a few rooms away.

But then her head swooshed off his shoulder. "Shannon lied."

Jackson nodded, and he tossed the envelope Shannon had given him onto the nightstand. "I figure her so-called maternity study is completely bogus. She is a nurse after all, so she probably used her medical training to fake a report that she thought would convince me to pony up some cash."

"But wouldn't Shannon have realized that you'd run your own tests to prove or disprove what she was claiming?" Bailey asked.

"Yeah, but maybe she thought I wouldn't be thinking too clearly after I saw that maternity study. She had her eyes set just on getting the money."

The relief and the joy were suddenly darkened by the anger that slammed through Bailey. "I want her arrested."

Jackson nodded again. "I'll deal with Shannon. And with Ryan, if he's had any part in this."

Of course. Ryan. A greedy adoption attorney could have helped set this up. It sickened and infuriated Bailey to think that either or both were willing to use her baby to extort money from Jackson.

He put his fingers beneath her chin, lifting it. "I owe you an apology. When I got that call last night, I intended to tell you, but I needed time to come to terms with what all of this meant."

His apology certainly seemed sincere enough, but Bailey remembered something else. "You told the person on the phone to destroy the samples and to keep the results a secret."

"I did," he readily admitted. "Because I didn't want anyone but us to know the truth. For now," Jackson added. "If the person who stole Caden from you realizes that you've found him, there might be other attempts to kill you. Other attempts to take him so this person can cover up his or her crime."

She couldn't argue with that. "But for hours you kept this to yourself."

"Yes." He paused, shook his head. "Like I said, I was

trying to come to terms with it. I wouldn't have kept it from you much longer."

Bailey believed him and wondered if she was a fool for doing so. After all, Jackson was a wealthy, powerful man, and he loved Caden. Just how far would he go to make sure he remained Caden's father?

The image of her precious little boy flashed into her mind. "I need to see him."

Bailey expected Jackson to try to stop her. She figured he would insist they talk before she went racing to her baby. But he didn't. Jackson got off the bed and stepped aside so that Bailey could race toward the suite door.

Her feet suddenly couldn't go fast enough, and she ran down the hall to the nursery. For several terrifying moments, she thought he might not be there, that Jackson had already sent Caden off somewhere so Bailey couldn't take him. But when she threw open the nursery door she saw that her son was in the nanny's arms. Tracy was seated in the rocking chair, an empty baby bottle next to her, and she was burping Caden.

Bailey obviously wasn't able to hide her raw emotions, and she moved much too quickly toward them. Tracy's eyes registered the alarm, and Caden turned his head, no doubt to see what the commotion was about.

Tracy looked past Bailey and to Jackson, and he simply nodded. That was it. His approval for Tracy to stand up and hand over Caden.

Of course, Bailey had held him before, but this time it was different. This time she wasn't holding Jackson's adopted son, she was holding her own baby.

She couldn't stop the tears and didn't even try. Bailey hugged Caden close and held on tight.

Finally. She had him, and she had no plans to let go.

"Give us some privacy, please," Jackson said to Tracy.

Tracy waited a moment, probably trying to figure out what was going on, but the woman finally gathered up the empty bottle and the bib and headed out the door.

Jackson didn't say anything else. He merely leaned against the wall and watched them.

Bailey didn't mind the audience. Heck, she didn't mind anything right now. She sank down into the rocking chair and sat Caden on her lap so she could see his precious little face.

He was perfect of course, and she went through the visual exam that most new mothers did of their newborns. She was four months late with this, but that didn't lessen her joy of counting ten little fingers and ten little toes.

Caden laughed when she wiggled his pinkie toe.

Bailey was certain that was the most miraculous sound she'd ever heard.

"He has my eyes," Bailey confirmed. There were pieces of her ex there, too, but they didn't bring back bad memories of a stormy relationship. On Caden, they were incredible features.

Caden reached for her hair, his chubby fingers pulling at the strands. Bailey laughed, too. These were the little miracles she had missed; but she would make up for all that lost time.

"D-d-d," Caden blurted out, and he looked at Jackson and gave him a big grin.

Jackson grinned back, but Bailey could see the pain in his eyes. It was a pain she understood all too well. She knew what it was like to lose a baby.

"Caden obviously loves you," Bailey mumbled.

"Yeah," Jackson said, but nothing else.

Bailey wasn't immune to what he was he feeling. Her own joy didn't make her blind or unfeeling to what Jackson was now experiencing. In fact, it only reminded her more that Jackson had risked his life for her son. He'd taken extreme measures and more to make sure Caden stayed safe. And in addition to that, Jackson loved Caden as much as her son loved him.

And that love caused Bailey's heart to sink a little.

What the heck was she going to do?

"Don't overthink it," Jackson warned, as if reading her mind. "For now, just get to know your son. We can talk later."

His generosity stunned her. Of course, she already knew he was an exceptional man, but that offer had no doubt cost him dearly. If their positions had been reversed, Bailey would have probably been doing everything within her power to hang on to Caden.

Jackson started to leave.

"Thank you," Bailey called out.

He turned back, gave her a slight smile and reached for the door. However, his phone rang before he could open it. He glanced down at the caller ID screen and groaned softly.

"It's the lab that Evan used to run Caden's DNA," Jackson let her know. He put the call on speakerphone and moved closer so she could hear. "Jackson Malone," he answered.

"Will Delaney. I'm the tech from Cyrogen Labs in San Antonio. Evan Young asked me to call you with the test results."

"And?" Jackson pressed when the tech didn't continue. Was it her imagination, or did the tech seem rattled?

"The two samples weren't a match," the tech informed them.

Bailey sucked in her breath. She couldn't believe what she'd just heard.

"The female's DNA that I tested couldn't possibly be related to the infant male," the tech continued. He hesitated again. "I hope these results are satisfactory?"

"Not really." Jackson tipped his eyes to the ceiling and mumbled something under his breath. "I'll get back to you. I need to call someone first."

Jackson slapped his phone shut and mumbled some harsh profanity, but he kept it at a whisper, probably because he didn't want Caden to hear his da-da curse a blue streak.

With Caden firmly in her arms, Bailey got to her feet. "You don't believe those results, do you?" And for one horrifying moment, she thought he might.

"No," Jackson assured her. "Evan no doubt told the lab to fake the results. If they ran the test at all. I'm sure he wanted to get the results he thought I wanted to hear." He met her gaze. "I wanted the truth, not a cover-up."

She released the breath she'd been holding. "Does Evan often do things like this?" Bailey thought of the threatening letter and Evan's strange behavior.

"Never." A moment later, Jackson repeated it and remained deep in thought. It wasn't so deep, however, that he didn't kiss Caden's hand when the little boy reached for him. Jackson didn't take the baby, but he stayed close and tickled Caden. Caden giggled.

"So we have both Evan and Shannon lying," she commented. The serious discussion seemed totally out of place with Caden's laughter and smiles, but Bailey knew this discussion had to happen. "A coincidence?"

Jackson shrugged. "Maybe. What I need is more information, and I need to figure out if Evan, or even Ryan Cassaine, had some part in this illegal adoption."

Yes, Ryan had seemed uncomfortable as well during his visits. Did the man have something to hide?

"Who's more likely to give you the answers you need—Evan or Ryan?" she asked.

He shook his head. "I'm not sure I trust either of them anymore to tell me the truth." Still, he opened his cell and made a call.

It was Ryan Cassaine who answered. "Jackson, I was hoping you'd call so I could apologize again for Shannon demanding money—"

"Is Shannon with you right now?" Jackson interrupted.

"No. We didn't drive out to your estate together, and she left her car by your front gate. When Steven drove us back down, Shannon and I went our separate ways. Don't worry, Jackson, I'll make sure she doesn't bother you again with demands for money."

"Why did she lie?" Jackson demanded. Good. Bailey was glad that he got right to the heart of the matter.

"Lie? I don't think she's lying about the baby—"

"She is. And I have proof. What I want to know is why. Is this just about money, or is it something more?"

Ryan stayed quiet for a moment. "What do you mean by *more?*"

"I mean, are you involved in this little scheme of hers?"

"No!" Ryan jumped to answer that. "Are you sure she's lying?"

"Positive."

"But she gave you a copy of the maternity test results," Ryan reminded him.

"She, or someone else, faked them. It's as simple as that. Come on, Ryan. Do you honestly think I would take her word, or yours, that the results are legit without verifying it? And I did verify that she was lying. She's not Caden's birth mother."

More silence, and the lawyer made a sound of frustration. "I don't know what to think. You obviously believe I've done something wrong, and I haven't. When you asked me to help arrange for a private adoption, that's what I did. I put out feelers and contacted other adoption attorneys to see if they had any leads. I worked my butt off to find Caden for you."

Jackson gave an impatient huff. "I don't doubt that, but I need to know if you cut any corners."

"None," Ryan insisted. "The only mistake I made was listening to Shannon and her apparent pack of lies."

"How did you meet Shannon?" Jackson asked, taking the question right out of Bailey's mouth.

"Shannon and some of the other maternity hostages are being represented by another attorney in my firm. The hostages are suing the hospital for poor security measures. I met Shannon while she was doing some paperwork here, and that's when she confessed that she was Caden's birth mother."

Bailey shifted Caden in her arms so she could get closer to the phone. "But when you first set up the adoption, you were in contact with another woman, the student, who claimed that Caden was hers."

"Yes," Ryan readily admitted. "I didn't actually meet her, though, and I never spoke directly with her. I dealt with her attorney, Phillip Dalkey."

"I want his number," Jackson demanded.

"I can give it to you, but it won't do any good. I've been trying to contact him for two days, and he's not answering his phone. His office insists they don't know where he is."

Oh, mercy. Did this Phillip Dalkey have a run-in with the person who'd hired those gunmen, or was Ryan lying about this as well?

"Go back four months ago," Jackson continued. "You said you put out feelers to find a baby for my private adoption. Was it Phillip Dalkey who first contacted you about Caden?"

Ryan made a sound to indicate he was giving that some thought. "No. Actually, it was someone else, someone we both know."

"Shannon?" Jackson asked, his voice loaded with sarcasm.

"Not Shannon either. The person who called to tell me about Caden was your business manager, Evan Young."

Chapter Twelve

Evan.

Jackson didn't like the way his business manager's name kept popping up in this investigation. Evan shouldn't have had anything to with the adoption; but according to Ryan, Evan had been the one who started the ball rolling when it came to finding Caden.

If Ryan was telling the truth.

After all, Ryan had actually profited from the adoption. Jackson had proof of that, since he'd paid the attorney a large amount in legal fees. As far as Jackson knew, Evan hadn't received a dime for anything related to the adoption.

Of course, maybe this wasn't about money.

"You think Evan is playing some kind of mind game with you?" Bailey asked.

She had worry written all over her face, and it shouldn't have been there. This should have been a time for celebration. For Bailey anyway. She'd found her missing baby and was holding him in her arms. Jackson figured this was the best moment of her life, and yet that moment was clouded with the possibility that the person who'd orchestrated the illegal adoption might be planning something worse.

Since both Caden and she were staring at him, Jackson went to them and gathered both in his arms. He kissed Caden's cheek and intended to do the same to Bailey. A simple, reassuring peck. But hell, he needed more than that, and judging from her expression, so did she.

So Jackson kissed her on the mouth.

He hadn't planned for it to go on, but it did. And despite the fact that Caden was right there, Jackson still felt the heat from the attraction. Even the danger couldn't make that go away.

Soon, very soon, he would have to figure out what to do about the attraction. And about Caden. He didn't think Bailey was ready to jump into a custody battle with him, but she would want to claim her son.

At that thought, Jackson pulled back and took a deep breath. Caden laughed, apparently amused with the kiss and his daddy's reaction. Jackson pressed his forehead to Caden's and hoped his son wasn't also aware that his daddy's heart was breaking.

He couldn't lose Caden.

Jackson opened his phone again and called Steven so he could ask the man to track down numbers for Shannon and the attorney, Phillip Dalkey. Normally, that would be an assignment he would give to Evan, but Jackson wanted to keep his business manager, and anyone else from the office, out of the information loop until he was sure Evan had no part in any of this. Steven assured Jackson that he would get back to him with the contact numbers as soon as possible. Jackson ended that call and made another one.

To Evan.

Evan's phone rang. And rang—five rings before it

went to voicemail. Strange. In the seven years that Evan had worked for him, Jackson couldn't remember once, not even on Christmas Eve, that the man hadn't answered on the first ring. Evan often joked that he even showered with his phone close enough to reach.

"Something's not right," Jackson mumbled.

"I agree." Bailey kept Caden close to her. "Part of me wishes they'd all just disappear. But we have to know who's behind all of this."

Yeah. And then they had to figure out how to deal with the aftermath.

Bailey stared at him, huffed and dropped her head on his shoulder. "I know what this is doing to you."

"And I know what you've been through for the past four months," Jackson countered. "Don't worry. We'll work out something."

Though he had no idea what.

He could ask Bailey to move onto the estate. There was plenty of room. That way, they could share custody. Of course, Bailey would almost certainly want full custody, and Jackson was afraid the law would be on her side, especially since the adoption wasn't final yet.

That got his mind and heart racing.

All she had to do was go to the police and tell them the DNA results. Family services would step in and probably take Caden and place him in foster care until they got this mess all sorted out. That could take months or longer.

Jackson had never felt this kind of panic before, and it shocked him when Bailey came up on her toes and kissed him.

"We'll work it out," she promised. And because Jackson desperately needed something to hang on to, he believed her.

He was about to seal that promise with another kiss, but his phone rang, and since the call was from Steven, Jackson answered it right away.

"I got the numbers for Shannon and Phillip Dalkey," Steven explained, "but neither is answering their phones."

Great. First Evan and now Shannon. Ryan had already told him that Phillip seemed to be missing, but Jackson had hoped he would get lucky.

"Robin Russo is back," Steven added. "She showed up at the gate about five minutes ago. Sir, she's practically hysterical and says someone's trying to kill her."

On most days, Jackson would have been alarmed by that, but this wasn't most days.

Welcome to the club, Robin.

"Should I let her in?" Steven asked.

Jackson didn't even have to think about it. "No. I don't want her inside the estate, and it's too cold for an outdoor meeting. Are you at the gate with her now?"

"Yes, sir."

"Then use the security camera to set up a video feed into my office." Jackson ended the call and looked at Bailey. "I doubt I'll learn anything from her—"

"I want to be there when you talk to her," Bailey insisted.

Jackson hesitated, figuring, at best, this conversation with Robin would be a waste of time, but he understood Bailey's need to get to the truth. "Come on. We'll leave Caden in the nursery with Tracy. It's time for his bath anyway."

Since Tracy was already in the nursery waiting for

them, it didn't take long for Bailey to give her Caden so they could then head to his office. By the time they arrived, Steven had already set up the video feed, and Jackson saw Robin on his laptop screen.

The woman was indeed waiting by the massive front gates. She had also gotten out of her car and was staring directly into the camera. She had her coat wrapped tightly around her and had ducked her head against the bitter winter wind. Judging from her red, swollen eyes, she'd been crying.

Jackson hit the button on his laptop that would allow two-way communication. "Robin," he greeted. "Back for round two already?"

"I'm back because I need your help." She moved even closer to the camera so that her face took up the entire screen. "Please let me in."

"You can say what you need to say right where you are," Jackson insisted.

Robin didn't get angry. She fired several glances over her shoulder as if she expected someone was about to ambush her. Jackson hoped that wasn't true, but he couldn't risk Bailey's and Caden's lives by allowing this suspect back onto the property.

"Could you get your man to leave?" Robin asked. "I don't trust him. I don't trust anyone right now."

Jackson thought about that a moment. "Is the gate locked and the security system activated?" he asked Steven.

"They are," Steven answered. "Should I go?"

Again, Jackson gave it some thought. The fence was crash-proof, something he'd never thought he would need, but he was glad he had it now. "Leave her there and drive back up the estate. I need you to keep checking those numbers for me."

For Shannon, Evan and the attorney, Phillip Dalkey. Plus, if there truly was a threat to Robin's life, Jackson didn't want Steven out there in the open.

Jackson did a split screen so he could watch as Steven got back into his vehicle and drove away. Robin didn't utter a word until the man was out of sight.

"After I left your estate, someone tried to run me off the road," Robin continued, her voice and expression a tangle of nerves. "At first I thought it was an accident. But about an hour ago, someone tried to do it again." Her mouth was trembling so hard now that it was difficult to make out her words. "If you or Bailey set someone on me, please call him off. I didn't do anything wrong."

"Neither Bailey nor I set anyone on you," Jackson let her know. "You've been to the police?"

"I just called them, and I'm going there after I leave here. But if you're behind this, I don't think San Antonio PD will be able to stop it."

Jackson and Bailey exchanged glances. Since Bailey and he knew they hadn't hired anyone to go after Robin, that meant someone else might have, or else the woman was lying.

Either was possible.

Bailey moved next to Jackson so that Robin would be able to see her on the monitor. "Maybe this is because of the house you purchased. Did you borrow the money from the wrong people?"

"No!" Robin practically shouted, but then just as quickly, the fight seemed to take everything out of her. "If you must know, I got a legal settlement with the hospital, but I signed a confidentiality statement. That's why I couldn't say where I got the money."

Convenient. That wouldn't be an easy thing to verify or disprove.

"You've come to the wrong people," Bailey explained. "Jackson and I don't want you dead."

"Well, somebody does." Robin looked over her shoulder again and swallowed hard. "Maybe it's Shannon. Maybe she's trying to kill us all."

"Why would she want to do that?" Jackson asked.

Robin opened her mouth as if she were about to blurt out something, but then she glanced around her again. Either she was a good actress, or she truly thought she was in danger just by being there.

When she turned back to the camera, her breath was uneven, and she was trembling even more than when this bizarre conversation had started.

"You're positive you're not trying to kill me?" Robin repeated.

"Positive," Jackson assured her.

She nodded and swallowed hard again. "Then it has to be Shannon."

Jackson couldn't assure her that Shannon wasn't guilty, especially after the stunt she'd pulled about saying she was Caden's biological mother.

Robin moved even closer to the camera, so close that her breath fogged-up the screen. "I think Shannon was having an affair with one of the gunmen who took the hostages."

One look at Bailey, and her shocked expression confirmed that this was something she hadn't heard before. But like the other things Shannon and Robin had said, it didn't necessarily make it true.

"Did you hear me?" Robin pressed. "Shannon was sleeping with one of the gunmen, and she probably helped him set up the entire hostage mess."

"You have proof?" Bailey asked.

Robin shook her head and the tears returned. "No. But I heard her talking about him one day. Danny Monroe. And I don't think it's a coincidence that one of the gunmen had the same name."

Jackson immediately saw a flaw in Robin's accusation. Two of them, in fact. "Why didn't SAPD find this connection, and why didn't you tell them?"

"I didn't remember until yesterday. Maybe it's the danger, but that conversation I had with her just came back to me. Here's what I think—we know that the gunmen wanted to kill Bailey that day...."

"They did," Bailey confirmed in a whisper. "They thought I'd seen them without their ski masks."

"Exactly!" Robin continued. "So I think Shannon hid you because of the baby. She didn't want her boyfriend coming after you and hurting the child."

That turned Jackson's stomach, but he couldn't dismiss that part. The mystery woman had told Bailey to keep quiet or the gunmen might try to use the baby to get to her. And by getting to her, the gunmen no doubt wanted to silence her permanently.

"So if Shannon took my baby, then why didn't she return him after the gunmen were killed?" Bailey asked.

"I'm guessing greed," Robin readily supplied. "I figure she sold the baby or something."

Jackson slipped his arm around Bailey. It was obvious this nightmare was difficult to relive.

"Robin, you should tell the police everything you just told us," Bailey insisted.

"I will, but for now I need your help to stop Shannon from trying to kill me."

"I'm not letting you in," Jackson repeated. "Leave now and go to the sheriff or SAPD."

Robin cursed, and she was still cursing when she made another glance over her shoulder. The profanity died on her lips. Her eyes widened, and she screamed.

But Robin's scream didn't drown out the loud blast. Someone had just fired a shot.

Chapter Thirteen

Bailey broke into a run, headed for the nursery. She didn't wait to see what was happening to Robin. She had to get to Caden and make sure he was safe.

Jackson was right behind her, but he had already grabbed his gun and then taken out his phone, no doubt to call and make sure no one had breached security.

"The gate's still closed," Jackson reminded her, shoving his gun into the waist of his pants.

Yes, but there could still be another attack on the estate.

Bailey raced into the nursery, and her heart dropped when she didn't see Caden. She hurried through the massive room and to the adjoining bathroom.

And there he was.

He was sitting in a yellow safety ring in the center of the bathtub. He was splashing water and laughing.

"What's wrong?" Tracy asked.

"Someone fired a shot near the gate," Jackson answered. "Go ahead and take Caden to the panic room."

Tracy had already started to do that before Jackson even finished. The nanny grabbed a thick terry cloth towel and swirled it around the soaking-wet baby.

Caden obviously didn't like having his bath interrupted, because he started to fuss and squirm.

"You should go with them," Jackson told Bailey while he still had his phone pressed to his ear.

It was tempting to be safely tucked away with her son, but she didn't want anyone breaking into the estate. Jackson would need all the backup he could get.

"I can help you keep watch," Bailey insisted. But it nearly brought tears to her eyes to see Tracy whisk Caden in the direction of the panic room. "We need to put an end to this."

Yes, it was stating the obvious. They did need to end it. But how? The only way to stop the attacks was to figure out who was behind them. Could Robin possibly help with that?

"Steven," Jackson said when the man came back on the line. "What's happening out there?" Jackson grabbed Bailey's hand and headed back to his office. The moment they were inside, he locked the door and used a keypad to engage the room's security system.

Bailey couldn't hear Steven's response, but she could see the security monitors when they got to his desk. He still had the split-screen images, and on the one by the gate, she saw the car speeding away. Robin's car perhaps.

But Bailey didn't see the shooter.

Jackson took out his handgun, put it on the desk and typed in something on his keyboard. He pulled up six more images on the screen. Both of them moved closer, examining the various camera angles.

"I don't see anyone either," Jackson relayed to Steven. "Maybe the person followed Robin. Call the sheriff so he can get someone out there on the road to protect her."

Of course, it might be too late for that. Robin could already be dead. And if so, the shooter might come back to the estate.

"Make certain everything is locked up tight," Jackson told Steven. "No one is getting in or out of the estate until the sheriff has the shooter in custody."

Jackson ended the call and sank down behind his desk so he could continue to scan the security feed. Bailey's heart was pounding now, and the adrenaline was raging through her. Her body was preparing itself for a fight. A fight she prayed wouldn't be necessary.

"What do we do?" she asked.

"We wait. Steven and his men will patrol the grounds and make sure no one gets onto the property. Then we let the sheriff do his job. It wouldn't be smart for me to go out there and leave Caden and you here."

"I agree." There was no way she would let Jackson leave. She was still recovering from the last time he'd done that, and they hadn't been—well—as close as they were now.

The stakes were so much higher on many levels.

Bailey sat on the armrest of his chair so she could have a better view of the computer screen. And so she could be near Jackson. It was stupid, but just being near him made her feel safer. He must have sensed that, because he slipped his arm around her and drew her closer.

There. She felt it. That click in her head that turned off some of the adrenaline rush. Her breathing began to slow down. She wondered if Jackson knew just how much he could soothe her with a mere touch.

For now, anyway.

It was highly probable they had their own personal storm brewing over Caden. Would they be enemies before this was over? Bailey hated the thought of never being able to sit with him like this again, but she had to put her baby first. She'd already lost so much time with Caden, she wouldn't let anyone, including Jackson, rob her of another day.

She forced her attention back on the screen, but there were still no signs of attack. Steven and some of the men were moving around outside, and they were all armed, bracing themselves for the worst.

Thankfully, the worst didn't seem to be coming.

"I think Caden and Tracy should stay in the panic room," Jackson mumbled. "He'll be ready for a nap soon anyway, and he can take it in there."

Bailey couldn't argue with that. The panic room was the safest place to be.

"Are you all right?" Jackson asked.

She looked over at him to see what had prompted that question and noticed he was staring at her.

"It'll be okay," he added.

Of course, Bailey knew he couldn't possibly guarantee that, but again, it made her feel good just to hear it.

She was obviously in big trouble here.

In the past two days, people had tried to kill them and kidnap Caden. A woman had been shot at just minutes earlier. But she couldn't stop feeling all warm and comforted because of Jackson.

With his attention fastened back onto the screen, he took her hand, brought it to his mouth and brushed his lips over her skin. "It'll be okay," he repeated.

"I don't know how," she mumbled.

Jackson kept hold of her hand. "You have to trust that we can get through this and work out everything. We're not enemies, Bailey. Far from it," he added.

Was that true? Yes, there was this attraction that seemed to be getting hotter and heavier every time they were together. Or apart. Heck, it just kept growing, even when they needed to focus all their attention on other things.

"We can't work this out in bed," she added.

He glanced up, and the corner of his mouth lifted. "No. But we can work out plenty of other things there."

That smile nearly melted her.

She shook her head. "I don't understand this."

"Simple." Jackson touched his mouth to her hand again. "You're a beautiful woman and I want you. That's all there is to it."

"Really?" she questioned. "Caden isn't part of this?"

"No," he said with complete conviction.

Jackson's phone rang, the sound slicing through the awkward silence.

"It's Steven," Jackson said after glancing at the caller ID screen.

Maybe this was the good news she'd been praying for. Maybe Steven or the sheriff had caught the person who fired the shot at Robin.

"Interesting," Jackson said, after at least a minute of silence. Another minute passed. "Dig into the accusation Robin made about Shannon being involved with one of the gunmen who took the hostages. Danny Monroe is the name. Let me know if you learn anything."

Jackson hung up and looked at her. "Steven has someone reviewing all the security feed, and he's not convinced there is a gunman."

"What? But we heard the shot."

"Yeah," Jackson agreed. "But remember, Robin kept moving close to the camera so we couldn't see what was going on around her."

Of course. Bailey had thought that was because the woman only wanted Jackson and her to hear what she was saying. "You think Robin could have set this all up and fired the shot herself?"

He shrugged. "It's possible. Maybe this was her plan, so we'd no longer be suspicious of her. She could be trying to gain our sympathy and trust."

And it nearly worked. Bailey had indeed been terrified for Robin's safety. Now she was riled to the core that Robin would try to manipulate them that way.

"Steven's already called the sheriff and SAPD," Jackson added, and his phone rang again. "It's Evan." He opened the phone and put it on speaker. "I tried to reach you."

"Yes, I got your message." And that's all he said for several moments. "I was out of the office when you called."

"Obviously." Jackson paused, too. "I wanted to ask you a couple of things. First, why did you have the lab fake the results of the DNA test?"

"Who said I did?" Evan immediately countered.

"Me. I know they're fake because I ran another set."

Evan cursed. "You didn't trust me?"

"No. And apparently my instincts were right."

"I did it to protect you," Evan insisted. "I didn't want you to lose Caden."

"That wasn't your call to make," Jackson insisted. "Now, talk to me about Ryan Cassaine. He said you're the one who told him about the college student who wanted to put up her baby for adoption."

"Yes, it was me. What about it?"

"Well, considering that I now know there are some questionable aspects about Caden's adoption—"

"Wait a minute," Evan interrupted. "You think I had something to do with stealing Bailey Hodges's baby?"

"Did you?" Bailey demanded.

"No." A moment later, Evan cursed and repeated his adamant denial. "I can't believe I have to defend myself like this. Jackson told me he wanted to adopt a baby, so I started asking around. This lawyer called out of the blue. Phillip Dalkey. And he said he had a client who might be willing to give up her child, but that she would need compensation. So I called Ryan and gave him the contact info. That's all. That's the only part I played in all this."

"And it has nothing to do with your fiancée's death?" Bailey prompted.

"No. Jackson, please tell me you don't believe any of this."

"I don't want to believe it, but I have to check out all the angles. Someone sent a man here to kill Bailey and me and kidnap Caden. I have to make sure that everyone around me is someone I can trust."

"Bailey's around you," Evan snapped.

"Yes, because I trust her. She has as much to lose here as I do."

"And she has everything to gain. That includes her son and your money." Evan's words were rushed now, and laced with bitterness. "Have you ever considered that she might have been the one to set up the illegal adoption? Bailey gets a cool million for turning over her baby to you, temporarily, and then a few months later she comes to the estate with DNA results and a sob story about someone stealing her baby. She takes Caden. It's a win-win for her."

Bailey frantically shook her head and turned to Jackson to defend herself, but Jackson gently tightened the grip he had on her.

"If Bailey had been trying to scam me, she would have showed up weeks ago. And she damn sure wouldn't have hired a gunman who'd get so close to Caden."

Bailey still held her breath. She couldn't afford to have Jackson think she was guilty of anything, because he might toss her out. God knows how long it would take for her to get Caden then.

"You'll lose Caden to her," Evan said a moment later.

"Probably. Merry Christmas, Evan. We'll talk after the holidays." Jackson closed his phone and dropped it onto his desk.

"Probably," Bailey repeated under her breath. She certainly hadn't expected that admission from Jackson.

Here she'd been trying to mentally prepare herself for a custody battle with one of the richest men in the country, and that "probably" had sounded like…surrender.

And it touched Bailey the way nothing else could have.

Jackson loved Caden. She was positive of that. Just

as positive as she was that Caden loved Jackson. Yet, that "probably" meant he was at least willing to consider losing the child he loved.

"I didn't come here to scam you," she reminded him.

But Jackson waved her off before she even finished. "I know."

He stood, pulling her to her feet. In the same motion, he drew her into his arms. "Evan's on the back burner for now. If he's the one behind this, then eventually he'll try to strike again. He won't succeed, with all the security precautions we've put in place. Eventually, he or the person responsible will be caught."

The idea sounded so simple. So convincing. And maybe that's why Bailey didn't pull back and launch them into a conversation that neither of them was anxious to have. Or maybe she just stayed there because it felt good to have him hold her.

"Can we get Caden from the panic room?" she asked. But she still didn't move out of his arms.

"Soon." Jackson didn't let go either. He held her and kissed the top of her head.

The air changed between them. Or something changed. Maybe it was all happening inside her and had nothing to do with the air. Bailey didn't care. She only wanted this moment and all the feelings that came with it.

It wasn't exactly hot passion that sent her in search of his mouth. Something else was going on here. Something that seemed to go bone-deep. Maybe deeper. Something that stirred her heart and blood even more than this fierce attraction could have.

She was falling hard for Jackson Malone.

That was it. More than the fire in her blood, there were the flames in her heart. It was probably stupid to fall for a man like him. A man who could cost Bailey her son and everything else. But her heart wasn't going to let her back out of this. In fact, her heart was the part of her that urged her to kiss him. Really kiss him—until any doubts that she had simply melted away.

"You're sure?" she heard Jackson ask.

Bailey didn't even have to think about this. She had never been more certain of anything in her life.

Chapter Fourteen

Jackson wasn't sure about this at all.

The timing was all wrong, but then the timing had sucked ever since Bailey had come into his life. They had so many things to work out—and he'd already insisted they wouldn't be able to work them out in bed—but here they were, heading in that direction.

Well, in the direction of his desk anyway.

Judging from the heat of the kiss she had initiated, they wouldn't make it out of his office, much less all the way to the bedroom.

He forced himself to think of the consequences, but those consequences kept getting bogged down in the hazy passion that was slamming hard and fast through his body. He blamed that on Bailey's kiss. On the way her breasts were brushing against his chest. Everything seemed to be coming down to sex, and it didn't seem to matter if Jackson wasn't convinced that sex should happen.

"This is more than I thought it would be," Bailey mumbled against his mouth.

Her words made it through the haze somehow, and he shook his head trying to figure out what she meant.

More than sex?

Jackson was about to stop, to tell her that it couldn't be more. They had too much to work out. Too much to do. Hell, someone was trying to kill them, or at least make them believe that. Life was so far from perfect that *perfect* didn't even seem to be on their radar.

Did that stop him from kissing her?

No.

He deepened the already too-deep kiss and tightened his grip around her. He slid his hand between them so he could cup her breast.

"I'm falling for you," Bailey whispered.

Even though her voice barely had sound, he heard it loud and clear. And that caused him to stop.

Jackson pulled back and stared down at her, trying to figure out what he could possibly say to that. Her words were like red flags because of his old wounds and baggage. He'd spent years avoiding words like that. Years making sure that no one ever got close enough to hurt him again.

Bailey's warm breath hit his mouth. Her eyes were half closed. Dreamy. And waiting. Either he had to dive right into this or step back. Stepping back was in his comfort zone. Years of practice had made it almost a rote response.

Don't get too close.

But this was Bailey. Hadn't he known from the moment they'd met that nothing between them would ever be ordinary?

"If you want to stop…" she whispered.

He laughed, but there wasn't an ounce of humor in it. "The last thing I want to do is stop. I want you more than my next breath."

She nodded, as if that was all there was to this. She

slid her hand around the back of his neck and pulled him in for another kiss.

"Later, we'll deal with the *later,*" she said, just as her mouth touched his. That simple touch shot through him, turning his body into a furnace all over again.

Later would no doubt be harder than hell, but it would be easier than resisting her now. Jackson knew he stood zero chance of that. So he just took charge and went with it. When *later* came around, he would accept the responsibility for letting his heart and libido rule his head.

Jackson kissed her, and he didn't hold anything back. He put all of his feelings, his frustration and the white-hot heat into that kiss. And he didn't stop there. The need had already made him crazy, so he decided to make Bailey crazy right along with him.

He dropped test kisses on her neck and listened for her response. She moaned when he got to the base of her neck, so he lingered there long enough to please her and himself.

She tasted like all of the best parts of Christmas.

If the need hadn't been driving him to speed things up, he would have taken more time to savor her, to watch her respond to the kisses that he trailed down her neck and to the tops of her breasts. But this wasn't a simmering fire. It was a full blaze for both of them.

Jackson pushed down the top of her stretchy dress. Pushed down her lacy bra. Maybe the *later* part would involve a second round so he could taste and sample and touch every part of her. But for now, he settled for wetting his fingers in his mouth and circling her right nipple.

She moaned, arched her back. The change in positions

sent her sex pushing against his. Jackson was already hard and ready to take her, but that was just a reminder that the taking couldn't wait.

Bailey began to fight with her clothes, shoving up her dress and then going after his zipper. Yeah, the heat was making them crazy and speeding up everything until it was a blur. But what he was feeling wasn't a blur. The need just kept slamming into him, until all he could do was pull her to the floor.

Later, he would apologize for taking her like a sex-starved teenager.

The moment her back was on the floor, Bailey reached for him, pulling him onto her. The location and the timing no longer seemed important. Nothing did, except for what was about to happen.

Jackson kept kissing her, hoping that her taste would satiate him enough so he would slow down. No such luck. Her taste and her eager hands just fueled the already-raging heat, and when he found the top of her panties, he peeled them off her.

He had to touch her. Couldn't resist. So, as he'd done with her breasts, he eased his fingers inside her. Into all that slick heat that was a primal invitation to his aroused body.

Bailey obviously thought turnabout was fair play. She unzipped him and took him into her hands. Jackson could have sworn his eyes crossed, and he heard himself curse. The need was shouting for him to take her *now now now,* but, man, he wanted this to last for hours.

Lasting hours was obviously a pipe dream.

He drew back his hand and entered her slowly. Or rather, that's what he tried to do. But Bailey made the intimate contact complete by lifting her hips.

Whatever was better than Christmas, this was it.

Any coherent thought that was left in his head was toast now. He was beyond thinking, and he moved inside Bailey, taking them both to the only place their bodies needed to go.

She made a sound of pure pleasure. A sound Jackson was positive he would never forget. He wouldn't forget that look on her face either. Part relief, part surprise.

All Bailey.

Her hands were frantic, reaching for him, dragging him closer, even though getting closer wasn't possible. There was a flicker of panic in her eyes, as if she thought for just a split second that she wasn't going to get the relief she needed.

But she came in a flash.

Jackson didn't stop. He was already too close to taking the leap himself, but that didn't prevent him from savoring the incredible woman in the throes of her orgasm.

It was Bailey who drew him deeper into her. Bailey who urged him on. Bailey who took him right over that cliff with her.

The French were right. It was a little death. Everything slammed toward that one moment. That overwhelming moment where everything became crystal clear. Where everything was reborn. And in that moment Jackson could see and feel only one thing.

Bailey.

He whispered her name as he buried his face against her neck and let himself go.

Jackson tried to move, to readjust their positions so that he wasn't crushing Bailey, but his body seemed reluctant to break the intimate connection. He finally managed to roll to the side, but he kept her in his arms. She rolled right along with him, and they landed on their sides and face-to-face.

Somehow, this was more intimate than when he'd been inside her.

Jackson considered himself a strong, occasionally ruthless man, but Bailey had a way of bringing him to his knees.

He wanted to tell her that she was beautiful and that what had just happened was pretty damn amazing. But he heard the ringing sound. For a moment, Jackson thought it was all in his head.

It wasn't.

It was his cell.

He hated the interruption, but since this could be a critical call from Steven or the sheriff, he reached up to the desk and answered the phone.

The caller ID flashed Captain Shaw Tolbert.

Jackson knew the name. Tolbert was a bigwig in the San Antonio Police Department, and that meant the captain might have news about the gunmen and the investigation.

Jackson took the call while he helped Bailey up from the floor. He sandwiched the phone between his ear and shoulder so he could talk while he fixed his clothes.

"Captain Tolbert," Jackson greeted. Judging from Bailey's suddenly alert expression, this was a conversation she wanted to hear, so Jackson put it on speaker. "What can I do for you?" But Jackson was hoping it was the other way around, and that the captain would help end this danger breathing down their backs.

"I got a call from your estate manager and he told me about the latest attack. Or the ruse, if that's what it turns out to be. We're looking into the matter. And we're looking for Robin Russo because she's still a suspect in the disappearance of Bailey Hodges's baby."

Jackson and Bailey exchanged glances. While it was a glance on her part, since she was putting her panties back on, Jackson did more than glance. Then he forced his attention back to the phone call. "And what about Shannon Wright?"

"Also a suspect. Both women were in the hospital the day of the hostage crisis, and both have some critical time gaps that they can't or won't account for. I also understand Robin accused Shannon of having an affair with one of the gunmen." The captain groaned softly. "We thought this case was over four months ago, when SAPD killed the gunmen who took the hostages. But things have happened. There have been other attacks."

"So I've heard. And witnessed firsthand. Twice, someone has come after Bailey while she's been at my estate. What I want to know is, is Shannon or Robin responsible for that?"

"We're not sure. Either or both could be innocent. We have no proof that Shannon and the gunman, Danny Monroe, were involved romantically or otherwise. We had her followed after the hostage incident ended, and she never met with Danny. There were no calls to him either, according to her cell phone records."

"So why would Robin accuse Shannon of something like that?" Jackson asked.

"Maybe to throw suspicion off herself," the captain suggested. "There are things going on. We've gotten wind of another possible hostage situation."

"Oh, God." Bailey pressed her fingers to her mouth, but it didn't suppress the sound of her words.

"Is that Miss Hodges?" Captain Tolbert asked.

"Yes." Her voice was shaky now, and Jackson knew why. She didn't want anyone else to go through the nightmare that she'd experienced.

"We're working with another hostage, a woman we're calling hostage number four, so that the media doesn't plaster her identity all over the press," the captain continued. "She has some memory loss, but we're hoping we can unleash those memories so she can tell us more about what happened in the hospital four months ago. Anything *you* can tell us?"

Bailey shook her head and inched closer to the phone. "No. I had just had a C-section when the gunmen came into the ward. I didn't know anything about it until after the fact. Until after my baby had been taken."

The captain stayed quiet a moment. "Someone's trying to kill this other hostage, too," he revealed. "That's why it's important that we get to the bottom of Shannon's or Robin's possible involvement."

"Both of them are liars," Jackson volunteered, "so I seriously doubt you'll get the truth from them."

"You're probably right, but I want to reinterrogate both women. I'm hoping your sheriff can locate Robin since we know she was just out at your place. But do you have any idea where Shannon is?"

"None," Jackson answered. "She came to the estate with some bogus papers and claimed she was my adopted son's biological mother. She's not. Bailey is."

Bailey expected the captain to jump right on that, but he calmly said, "I see. Well, that's resolved. And the baby is safe?"

Not really. But Jackson would remedy that.

"Someone sent a man out to kidnap him and probably kill Jackson and me as well," Bailey blurted out.

"Yes, Sheriff Gentry gave me an update on that. The guy's name was Melvin Cross, a hired gun. He was a big badass years back, but his love of the bottle put him off his game. He's been off our radar for nearly a decade."

So that meant someone could have hired him cheap. It also meant this drunken SOB could have harmed Caden by accident rather than design. Not that he needed it, but it gave Jackson even more reason to go after the person who was behind all of this.

"Talk to me about these threatening letters you've received," the captain said to Jackson.

Those. It was yet something else on his too-full plate. "I got another one yesterday morning. Someone left it outside my downtown office, but it was left in an area where there were no security cameras."

"Yeah, that's what the detective handling it told me. You think that threat is connected to everything else that's going on?"

"I have no idea." And he didn't. "But it can't be a coincidence." ·

"Well, we're looking into it," the captain explained, "because it might be connected. It's true, none of your security cameras were aimed in that area, but we're trying to tap into the ATM camera of the bank just up the street. We might get lucky."

Yes, but even if they identified the person who'd left it, Jackson couldn't see how it would be part of the attempts to kill him and kidnap Caden. A threatening letter was benign compared to those other attempts.

"What happens now?" Bailey asked the captain.

"We keep working with hostage number four, and we help her regain her memory. And get her to trust us. Things aren't going so well in that department," Captain Tolbert added in a mumble. "In the meantime, I'll keep pressing Shannon and Robin, because I damn sure don't want another hostage incident."

No. Neither did Jackson.

"You should interrogate my business manager, Evan Young," Jackson suggested. "He also tried to fake the DNA evidence for Bailey's son. I doubt he had anything to do with the original hostage incident, but he might have learned something from Shannon after the fact."

"Thanks for the tip. I'll get him in here today, right after I talk with Ryan Cassaine."

"Ryan Cassaine?" Bailey and Jackson repeated at the same moment.

"Yeah. I just had him brought into headquarters for questioning," the captain confirmed.

Jackson was having some doubts about the adoption attorney's innocence, but it surprised him to hear that the SAPD captain was having doubts as well.

"Why did you bring in Ryan?" Jackson asked. "Is it because he cut some corners when he handled the adoption?"

"No, but I will ask him about that. Right now, I want to speak to him about his relationship with Shannon. I've just learned that they're involved romantically."

Jackson cursed. "Yeah. He brought her to the estate when she told that lie about being Caden's birth mother."

"Well, that doesn't surprise me, but what I did find

surprising was that, according to a couple of witnesses, the relationship isn't a new one."

"What do you mean?" Bailey asked.

"According to my detectives, Ryan and Shannon have been seeing each other for a while now—even before the hostage incident at the maternity hospital. Now, I need to find out just how deep the adoption attorney is into this."

Chapter Fifteen

Bailey tried to pretend that everything was normal.

In some ways, it was easy to do. After all, she was spending time with her baby. She was literally holding Caden in her arms and reading to him. She'd dreamed about moments like this, and now she had them.

But for how long?

She tried to push aside that troubling question, and continued to read the Christmas book aloud. He was too young to understand the story itself, but he slapped at the colorful pages and babbled when he saw something that caught his attention.

From the other side of the nursery, Jackson smiled at the baby's antics, but the smile was too brief, because he immediately jumped back into his phone call. Bailey had lost count of how many calls there had been, but Jackson had been working hard to get updates on the case. No easy feat, considering the investigation was now splintered between Sheriff Gentry's office, SAPD and, apparently, another set of detectives who were trying to track down and protect the other hostage with the memory issues.

Jackson had been filling Bailey in as he ended each of the outgoing and incoming calls, but the bottom line was that no one had found Shannon or Robin, and both Evan and Ryan were still insisting they were innocent.

They were back to square one.

Except that she now had her son.

Despite the danger, it was hard to be pessimistic. Soon, her son would get to experience his very first Christmas, and even the investigation couldn't put a damper on that.

However, she couldn't say the same for Jackson.

Each call seemed to frustrate him even more than the last, and it couldn't help when every time he glanced in her direction, he saw her with Caden. It had to be tearing him apart to know that he might lose the baby he loved. And there were no doubts in her mind that Jackson loved Caden with all his heart.

"Still no sign of Shannon or Robin," Jackson relayed when he ended the call with Sheriff Gentry. "SAPD questioned Ryan and Evan, but they didn't have any evidence to hold either of them."

Yes, he was frustrated, and it was just as apparent in his tone as it was in his expression. Bailey decided to do something about it.

She put the book aside, stood, and with Caden in her arms, she went to Jackson. "Come on. Let's go to the foyer and see the Christmas tree."

He shrugged as if he might refuse, but then Caden reached out for him. Bailey let her son go into Jackson's waiting arms.

"You're right," Jackson said, giving Caden a kiss on the cheek. "He should see the Christmas tree. And tonight, after he's asleep, I can take his presents out of my office closet. There are about a dozen of them crammed in there."

She was betting it was more than that. It was clear Jackson had been planning this holiday for a long time.

"After he's in bed we can talk," Jackson added, as they headed down the stairs.

Uh-oh. Bailey knew what that talk was about—custody of Caden. Maybe they would even discuss the fact that they'd had sex—and what that meant.

If anything.

Bailey's body was still humming from the experience, but she had to accept that once was all she might get with Jackson. When the investigation, the danger and the custody were all resolved, he would almost certainly remain in Caden's life, but not necessarily hers.

And if so, that would break her heart.

"See the lights?" Jackson said to Caden.

"Ooo," Caden babbled, pointing to the tree. There were indeed lights to see. Hundreds of them, and they glittered and twinkled from top to bottom, the sparkles dancing off the glass ornaments and tinsel. Someone had obviously finished the decorating and cleaned up the lights she'd broken.

It was perfect now.

Jackson and she had met by this tree, and that alone made it special, but the magical look in her son's eyes made this a moment Bailey would never forget. One glance at Jackson, and she realized he felt the same. But with a twist. He was no doubt wondering if this would be the one and only Christmas he would have with Caden.

Bailey wanted to start the discussion regarding

custody. Maybe they should just have it here and now, but then Caden babbled more of those precious sounds and waggled his fingers at the tree. Jackson took him closer for a better look.

Jackson's phone rang—again. The irritation flashed through his eyes, but because he had no choice, he handed Caden back to Bailey, took out the phone, glanced at the screen and then answered it.

"The police are looking for you, Shannon," he greeted the caller.

Shannon? So she'd turned up after all, just in time to spoil this moment with Caden and his first Christmas tree.

"You should go to SAPD," Jackson added. "They want to talk to you." He clicked the speakerphone button and held out the cell so that Bailey would be able to hear.

"I know, and when I was on the way to the police station, someone tried to run me off the road. I swear, someone's trying to kill me."

"Trust me, you're not the only one," Jackson mumbled in frustration. Unfortunately, Bailey felt the same. She wasn't just frustrated. She was weary from the attacks and the danger. She only wanted a little bit of normalcy.

"I want to come to the estate so we can talk," Shannon insisted.

Bailey shook her head, praying that Jackson would refuse, but it was obvious he didn't intend to grant Shannon's request. "We can talk now, on the phone," Jackson let the woman know, "but I'm not letting you come here. Not a chance."

Good. Bailey didn't want any of their suspects near the estate.

"I'm sorry I lied about your son being mine," Shannon continued, her voice weepy. "I was desperate, you see. I owe a lot of people money."

"So you conspired with Ryan to extort that money from me?" Jackson asked point-blank.

"No. Ryan had no part in this, I swear."

"And coming from you, that means a lot," Jackson said sarcastically. "Ryan is your lover, so I figure he'll do anything you ask."

"You're wrong. He's an honest man. The only mistake he made was getting involved with me."

Shannon sounded as if she was telling the truth, but the woman had told so many lies that Bailey wasn't about to believe her now.

"You're not denying that Ryan's your lover?" Jackson asked, pressing her.

"No, but I doubt he'd want me to confess that to anyone, especially you. He's trying to distance himself from me. And he should. I'm bad news. I can't seem to keep myself away from the wrong people."

Bailey couldn't agree more. The woman was indeed bad news. But had she really orchestrated a baby snatching and an illegal adoption?

"Talk to me about your involvement with the hostage gunman, Danny Monroe," Jackson continued.

Bailey thought she heard Shannon gasp. "Who told you I was involved with him?"

"Robin," he readily admitted.

Bailey wished she could see Shannon's face, because the woman's silence was causing Bailey to be even more suspicious of her.

"Robin," Shannon snarled. "You know why she's doing this, right?" But she didn't wait for an answer. "She wants to make me look guilty."

"Did you have an affair with Danny Monroe?" Jackson demanded.

"No. It was Robin who was having the affair. Not me."

Bailey huffed. She wanted to lock Robin and Shannon in a room and make them argue it out until they finally told the truth.

"Robin had the affair?" Jackson repeated. He was obviously skeptical.

"Yes. But I know you don't believe it. That's okay. Just stop Robin. When she's stopped, her lies will stop, too." And with that, Shannon hung up.

"I need to give Shannon's number to the SAPD," Jackson said immediately. He scrolled through his list of recent calls. There were so many of them. And he located Captain Shaw Tolbert. He pressed redial.

"Mr. Malone." The captain answered on the first ring.

"Shannon Wright just phoned me, and here's where you can reach her." Jackson read off the numbers. "She also admitted to having an affair with Ryan Cassaine."

"Thanks—I'll get someone right on that." He paused. "I'm glad you called. I needed to speak to you anyway. There's been a development in the case."

Bailey slowly drew in a breath and tried not to jump to any bad conclusions. Unfortunately, the captain's tone made that impossible. He didn't sound as if he had good news to relay.

"Remember I told you we were trying to use the

security cameras up the street from your office to determine who had left that threatening letter?"

"Yeah, I remember," Jackson said cautiously. "Did you find anything?"

"We got some images. The tech enhanced them and cleaned them up, and a few minutes ago, he managed to ID the person responsible." The captain paused again. "It was one of our suspects, Robin Russo."

JACKSON CHECKED HIS MESSAGES again to see if he had an update about Robin and her whereabouts. He didn't. And that made his temper boil to the point of exploding.

Robin better have a damn good excuse for leaving that letter, but what excuse could there be?

None.

Unless this was some kind of sick game. Pretend she was the one in trouble. Lie like crazy. And then leave him threatening letters. Hell, he could probably add baby-snatching to her list of wrongdoing.

No matter which way he looked at it, Robin Russo couldn't be trusted and could be dangerous.

And that's the reason Jackson had his laptop on the table next to him. He was using a split screen so he could easily check all the security cameras. Steven and his men were doing the same, and all of them had set their monitors to show any detection of motion. Any movement outside should register and alert them all.

Hopefully, their vigilance and the new security measures would pay off.

The grounds were lit up with both the Christmas decorations and the security lights. There was a light, misty rain falling, and it made the lights glitter even more. Everything looked festive. But the heavy illumination was also another precaution. Even if someone managed to get past the motion detectors, it wouldn't be long before someone saw them.

Jackson put away his phone and glanced first at Caden, who was sleeping in his crib, then at Bailey. She was sleeping, too. *Finally.* She was curled up on the comfy sofa in the nursery, but the blanket Jackson had draped over her earlier was now halfway to the floor, proving that her sleep was restless at best.

Neither Jackson nor she had wanted to leave Caden, so they'd agreed to stay put, with Jackson in a recliner next to the crib, and Bailey on the sofa a few feet away.

Jackson thought about joining her there. It would be a tight fit, just the right amount of space for cuddling. His body was begging for that, but it was also begging for more. If he got onto that sofa with Bailey, it wouldn't be just for cuddling.

They'd have sex.

No. They'd make love, he mentally corrected himself.

And even though he was aroused by just looking at her, Jackson understood the difference. Being with Bailey couldn't be casual. It couldn't be temporary. So it was best to sort out his feelings before…before anything else happened between them.

He checked the time. It was just past midnight, and that meant it was finally Christmas. This wasn't exactly the way he'd envisioned his first Christmas with his son, but at least Caden was here with him. Considering everything that'd happened, that was a holiday gift he was extremely grateful to have.

Jackson got up and gave Bailey's blanket an adjustment. He kept his movements light, hoping she would stay asleep, but she stirred anyway.

Her eyelids fluttered open and she looked at him. Not a startled where-am-I? look. She smiled as if his face was exactly what she'd wanted to see.

Man, that didn't help his begging body.

Nor did it help when she reached out and slid her hand around the back of his neck. Bailey pulled him to her for a kiss.

"Hmmm," she mumbled against his mouth. "Merry Christmas."

Everything about that moment, that kiss and her words, seemed so right. She was welcoming him home, right into her arms. And even though Jackson knew they should talk first and kiss later, that's not what happened.

He pulled her closer and returned the kiss, as if Bailey was his for the taking.

"Caden's asleep?" she asked, glancing over his shoulder.

Jackson nodded. Caden was asleep and would almost certainly stay that way through the entire night. That cleared a path to sex with Bailey that didn't need any more clearing.

"We'll talk later," she murmured.

Had she read his mind? Maybe she had just sensed his hesitation. But that suggestion of "we'll talk later" zapped what little hesitation he had left.

Jackson hooked his arm around her and pulled her to him. If he was going to make a mistake by being intimate with her, then he sure as hell intended to make it a mistake worth remembering.

He angled her back farther. And farther. Until she pulled him down onto the sofa and onto her. Jackson was getting ready to take this to the next level and indulge in some foreplay.

But his phone vibrated.

Jackson silently cursed. He had turned off the ringer so the sound wouldn't wake Caden, but the buzzing was still audible.

They froze, both of them obviously trying to pull themselves from the hazy passion, but Jackson didn't delay. The buzzing sound was also a reminder that all calls could be critical.

Especially this one.

"Steven," he whispered, answering the cell. Jackson got up from the sofa and went to the other side of the room.

Bailey got up as well, and with her face showing her concern, she followed him.

"Check screen six," Steven instructed.

That sent Jackson racing back across the room to the table that held his laptop. His attention went right to screen six, just as Steven had directed.

This was the back section of the property, where there was a pond and shrubs covered in Christmas lights. Jackson moved closer to the screen, trying to pick through the landscape and decorations.

"Hell," he mumbled under his breath.

Jackson spotted something.

Or rather some*one*.

Chapter Sixteen

From the moment Jackson answered Steven's call, Bailey's heart had started pounding. It was too late for this to be a casual, how-are-you check-in; and since Jackson had been getting message and text updates throughout the night, this call meant something out of the ordinary had happened.

"There," Jackson said, pointing to the spot on the screen.

Even with him pointing, it still took her a moment to see what had put the alarmed expression on his face.

There was someone scaling the fence.

Oh, God. Not again.

The person was dressed all in black and blended right into the night. In fact, if it hadn't been for the multicolored Christmas lights, she might not have seen him at all. But she did see him, and she saw the rifle he was carrying.

"I have someone on the way to intercept him," Steven explained. "The house is locked down and every inch of it wired, in case someone tries to break in. I'll call when I have more info."

Jackson shut his phone and reached for the intercom button on the wall. "Tracy?" he said.

When the nanny answered, Jackson told her to get to the nursery immediately, but Bailey didn't wait for Tracy to arrive. She gathered up Caden in his blanket so he would be ready to go. Her son obviously didn't appreciate being awakened, because he started to fuss.

Jackson made another call, to someone on his staff, and he told everyone to go to their panic room. He also called the sheriff and asked him for assistance. Maybe, just maybe, that would be enough to stop whatever was happening.

Bailey tried to console Caden by kissing his cheek and gently rocking him, but perhaps the child could feel the tension in her body. Even though Steven seemed to have this situation under control, she couldn't help but be terrified for her baby's safety.

"It's just one person," Jackson reminded her. He put his arm around Caden and her.

"One desperate person," she said under her breath.

Maybe Shannon or Robin. Maybe Evan or even Ryan. But one desperate person could do a lot of damage with a rifle.

"How many men do you have out there?" Bailey asked.

"Four, including Steven. All of them are armed. Plus, we can track this person's every move with the new security system that was just installed. He won't get far."

Or maybe *she* wouldn't get far, because it very well could be a woman beneath all those dark clothes.

"Go to the panic room," Jackson insisted, the moment Tracy rushed into the room.

But he wasn't just directing the order at Tracy, Bailey realized. He was talking to her as well.

"We've been through this before, and I'd rather stay out here in case you need help," Bailey insisted right back.

She braced herself for an argument, but his attention went back to the laptop screen. Bailey saw the shadowy figure make its way through the shrubs, and each step brought it closer to a confrontation with Steven and his men.

Each step also brought the intruder closer to the house where he or she would be in firing range with that rifle.

"Go ahead to the panic room," Bailey told Tracy. "If things get worse, I'll join you."

Tracy gave a shaky nod and took Caden from her arms. Bailey gave her son several kisses, which he tried to bat away. Obviously, he was cranky and still sleepy.

Jackson kissed the baby as well, and motioned for Tracy to leave, but he kept his attention on the monitor.

"Here," he said, handing her the gun he had next to his laptop. "I'll grab another one from my office. Keep watch on the screen, and if anything happens, yell for me."

Oh, she would do that all right. Bailey didn't want this monster anywhere near the house.

She heard Jackson run down the hall toward his office, and she saw more movement on the screen. Steven and his men were forming a circle around the intruder. It shouldn't be long before they had him. Then they'd know the identity of the person who'd been making their lives a living hell.

The intruder froze. Maybe because he heard Steven. He lifted the rifle, taking aim.

Oh, God.

She prayed he didn't shoot one of the men before they could take him down.

Bailey was still praying when she heard the sound. At first she thought it was Jackson hurrying back from his office. But it hadn't come from the hall, it came from the front of the estate. It sounded as if someone had slammed a car door. Had one of the servants gone out for something? If so, Jackson wouldn't be happy about that, because he'd ordered them all to the panic room.

She glanced in the direction of the window, but it was too far on the other side of the room. If she went there to look out, she wouldn't be able to see the computer screen. Right now, the screen was critical, because it seemed as if Steven was only seconds away from reaching the intruder.

She heard Jackson's footsteps. *Finally!* Bailey didn't like him being out of sight at a time like this. She volleyed her attention between the laptop and the open door of the nursery. Waiting.

The next sound she heard, however, sent her heart to her knees.

There was a blast. Some kind of an explosion. And it seemed to rock the entire house.

Everything inside her froze for a moment. The windows hadn't broken. There didn't seem to be any signs of damage to the nursery.

"Bailey?" Jackson called out, and he raced into the room. He had a gun in each hand. "What happened?"

She shook her head, studied the images on the screen,

and it didn't take her long to find what she was looking for. There, at the back of the house, one of the utility vehicles was on fire. That was obviously the source of the explosion.

"Where's Steven?" Jackson asked, but he didn't wait for her to answer. He hurried to the computer and looked at the images.

Steven was still there, near the intruder in the dark clothes, but he'd stopped, as if trying to figure out what was going on.

Bailey was trying to figure out the same thing.

There was another deafening blast that rattled the windows and sent things falling from the walls and tables. She held onto the laptop and frantically searched the screen. It would have been impossible to miss.

Another vehicle was in flames.

"The intruder couldn't be doing this," Jackson mumbled, and he cursed. "There must be two of them."

In the back of her mind Bailey had already come to that conclusion, but hearing it spoken aloud turned her blood to ice. This wasn't a simple trespassing. And worse, it was possible the intruder had been a decoy to draw Steven and the others away from the estate.

It'd worked.

"I need you to go to the panic room," Jackson insisted, and he put one of the guns into her hands.

This time Bailey didn't intend to argue with him. She wouldn't go into the panic room itself, but she would instead stand guard outside to make sure no one got in.

"Don't do anything dangerous," she heard herself say. And she pressed a quick kiss to Jackson's lips.

She turned to run into the hall, but Bailey didn't get far.

A bullet came crashing through the nursery window.

Jackson cursed and pulled Bailey to the floor.

Hell. This couldn't be happening again. He'd taken too many precautions for this, and no one should have been able to fire shots into the house again.

The new security alarm went off, the shrieking sound piercing the room, and the cold winter wind started to howl through the gaping hole in the broken glass.

He grabbed the laptop from the table and pulled it onto the floor with them. First he had to silence the alarms so he could hear what was happening. He didn't want an intruder to use the shrill noise to cover up an actual break-in.

Jackson punched in the codes for the security system and temporarily disengaged the alarm. Only for a few seconds. Just to stop the sound. And then he rearmed the entire system so that it would alert them if another window was broken or a door opened in any part of the estate.

"Find the shooter on the screen," he told Bailey, and keeping low, he scrambled toward the window.

"Stay away from there," Bailey warned.

But he couldn't. Since the bullet had come through the window, that meant the shooter was out there, and not on the fence this time, or it would have tripped the sensors. Or it should have anyway.

"See if you can pinpoint the gunman's location for me," Jackson asked. He stood, staying to the side of the window and peeked out.

Nothing.

"I see Steven and his men but not the gunman," she said. "Oh, God, the man wearing the dark clothes is running. I think he's heading back to the fence."

He was probably getting away or creating a diversion so the shooter could get closer to the house. Had the two crossed the fence together? That would have tripped the sensors and alerted Steven, but maybe then the pair had split up. Steven and the others might not even know they were dealing with more than one intruder, but Steven had no doubt heard those blasts and the shot.

Another bullet came crashing through the window.

Jackson jumped to the side and tried to dodge the shards of glass that spewed across the room.

Yes, there were definitely two culprits.

Maybe more.

"Stay down!" Bailey shouted.

Jackson would for now; but soon, very soon, he had to return fire to keep this person from getting closer. However, he couldn't just blindly fire shots into the night, because his own men were out there.

"Where are Steven and the others?" Jackson asked Bailey. "And what about the sheriff?" But it was still too early for the sheriff to arrive. He was a good twenty, maybe twenty-five minutes out, and while it'd felt like an eternity, this ordeal was only about ten minutes old.

He glanced at her and saw she had her gaze nailed to the laptop. "Steven and one other man are running after the intruder. Two of your men are coming back toward the house."

Good. "Where are they?"

She shook her head. "Somewhere on the grounds at

the rear of the house. It's hard to tell exactly where they are."

Hell. "Hard to tell" meant he couldn't shoot and try to end this situation.

But that wasn't true for the gunman.

He sent three rounds, one right behind the other, slamming into what was left of the window.

"I need an exact location," Jackson pressed. Because the sooner he had that, the sooner he could fire, and then he could get Bailey out of there and on the way to the panic room where she belonged.

It sickened him and riled him to the core that she was in danger again. Bailey had already been through way too much to have to deal with bullets coming at her again.

"I see your men," she finally said. "They're approaching the estate from the back, where that car is still burning."

Good. That meant they weren't on the west side of the house where the shots were coming from.

"Don't get up," Jackson reminded her.

He took a deep breath, darted out from cover, and fired through the gaping holes in what was left of the window. He figured it would take a miracle for him to hit the shooter, but that wasn't what this was all about. He needed his own diversion, a way of getting the shooter to back down so it would buy Bailey some time.

Jackson fired two shots, keeping track of how much ammunition he used. He had several magazines in his pockets, but he didn't want to go bullet-to-bullet with someone hell-bent on killing them.

Four shots came tearing right at him.

He cursed and ducked back against the wall. So much for his plan of buying some time. More shots came one right behind the other.

Jackson glanced at Bailey to make sure she was okay. She wasn't. She was on the floor, shaking, and had a death grip on the gun and the laptop. However, despite the chaos all around them, she was still focusing on the computer screen.

"I see the shooter!" she shouted over the din of the bullets.

Since this guy didn't seem to be letting up, Jackson made his way back across the room and to Bailey. Somehow, he was going to have to get her into the hall despite the fact that the bullets all seemed to be landing right around the door they would have to use to make their exit.

First though, Jackson needed to try to get a visual on everyone so he didn't end up shooting the wrong person.

He kept his ear pinned to the sound of the shots so he could tell if they changed directions, and he also studied the computer monitor. He saw who he thought must be Steven. The Christmas lights helped with the illumination, but it was still night, and everyone was wearing dark clothes. From what he could tell, two of his men were definitely at the rear of the house, and they appeared to be trying to sneak up on the gunman.

"What now?" Bailey asked, her voice trembling.

Jackson was about to tell her they were moving to the panic room. Or rather, she was.

But just like that, the shots stopped.

So did Jackson's heart.

He damn sure hadn't wanted bullets coming at them,

but if the shooter was firing, they had a good idea where he was.

"The doors and windows are all locked," Jackson reminded Bailey, hoping it would help level her breathing.

Or were they?

He'd turned off the alarm after the glass had shattered. There'd only been—what?—a minute at the most between the time the first shot was fired and his cutting the sound of the alarm so he could hear if anyone broke in. Hell. He hoped someone hadn't managed to get through one of the doors or windows during that short time before he reengaged the system.

If so, Bailey and he could be ambushed.

Jackson reached up and turned off the lights. It probably wouldn't help at this point, because the shooter obviously knew where they were; but he didn't want the overhead light to make it easier for the shooter to see them if and when he got Bailey out of there.

"Come on," Jackson instructed. "Stay down and move fast. I want to get out into the hall as quickly as possible."

She pulled in a hard breath and nodded. Her eyes were wide with fear, but she didn't panic. Far from it.

"We'll protect Caden," she insisted.

Yes, they would.

"Leave the laptop," he told her.

He wanted their hands free so they could use their weapons if it became necessary. But Jackson hoped they wouldn't have to be long without another computer tied to the surveillance system. The security feed could be transferred to his phone, and he could do that as soon as he got Bailey out of there. Then, he could keep an eye on Steven and whatever was going on at the back of the estate. He could also monitor his two men, who were no doubt trying to provide some sort of backup.

Plus, there was the sheriff. The gate was closed, but the sheriff had the security codes to open it. Still, Jackson wanted to make sure where everyone was at any given moment.

Jackson helped Bailey get into a crouching position. There were no other shots. No other sounds to indicate the location of the shooter.

"Now," Jackson instructed.

He maneuvered himself so that he was behind Bailey. It was a risk because it meant she would go first into the hall. But since the bullets had come through the window, he didn't want her in the direct line of fire either.

Jackson nudged her forward, trying to hurry. The first step was to get out of the nursery and to the back stairs. From there they could reach the library, and then the panic room. Once they were there, he would force Bailey inside where she'd be safe, so he could deal with this armed SOB.

This ended tonight.

He wasn't going to allow Bailey or Caden to be in danger any longer.

"Stay down," he reminded Bailey. After all, there were windows at the front of the hall. "And once you're out there, go to the left."

She nodded and gave him one last glance over her shoulder before she darted into the hall. Jackson was right behind her. But they only made two steps before there was a sound that Jackson didn't want to hear.

A shot.

It was a loud deafening blast.

But it hadn't come from the nursery window, and there'd been no sounds of breaking glass.

None.

And Jackson knew why.

The shooter was inside the house.

Chapter Seventeen

Bailey dropped down and flattened her body on the floor in the hall.

Oh, God.

Things had just gone from bad to worse. The shot had come from inside. How the devil had this person gotten in and brought the danger so close?

She tried to keep her gun ready, but she also pulled Jackson to the floor with her.

He didn't go willingly.

Jackson was obviously looking for the shooter so he could return fire. She knew that was necessary, but Bailey didn't want him risking his life like this. No. There had to be another way. They needed to find a place to take cover so they could try to decide how to get out of this situation.

If there was a way out.

She suddenly had a terrifying thought. Or rather several of them. What if there were more than two intruders? What if they'd already neutralized Steven and his men? And what if the sheriff couldn't get onto the grounds?

Bailey was pretty sure someone would have to open

the gate for Sheriff Gentry, and without computer access there was no way Jackson or she could do that.

"The shooter's in the foyer," Jackson mumbled under his breath.

Bailey's heart dropped.

The foyer was just below them.

She lifted her head slightly. Bad idea. A bullet went slamming into the wall directly above them.

Jackson cursed and rolled her to the side until he was in front of her. He was protecting her again, and in doing so he was placing himself in grave danger.

He levered himself up and sent a single shot down into the foyer.

Bailey looked down the hall in the direction of the back stairs. She couldn't actually see the stairs from her location, but she knew they were just on the other side of the wall. Probably a good forty feet away. Of course, once they got out of the open area where they were now, the hall might actually provide them some cover.

First though, they would have to move a couple of yards, out in the open, where the shooter would easily be able to see them.

Her heart was pounding in her ears, and her hand started to shake. Bailey thought of her precious son, and she fixed Caden's face in her head. She used that to fight off the fear. She would protect him because the alternative was unthinkable. She'd lost him for four months, and she didn't intend to lose him again.

She was about to suggest to Jackson that they just make a run for the covered part of the hall.

But then she heard a different sound.

Not a shot this time, but it was a sound that tore through her worse than any bullet ever could.

She heard a baby crying.

Bailey tried to get to her feet, but Jackson jerked her back down.

"Just listen," he whispered, his voice strained and hard as the grip he had on her.

She tried to do that. Bailey tried to latch onto any information that would help them. But the only thing she could think of was getting to Caden. Her baby was in danger.

"Caden's in the panic room," Jackson reminded her.

Was he? Tracy had certainly intended to take him there, but maybe they hadn't made it. Maybe an intruder had managed to stop them and was now holding them hostage.

"It's probably a trick," Jackson added.

Before Bailey could wrap her mind around that, another bullet slammed into the wall just a few feet away. Then another. However, over the thick blasts, she could still hear the baby crying.

Bailey struggled to get up again, and she batted away Jackson's hand. He didn't give up. He grabbed her gown and dragged her back to the floor.

"That's not Caden," he insisted.

Maybe because she could see the certainty in his eyes and on his face, Bailey forced herself to listen harder. Yes, it was a baby crying all right, but she had heard Caden cry.

Those sobs didn't belong to her son.

"It's a recording," Jackson told her. "A loop. It's the same sound being played over and over."

He was right. It was a recording. And not of Caden. This was indeed a trick, and it had come very close to working. She had nearly left what little cover they had so she could race downstairs and get to the source of those baby sobs.

The relief instantly flooded through her, even as the bullets continued to come their way. But in between the shots and the recorded sounds of a baby crying, Bailey heard something else.

Footsteps.

Jackson must have heard them, too, because his gaze whipped in that direction. Not to the steps in front of them, but to the nursery behind him. My God. Had someone used a ladder to climb up and get into the room? There wasn't a way to access it from another point in the house.

The relief that Bailey had felt just seconds earlier evaporated.

In addition to the dark-clothed intruder they'd seen on the monitor, there was a gunman in the foyer and now another, perhaps in the nursery right behind them. Three of them. Unless it was one of Jackson's guards or a servant who hadn't made it to the panic rooms. One thing was for certain. They couldn't just lie there and wait to see who might be coming out of the nursery. If it was another shooter, they'd be sitting ducks.

Jackson reached up and slapped off the hall lights. It didn't plunge them into total darkness, because there were lights on below in the foyer, but hopefully it wasn't illuminated enough for the shooter to see them clearly.

The bullets continued to tear through the walls and

the stair railings, each of them robbing Bailey of what little breath she had left.

"We need to get to the back stairs," Jackson mouthed.

Yes. Away from the foyer and away from the nursery. It would also get them closer to reaching Caden. Of course, they couldn't go in the panic room, not with the threat of danger so close. But Bailey wanted to be directly in front of that panic room door so she could be a last line of defense, if it came down to it.

"Now," Jackson whispered. "Run and don't look back."

"What are you going to do?" she demanded.

"Go now!" he demanded.

Jackson levered himself up, and in the same motion, he slammed the nursery door shut. It certainly wouldn't stop bullets, but it might slow down the person they'd heard inside the room.

Bailey stayed in a crouching position, and while she tried to keep her gun ready to fire, she started down the hall.

She didn't get far.

The barrage of shots came right at them, and she dropped back down. But not Jackson. He took aim at the person in the foyer.

And fired.

The sound seemed to echo through the entire estate, but just like that, the shots stopped.

"I think I got him," Jackson said, reaching for her.

But before Jackson could take hold of her, someone opened the nursery door. It happened in a flash. Too soon for Bailey to move out of the way.

She felt someone grab her from behind and jerk her into the dark nursery.

And then that someone jammed a gun against her head.

Everything seemed to happen at once.

Jackson saw the gunman in the foyer drop, his weapons clattering to the floor. He caught a glimpse of two of his own guards who were making their way up the back steps. He also heard a siren, probably from Sheriff Gentry's vehicle.

But all of those details melted away when he saw Bailey.

There was just a flash of movement from behind her, and then she seemed to vanish. Someone had pulled Bailey into the nursery. Jackson thought it was too much to hope that it was one of his own men.

Keeping his gun lifted and aimed, Jackson bracketed his right wrist with his left hand. He walked toward the open doorway of the nursery where Bailey had disappeared.

He saw her, right in the middle of the darkness and the cold. Her pale skin gleamed like a beacon.

So did the gun.

Not hers. Bailey's weapon was on the floor.

The one that grabbed every bit of Jackson's attention was jammed right against Bailey's temple.

"The gunman's dead," one of Jackson's guards shouted from the foyer. "We're coming up."

But Jackson shook his head, hoping they would see his response and back off. He didn't want anything prompting Bailey's captor to pull that trigger.

"It's over," Jackson said to both Bailey and the armed person hiding in the shadows behind her. "The sheriff's here. So are my men. Your partner is dead, and my guards have the other one cornered on the grounds."

He hoped.

Jackson had to take a deep breath to keep his voice steady. "Put down your gun and we can talk."

Though talking was the last thing Jackson wanted to do. Right now, he just wanted Bailey safe and in his arms. That meant he first had to get her away from that armed SOB who was likely responsible for all the hell that'd been happening over the past few days.

Jackson inched closer. "Put down the gun," he repeated.

"Don't move," the gunman ordered.

And Jackson knew exactly who'd given that order.

"Evan," Jackson growled, and he fought hard to stop himself from cursing. Even though he wanted to throttle Evan for putting the gun to Bailey's head, he couldn't antagonize the man. "There's nothing you can gain from holding Bailey. Let her go."

"Oh, there's something." Evan tried to laugh, but the sound was broken and hollow.

Hell. Evan was in way over his head here, and if he decided to fight so he could escape, Bailey could be shot. Evan's gun was literally point-blank against Bailey's temple. She wouldn't survive a shot fired at that range.

"I need a car," Evan demanded. "And some cash."

Jackson moved a fraction of an inch closer, all the while keeping watch on Evan's trigger finger. "What happened to the million dollars you got from selling Caden?"

"Most of it's gone. I had to use most of it to cover up what I did."

"And what exactly did you do?" Jackson asked, fighting to keep his voice and body calm. He didn't have a clean shot because Evan had ducked down behind Bailey.

"Robin got in touch with me when she heard you were looking to adopt a baby. She was scared and thought she would be arrested, that no one would believe she was just trying to save Bailey and her son. After all, she'd been having an affair with one of the gunmen."

"So, you convinced her to turn the baby over to you." Jackson wanted to keep Evan talking so he could hopefully distract him. If Evan moved just a little to either side, he would have a clean shot.

A shot he *would* take.

He would do anything to save Bailey.

"I gave Robin money," Evan continued. "Part of the money you forked over for the adoption."

"You sold my baby." Bailey shook her head, and that caused Evan to jam the gun even harder against her skin. Bailey winced in pain.

Every muscle in Jackson's body reacted to that wince. *How dare this SOB hurt Bailey.*

"Yes, I sold him," Evan admitted. "But it had nothing to do with you or your son. This was the way I could get back at Jackson and punish him."

Bailey swallowed hard. "Why punish Jackson? He wasn't responsible for Sybil's death."

"To hell he wasn't." Evan was frantic now, and sounded on the verge of losing it completely. "It was because of Jackson she was on that plane. If he hadn't been trying to do another hostile takeover of a company, it would have never happened. Never."

"You're right," Bailey said, her voice broken but

somehow calm. "Jackson walked away from that crash. It doesn't seem fair, does it?"

Good. Bailey was playing along and trying to keep Evan from going completely berserk.

"That's why I'll go with you," Bailey continued. "We'll get the money and the car, and you can hold me hostage until you're away from the estate."

Jackson cursed despite his attempt to stop it. "No, Bailey. Don't do this."

"I have to do it. We owe Evan that much. And besides, he doesn't want to fire any more shots, because someone could get hurt."

"You can't let Evan take you from here," Jackson said through clenched teeth.

Bailey winked at him.

Jackson tried not to show any relief, but he felt a ton of it. Bailey and he were on the same page here, thank God. Pretend to cooperate but look for the first opportunity to stop this madman.

"If you hate me so much," Jackson said to him, "then why fake the DNA results?"

"Simple. I had to make you keep trusting me. What better way than for you to believe I would lie for you."

Yeah. It was a good plan. "And if all of this blew up in your face, then you could lie to the cops and tell them that I faked the DNA results."

"Good plan, huh?" Evan said with some amusement.

Right. A good plan. The plan of a sick mind. "What about the threatening letters that Robin left for me?"

"Just another layer to make you miserable. Like I am. But I'm tired of talking about this. Tired of trying to justify myself to you. Call down to your men," Evan ordered. "Tell them to get that car and the cash. And tell them to hurry. My patience is wearing thin."

Jackson didn't move and didn't look back, but he relayed the demand from over his shoulder. He asked them to take the cash that they kept in Steven's office. His men would do as they were told, which meant within minutes Evan would have what he wanted.

And within minutes, Jackson would be ready to take him down when he tried to get out of the house. It was a long way down those stairs. Longer still for Evan to reach the car that would be brought to the driveway. If by some miracle the man did make it to the vehicle, it had a GPS tracking device.

"I had to make you feel how much it hurts to lose someone you love," Evan snarled, his words angry again. "That's why I let you have Caden all this time. I wanted you to love him, and I want your heart ripped to pieces when you lose him."

"Then why take Bailey?" Jackson challenged. He took another step closer. "She had nothing to do with that plane crash. You hurt, and are continuing to hurt, an innocent woman. Let her go."

"No. I can't. She's collateral damage since she gave birth to Caden. I've been following her, you know, and making sure she didn't come to you too soon."

Jackson kept trying. "Too soon?"

"I wanted to drag this out longer. I wanted you to be with Caden a few more months, but then Bailey decided to come here, and that moved up all my plans."

So, Evan had been the one following her, and that's how he knew when to send the first hired gun out to the estate. Since Evan had access to the security cameras both inside and outside the house, that explained how he had been able to pinpoint them so easily during the attacks. It made Jackson sick to think that Evan had been watching all this time.

"Bailey didn't know about your plans," Jackson pressed. "You can make it so she's safe. You too."

"Right." Evan gave another hollow laugh. "The only thing you want is for me to be arrested. Well, that's not going to happen. SAPD would charge me as an accessory to the hostage incident. People were murdered that day, and you and I both know that accessory to murder is the same sentence as murder itself."

Jackson wasn't sure of that at all, but he was certain that Evan would be charged with a whole host of other things that he'd carried out in the past forty-eight hours.

"I have the cash," one of Jackson's men called out from the foyer. "And the car is in front of the house."

"Time to go," Evan said, obviously not wasting any time. "Back up, Jackson. And don't try anything stupid. I have nothing to lose here."

Oh yes he did. Evan was about to lose his life.

But then Jackson saw something that could give this an ugly turn.

Behind Evan and Bailey, there was some movement, and a moment later, he spotted Sheriff Gentry. He was easing up the ladder that Evan had apparently used to gain entry into the nursery. Of course, Evan had been able to do that because he'd shot out the window.

Jackson shook his head slightly so the sheriff would stop. He wanted Gentry's help, but he didn't want Evan getting spooked. Best to get the man onto the stairs where there would be more room to maneuver.

"What?" Evan demanded. It was obvious something alerted him.

Jackson didn't look at the sheriff because he didn't want Evan to follow his gaze. But he must have sensed that someone was behind him.

A sound tore from Evan's mouth. Not exactly a shout. Something that sounded more animal than human.

Evan turned, dragging Bailey with him. Both of them moving to face the sheriff.

Hell.

Evan's hand tightened, poised to pull the trigger of the gun still pointed at Bailey's head.

Jackson still didn't have a clean shot, so he lowered his head and dove toward Bailey and Evan. It was a huge risk. The biggest one he'd ever taken, but he couldn't just stand there while Evan fired.

He plowed right into them and sent all three of them crashing against what was left of the window frame. Bits of wood and glass flew everywhere. So did Evan's hands. The man was trying to bash the gun and his fist into anything close enough for him to hurt.

Jackson couldn't stop Evan's fist from bashing into Bailey's stomach.

And then there was the shot.

The sound of it blasted through the room.

Bailey gasped, as if fighting for air, and Jackson saw her crumple to the floor. God, had she been hit? Had he lost her?

And in that moment of fear and panic, he realized just what she meant to him.

"Bailey!" Jackson shouted, but his voice was drowned out by the other sounds.

The echo from the gunshot. The chaos that followed.

The rustling of the sheriff diving through the window to grab hold of Evan. But Jackson didn't hear the one sound he wanted to hear.

He didn't hear Bailey's voice.

Chapter Eighteen

Bailey heard everything, every sound of the struggle going on around her. She could see, too. But what she couldn't do was speak. That's because the breath had been knocked out of her when Evan punched her in the stomach.

Jackson cursed, something raw and filled with fury. He came at Evan and latched onto the man's hand so he couldn't fire his gun again. Jackson bashed Evan's hand against the floor, and when he didn't let go of the weapon, he bashed it again.

Finally, Evan dropped the gun.

The sheriff was right there to grab the man and pin him down so that he couldn't move and go after that gun again.

Bailey tried to get up, but Jackson beat her to it. He raced to her and scooped her up into his arms.

"Are you hurt?" he demanded.

She managed to shake her head, but her voice still wouldn't cooperate.

That's because she saw the blood.

It was trickling down the side of Jackson's face.

"But *you're* hurt," she said.

It seemed to take much too long for her to reach up

and wipe away the blood. Not a gunshot wound, thank God. It had likely come from the broken glass.

The relief was overwhelming. Maybe because it was mixed with the adrenaline and the realization that they had both come out of this alive.

Bailey grabbed Jackson and kissed him.

She didn't bother to keep it simple and sweet. It was a kiss filled with the powerful emotions coursing through her.

"She's okay, I guess," the sheriff mumbled, sounding mildly amused. He hauled Evan to his feet. "I got an update from SAPD on the way over. They have the woman they're calling hostage number four, and everything seems resolved. She's safe, and there isn't going to be another hostage incident. Turned out to be a ruse."

Thank God. It was all over, except for dealing with the aftermath of the situation that Evan and his hired guns had created.

"Your men got the third intruder," the sheriff continued, "and he's spilling his guts, already trying to work out a deal so he can testify against Mr. Young here in exchange for immunity."

"That little weasel," Evan snarled. "I knew I couldn't trust him."

"He said you didn't pay him nearly enough." The sheriff handcuffed Evan. "He also said you were the mastermind of this disaster, that you'd hired not just him but the other gunman, and that you came here to kill Bailey and then kidnap the child."

Evan cursed, but he didn't deny any of it. Good reason. There was a ton of evidence against him.

"And the explosions?" Jackson asked. Bailey was

thankful he'd asked. She wanted to know about those as well.

"I wanted to distract you so I could get inside," Evan spat out. "I should have blown up the house and everyone in it instead."

The man's venom caused Bailey to shudder.

"We have Shannon Wright and Robin Russo down at my office," Sheriff Gentry added. "I put them in protective custody just about the same time I got a call about this attack here at the estate. I don't think either woman had any part in this."

Well, that was something, at least. Still, it would no doubt take a while for Shannon to get her life back in order. And of course, Robin would face charges for taking Caden and for leaving those threatening letters.

"What about Ryan Cassaine?" Bailey asked.

The sheriff shook his head. "No links to this one here," he said, tipping his head to Evan. Sheriff Gentry mumbled something about that being a good thing, and he led Evan out the door.

Bailey looked away from the man who'd made her life a living hell. She didn't want another glimpse of him. She only wanted Evan and his dead henchman out of the house.

"I'm so sorry," Jackson whispered.

"For what? This wasn't your fault."

"Evan worked for me," Jackson pointed out.

"And you had no idea that his fiancée's death made him crazy. No. I won't let you take the blame for this."

"Thank you for that." Jackson gathered her in his

arms and kissed her right back. That robbed her of what little breath she'd managed to gather.

He pulled back. Met her gaze. "Let's check on Caden." Jackson took her hand and hurried out the door and toward the back stairs.

Bailey suddenly couldn't get to Caden fast enough. The only consolation in all of this was that her baby was too young to remember the attack that had almost cost him his parents.

"We're his parents," she mumbled.

Jackson's grip tightened on her hand. "What did you say?"

"We're Caden's parents," she said a little louder.

She hadn't expected him to come to a dead stop outside the panic room and whirl around to face her again. He suddenly looked like a dark warrior ready for another battle. The muscles in his jaw stirred, and he stared at her with narrowed, waiting eyes.

"Yes. We are." His voice was as clogged with emotion as hers. Jackson didn't seem the ruthless businessman now. He seemed humbled. "You aren't going to take him from me, are you?"

It was such a heartfelt question that it brought tears to her eyes. "No." But until she heard her answer, she hadn't been sure what was going to happen next.

She still wasn't.

It was almost as if she were still out of breath, waiting. Because Bailey figured what she said and did here in the next few minutes would change her life forever.

A scary thought.

Her head was filled with all the images of the attack, and there was still some blood on Jackson's forehead.

She could hear Evan's threats. The explosions. The shots that had been fired.

But for some reason, her mind was crystal-clear.

"We can share custody," she suggested, though that didn't sound as good as it should have. "It's a reasonable solution."

"Reasonable," Jackson repeated. He shook his head, cursed. "What if I don't want reasonable?"

Bailey blinked, and there went the air again. "You can't want full custody?"

He shook his head again. Cursed again. He reached for the button that would open the monitor for the panic room but then jerked back his hand.

"I do want full custody," he insisted. "And I also want you."

Because she was gearing up for a fight, and trying to figure out how she was going to deal with a broken heart, it took a moment for that to sink in.

"You want me?" she clarified, not sure exactly what he meant by that.

He put his hands on his hips. "Not an affair. Not just sex. *You.*"

Which still didn't clarify everything.

She must have looked confused, because he grasped her shoulders and stared at her. And it seemed as if he just couldn't find the right words. Strange. Jackson had a knack for saying and doing the right thing at the right time.

"I'm in love with you," Bailey blurted out. Yes, it was a massive risk. It could be too much too soon for the Texas tycoon, but Bailey didn't regret it. He needed the facts, and the facts were that she was desperately in love with him.

He didn't respond. Instead, he let go of her and pushed the button so the monitor would drop down.

"How's Caden?" Jackson asked, the moment that Tracy's image appeared on the screen.

"Sleeping." Tracy stepped back so they could see him.

Caden was indeed asleep, snuggled into his blanket as if this was an ordinary night. It wasn't. They'd just been attacked, and she'd just poured out her heart to Jackson and had gotten no response.

"Is it safe to come out?" Tracy asked.

Jackson nodded, and a moment later the thick steel door opened. "Could you let everyone know that the crisis is over, that they can return to their quarters?"

"Certainly." Tracy didn't linger. She hurried away, obviously relieved that the danger was gone.

She and Jackson stepped inside and tiptoed across the room. Bailey went to the crib and stared down at her son. She got that same warm jolt every time she looked at Caden, and it was even stronger now.

"I wanted to say this here, with Caden in the room," Jackson whispered. He slid his hand over hers.

Since he didn't seem eager to continue, Bailey just decided to put her fear right out there so she could try to deal with it. "You're dumping me?"

Jackson looked as if she'd slapped him. "No." He didn't have any trouble getting that out. Nor moving. He pulled her closer to him and turned her so they were face-to-face.

"Dumping you?" he asked, making it sound like the last thing on his mind. "I was going to tell you that I'm in love with you, too. And then I was going to ask you to marry me."

Now it was Bailey's turn to be stunned. *Mercy.* She hadn't seen that coming.

"You really were going to do those things?" she asked.

Jackson winced. "I still am." He stared at her. "I love you. And—will you marry me?"

Bailey wanted to say yes. Heck, she wanted to jump for joy, kiss Jackson and then haul him off to bed somewhere. But she couldn't just go blindly into this.

"No," Jackson interrupted before she could say anything. "I'm not doing this for Caden. Or even for us. I'm doing it for me. I want you, not just for tonight. And not just to be Caden's mother. Bailey, I want *you* because I love *you*."

She studied his eyes, looking for any signs of doubt, but there weren't any.

Bailey only saw the love, and it was the same love that she felt in her heart.

She smiled, slid her hand around the back of Jackson's neck and pulled him down for a kiss. It wasn't the frantic kiss of relief she'd given him in the aftermath of the attack. This one was meant to say only one thing.

I love you.

Still, Bailey gave him the words to go along with the kiss. "I love you, Jackson. And yes, I'll marry you."

He smiled, but she caught that smile with her mouth and tasted it with another kiss.

Like their other kissing sessions, this one turned hot very fast, and Jackson hauled her against him so they were body-to-body and touching everywhere. It left her breathless and wanting a whole lot more.

"I have no doubts that this is how I want to spend the rest of my life," she whispered. "With you and Caden."

At the sound of his name, Caden started to fuss. But

not just fuss. He woke up and started to wail. It was loud and a complete attention-getter.

At the same time, they reached for him—and then laughed when they bumped into each other. Caden stopped crying and stared at them as if trying to figure out why they were so darn happy when he was cranky over having his sleep interrupted with a marriage proposal and a declaration of love ever after.

Bailey stepped back a little so that Jackson could pick up the baby. He kissed Caden's cheek and then handed the baby to her.

"She said yes," Jackson whispered in Caden's ear. "Your mom is going to be my wife. And if we play our cards right, one day you might get a little sister or brother out of this deal."

Even though Caden couldn't have possibly understood what he meant, he must have picked up on his dada's happy tone and expression.

Caden smiled, a big gummy grin complete with a "Coo."

Their son obviously approved, and to celebrate, Bailey gave both of them another kiss.

This was her dream come true. The life she had always wanted. And it was right in her arms, and in her heart, forever.

* * * * *

UNFORGETTABLE

BY
CASSIE MILES

All the characters in this book have no existence outside the imagination of the author, and have no relation whatsoever to anyone bearing the same name or names. They are not even distantly inspired by any individual known or unknown to the author, and all the incidents are pure invention.

First published in Great Britain 2012
by Mills & Boon, an imprint of Harlequin (UK) Limited,
Eton House, 18-24 Paradise Road, Richmond, Surrey TW9 1SR

© Kay Bergstrom 2011

ISBN: 978 0 263 89501 8

46-0212

Harlequin (UK) policy is to use papers that are natural, renewable and recyclable products and made from wood grown in sustainable forests. The logging and manufacturing processes conform to the legal environmental regulations of the country of origin.

Printed and bound in Spain
by Blackprint CPI, Barcelona

Though born in Chicago and raised in L.A., **Cassie Miles** has lived in Colorado long enough to be considered a semi-native. The first home she owned was a log cabin in the mountains overlooking Elk Creek, with a thirty-mile commute to her work at the *Denver Post*. After raising two daughters and cooking tons of macaroni and cheese for her family, Cassie is trying to be more adventurous in her culinary efforts. Seviche, anyone? She's discovered that almost anything tastes better with wine. When she's not plotting Intrigue books, Cassie likes to hang out at the Denver Botanical Gardens near her high-rise home.

To Sara Hanson, the next writer in the family.
As always, to Rick.

Chapter One

Morning sunlight sliced into the rocky alcove where he had taken shelter. A blinding glare hit his eyes. The sun was a laser pointed directly into his face. He sank back into the shadows.

If he stayed here, they'd find him. He had to move, to run…to keep running. This wasn't the time for a nap. He shoved himself off the ground where he'd been sleeping and crouched while he got his bearings.

Behind him, the rock wall curved like bent fingers. Another boulder lay before him like a giant thumb. He had spent the night curled up inside this granite fist.

How did I get here?

Craning his neck, he peered over the edge of the thumb. His hideout was halfway up a slope. Around him were shrubs, lodgepole pines, more boulders and leafy green aspen trees. Through the trunks, he saw the opposite wall of a steep, rocky canyon.

Where the hell am I?

His head throbbed. The steady, pulsating pain synchronized with the beating of his heart.

When he raised his hand to his forehead, he saw a smear of dried blood on the sleeve of his plaid, flannel shirt. *My blood?* Other rusty blotches spattered the front of his shirt. *Was I shot?* He took a physical inventory. Apart from the killer headache, he didn't seem to be badly hurt. There were scrapes and bruises but nothing serious.

By his feet, he saw a handgun. A SIG Sauer P-226. He checked the magazine. Four bullets left. *This isn't my gun.* He preferred a Beretta M9, but the SIG would do just fine.

He felt in his pockets for an ammunition clip and found nothing. No wallet. No cell phone. Not a useful packet of aspirin. Nothing. He wasn't wearing a belt or a holster. Though he had on socks, the laces of his steel-toed boots weren't tied. *Must have dressed in a hurry.*

He licked his parched lips. The inside of his mouth tasted like he'd been chewing on a penny. The coppery taste was a symptom, but he didn't know what it meant. *I could ask the paramedics. Oh, wait. Nobody's here. Nobody's coming to help me.*

He was on his own.

His fingers gingerly explored his scalp until he found the source of his pain. When he poked at the knot on the back of his head, his hand came away bloody. Head wounds tended to bleed a lot, but how had that blood gotten on the front of his shirt?

He remembered shots being fired in the night. A fist-fight. Running. Riding. On a horse? *That can't be right.* He wasn't a cowboy. Or was he?

No time for speculating. He had to move fast. In four days…

His mind blanked. There was nothing inside his head but a big, fat zero.

In four days, something big was going down, something life-changing and important. Why the hell couldn't he remember? What was wrong with him?

The chirp of a bird screeched in his hypersensitive ears, and he was tempted to go back to sleep. If he waited, the truth would catch up to him. It always did. Can't escape the truth. Can't hide from reality.

He closed his eyes against the sun and gathered his strength. A different memory flashed. He wasn't in a forest but on a city street. He heard traffic noise and the rumble of an overhead train. Tall buildings with starkly lit windows loomed against the night sky. He fell on the pavement. Shadows devoured him. He fought for breath. If he lost consciousness, he would die.

His eyelids snapped open. Was he dead? That was as plausible an explanation as any.

This mountain landscape was the afterlife. Through the treetops, he saw a sky of ethereal blue. One thing was for damn sure. If he was dead, he needed to find an angel to tell him what came next.

CAITLYN MORRIS STEPPED onto the wide porch of her cabin and sipped coffee from her U.S. Marine Corps skull-and-crossbones mug. A crisp breeze rustled across the open meadow that stretched to the forested slopes. Looking to the south, she saw distant peaks, still snowcapped in early June.

A lock of straight blond hair blew across her forehead. She probably ought to do something about her messy pony-tail. Heather was going to be here any minute, and Caitlyn didn't want to look like she was falling apart.

She leaned her elbows on the porch railing and sighed. She'd moved to the mountains looking for peace and solitude, but this had been a busy little morning.

At daybreak, she'd been awakened by an intruder—a dappled gray mare that stood outside her bedroom window, nickering and snorting, demanding attention. The mare hadn't been wearing a bridle or saddle, but she had seemed tame. Without hesitation, she'd followed Caitlyn to the barn. There, Caitlyn kept the other two horses she was renting for the summer from the Circle L Ranch, which was about eight miles down the winding dirt road that led to Pinedale.

After she'd tended to the wayward horse, sleep had been out of the question. She'd gotten dressed, had breakfast, put in a call to the Circle L and went back to the horse barn to check the inventory slip for the supplies that had been delivered from the hardware store yesterday.

A handyman was supposed to be starting work for her today, even though it was Saturday. Most of her projects didn't require two people, but she needed help to patch the barn roof. She checked her wristwatch. It was almost nine o'clock, and the guy who answered her ad had promised to be here by eight. Had he gotten lost? She really hoped he wasn't going to flake out on her.

When she saw a black truck coming down the road, her spirits lifted. Then she noticed the Circle L logo and the horse trailer. This wasn't her handyman.

The truck pulled into her drive and a tall, rangy brunette—Heather Laurence, half-owner of the Circle L—climbed out. "Good to see you, Caitlyn. How are you doing?"

There was a note of caution in the other woman's voice. Nobody from this area knew exactly why Caitlyn had come to live at this isolated cabin, which had been a vacation home for her family since she was a little girl with blond pigtails and freckles.

She hadn't wanted to tell her story, and folks from around here—even someone like Heather, whom she considered a friend—didn't push for explanations. They had a genuine respect for privacy.

Caitlyn held up her skull-and-crossbones mug. "Would you like some coffee?"

"Don't mind if I do."

The heels of Heather's cowboy boots clunked on the planks of the porch as they entered the cabin through the screen door.

When Caitlyn arrived here a month ago, it had taken a week to get the cabin clean enough to suit her. She'd scrubbed and dusted and repainted the walls of the front room a soothing sage green. Then she'd hired horses for company. Both were beauties—one palomino and the other roan. Every day since, she'd made a point of riding one in the morning and the other in the afternoon. Though she certainly didn't need two horses, she hadn't wanted to separate one from the others at the Circle L. No need for a horse to be as lonely as she was.

Sunshine through the kitchen windows shone on the clean-but-battered countertops and appliances. If she decided to stay here on a more permanent basis, she would resurface the counters with Turkish tile.

"Looks nice and homey in here," Heather said.

"It had been neglected." When she and her brother were living at home, the family spent every Christmas vacation and at least a month in the summer at the cabin. "After Mom and Dad moved to Arizona, they stopped coming here as often."

"How are they doing?"

"Good. They're both retired but busy." Caitlyn poured coffee into a plain blue mug. "Cream or sugar?"

"I take it plain and strong." Heather grinned. "Like my men."

"I seem to remember a summer a long time ago when you were in love with Brad Pitt."

"So were you."

"That sneaky Angelina stole him away from us."

Heather raised her coffee mug. "To Brad."

"And all the other good men who got away."

They were both single and in their early thirties. Caitlyn's unmarried status was a strategic career decision. She couldn't ask a husband to wait while she pursued her work as a reporter embedded with troops in war zones around the globe.

"That crush on the gorgeous Mr. Pitt must have been fifteen years ago," Heather said. "A simpler time."

Fifteen years ago, September eleventh was just another day. Nobody had heard of Osama bin Laden or the Taliban. "Before the Gulf War. Before Afghanistan."

"You've been to those places."

"And it doesn't look like I'll be going back any time soon." A knot tightened in her throat. Though Caitlyn wasn't ready to spill her guts, it wouldn't hurt to tell her old friend about some of the issues that had been bothering her. "The field office where I was working in the Middle East was closed down due to budget cuts."

"Sorry to hear it. What does that mean for you?"

"I've got a serious case of unemployment." And a lot of traumatic memories. Innumerable horrors she wanted to forget. "I'm not sure I want to continue as a journalist. That was one of the reasons I came here. I'm taking a break from news. No newspaper. No TV. And I haven't turned on my laptop in days."

"Hard to believe. You were always a news junkie, even when we were teenagers."

"Your brother used to call me Little Miss Know-It-All." Her brother was four years older and as cute as Brad Pitt. "I had such a huge crush on him."

"You and everybody else." Heather shook her head. "When Danny finally got married, you could hear hearts breaking all across the county."

Danny was still handsome, especially in his uniform. "Hard to believe he's a deputy sheriff."

"Not really. Remember how he always played cops and robbers?"

"Playing cowboy on a ranch is kind of redundant."

After days of solitude, Caitlyn enjoyed their small talk. At the same time, she felt an edge of anxiety. If she got too comfortable, she might let her guard down, might start welling up with tears, might turn angry. There was so much she had to hold back.

She looked through her kitchen window. "Do you know a guy named Jack Dalton?"

"I don't think so. Why?"

"He answered my ad for a handyman. And he was supposed to be here over an hour ago."

"Caitlyn, if you need help, I'd be happy to send over one of the hands from the ranch."

She wanted to remain independent. "This guy sounded like he'd be perfect. On the phone, he said he had experience as a carpenter, and he's a Gulf War veteran. I'd like to hire a vet."

"You spent a lot of time with the troops."

"And I don't want to talk about it. I don't mean to be rude, but I just can't." Suddenly flustered, she set down her mug on the countertop. "Let's go take a look at the horse that showed up on my doorstep."

After years of being glib and turning in daily reports of horrendous atrocities, she hated to find herself tongue-tied. Somehow, she had to get her life back.

WEAVING THROUGH THE BOTTOM of the canyon was a rushing creek. He sank to his knees beside it and lowered his head to drink. Ice-cold water splashed against his lips and into his mouth. It tasted good.

No doubt there were all kinds of harmful bacteria in this unfiltered water, but he didn't care. The need for hydration overwhelmed other concerns. He splattered the cold liquid into his face. Took off his flannel shirt and washed his hands and arms. His white T-shirt had only a few spots of dried blood.

As far as he could figure, he'd been sleeping in his boxers and undershirt. He'd been startled awake, grabbed his flannel shirt and jeans, jammed his feet into his boots and then...

His scenario was based on logic instead of memory. The remembering part of his brain must have been damaged by the head wound. His mind was like a blackboard that had been partially erased. Faint chalk scribbles taunted him. The more he concentrated, the more they faded. All he knew for sure was that somebody was trying to kill him.

This wasn't the first time he'd been on the run, but he didn't know why. Was he an innocent victim or an escaped felon? He suspected the latter. If he'd ever rated a guardian angel, that heavenly creature was off duty.

His first need was for transportation. Once he'd gotten away from this place, he could figure out what to do and where to go.

He tied the arms of his flannel shirt around his hips, tucked the SIG into the waistband of his jeans and started hiking on a path beside the creek. Though it would have been easier to walk along the nearby two-lane gravel road, his instincts warned him to avoid contact.

The canyon widened into an uncultivated open field of weeds, wildflowers and sagebrush. This landscape had to be the Rocky Mountains. He'd come to the Rockies as a kid, remembered hiking with a compass that pointed due north. It was a happier time.

A black truck hauling a horse trailer rumbled along the

road. He ducked behind a shrub and watched as the truck passed. The logo on the driver's side door read: Circle L Ranch, Pinedale, Colorado.

Good. He had a location. Pinedale. Wherever that was.

He trudged at the edge of the field near the trees. His head still throbbed but he disregarded the pain. No time for self-pity. He only had four days until…

He approached a three-rail corral fence in need of repair. Some of the wood rails had fallen. Two horses stood near a small barn which was also kind of dilapidated. The log cabin appeared to be in good shape, though.

He focused on the dark green SUV parked between the cabin and the horse barn. That would be his way out.

A woman with blond hair in a high ponytail came out of the barn. Around her waist, she wore a tool belt that looked too heavy for her slender frame. At the porch, she paused to take a drink from a water bottle. Her head tilted back. The slender column of her throat was pure feminine loveliness. That image dissolved when she wiped her mouth on the sleeve of her denim shirt.

He didn't want to steal her SUV. But he needed transportation.

Coming around the far end of the corral, he approached.

When she spotted him, she waved and called out, "Hi there. You must be Jack Dalton."

It was as good a name as any. "I must be."

Chapter Two

Caitlyn watched her new handyman as he came closer. Tall, lean, probably in his midthirties. He wasn't limping, but his legs dragged as though he was wading through deep water. Rough around the edges, he hadn't shaved or combed his thick, black hair. His white T-shirt was dirty, and he had a plaid shirt tied around the waistband of his jeans.

When he leaned against the corral fence, he seemed to need the rail for support. Was he drunk? Before ten o'clock in the morning? She hadn't asked for references. All she knew about Jack Dalton was that he was a veteran who needed a job.

"On the phone," she said, "you mentioned that you were in the army."

"Tenth Mountain Division out of Fort Drum, New York."

Colorado natives, like Caitlyn, took pride in the 10th Mountain Division. Founded during World War II, the original division was made up of elite skiers and mountain climbers who trained near Aspen. "Where were you stationed?"

"I'd rather not talk about it."

After the time she'd spent embedded with the troops, she had a great deal of empathy for what they had experienced. To be completely honest, she had self-diagnosed her own low-grade case of post-traumatic stress disorder. But if Jack Dalton had come home from war an alcoholic, she had no desire to be his therapist. "Have you been drinking, Jack?"

"Not a drop, ma'am."

In spite of his sloppy clothes and posture, his gaze was sharp. He was wary, intense. Maybe dangerous.

She was glad to be wearing her tool belt. Hammers and screwdrivers were handy weapons. Just in case. She looked behind him toward the driveway leading up to her house. "Where's your car?"

"I had an accident. Walked the rest of the way."

"Are you hurt?"

"A bit."

"Oh my God, I'm a jerk!" She'd been treating him with suspicion, thinking he was a drunk when the poor guy was struggling to stay on his feet after a car accident. "Let's get you inside. Make sure you're okay."

"I'm fine, ma'am."

"Please, call me Caitlyn. I feel terrible for not realizing—"

"It's all right." He pushed away from the fence, obviously unsteady on his feet. "I was hoping you could loan me your car and your cell phone so I could go back to my truck and—"

"You're not driving in your condition." She went to him, grabbed his arm and slung it over her shoulder. "Come on, lean on me."

"I'm fine."

He tried to pull away, but she held on, adjusting his position so none of her tools poked into his side. Jack was a good seven or eight inches taller than she was, and he outweighed her by sixty or seventy pounds. But she could support him; she'd done this before.

As they moved toward the back door to her cabin, she flashed on a memory. So real, it felt like it was happening again, happening now.

The second vehicle in their convoy hit a roadside bomb. The thunder of the explosion rang in her ears. Still, she heard a cry for help. A soldier, wounded. Reporters weren't supposed to get involved, but she couldn't ignore his plea, couldn't stand by impartially and watch him suffer. She helped him to his feet, dragged him and his fifty pounds of gear to safety before the second bomb went off.

Her heart beat faster as adrenaline pulsed through her veins. If she closed her eyes, she could see the fiery burst of that explosion. Her nostrils twitched with the remembered stench of smoke, sweat and blood.

At the two stairs leading to the door, Jack separated from her. "I can walk on my own."

With a shudder, she forced her mind back to the present. Her memories were too vivid, too deeply carved into her consciousness. She'd give anything to be able to forget. "Are you sure you're all right?"

His shoulders straightened as he gestured toward the door. "After you."

The back door opened into a smallish kitchen with serviceable but elderly appliances and a beat-up linoleum floor of gray and pink blobs that she would certainly replace if she decided to stay at the cabin through the winter. Mentally, she started listing other projects she'd undertake. Repair roof on the horse barn. Replacing the railing on the porch. Staying busy kept the memories at bay.

She led Jack to the adjoining dining room and pointed to a chair at the oblong oak table. "Sit right there, and I'll bring you some water."

"Something's wrong." It was a statement, not a question.

"I don't know what you mean."

"Yes, you do."

He stood very still, watching her, waiting for her to talk. *Not going to happen.* She knew better than to open the floodgate and allow her nightmare memories to pour into the real world.

Deliberately, she changed the subject. "Are you hungry?"

"I could go for a sandwich."

Up close, he was disturbingly handsome with well-defined features and a dark olive complexion. His eyes were green—dark and deep. Not even his thick, black lashes could soften the fierceness in those eyes. He'd be a formidable enemy.

She noticed a swelling on his jaw and reached toward it. "You have a bruise."

Before her fingers touched his face, he snatched her wrist. His movement was so quick that she gasped in surprise. He had the reflexes of a ninja. Immediately, he released his grasp.

As he moved away from the table, she could see him gathering his strength, pulling himself together. He went through the dining room into the living room. His gaze darted as though assessing the room, taking note of where the furniture was placed. He ran his hand along the mantle above the fireplace. At the front door, which she'd left open, he peered outside.

"Looking for something?" she asked.

"I like to know where I am before I get comfortable."

"Reconnaissance?"

"I guess you could say that."

"Trust me, Jack. There's nothing dangerous in this cabin." He wasn't entering an insurgent hideout, for pity's sake. "I don't even have a dog."

"You live alone."

Women living alone were never supposed to admit that they didn't have anyone else around for protection, especially not to a stranger. Her hand dropped to the hammer on her tool belt. "I'm good at taking care of myself."

"I'm sure you are."

Though he kept his distance, she didn't like the way he was looking at her. Like a predator. "Would you please stop pacing around and sit?"

"Before I do, I need to take something out of my belt." He reached behind his back. "I don't want you to be alarmed."

Too late. "Of course not."

He pulled an automatic pistol from the waistband of his jeans. The sight of his weapon shocked her. She'd made a huge mistake by inviting him into her cabin.

THE THROBBING IN HIS HEAD made it hard to think, but he figured he had two options. Either he could shoot Caitlyn and steal her car or he could talk her into handing over the car keys voluntarily.

Shooting her would be easier.

But he didn't think he was that kind of man.

He reassured her again, "Nothing to worry about."

"I'd feel better if you put the gun down."

"Not a problem." He placed the SIG on a red heart-shaped trivet in the center of the table, took a step to his left and sat in the chair closest to the kitchen. From this angle, he had a clear view of the front door.

She asked, "Do you mind if I check your weapon?"

"Knock yourself out."

She wasted no time grabbing the gun. Expertly, she removed the clip. "Good thing you had the safety on. Carrying a gun in your waistband is a good way to shoot your butt off. Why are you carrying?"

There were plenty of lies he could tell her about why he was armed, but an efficient liar knows better than to volunteer information. "It never hurts to be prepared."

She gave a quick nod, accepting his response.

Apparently, he was good at deception. When she'd asked about his military service, he hadn't hesitated to cite the 10th Mountain Division, even though he didn't remember being in the army or being deployed.

His story about the car accident had been a simple and obvious lie. Everybody had car trouble. Claiming an accident prompted automatic sympathy.

If he'd planned to stick around for more than a couple more minutes, he would have felt bad about lying to her. She was a good woman. Kindhearted. When he'd said he was hurt, she'd rushed to help him, offered her shoulder for support.

Taking his gun with her, she headed toward the kitchen. "I hope egg salad is okay."

"Yes, ma'am."

"I told you before, call me Caitlyn. I'm not old enough to be a ma'am."

And you can call me Jack, even though I'm pretty sure that's not who I am. He rolled the name around in his memory. Jack Dalton. Jack. Dalton. Though the syllables didn't resonate, he didn't mind the way they sounded. Henceforth, he would be Jack Dalton.

Caitlyn poked her head into the dining room. "If you want to wash up, the bathroom is the first door on the right when you go through the living room."

He followed her directions, pausing to peek into the closet near the front door. If he was going to be on the run for any period of time, he'd need a jacket. A quick glance showed a couple of parkas and windbreakers. Nothing that appeared to be his size. A rifle stood in the corner next to the vacuum cleaner.

At the bathroom, he hesitated before closing the door. If the men who were chasing him showed up, he didn't want to be trapped in this small room with the claw-footed tub and the freestanding sink. He checked his reflection in the mirror, noting the bruises on the right side of his face and a dark swelling on his jaw. Looked like he'd been in a bar fight. Was that the truth? Just a bar fight? The simplest answer was usually the correct one, but not this time. His problems ran deeper than a brawl. There were people who wanted him dead.

He searched the medicine cabinet. There was a wide selection of medical supplies. Apparently, a woman who swaggered around with a tool belt slung around her hips injured herself on a regular basis. He found a bottle of extra-strength pain reliever and took three.

After trekking through the forest, his white T-shirt was smeared with dirt, and he didn't exactly smell like a bouquet of lilacs. He peeled off the shirt and looked in the mirror again. In addition to patches of black and blue on his upper right arm and rib cage, a faded scar slashed across his chest from his clavicle to his belly button. He had a couple of minor scratches with dried blood. A deeper wound—newly healed—marked his abdomen. *What the hell happened to me?* These scars should have been a road map to unlock his memory.

Still, his mind was blank.

He washed his chest and pits. His worst injury was on the back of his head, but there wasn't much he could do about it. No matter how he turned, he couldn't see the damage.

There was a sound outside the bathroom door. A car approaching? They could be coming, could be getting closer.

Damn it, he didn't have time to mess around with bandages or sandwiches. He needed to get the hell away from here.

He slipped through the bathroom and looked out the front window. The scene in front of her house was unchanged. Nobody was coming. Not yet.

Caitlyn called out, "Hey, Jack."

"I'll be right there."

She charged into the living room and stopped when she saw him. A lot of women would be repulsed by his scars. Not Caitlyn. She stared at his chest with frank curiosity before lifting her gaze to his face. "White or rye?"

"Did you get a good look?"

She shrugged. "I've seen worse."

Her attitude intrigued him. If he hadn't been desperate to get away from this area, he wouldn't have minded spending time with her, getting to know what made her tick. "Are you a nurse?"

"I used to be a reporter, embedded with the troops." She moved closer. "I know some basic first aid. I could take care of those cuts and bruises."

He didn't like asking for assistance, but the head wound needed attention. He went to his chair by the table and sat. "I got whacked on the back of my skull."

Without hesitation, she positioned herself behind him. Her fingers gently probed at the wound. "This looks bad, Jack. You should be in the hospital."

"No doctors."

"That's real macho, but not too smart." She stopped poking at his head and pulled a chair around so she was sitting opposite him. Their knees were almost touching. "I want you to look at my forehead. Try to focus."

"You're checking to see if my pupils are dilated."

"If you have a concussion, I'm taking you to the hospital. Head injuries are nothing to fool around with."

He did as she asked, staring at her forehead. Her eyebrows pulled into a scowl that she probably thought was tough and authoritative. But she was too damn cute to be intimidating. A sprinkle of freckles dotted her nose and cheeks. Her wide mouth was made for grinning.

In her blue eyes, he saw a glimmer of genuine concern, and it touched him. Though he couldn't remember his name or what kind of threat brought him to this cabin, he knew that it had been a long time since a woman looked at him this way.

She sat back in her chair. "What really happened to you? You didn't get that head injury in a car accident."

How could he tell her the truth? He didn't have the right to ask for her help; he was a stranger. She didn't owe him a damn thing. "I should go."

"Stay." She rested her hand on his bare shoulder. Her touch was cool, soothing. "I'll patch you up as best I can."

For the first time since he woke up this morning, he had the feeling that everything might turn out all right.

Chapter Three

Caitlyn only knew one thing for sure about Jack. He was stoic—incredibly stoic. His ability to tolerate pain was downright scary.

Moments ago, she'd closed the wound on his head with four stitches. Though she'd used a topical analgesic spray to deaden the area, the effect wasn't like anesthetic. And she wasn't a skilled surgeon. Her clumsy stitching must have hurt a lot.

He hadn't flinched. When she had finished, he turned his head and calmly thanked her.

After that, he had wanted to leave, but she insisted that he stay long enough to eat something and have some water. After sewing him back together, she was invested in his survival.

Also, she was curious—an occupational hazard for a journalist. She wanted to get Jack's true story.

They sat at her dining room table, and she watched as he devoured an egg salad on light rye. She'd found him a faded black T-shirt that belonged to her brother, who wasn't as big as Jack but wore his clothes baggy. The fabric stretched tight across Jack's chest. Underneath were all those scars. How had he gotten wounded? In battle? The long ridge of puckered flesh on his torso was still healing and couldn't have been more than a couple of months old.

If he'd been injured in military service, he wouldn't have been discharged so quickly.

She nibbled at her own sandwich, trying to find a non-intrusive angle that might get him talking. In her work, she'd done hundreds of interviews, some with hostiles. The direct question-and-answer approach wouldn't work with Jack.

"You're not from around here," she said, "What brought you to the mountains?"

"Beautiful scenery. Fresh air."

Spare me the travelogue. "Where did you grow up?"

"Chicago."

Was he a kid from the burbs or a product of the mean streets? Instead of pushing, she offered an observation of her own. "One of the best times I had in Chicago was sailing on Lake Michigan at dusk, watching as the lights of the city blinked on."

He continued to eat, moving from the sandwich to a mouthful of the beans she'd heated on the stove.

"Your turn," she said.

"To do what?"

"I tell you something about me, and then you share something about yourself. It's called a conversation."

His gaze was cool, unreadable and fascinating. The green of his eyes contained dark prisms that drew her closer. "You have questions."

"We're just having a chat. Come on, Jack. Tell me something about growing up in the Windy City."

"The El," he said. "I don't care for underground subways, but I always liked riding the elevated trains. The jostling. The hustle. Made me feel like I was going someplace, like I had a purpose."

"Where were you going?"

"To see Mark." As soon as he spoke, his eyebrows

pinched in a frown. He swallowed hard as though he wanted to take back that name.

"Is Mark a friend?"

"A good friend. Mark Santoro. He's dead."

"I'm sorry for your loss."

"Me, too."

His friend's name rang a bell for her. Even though she hadn't been following the news regularly, she knew that the Santoros were an old-time but still notorious crime family. For the first time in weeks, she glanced longingly at her laptop. Given a few minutes to research on the internet, she might be about to solve the mystery of Jack Dalton.

"I haven't been honest with you, Caitlyn."

"I know."

"I didn't have a car accident."

"What else?"

"There are some guys looking for me. They've got a grudge. When I came here, I thought I could use your car for a getaway. But that's not going to work."

"Not that I'm volunteering my SUV for your getaway, but what changed your mind?"

"If I have your car, it connects you to me. I don't want anybody coming after you."

She agreed. Being targeted by the Santoro family wasn't her idea of a good time. "We should call the police. I have a friend, Danny Laurence, who's a deputy sheriff. He's somebody you can trust."

"I'm better off on my own."

He rose from the table, and she knew he was ready to depart. She hated the thought of him being out there, on his own, against powerful enemies. She bounced to her feet. "Let me call Danny. Please."

"You're a good person, Caitlyn." He reached toward her. When his large hand rested on her shoulder, a magnetic pull urged her closer to him. Her weight shifted forward, narrowing the space between them. He leaned down and kissed her forehead. "It's best if you forget you ever saw me."

As if that would happen. There weren't a whole lot of handsome mystery men who appeared on her doorstep. For the past month, she'd been a hermit who barely talked to anyone. "You won't be easy to forget."

"Nor will you."

"For the record, I still think you need to go to the hospital."

"Duly noted."

From outside, she heard the grating of tires on gravel.

Jack had heard it, too. In a few strides, he was at the front window, peering around the edge of the curtain.

A 1957 vintage Ford Fairlane—two-toned in turquoise and cream—was headed down her driveway. She knew the car, and the driver was someone she trusted implicitly. His vehicle was followed by a black SUV with tinted windows. "Do you see the SUV? Are these the people who are after you?"

"Don't know," he said. "They've seen your car so you can't pretend you're not here. Go ahead and talk to them. Don't tell them you've seen me."

"Understood." She gave him a nod. "You stay in the house. I'll get rid of them."

Smoothing her hair back into her ponytail, she went to the front door, aware that she might be coming face-to-face with the enforcers for a powerful crime family. Panic fluttered behind her eyelids, and she blinked it away. This wasn't her first ride on the roller coaster. She'd gotten through war zones, faced terrorists and bloody death. A couple of thugs from Chicago shouldn't be a problem.

From the porch, she watched as the Ford Fairlane parked

near her back door. The black SUV pulled up to the rear bumper of her car before it stopped.

She waved to Bob Woodley—a tall, rangy, white-haired man who had been a longtime friend of her family. He was one of the few people she'd seen since moving back to the cabin. A retired English teacher, he had been a mentor to her when she was in her teens. "Hi, Mr. Woodley."

He motioned her toward him. "Get over here, Caitlyn. Give an old man a proper hello."

When she hugged him, he must have sensed her apprehension. He studied her expression. His bushy eyebrows pulled into a scowl. "Something wrong?"

"I'm fine." She forced a smile. "What brings you here?"

"I was visiting Heather at the Circle L when these two gentlemen showed up. Since I'm a state congressman, I figured it was my duty to extend a helping hand to these strangers by showing them how to find your cabin."

She looked past him toward the SUV. The two men walking toward her were a sinister contrast to Mr. Woodley's open honesty. Both wore jeans and sports jackets that didn't quite hide the bulge of shoulder holsters. Dark glasses shaded their eyes.

Woodley performed the introductions. "Caitlyn, I want you to meet Drew Kelso and Greg Reynolds."

When she shook their hands, their flesh was cold—either from the air-conditioning in their car or because they were reptiles. "What can I do for you?"

Woodley said, "We understand that you had a visitor this morning."

How did they know about Jack? Had her cabin been under surveillance? "I'm not sure what you're talking about."

"The dappled gray mare," Woodley said. "You had Heather come over and pick it up."

"Oh, the horse." She rolled her eyes in an attempt to look like a ditzy blonde. She didn't want these men to take her seriously, wanted them to dismiss her as harmless. "Silly me, I'd already forgotten about the horse."

The one named Reynolds said, "It belongs to someone we know."

"Your friend needs to be more careful," she said. "The horse showed up on my property without a saddle or a bridle or anything."

The friendly smiles she offered to the two thugs went unanswered. They meant business.

The taller, Drew, had sandy hair and heavy shoulders. His mouth barely moved when he spoke. "We're looking for the guy who was riding that horse."

"I didn't see anybody." She widened her eyes, even fluttered her lashes. "Like I said, no bridle or saddle."

Drew said, "If you saw him, it'd be smart to tell us."

His comment sounded a bit like a threat. "Who is this person? What's his name?"

"Tony Perez."

With complete honesty, she shook her head. "Never heard of him. But I'll be on the lookout. Is there a number I should call if I see him?"

Drew handed her a business card that contained only his name and a cell phone number.

"I guess that wraps up our business." Woodley checked his wristwatch. "I'd better shove off."

She wanted to cling to him and plead for him to stay until these two men were gone. "Can't you stay for coffee?"

"Sorry, kiddo. I'm running late for an appointment in Pinedale." He strolled toward his vintage Ford Fairlane. "I hope you gents can find your missing friend."

They gave him a nod and headed toward their SUV. Caitlyn breathed a little sigh of relief. They were leaving. The crisis was averted.

Before Woodley climbed behind the steering wheel, he said, "Don't be a stranger, Caitlyn."

He drove down her driveway and turned onto the road. The two men stood beside their SUV talking. With every fiber of her being, she wanted them gone. These were two scary guys. Why hadn't Mr. Woodley been able to see it?

They came back toward her. Drew said, "We want to take a look around. To make sure he's not hiding around here."

"That's not necessary." She positioned herself between him and her front porch. "There's nobody here but me."

Drew glanced over his shoulder at the other man, Greg Reynolds. He was neat and crisp. His boots were polished. His charcoal sports jacket showed expensive tailoring, and his thick black hair glistened in the sunlight. She guessed that he was a man of expensive tastes, definitely the boss.

Greg gave a slight nod, and Drew walked toward her cabin. Short of tackling him, there was no way Caitlyn could stop him. Still, she had to try.

"Hey." She grasped his arm. "I told you. There's nobody here."

Slowly, he turned toward her and removed his sunglasses. He didn't need to speak; the curl of his upper lip and the flat, angry glare from his eyes told her that he wouldn't hesitate to use violence. And he would most likely enjoy hurting her.

She stepped back. Silently, she prayed that Jack had hidden himself well or had managed to slip out the back door.

"This is for your own safety," Drew said. "Tony Perez is dangerous."

As she entered her cabin, her heart was pumping hard. She shoved her hands into her pockets so no one would notice the trembling.

Jack had cleaned up every trace of his presence. On the dining room table, there was only one plate and one bottled water. She watched as Drew went into the bathroom. Jack's discarded clothing had been in there. Apparently, his shirt and undershirt were gone because Drew emerged without saying anything.

When Tony brushed past her, she caught a whiff of his expensive cologne. It smelled like newly minted hundred-dollar bills. He rested his hand on the door handle of the front closet and yanked it open. She noticed that her rifle was gone.

IN THE LOFT ABOVE the stalls in the horse barn, Jack lay on his belly and sighted down the barrel of Caitlyn's rifle. This weapon lacked the sophistication of the sniper equipment he was accustomed to using. Her rifle scope was rudimentary and so poorly mounted that he had removed it. At this range, he trusted his marksmanship. His first shot would show him the correction for this particular weapon, after which he would be accurate.

His plan was simple. Take out the tall man with sandy hair; he was the most deadly. Then the boss.

Holding the rifle felt natural, and he easily comprehended the necessary strategy in an assault situation. These skills weren't inborn. He couldn't remember where he'd learned or who taught him. But he knew how to kill.

When Caitlyn and the men entered the house, Jack adjusted his position, trying to keep track of their movements through the windows. So far they hadn't threatened Caitlyn, except for that moment when she touched the sandy-haired thug. The bastard looked like he wanted to kill her. If he'd hurt her, Jack would have squeezed the trigger. He'd gotten Caitlyn into this mess, but he wouldn't let her be harmed.

The optimum scenario would be for them to make their search and then go. She wasn't a part of this.

Not being able to see what was going on inside the house made him edgy. If they didn't come outside soon, he needed to move in closer to protect her. He started a mental timer for five minutes.

In the corral below him, the two horses—one light and one dark—stood at the railing. Their ears pricked up. They nickered and shifted their hooves. Animals could sense when something was wrong. The horses knew.

He was nearing the end of his countdown when the small group emerged from the back door. Caitlyn looked angry. Earlier, she'd tried to act like a dumb blonde and had failed miserably. Her intelligence showed in every move she made and every word she spoke.

The two men walked ahead of her toward the barn. Jack got ready to shoot. His position gave him an advantage, but he needed to time his shot so there was no chance they could retaliate. He wished there was some way to signal Caitlyn to keep her distance from them.

They walked toward the corral. Coming closer, closer. They were less than fifty yards from his position. The tall man was in front. His hand slid inside his jacket, and he pulled his handgun.

Jack aimed for the center of his chest, the largest target. If he'd been using a more sophisticated weapon, he would have gone for a head shot.

He heard Caitlyn object. "What are you doing? Why do you have a gun?"

The other man assured her, "We have to be prepared. The person we're looking for is extremely dangerous."

Damn right. Jack knew he was capable of lethal action. A trained killer. *Damn it, Caitlyn. Get out of the way.* The slick-looking man with black hair, the boss, stayed close to her. Too close.

Jack adjusted his aim. He'd kill the boss first. As he stared, he realized that he knew this man. Gregorio Rojas. He was the younger son of a drug cartel family that supplied the entire Midwestern United States.

Hatred flared in Jack's gut. His finger tensed on the trigger. Rojas was his sworn enemy. *Take the shot. Rid the world of this bastard whose actions have been responsible for so much misery, so much death.*

Rojas paused, took a cell phone from his pocket. After a brief conversation, he motioned to the other man. They headed back toward their vehicle.

Still, Jack didn't relax his vigilance. Rojas was still within range.

His memory was returning. The blank spaces knitted together in a tapestry of violence. *Take the shot.*

Chapter Four

Jack knew he had killed before. As he stared down the barrel of Caitlyn's rifle, his vision narrowed to his target. The center seam of Rojas's tailored jacket. His hands were steady. He was focused. Cool and calm, as always.

He remembered another time, another place, another killing.

He was in the city, the seedy part of town. On the fourth floor of a dirty brick hotel that rented rooms by the hour, he set up his sniper's nest and assembled his precision rifle with laser scope, silencer and tripod. With high-power, infrared binoculars, he observed the crappy apartment building directly across the street. Fourth floor, corner unit. Nobody home.

He checked into the hotel at sundown. Hours passed. Dusk turned to nightfall when lights flickered on throughout the city. Not that he had a glittering view.

When the lamp in the apartment across the street came on, he eased into position. Though he sat in the dark, the glow from a streetlight reflected dully on the barrel of his rifle and silencer.

He peered through his scope. Through the uncurtained window of the apartment across the street, a man with fiery red hair paced from room to room with his gun in his hand, looking for danger.

"I'm here," Jack whispered. *"Come to the window, you bastard."*

This man deserved to die.

But his target hadn't been alone. A small woman with brassy blond hair and a child entered Jack's field of vision. Two witnesses.

The killing had to wait.

From the loft in the barn, Jack watched as Rojas and his companion got into the SUV and drove away from Caitlyn's cabin. She turned on her heel and rushed back into her house, moving fast, as though she had something burning on the stove.

When the black SUV was out of sight, he rolled onto his back and stared up at the ceiling in the barn that needed patching.

He knew who he was.

A stone-cold killer.

INSIDE HER CABIN, Caitlyn wasted no time. She dove into the swivel chair behind her small desk in the living room and fired up her laptop. It felt good to see the screen come to life. Back when she was a working journalist—especially in the field—her computer had been an ever-present tool, almost an extension of her arm.

Her hands poised over the keyboard. *But I'm not a journalist anymore. Not right now.* She had no assignment, no story to investigate, and she wasn't entirely sure that she wanted to go back into the fray.

Her main reason for moving to this cabin had been to purposely distance herself from the 24-hour-a-day news cycle. During this time of self-imposed seclusion, she hoped to regroup and decide what to do with the rest of her life.

Her parents and nearly everyone else who cared about her had encouraged Caitlyn to seek out a safer occupation.

Not that they wanted her to quit writing, but they hoped she would leave the war zones to others. As if she'd be satisfied reporting on garden parties? Writing poetry about sunshine and lollipops?

She wasn't made that way. She thrived on action.

Jack's arrival at her doorstep might be fate. She hadn't gone looking for danger, but here it was. She had armed thugs searching her cabin. If Jack Dalton had a story to tell, she wouldn't turn away.

She jumped on the internet and started a search on the name of Jack's supposed "friend," Mark Santoro. Expertly, she sorted through news stories, mostly from the *Chicago Tribune,* and put together the basic facts.

As Jack had said, Mark Santoro was dead. He and four other members of the Santoro crime family had been killed in a shootout on a city street five months ago. One of the men had his hands cut off. Mark had been decapitated. A gruesome slaughter; it was intended to send a message.

Allegedly, the Santoro family handled narcotics distribution in the Midwest, and they had angered the powerful Rojas drug cartel—the suppliers of illegal drugs.

Agents from the DEA and the Bureau of Alcohol, Tobacco, Firearms and Explosives were all over this incident. They arrested and charged several members of the Rojas cartel, including the top man, Tom Rojas. The federal murder trial was due to start on Tuesday, four days from now, at a district court in Chicago.

Reading between the lines, Caitlyn suspected that much of this story never made it to print. She used to date a reporter who worked at the *Trib*—a sweet guy who had taken her for that romantic sailboat ride on Lake Michigan and begged her to stay in the States. She'd refused to settle down, and he'd moved on. A typical pattern for her relationships. The last she'd heard, her former beau was happily married with an infant daughter. If she needed to find out more about the trial, she could contact him.

Rapid-fire, she typed in the names of the two thugs: Drew Kelso and Greg Reynolds. A quick search showed several people with those names, but nothing stood out. She wasn't surprised. Drug lords and thugs don't generally maintain websites.

Next, she searched for Tony Perez. After digging through a lot of worthless information, she tightened her search and linked it to Mark Santoro. In one of the articles about the shootings, Tony Perez was mentioned as a bodyguard for Santoro. Perez had been killed at the scene.

But Jack Dalton was very much alive.

Slowly, she closed her laptop. Though she hadn't heard him enter the house or walk across the living room floor, she sensed Jack's nearness. She knew that he was standing close, silently watching her.

A shiver prickled down her spine. She wasn't afraid that he would physically harm her. There wasn't a reason, and he was smart enough to avoid unnecessary violence. But she was apprehensive. Jack was pulling her toward a place she didn't want to go.

"Did you find what you were looking for?" he asked.

She swiveled in her desk chair to face him. "You look pretty healthy for a dead man."

He crossed the room and returned her rifle to the front closet. "I brought your gun back."

The smart thing would be to send him on his way and forget she ever saw him. But finding the truth was a compulsion for her. "Those men were looking for Tony Perez. Is that your real name?"

"Tony's dead. Call me Jack."

"They said you stole a horse, and that you're dangerous."

"Half right."

"Which half?"

"I didn't steal the horse. I borrowed it."

He approached her, braced his hands on each of the arms of her swivel chair and leaned down until his face was on a level with hers. "Those men are unpredictable. There's no telling what they might do. I strongly advise that you stay with a friend for a couple of days."

"What about you? Where are you going?"

"Not your problem."

He was so close that she could see the rise and fall of his chest as he breathed. She wanted to rest her hand against his black T-shirt, to feel the beating of his heart. Instead, she picked a piece of straw off his shoulder. "You were hiding in the barn. In the loft."

"I couldn't leave until I knew you were safe."

"Who were those guys?" She searched his eyes for a truth he might never tell her. "They said their names were Drew Kelso and Greg Reynolds."

"Not Reynolds. That was Gregorio Rojas." He reached toward her desk and flipped her computer open. "You know the name. You were reading all about him and his pals."

"And his brother, Tom. His murder trial starts in four days."

He stepped away from her. "I have to go."

"Not yet. I'm still putting the pieces together." She left her chair and stood between him and the front door. "I'm asking myself why Rojas is after you. Something to do with his brother's trial, right?"

"You don't need to know."

"But I do, Jack. I'm a reporter." And she was damn good at her job. He'd thrown out just enough bread crumbs for her to follow this trail. "Let's suppose that you are this

Tony Perez and that you survived the attack on the street. That makes you a witness."

"I told you before. Tony is—"

"Dead." *Yeah, sure.* "I'm just supposing here. I can only think of one reason that an eyewitness to a crime in Chicago would be hiding in the Colorado mountains. WitSec."

The Witness Security Program provided protection for those who might be in danger before a trial. There must be a safe house in the area.

"Suppose you're correct," he said. "If a protected witness was attacked at a safe house, it must mean that he was betrayed by the marshals who were supposed to be looking out for him. They gave the location of the safe house to Rojas."

She hated to acknowledge that law enforcement officials—in this case, U.S. Marshals—could be corrupted. But she knew it was possible. While embedded with the troops, she'd run across similar instances. Somebody taking a payoff. Somebody acting on a grudge instead of following orders.

With a shrug, she said, "It happens."

"If it did happen that way, there's nobody this witness can trust. Rojas is after him. And the marshals can't let him report them. He has to go on the run and find his own way to make it to the trial in Chicago."

"I can help you."

"I don't want your help."

He stepped around her and went out the front door.

JACK STRODE AWAY FROM her house toward the corral fence. Angry at himself for telling too much. Angry at her for wanting to know. How the hell could she help him? And why? Why should she give a damn? As a reporter with the troops, she was accustomed to being surrounded by heroes. Not somebody like him.

At the fence, he paused to settle his mind into a plan. He wasn't sure how he'd make his way out of this sprawling mountain terrain where a man could disappear and never be seen again. That might be the solution. *Drop out of sight and start over.*

But he had promised to appear in court. His eyewitness testimony would put Tom Rojas and some of his top men behind bars. Little brother Gregorio didn't have the guts or the authority to hold the cartel together. Jack's testimony could make a difference.

He looked toward the road that ran past her house—the only direct route into and out of this area. His enemies would be watching that road. He'd be better off taking a cross-country path, walking until... Until he got to Chicago?

"Jack, wait!" Caitlyn dashed toward him. She thrust a canvas backpack into his hands. "Take this."

Inside the pack, he saw survival supplies: a couple of bottled waters, some energy bars, a sweatshirt and a cell phone. He'd be a fool to refuse these useful items, but he wasn't going to admit that she'd been right about him needing her help.

She dug into the pocket of her jeans and pulled out a wad of cash. "It's a hundred and twenty-seven bucks. That's all I have on hand."

"Caitlyn, why—"

"And this." She handed him a cowboy hat. "To protect the wound on your head."

Jack tried on the battered brown hat with a flat brim. Not a bad fit. "Why are you so determined to help me?"

Her face was as open as a sunflower, deceptively innocent. "Why shouldn't I?"

"You don't know me. You don't know the life I've led."

"You were part of the Santoro crime family," she said. "I'm assuming that you've done a lot of things I wouldn't condone. You could have been a hit man, an assassin or even a drug pusher."

"No," he said, "never a pusher. I hate drugs."

"That's the past, Jack. You made a change. You decided to testify against some very bad men."

"Maybe I didn't have a choice."

"I don't care."

He was surprised to hear a tremble in her voice, an undercurrent of strong emotion. She was feeling something intense. About him? He didn't think she was the kind of woman who formed sudden attachments. Over and over, she'd said she was a reporter. In her profession, she couldn't allow her passions to rule. "What's going on with you?"

"You're risking your life to testify, to do the right thing." She inhaled so deeply that her nostrils flared. As she exhaled, she regained control of herself. "I need to believe that when people fight for the right thing and put their lives on the line, it's not for nothing. Their sacrifice has significance."

Spoken like someone who had been to war and had seen real suffering. His irritation faded behind a newfound admiration. She was one hell of a woman. Strong and principled. For the second time, he wished they had met under different circumstances. "Don't make me into something I'm not."

"Fair enough," she said. "As long as you don't downplay what you're doing. You're giving up your former life to do the right thing."

"I'm no hero."

She cocked her head to one side. A hank of straight blond hair fell across her forehead. "Neither am I."

"I have to go."

"First, let me show you how to use the GPS on the cell phone. It won't give you a detailed topographical map, but you'll have an idea where the roads are."

Instead, he handed the phone back to her. "If the GPS shows me where I am, it'll show other people my location. They can track me from the signal."

"Of course. I knew that." She shoved the phone into her pocket. "You said you didn't want to use my car, but you could take one of the horses."

On horseback, he'd make better time than if he was on foot. He nodded, accepting her offer. "I'll find a way to return the horse to you."

"You should take the stallion. His name is Fabio because of his blond mane. And he's a real stud."

Entering through the corral gate, she motioned to the handsome palomino horse and made a clicking with her tongue. Both animals responded and obediently trotted toward the barn door.

As he followed, he noticed her athletic stride. There was nothing artificial about her. No makeup. No fancy styling to her hair. Her body was well toned, and he suspected that her fitness came from outdoor living rather than a regular workout at a gym. Her jeans fit snugly, tight enough to outline the feminine curve of her ass.

Until now, he hadn't really taken the time to appreciate how attractive she was. When he first stopped at her cabin, he thought he'd be there for only a couple of minutes. He hadn't expected to know anything about her.

While she saddled the stallion and rattled off instructions for the care of the horse, he watched. Her energy impressed him. She was unlike any woman he'd known before. He regretted that after he rode away from her cabin, he would never see her again.

He harbored no illusions about coming back to her after the trial. His life wasn't his own. He'd be stashed away in witness protection, which was probably for the best. Right now, Caitlyn had a high opinion of him. If she knew the reality of his life, she wouldn't want to be in the same room with him.

She finished with the saddle and came toward him. "Fabio is ready to go."

"I'm not."

He placed his hand at the narrowest part of her body and gently pulled her closer.

Chapter Five

When Jack laid his hand possessively on her waist, Caitlyn knew what was coming next. Awareness gusted through her like a moist, sultry breeze that subtly pushed her toward him.

His green eyes shone with an unmistakable invitation, but he gave her plenty of time to back off and say no. During the past several years, she'd spent most of her days in the company of men and had learned how to make it clear that she wanted to spend her nights alone. But she wanted Jack to kiss her. His story had touched the very core of her being and reminded her of important truths. As if she wanted to kiss him because of her principles? *Yeah, right.* There was a whole lot more going on when she looked into Jack's handsome mug. The man was hot. Sexy as hell.

She leaned toward him. Her breasts grazed his chest as she tilted her head back. Her lips parted. Her eyelids closed.

The firm pressure of his mouth against hers started an earthquake inside her. She gasped, enjoying the tremors. Her arms wrapped around him, her body molded to his and she held on tight. It had been a long time since she felt so totally aroused. Way too long.

His big hands slid down her back and cupped her bottom.

He fitted her tightly against his hard body. The natural passion that she usually suppressed raced through her.

If they had more time, she would have gone to bed with him. But that was purely hypothetical. He had to depart immediately. Maybe that was why she could kiss him with such abandon. She knew she'd never see him again.

With obvious reluctance, he ended the kiss and stepped back. "I should go."

Every cell in her body wanted him. She struggled to be cool. "I wish you'd let me call my friend Danny."

"The deputy?"

She nodded vigorously, trying to ignore her intense desire and be logical. "After what you told me, I understand why you don't want to contact anybody in law enforcement. But I've known Danny since we were kids. I trust him."

"That's exactly why you shouldn't call him." He reached toward her and tucked a piece of hair behind her ear. "If he helped me, I'd be putting him and everyone he knows in danger."

"From Rojas," she said.

"You're a reporter. You know how the drug cartels deal with people who get in their way."

Though it was difficult to imagine grisly violence in the Colorado mountains under peaceful blue skies, she knew he was right. Revenge from the drug cartels was equal to the horrors she'd seen in the Middle East. Whole families—women and children—were brutally slaughtered, their bodies dismembered and left to rot.

Those images completely doused her desire. Jack had to go. He had to find his way to safety.

"I'm worried for you," she said. "I don't suppose you'd consider taking me along."

"Not a chance." He grinned, and she realized that it was

the first time she'd seen him crack a smile. "Why would you even ask?"

"A federal witness on the run? It's a damn good story."

"Not unless it has a happy ending."

He mounted the palomino stallion. Though Jack wasn't a cowboy, he looked real good on horseback. She hated that he was on the run, couldn't accept that she'd never be with him. There had to be a way to see him again.

Of course there is. She knew where the trial was taking place. If she pulled some strings and used her press credentials, she could wangle a seat inside the courtroom. "I'll see you in Chicago."

"If I make it."

With a wave, he rode from the barn.

She was left standing in the corral, watching as Jack rode into the forest behind her cabin. If she'd been riding beside him, she would have told him to go the other way. Across the meadow, he should have headed southeast. The terrain was less daunting in that direction, and there was water. Eventually, he would have found the Platte River. *What if he doesn't make it?*

Being left behind while someone else charged into danger wasn't the way she operated. She had to do something.

Taking the cell phone from her pocket, she called Heather to get her brother's phone number.

DANNY LAURENCE WASN'T as yummy as she remembered from her high school years. Though he looked sharp in his dark blue deputy uniform shirt, he was developing a bit of a paunch—a testament to being settled down and eating home-cooked meals every night.

He took off his cowboy hat as he sat at the head of her

dining room table. His short hair made his ears look huge. Had he always had those ears?

"Good to see you," he said. "I've been meaning to drop by and talk about old times."

"Same here. And I want to meet the woman who finally got Danny Laurence to take that long walk down the aisle."

"Sandra." He spoke her name fondly. "You'd like her. She's kind of a goofball."

"Is she Baby Blue or Green Light?"

He laughed. "It's been a long time since I heard those code words you and Heather made up to describe the guys you met. Baby Blue means a sissy, right? And Green Light is good to go."

"And Red Fire means trouble ahead." A particularly apt description. The English translation for *Rojas* was "red."

"My Sandra is Green Light all the way."

She was glad he'd found happiness. Not that a rosy future was ever in doubt; Danny had always been the most popular guy around—the captain of the football team, the president of the senior class.

Joining him at the table, she set a glass of fresh-squeezed lemonade in front of him. This was exactly the same seating arrangement she'd had with Jack, but the atmosphere was utterly different. With Danny, she felt friendly—as if they should tell dumb jokes and punch each other on the arm. There was none of the dangerous magnetism she experienced with Jack. The thought of him reminded her of their kiss and made the hairs on her arm stand up. Somehow, she had to help him.

She wished that she could come right out and ask Danny the questions she needed answered: Was there a WitSec safe house in the area? Did he know about a federal witness on the run? How could Jack be protected from a drug lord bent on revenge?

The direct approach wasn't an option. If Danny knew nothing, she wouldn't be the one to tell him and bring down the wrath of the Rojas. Caitlyn didn't want to be responsible for a bloodbath in Douglas County.

Danny took a swallow of lemonade. "What's up?"

"I was concerned about that horse I found." Jack had used the gray mare for his escape. Finding the owner meant locating the safe house. "Has anybody claimed her?"

"We haven't had a report of a stolen horse. Which isn't surprising. Livestock gets loose now and then. Nobody wants to make a big fuss only to have the horse come trotting back home."

"Have you checked the brand?"

"Not yet. A runaway horse isn't top priority. I've got other things to do."

"Such as?"

"The usual."

His attitude was way too laid-back to be dealing with the aftermath of a shootout at a WitSec safe house. She doubted that the marshals had reported Jack's disappearance, especially not if they were in collusion with Rojas. As far as she knew, federal marshals weren't required to check in with local law enforcement. It defeated the purpose of a safe house if too many people were aware of its existence.

"I was wondering," she said, "if there's been any kind of unusual activity around here?"

"Like what?"

"Oh, you know. Strangers in town. Suspicious stuff."

"You're working on some kind of news story, aren't you? You haven't changed a bit, Caitlyn. Always have to have the scoop." He sipped his lemonade and licked his lips. "Little Miss Know-It-All."

His teasing annoyed her. "You haven't changed, either. You're still the mean big brother, looking down his nose."

"I remember that time when you and Heather followed me and my date to a party in Bailey and I ended up having to escort you home. You two used to drive me crazy."

"Ditto." She actually did punch him on the arm. "Suppose I was working on a story. I'm not saying I am, just suppose. Would you have anything to tell me?"

"Could you be more specific?"

Not without putting him in danger. "I'm wondering if the FBI or maybe the federal marshals have any current operations in our area."

His expression turned serious. "If you have some kind of inside track on FBI activity, I want to hear about it."

"Nothing. I've got nothing."

"Why did you want me to come over?"

Aware that she'd already said too much, Caitlyn changed directions. "Do you know a guy named Jack Dalton?"

"As a matter of fact, I arrested that sorry son-of-a-gun last night at the Gopher Hole. Drunk and disorderly. He's sleeping it off in jail."

That solved the mystery of her missing handyman—the *real* Jack Dalton. "I almost hired him to work for me."

"Aw, hell, Caitlyn. Don't tell me this Dalton character is some kind of FBI agent."

"He's just another troubled soul." And not her responsibility. "When he wakes up, tell him he lost the job."

"You're acting real weird. You want to tell me what's wrong?"

"I'm just nervous. Because of the horse." She thought about mentioning the two armed thugs and decided against it. There wasn't anything Danny could do about them. "Lately, I've been jumpy."

As he studied her, his expression changed from irritation to something resembling compassion. He reached over and gently patted her arm. "Heather told me that you'd been through a lot, reporting on the war. She's kind of worried about you."

The last thing she wanted was pity. "I'm fine."

"It's okay to be nervous."

"I told you. I'm doing just fine."

"Whatever you say." He drained his glass of lemonade, stood and picked up his hat. "I want you to know, it's all right for you to call me any time."

"If I run into any Red Fire situations, I'll let you know."

He stepped outside onto the porch and waited for her to join him. "The sheriff just hired a new guy who was in Iraq. He happens to be single. If you want to talk, he'd—"

"Whoa." She held up her hand. "I never thought I'd see the day when Danny Laurence started playing match-maker."

"That's what happens when you get settled down. You want everybody else to pair up."

"When I'm ready to jump into the singles pool, I'll let you know."

"Fair enough."

"Thanks for coming over." She gave him a warm smile. "Be careful, Danny."

"You, too."

She watched as he drove away in his police vehicle with the Douglas County logo on the side. Asking him to come here hadn't given her any new information, except to confirm the identity of Jack Dalton. The *real* Jack Dalton was not the man who had showed up on her doorstep. *Her* Jack

Dalton was actually Tony Perez. But he didn't want to use that name. Because he'd changed? She wanted to believe that when Tony Perez agreed to testify, he abandoned his old life.

Her gaze wandered to the hillside where she'd last seen him. By now he'd be miles away from here.

She missed him.

For that matter, she also missed the real Jack Dalton. Without a handyman, patching the barn roof was going to be nearly impossible. *Who cares?* Did it really matter if her barn leaked? Earlier today, she'd thought so.

For the past weeks, she'd filled her waking hours with projects—cleaning, painting, doing chores and making repairs. Those jobs now seemed like wasted energy. Not like when she'd been talking to Jack, figuring out his identity. Tracking down a story made her feel vital and alive. At heart, she was a journalist. That was what she needed to be doing with the rest of her life.

Her decision was made. The time had come for her self-imposed seclusion to end. Looking across the road, she scanned the wide expanse of sagebrush and prairie grass that led to the rugged sweep of forested hillsides. A rich, beautiful landscape, but she didn't belong here.

Her job was to follow the story. Packing a suitcase would take only a couple of minutes; she was accustomed to traveling light. She could be on her way in minutes, driving toward Denver International Airport, where she could catch the next flight to Chicago.

But what if Jack ran into trouble and came back to the cabin? She needed to stay, if only for twenty-four hours. As long as she was here, she might as well patch the barn roof.

She went back into the cabin and picked up her tool belt. Though she never locked her house when she was home, the recent threats emphasized the need for security. After she'd locked the front and back doors, she headed toward the barn.

The midday sun warmed her shoulders. Her life here was idyllic, but it wasn't where she needed to be. Why had she doubted herself? It was so obvious that she was a reporter. What was she afraid of? *Oh, let's see. A million different things.* Not that she was Baby Blue—a sissy. She'd always been brave, and living in a war zone had hardened her to the sight of blood and gore. She had faced unimaginable horror, and she'd learned to stifle her terror. But those fears never truly went away.

Though she'd never told anyone, she had experienced fits of uncontrolled sobbing, nightmares, even delusions. Once, she'd heard a helicopter passing overhead and panic overwhelmed her. She'd dropped to her knees and curled into a ball. Her mind wasn't right; she wasn't fit to be on the front line.

But she could still be a reporter; not every assignment required her to rush headlong into danger.

Inside the barn, she fastened the tool belt around her hips and looked up at the roof. One of the holes was so big that she could see daylight pouring through.

From the stall nearest the door, the bay mare snorted and pawed at the earthen floor.

"Oh, Lacy." Caitlyn went toward the horse. "I'm sorry. We missed our morning ride. Maybe later, okay?"

Lacy tossed her head as though angry. When she looked sadly at the empty stall beside her, Caitlyn felt guilty. Poor Lacy had been left behind, locked in her stall and deprived of her morning exercise.

"All right," Caitlyn said, "a short ride."

She had just gotten the horse saddled when she looked
out the front door of the barn and saw the black SUV approaching her driveway. Rojas was back.

Chapter Six

After Jack left Caitlyn's cabin, he continued to discover more of his innate skills. Horseback riding wasn't one of them. Every time he urged Fabio into a pace faster than a walk, Jack bounced around in the saddle like a broken marionette. How did cowboys do this all day? His ass was already sore.

Lucky for him, Fabio was a genius. The big palomino responded to his clumsy tugging on the reins with impressive intelligence as they wove through the pines and leafy shrubs in the thick forest. They found a creek where the horse could drink, and a couple of rock formations that could be used for hideouts.

After getting repeatedly poked in the arms by branches, Jack put on the sweatshirt Caitlyn had so thoughtfully packed for him. He hadn't expected her help. Her kindness. Or her kiss. It meant something, that kiss. Beyond the pure animal satisfaction of holding a woman in his arms, he'd felt a stirring in his soul as though they were deeply connected. He had a bright fleeting memory of what it was like to be in love, but the thought quickly faded into the darker recesses of his mind.

There could never be anything significant between him and Caitlyn. If he survived the next four days and made it to the trial, he'd have a new life in witness protection. And it wouldn't include her.

Looking up at the sky through scraggly branches, Jack noted the position of the sun and determined which way was north. This ability to get his bearings came from outdoor training in rugged, arid terrain. He remembered a desert. And an instructor who spoke only Spanish and—surprise, surprise—Jack was able to translate. He was bilingual. Another useful skill.

Also, he had a sharp comprehension of strategy. He knew that Rojas and his men were looking for him, as were the marshals at the safe house who had betrayed him. They might have access to advanced technology. Though Jack didn't see or hear a chopper overhead, it was entirely possible that this whole area was under aerial surveillance. His plan was to stay under the cover of the trees until nightfall.

He headed northwest, roughly following the direction of the horse trailer he'd seen on the road to Caitlyn's cabin. The logo on the side of that truck said: Circle L Ranch, Pinedale, Colorado. Locating the nearby population center could prove useful, and Fabio seemed to know where they were going. The big horse moved smoothly through the forest until they came to a ridge overlooking a meadow.

From this vantage point, Jack looked down on a small herd of fat black cattle, twenty-five or thirty head. As he watched, cowboys in a truck pulled up to a feeding area. Another ranch hand on a dirt bike joined them. None of these men were on horseback.

Jack patted Fabio's neck beneath his flowing blond mane. "Don't worry, buddy. A truck will never replace you. You're too pretty."

For a moment, he considered riding down and asking for shelter. On a ranch, there would be a number of places to hide. But he didn't want to put these people in danger. If Rojas suspected they were helping him, he'd gun down every person on the ranch and probably shoot the cattle as well. Fear was how the cartel ran their business; violence was their methodology.

Had Mark Santoro been the same way? Jack had respected Mark. He liked him, but that didn't mean either of them were upstanding citizens.

A clear thought unfurled inside his head. *No crime justifies taking the law into your own hands.* He believed this principle. At the same time, he knew that he had violated it. He had performed an execution. The circumstance wasn't clear, but Jack had killed an unarmed man.

He tugged on Fabio's reins, and they went back into the forest, heading toward Caitlyn's cabin. Thinking about Rojas made him worry. What if the thugs returned to her place? Gregorio Rojas was notorious for taking rash action. He lashed out violently. If he couldn't find another lead, he might return to Caitlyn with the idea that he could make her talk. Even if she didn't know anything. Even if she was innocent.

With Fabio tethered to a tree, Jack settled down to watch the cabin. An open space in a roughly triangular shape stretched downhill to her back door. The back of the barn was only a couple hundred yards away. Leaning against a sun-warmed boulder, he opened one of the bottled waters and ate a crunchy energy bar. A full meal would be nice. A rare steak with baked potato. Maybe a nice Chianti. And a cigar.

The memory of those rich flavors teased his palate. His mouth watered. The rest of his past was sketchy, but he knew what he wanted for his last meal. He inhaled the remembered fragrance of mellow tobacco. A Cuban cigar, of course.

When he saw the police vehicle arrive at Caitlyn's cabin, he supposed this was the friend she kept talking about. Danny the deputy appeared to be a tall, good-looking guy. Standing on the porch, he gave her a hug that lasted a bit longer than a casual greeting. A boyfriend? Hopefully, she wouldn't feel compelled to tell Danny Boy all about him. The last thing Jack needed was the local cops putting out an APB. There were enough people after him already.

Jack was disappointed to see Danny drive away by himself. If Caitlyn had gone with him, she'd be safe. At least, she'd have an armed cop at her side.

Alone, she was vulnerable.

He considered sneaking down the hill and telling her to come with him. *Bad idea.* With him, she'd be in danger for sure. Without him, she had a chance. *Sit tight. This might all go away.*

Caitlyn seemed to be getting back to her routine. She came out the back door carrying her tool belt. Her single-minded determination made him grin; nothing was going to stop her from patching that roof.

He almost relaxed. Then he saw the black SUV. They were driving too fast on the two-lane gravel road. Reckless. Dangerous.

He had to get Caitlyn out of there. He pushed himself to his feet and ran. Instinctively, he dodged and stooped, staying away from the open area, keeping his approach camouflaged.

The SIG was in his hand. He'd checked the clip and knew he had only four bullets. That should be enough. If he got to the rear of the barn, he'd be in range. First, he'd take out the big bodyguard, the guy who called himself Drew Kelso. Then, he'd shoot Rojas.

The SUV parked in her driveway. Four men and Rojas

emerged. Five targets and only four bullets. Jack didn't like the odds.

Kelso led the way. The bodyguard yanked his handgun from the shoulder holster as he stormed toward the cabin. He yelled, "Hey, bitch. Get out here."

The others followed.

The fact that Caitlyn was in the barn might save her. If she moved fast enough, she could get away without having them notice.

Jack crouched at the edge of the trees. There was no cover between him and the back wall of the barn. He stared at the weathered wood. No back door. That would have been too easy.

Caitlyn came through the big door in the front. She was astride the bay mare and, for some reason, wearing her tool belt. If she rode toward the corral gate, it would bring her closer to Rojas. She wheeled the horse in the opposite direction—toward where he was hiding in the trees—and rode across the fenced corral. At the far end was a gate that opened into the field.

She rode straight at it, leaning forward in the saddle and moving fast. Her expertise in handling her mount was obvious, and he admired her skill.

Rojas and his men hadn't spotted her. They were occupied with breaking into her cabin, yelling threats. Jack hoped they would keep up their posturing until she'd gotten safely away.

He sprinted down the rugged hill. When he got to the gate, he'd throw it open. And she'd ride through to safety. Caitlyn was close, almost there. *Come on, baby, you can make it.*

The shouting from the cabin changed in tone. Like hunting dogs on the chase, they'd seen their quarry and reacted.

In front of the others, Kelso ran from her house toward the corral. Gunfire exploded in wild bursts.

Caitlyn stiffened in the saddle. She reined her horse. What the hell was she doing?

He reached the gate, unfastened the latch and threw it open. "Caitlyn," he called to her. "This way. Hurry."

She turned her head toward him. All the color had drained from her skin. Her mouth was open, gasping. Had she been hit?

At the other end of the corral, he saw the five men pour through the gate, waving their guns, yelling, shooting.

Jack wanted to return fire, but he only had four bullets. Every shot had to count.

Kelso stopped and spread his legs in a shooter's stance. With both hands, he took aim.

Jack dropped to one knee, pointed the SIG and squeezed the trigger.

His bullet found its mark. Kelso roared in pain, clutched his thigh and toppled to the dirt inside the corral.

The men behind him stumbled to a halt. They'd thought they were dealing with an unarmed woman. Hadn't expected to be in danger.

Taking advantage of their momentary confusion, Jack fired a second time. Again, he aimed for the legs. Another man screamed and fell.

The others were in retreat. The cowards didn't know he had only two bullets left. He took advantage. Grabbing the reins on Caitlyn's horse, he pulled her toward the open gate.

"Wait." Her voice quavered. "Mount up behind me."

He didn't question her or argue. On horseback, their chances for escape were a hell of a lot better. As she scooted forward and out of the saddle, he stuck his toe into the stirrup and took her place.

Riding like this wouldn't be easy. He would have preferred holding his ground and shooting, picking them off one by one. But he didn't have the firepower. Jack dug in his heels, urging the horse forward. They made it through the gate.

"Where are we going?" she asked.

"Uphill," he said. "Take cover in the trees."

Behind his back, he heard another couple of shots. Leaning forward, he wrapped his arms around her. A screwdriver handle from her tool belt dug into his gut. He noticed that with every blast of gunfire, her body trembled.

They made it into the forest.

When he looked over his shoulder toward the barn, he saw Rojas, staring after them. Revenge was all he lived for. The bastard wouldn't quit until Jack was dead. And now, Caitlyn was another object for his hatred.

Jack felt like hell. It was his fault that she was in danger. Because of him, her peaceful life was torn to shreds. This counted as one of the worst things he'd done in his life as Tony Perez or whoever he was.

"Where's Fabio?" she asked.

"Up here. To the right."

Still within earshot of the shouting from her cabin, they approached the tree where he'd tethered the horse. The big palomino nickered a greeting to the bay mare.

Jack dismounted and went to his horse while she readjusted her position. She reached down to the tool belt. "Should I take this off?"

"Keep it." Some of those tools might be modified to use as weapons. "Never can tell when you might need a ratchet."

"I think we should go to the Circle L."

Though her voice was still shaky, the blush had returned to her cheeks. He didn't know what had happened to her when the shooting started, but the intensity of her reaction gave him cause for worry. It was almost like she'd gone into shock.

"We can't involve anyone else," he explained. "If the people at the Circle L help us, they'll be in as much danger as we are. Follow me."

Disappearing in this vast wilderness wouldn't be difficult, but hiding the horses presented a problem. Not only did they need to locate a cave big enough for Fabio and Lacy but they had to figure out a way to keep the animals quiet.

He turned to her and asked, "Do you have your car keys?"

"Why?"

"We might need to use your car."

"The keys are in my pocket. It's weird. I don't usually lock my cabin. For some reason, I did."

"Your instinct was right. The locked doors slowed down Rojas and his men. It gave you more time to escape."

"Oh, damn," she muttered. "I'll bet they kicked in my door. That's going to be a problem. You know, I've gone to a lot of trouble fixing up the place."

Her attitude puzzled him. Earlier, she'd frozen in terror. Now, she seemed more concerned about property damage than the fact that she was running for her life. "A broken door is the least of your problems. Rojas and his men are more likely to burn your cabin to the ground."

"That's terrible. A wildfire would devastate miles of forest." Her blue eyes snapped. "But I guess drug cartels aren't real concerned about environmental damage."

He couldn't believe she was composed enough to make a joke. Every muscle in his body was tense. Their plodding progress along the path beside the creek was driving him crazy. He wanted to fly, but they couldn't go faster without heading into open terrain. It was safer to stay within the shelter of the forest.

Single file, they ascended a ridge leading away from the creek. Direct sunlight hit Fabio's mane. The golden horse glowed like a beacon. "We have to ditch the horses. What will they do if we dismount and continue on foot?"

"They'll probably trot along behind us."

Exactly what he was afraid of. They were approaching an area he'd explored earlier. A rugged granite cliff rose above the tree line. If they climbed those rocks, there were a number of crannies where they could hide until nightfall.

"I have an idea," she said. "Fabio and Lacy don't actually belong to me. They're from the Circle L. If we get within sight of the ranch and shoo them away, they'll probably trot home to their stable."

"I told you before. We can't drag anybody else into danger." Why didn't she understand? "If the horses show up, the people at the ranch will know that something happened to you. They'll report it. Local police will be involved."

"As if that's a bad thing?"

Her sarcasm was the last straw. He wheeled around on Fabio and rode up beside her, confronting her face-to-face. She appeared to be blasé and cool.

"There's a time to be a smart-ass, Caitlyn. This isn't it."

"What do you want me to do? Burst into tears?"

Tears would be more normal than the facade she was putting up. He wanted an honest reaction from her. "Rojas wants us dead. Both you and me. If he gets his hands on us, death won't be painless. This isn't a game. It isn't a tidy little story you're writing for an article."

"You don't know anything about what I do for a living."

"Tell me," he challenged.

"I lived on the front lines of battle." Her eyes darkened. She wasn't joking, not anymore. "I've seen things you couldn't imagine."

"There's a difference between reporting on the shooting and being the target."

"Really? The incoming bombs didn't know the difference. An improvised explosive device couldn't tell that I was a reporter. I know what it's like to be in danger, Jack. I remember every minute, every horrible minute. Sometimes, I wake up at night and…"

He was beginning to understand her earlier reaction. "That's what happened to you when you heard the gunfire. You had a flashback. You froze."

"The only way I can handle the panic is to ignore it, pretend that it's erased. But it won't go away. I can't forget. That fear is branded into my brain."

If they were going to survive, he needed for her to be fully in control. She needed to be smart and conscious. To get beyond the flashbacks.

If they weren't careful, her memories would kill them.

Chapter Seven

Caitlyn couldn't help feeling the way she did. Her way of hiding fear was bravado. Cracking jokes and making snide comments gave her a buffer zone. One of the reporters she worked with in Iraq said that when it came to gallows humor she was the executioner. What else could she do? The alternative was to turn as hard as stone.

But the way she'd frozen when she heard gunfire wasn't typical. In other combat situations, she'd been able to respond and follow orders. The attack at her cabin had been unprovoked, unexpected. Because there hadn't been time to prepare herself, fear rushed in and overwhelmed her. She could never let that happen again. Her response had almost gotten them killed.

Jack reached toward her, spanning the space between their horses. She slapped his hand and turned her head away. "I'm fine."

"Listen to me, Caitlyn."

"You don't have to explain again. I've read the news stories. I know the cartels are famous for their vengeance. And brutal. Their victims are dismembered, beheaded, burned alive. I know what Rojas is capable of."

"Look at me."

Reluctantly, she lifted her gaze. His eyes narrowed to

jade slits. A muscle twitched in his jaw. He was fierce, a warrior. Quietly, she said, "I'm glad you're on my side."

"I don't make promises lightly." His voice had an edge of steel. "Believe me, Caitlyn. I won't let them hurt you."

How could he stop them? Sure, he was tough, and his marksmanship at the cabin had been nothing short of amazing, but he was only one man. "We need backup."

"Do you really think your friend Danny is a match for Rojas?"

"What do you know about Danny?"

"I'm assuming he's the cop who came to your house."

"You were watching my cabin." She appreciated his concern. Instead of putting miles between himself and Rojas, Jack stuck around to keep an eye on her. "Why?"

"Guilt," he said. "I feel like hell for putting you in danger."

"How did you know they'd come back?"

"I didn't. That was the worst-case scenario." His eyes scanned the forest impatiently. "I have a strategy. Plan for the worst and hope for the best."

"Something you learned while working for Santoro?"

"Santoro wasn't my first job. Let's get back to Danny. You gave him a long hug. Are you close?"

"I've known him since we were teenagers. He's like a big brother. And why do you care about who I'm hugging? Are you jealous?"

"Hell, no."

His denial came too fast. *He was jealous.* "Danny is happily married."

"Good for him. Now, here's the plan. We'll take the horses down to a field and leave them. Then we come back here, climb the rocks and find a place to hide until nightfall."

"I know this area better than you," she said. "Let me take the lead."

"Move fast."

As she rode down to an open area beyond a grove of aspen, she digested the very interesting fact that Jack cared enough about her to stay and watch her cabin, and he was jealous when he saw another man give her a hug. He must be attracted to her. He'd kissed her, after all.

Frankly, that attraction went both ways. He was handsome, aggressive, masculine and…totally unavailable. It was just her rotten luck to get involved with a guy who worked for a crime family and would be going into witness protection.

When they reached the creek at the edge of the meadow, she dismounted, removed the saddles and used a rope to lightly hobble the front legs of their horses. She didn't like to leave Fabio and Lacy alone for a prolonged period of time, but they'd be all right for a couple of hours. When she and Jack were safely on their way, she'd call Heather and tell her where to find the horses.

Jack slung the little backpack she'd prepared for him over his shoulder. "Give me the tool belt," he said. "We're going to be moving fast, and it's heavy."

She unbuckled the belt and held it toward him. "How much time do we have before they come after us?"

"Not much." While he fastened the belt around his hips, he transferred his gun to his hand. "They had to deal with two injured men and arrange for off-road transportation. Those things take time, but I'm assuming they're already on our trail."

She swallowed the fear that was bubbling inside her. "I suppose that's the worst-case scenario."

"Getting caught is the worst." He looked back toward the rocky cliffs. "Stay under the cover of the trees."

"Why?"

He gestured to the cloudless blue skies overhead. "Possible aerial surveillance."

He really was thinking of every contingency. "Really?"

"Start running," he said.

Though she didn't follow a regular exercise routine, Caitlyn was in good physical condition. She jogged at the edge of the forest, dodging between the tree trunks and ducking under low-hanging branches. The vigorous motion got her heart pumping. Though breathing heavily, she wasn't winded. After a month at the cabin, the altitude didn't bother her. But Jack probably wasn't acclimated to the thin air at this elevation. She glanced over her shoulder to check on him.

With the gun in his hand and ferocious determination written into every line of his face, he showed no indication of being tired. "Faster," he said.

"Need to be careful." She took a breath. "Don't want to trip. Sprain an ankle."

"You can move faster."

She spurred herself forward. When her family spent summers at the cabin, she and her brother climbed all over these rocks and hills. She knew the perfect place to hide. Her thigh muscles strained as she started the final uphill push.

Pausing, she caught her breath. "We'll climb down this sharp ravine, then up and over those boulders."

"Right behind you."

Her hideout wasn't actually a cave; it was a natural cavern formed by huge chunks of granite piled against each other. The most dangerous part was at the top. She flattened her back against the rock and crept along a ledge. "Be careful here. The drop wouldn't kill you, but it'd hurt."

Even with the tool belt, he managed easily.

At the far side of the ledge, she slipped through a slit between two boulders and climbed down, placing her feet carefully. A cool shadow wrapped around her.

She was inside a low cavern. The waters of the creek trickled through the rocks above and formed a pool, which then spilled down into another cavern that wasn't visible from where she crouched on a rock.

Jack sat beside her. There wasn't enough room for him to stretch his legs out straight without getting his feet wet in the pool. "You did good, Caitlyn. This cave is excellent."

Sunlight through the slit provided enough illumination for her to see him. When she sat on the rock beside the pool, she felt moisture seeping into her jeans. "The only way they can find us is to stick their heads down here. Have you got any bullets left?"

"Two." He unbuckled the tool belt and moved closer to her. "The sound of the creek will cover our voices if we talk quietly."

Her muscles tingled from the run, and his nearness started a whole other spectrum of sensation. In spite of the danger and the fear, she was thinking of how good it would feel to lean against him and have his arm wrapped around her shoulders.

He pointed toward the ledge where the water made a miniature Niagara Falls. "There's another cavern below this one, right?"

"Two others. A large one that can be reached by following the creek. Then another. Then this cubbyhole."

"How visible is the approach to the first cavern?"

"If they come after us on horseback, they'd have to dismount and walk in. Rojas didn't impress me as the kind of man who did that kind of search."

"We have to remember the other men at the safe house," he said, "the federal marshals who betrayed me."

She hated to think of that conspiracy but didn't have trouble believing it had happened the way Jack said. Rojas had plenty of money to use as an enticement. "After you were found dead, how do you think the marshals planned to cover it up?"

"They could say that unidentified men in masks burst into the safe house and grabbed me. Or they could claim that I turned on them and they had to shoot me."

"What about me? How can they explain killing me?"

In the dim light, the rugged lines of his face seemed softer. The rough stubble on his chin faded to a shadow. "Your death wouldn't be explained. You'd just disappear. There's no tangible link between us."

"Yes, there is. The gray mare." The horse that showed up on her doorstep belonged to the men at the safe house. "A good investigator would connect the horse to my disappearance. Plus, Rojas and his men tore up my cabin. Somebody would have to suspect foul play."

"They'd blame it on me." His quiet words blended into the rushing of the creek. "Or on the unidentified men who killed me. The marshals wouldn't necessarily come under suspicion."

Though Rojas and his men represented a direct threat, she was more concerned with those federal marshals. They wouldn't charge through her door with guns blazing. Their approach would be subtle and clever. "What if they contact Danny to help them search for me? He knows about this cavern. He could lead them to us."

"Think it through," Jack said. "In the first place, they won't want to involve local law enforcement. Not while Rojas is in the area."

Wishing that she felt safer, she leaned against him. The warmth of his body contrasted with the cool surface of the rocks. His arm slipped around her.

She looked up at him. Would he kiss her again? Though she wouldn't mind a repeat, she was too nervous to relax and enjoy the sensations. "How long do we wait?"

"After dark," he said, "we'll go to your cabin and take your car."

"Won't they be watching?"

"I'll know if they are."

He sounded so confident that she believed him, even though she had no reason to think that he was a surveillance expert. Being in the employ of the Santoro family meant he knew his way around firearms and was probably good with his fists. But he seemed to have a wider spectrum of experience.

"I don't know much about you." In the subtle light of the cave, she studied him. "You might say I don't know Jack."

"Funny." He touched the tip of her nose with his index finger. "And this is an appropriate time for a joke."

"So glad I can entertain you. Seriously, though. Do you have training in surveillance?"

"I watched your cabin for over an hour, and you didn't know I was there."

"True, but I wasn't looking for you."

"I know how to shadow, how to observe and how to do a stakeout. And I learned from an expert. An old man who lived in Arizona. He was a tracker, a hunter. He showed me how to disappear in plain sight and how to sense when someone was coming after me."

"Sensing a threat? How does that work?"

"Awareness." He pointed to a glow that flickered against the cavern wall. "That patch of light is rising from the cave below us. If I see a shadow, I'll know that someone is approaching and getting too close."

She nodded. Though his method was simple, it hadn't occurred to her. "What else?"

"Listen to the rippling of the water as it slips from this cave to the next. There's a pattern to the sound. A splash indicates an obvious disturbance, but even a stealthy approach can be heard."

Though she concentrated on the sound of the water, she only heard gurgling and dripping. "This awareness thing is a kind of Zen-like approach. Was your teacher a guru?"

"He'd never use that word, but yes." Jack rattled off a sentence in Spanish, then he translated: "Wisdom comes from an open mind and profound simplicity."

"You speak Spanish. Are you from Mexico?"

"Does it matter?"

"Not really." When she shrugged, her shoulder rubbed against his chest. The moist air in the cavern sank into her pores like a cool sauna. "You make me curious. How did you get those scars on your chest?"

"How do you think?"

"You're being deliberately evasive." And it was beginning to irritate her. "There's no reason for you to be secretive. I already know you're not the real Jack Dalton, because Danny told me he's sleeping off a drunk-and-disorderly charge in jail. I know you're a federal witness on the run. And I'm fairly sure that you're Tony Perez."

"I guess you know it all."

She doubted that she'd even begun to scratch the surface of this complicated and somewhat infuriating man. "When I ask a question, I want an answer. How did you get those scars?"

"I was in a motorcycle accident. And a knife fight. Twice I was shot."

He'd lived a dangerous life, but she'd known that. "What were the circumstances? Why were you injured?"

"I have enemies. They don't place nice."

"Enemies like Gregorio Rojas and his brother," she said.

With his thumb he tilted her chin so she was looking up at his face. Though his expression was unreadable, his eyes glimmered, and that shine was somehow reassuring. A few years ago she had interviewed a mercenary in Afghanistan and had seen a flat coldness in his eyes, as though his soul no longer inhabited his body. Jack wasn't like that. Though she had no doubt that he'd killed people, he still had a conscience.

The tension in his jaw relaxed as he leaned closer to her. She arched her neck and closed her eyes, waiting for his kiss. His lips pressed firmly against hers. He withdrew an inch, then tasted her mouth more thoroughly, nibbling at her lower lip and gliding his tongue across her teeth.

His subtlety tantalized her, and she pressed for a harder, deeper kiss. This wasn't wise. Not profoundly simple. But she experienced a wonderful awareness.

He tensed and pulled away. Without speaking, he pointed to the patch of light on the wall. The pattern had changed. She heard a difference in the splashing of the water.

Someone had entered the cave below them.

Chapter Eight

Moving cautiously so he wouldn't betray their hiding place by scraping his boot against the rock, Jack positioned her in the darkest corner of the cavern. He figured that if she froze in panic, he wouldn't have to maneuver around her. Though he didn't dare peek over the ledge overlooking the lower cavern, he stretched out flat on his belly on the rock beside the water. If the searcher got close, Jack could react effectively. The SIG was in his hand.

A voice echoed from the cavern below them. "This is a good hiding place. Not big enough for their horses, though."

Another voice responded from a distance. "Do you see anything?"

A beam from a flashlight reflected on the wall and ceiling of the lower cave. Jack wished that he'd done more reconnaissance. Should have explored the cave below them. Should have been more prepared.

Glancing toward Caitlyn, he saw her tension, but she wasn't frozen as she'd been when she heard the gunfire. She managed a nod. Her eyes were huge. Her hands clenched at her breast.

From below he heard a splash.

"Damn," the voice said, "I got my boots wet."

"Any sign of them?"

"Nothing."

"We'll move on. They're on horseback and would have gone farther away from the cabin than this."

Jack listened carefully to their voices. One of them had a Texas twang that sounded familiar.

The flashlight beam went dark. There was the sound of more splashing from the lower caves. As the searchers moved away from them, his voice faded. "Here's what I don't understand. If he was at that woman's house, he'd have access to a phone. Why didn't he call for backup?"

Jack strained to hear what they were saying. Why did they think he could call for backup? The Santoros were based in Chicago. They couldn't help him from halfway across the country.

"Who knows what's going on in his head," said the other voice. "We're not dealing with an average person. He's a legend."

"Yeah, I've heard. Tall tales," the Texan drawled. "They say he hid out for six weeks in a jungle before he completed his mission."

Though the men were still talking, they were outside the cave. Jack could hear only bits and pieces of their conversation. Something about a "loner" and "killed a man."

He didn't remember surviving in a jungle. What kind of mission had he been on? Reaching into his memory was like sticking his hand into a grab bag. He didn't know whether he'd pull out a gold medal or a piece of dung.

When he felt Caitlyn touch him, he rolled onto his back and looked up at her. He knew that she'd heard as much as he had. Therefore she'd have questions. Even if he'd known all the answers, Jack figured it wasn't wise to go into details. Some memories were better left unsaid.

He sat up. She was close to him, kneeling on the rock

beside his thigh. Her jaw was tight. In a barely audible whisper, she asked, "Are they gone?"

He nodded. "We're safe. For now."

Exhaling in a whoosh, she sat back on her heels. He had the sense that she'd been holding her breath the whole time the searcher had been in the cave below them. Still whispering, she asked, "What did they mean when they said you could call for backup?"

Damned if I know. Hoping he could defuse her curiosity, he grabbed the backpack, unzipped the flap and reached inside. "Energy bar?"

"I'm glad I packed these for you. I'm starving." She tore off the wrapping. "Tell me about this backup."

So much for distracting her. He peered into the backpack. There were two bars left. Like his bullets, their food would have to be rationed. He looked up at the sunlight slanting through the opening above them. "We've probably got three more hours of daylight before we can make our move."

"Were those the federal marshals?"

He shrugged, hoping against hope that she'd drop the topic.

She took a bite of the energy bar and chewed. Her eyes were suspicious. "Are you going to tell me? Were those the feds or not?"

"I can't say for certain."

"Why not?" Her voice was sharp. "This is getting really annoying."

"I'm not lying to you," he said.

"Hard to believe, Jack. That one guy had a distinct accent. Did you hear his voice at the safe house or not?"

Evading her inquiries wouldn't be easy. She was smart and determined. His glance bounced off the rocky walls of their hiding place. Spending the next couple of hours in this enclosed space with Caitlyn slinging questions every few seconds would make him crazy. Might as well tell her the truth and get it over with.

"I can't remember," he said.

"Can't remember the names of the marshals? Or can't—"

"I don't remember much of anything." He moved away from her, returning to his position against the cavern wall. He felt as if he was literally stuck between a rock and a hard place. "When I got hit on the head, a lot of memories fell out."

"Seriously?" She scrambled around until she was beside him, facing him. Anger sparked in her eyes as she braced her hand against the wall beside his head and leaned in close for her interrogation. "Are you telling me that you have amnesia?"

"Something like that."

"Oh, please. If you don't want to tell me the truth, just say so. Don't insult me by making up a ridiculous excuse."

The irony irritated him. When she'd thought he was a handyman, she'd been more than willing to accept his lies. The truth was harder to swallow. "Believe what you want."

"If you have amnesia, how did you remember Mark Santoro?"

"I watched him die on the street in Chicago. A hell of a vivid memory." Through his shirt he felt the ragged edge of the scar on his belly. He'd been shot on that street. "I was never a soldier, but I understand chain of command. Mark Santoro was my captain. I was supposed to protect him, and I failed. That memory is never going to fade."

"What about the safe house?" she asked. "You remembered being at the safe house."

"I have a recollection of the place." He might even be able to locate the house again. There was a shake shingle roof, a long porch, a red barn. He shook his head. "The only thing I know for certain is that I need to be at the trial on Tuesday."

"Uh-huh."

"True story."

"This amnesia of yours," she said, "it comes and goes. Is that right? You remember whenever it's convenient?"

"I wish." He glared back at her. "If I knew who to call for backup, I'd have been on the phone first thing. Playing hide-and-seek with Rojas isn't my idea of fun."

She backed off, but only a few inches. Her expression remained skeptical as she chomped on her energy bar. "Head injuries can cause all kinds of strange problems. I just don't know whether to believe you."

"I don't give a damn if you trust me or not. There's only one thing that's important—for us to get out of this mess in one piece."

"Why did you tell me about the amnesia?"

"Because you're a pain in the butt." He held her by the shoulders and confronted her directly. "I don't want to spend the next couple of hours being interrogated."

She shoved at his chest. "Get your hands off me."

"Gladly."

He moved around her and picked up the tool belt. There were screwdrivers, a file and a rasp. "I don't suppose there's a knife in this belt. Or a nail gun."

Her voice was quiet but still persistent. "You told me about the wise old man in the desert who taught you about awareness. A memory?"

"I remember him. He trained me, but I don't know why." Without looking at her, he continued, "I'm aware of speaking Spanish, but don't know how I learned the language. I have skills. Seems like I'm a pretty good marksman."

"I'll say. Back at my cabin you made every bullet count."

Though he was pleased that she'd noticed his ability, he didn't let down his guard. "I don't know how I learned to handle a gun. I have no memory of being trained."

"When you said—"

"That's it, Caitlyn. I'm done talking."

His ability to remember was far less important than their immediate problem. They needed to get as far away from Rojas as possible. And they needed to move fast.

NO MATTER HOW CAITLYN shifted around, she couldn't get comfortable. When she leaned against the wall of the cavern, her backbone rubbed painfully on the hard surface. Her butt was sore and cold from sitting on the damp rocks beside the water. With her knees pulled up, she wrapped her arms around her legs and watched Jack as he sorted through the various implements on her tool belt.

Who was this man? Reluctantly she decided to accept his explanation that he suffered from some form of amnesia. His head injury provided validation for that claim, and she was well aware of the unpredictability of trauma to the brain.

Okay, then. Amnesia.

The only identity that made sense was Tony Perez, member of the Santoro crime family who supposedly died on the streets of Chicago. As Perez, he'd be a witness— a protected witness—whose testimony could convict the elder Rojas brother.

But the searcher who poked around in the lower cave had mentioned a few things that didn't fit. Why would Tony Perez be able to call for backup? And what kind of jungle mission would he have been undertaking? She wished that she'd had more time on her computer to research his background.

Though Jack had made it very clear that he didn't want to answer questions, she wasn't the kind of passive woman who could simply sit back and take orders. She cleared her throat before speaking. "It seems to me that it might be extremely useful to know who you might call for backup."

He grunted in response.

"If you gave me a chance, I might be able to jog your memory. Maybe we could start with the last thing you remember and work backward."

He flipped a Phillips screwdriver in his hand and gripped the handle as if using it to stab. He stared at the tip and frowned. "I know you'd like a simple solution. So would I. But amnesia isn't like misplacing my keys or forgetting where I parked my car. There are empty spaces inside my head."

She didn't want to give up. "We could try. It wouldn't hurt."

"What if I don't like what I remember?" He flipped the screwdriver again. His hands were quick, his coordination excellent. "It might turn out that those blank spots are filled with nasty secrets."

"Are you saying that you'd rather not know?"

"I don't mind being Jack Dalton, a man with no past."

She understood that while he was working for Mark Santoro he might have done things he'd rather forget. But to throw away his entire history? "You're not a bad person. You have a conscience. You agreed to come forward and testify."

"I want Rojas to pay for the murder of Mark Santoro," he said.

"That's a starting place," she said, encouraging him to continue. "What else do you want?"

"To get you to safety."

He focused on her. In the dim light of the cavern, his features weren't clear. She felt rather than saw the heat emanating from him. He smoldered, and she felt herself melting. On a purely visceral level, it didn't matter where he came from or who he was. She knew, without doubt, that he was dedicated to rescuing her. Still, she persisted. "Your memories could help us. There might be someone you could call."

"Someone from the Santoro family?" The corner of his mouth lifted in a wry grin. "That might not be good news for you."

Probably not. The notorious crime family from Chicago wouldn't welcome a reporter into their midst. "Better them than Rojas."

"Leave my past alone, Caitlyn."

He returned his attention to the tool belt. She watched him as he evaluated each implement. In his hands, a paint scraper became a tool for slashing. The hammer was an obvious weapon, as was the crowbar. After discarding wrenches and small screwdrivers, he took the belt apart and reassembled it as a sort of holster.

She couldn't help asking another question. "Have you done this before?"

"Not that I remember. I seem to be good at improvising, using whatever comes to hand."

"Maybe you're MacGyver."

"Anything can be used as a weapon. A belt buckle or a shoelace. A mirror. A rock. It's all about intent."

"And what are your intentions?"

"To be prepared in case we're attacked. Frankly, I'm hoping I won't need a weapon. We'll get to your car and drive to a safe place where I can turn myself in to the authorities. How far are we from Denver?"

"About an hour. If we were going cross-country, we'd actually be closer to Colorado Springs."

He looked up at the sunlight that spilled through the opening in the rocks. "We still have a couple of hours before we can move. Might be smart to catch some shut-eye."

During the time she'd spent embedded with the troops, she'd learned to nap in difficult surroundings. She agreed that it was wise to be rested before they took on the final leg of their escape. "I don't think I can sleep."

Jack settled himself against the cavern wall and beckoned to her. "Lean against me. You'll be more comfortable."

Or not. Whenever she got close to him, her survival instincts were replaced by a surge of pure lust. Why did she have this crazy attraction to him? Sure, he was handsome, with that thick black hair and steamy green eyes. Definitely a manly man, he was her type. But she'd been around plenty of macho guys when she was with the troops. None of them affected her the way Jack did.

He noticed her hesitation. Again, he treated her to that sexy, wry grin. "Scared?"

"Of you?" Was her voice squeaking? "No way."

"Then come here. Use me for a pillow."

Pillows were soft and cuddly. Snuggling up against Jack's muscular body wouldn't be the least bit relaxing. She needed a different plan.

Reaching into her pocket, she took out her cell phone. "We could call the authorities in Denver right now."

"You know that phones can be tracked with a GPS signal."

"You said that before. I get it. But this is a secure phone. It was issued to me by my former employer. It's safe."

"Are you clear on that point?"

"Crystal."

He closed his eyes. "We wait until dark."

Chapter Nine

Jack always slept with one eye open. That wasn't a memory but a fact. Being a light sleeper was as indelible as being right-handed.

He leaned against the wall of the cavern. His body slipped into a state of relaxation, allowing his energy to replenish, but part of his mind stayed alert. Even when he was a kid, he knew it was important to be on guard so he would hear the staggering footsteps in the hallway outside the bedroom. His eyes were attuned to deal with the flash of light when that bedroom door crashed open. He knew the smell of the man who meant to hurt him—sweat and whiskey and hate.

Danger was ever present. Survival depended on being ready for the inevitable slap across the face or belt lashing. Or Rojas.

While sleeping, he remained aware of Caitlyn's movements. She tried curling up by herself at the edge of the water. Then she got another energy bar from the backpack. She stood and paced two steps in one direction then the other, like an animal in a cage that was too small. Finally, she settled beside him. Her head rested on his chest, and her slender body curved against him.

He pulled her close. The way she fit into his embrace gave him a sense of warmth and comfort that went beyond the sensual pleasure of holding a beautiful woman. Physically, they were well matched. And there was a deeper connection. Her unflagging curiosity drove him nuts, but he appreciated her intelligence, her wit and her stamina. When he'd given her the clear directive to run, she hadn't complained. Caitlyn wasn't a whiner. She'd been affected by her memories of war but hadn't been broken.

He'd been with other women, many others. One had been special, cherished and adored. He had loved before. Part of him longed to see his lover's face again and to hear her soft, sweet voice. But that was not to be. Without remembering the specifics, he knew his love was gone. Forever.

When Caitlyn moved away from him, he felt the empty space where her head should have been resting. His eyelids opened to slits. The sunlight filtering into the cavern had dimmed to grayish dusk.

He watched as Caitlyn climbed toward the ledge leading out of the cavern. "Where are you going?"

"I'll get better reception here. I need to call Heather at the Circle L Ranch and tell her where the horses are tethered."

"It's best if no one else gets involved. Don't tell her anything else."

"I understand." After she made the call, she looked down at her phone.

"I have a message from Danny. It came through about twenty minutes ago."

He stretched and yawned. The brief sleep had refreshed him enough to continue with his simple plan to get her car and drive to safety. He was aware of potential obstacles, especially since the federal marshals were involved. It might be useful to hear from the local deputy. "Go ahead and play back the message."

As she held the phone to her ear and listened, he watched her posture grow tense and angry. "You need to hear this."

She played back the message on speaker. Danny's voice was low. "Hey, Caitlyn. I found the owners of the gray mare. I thought I remembered seeing that horse."

Danny had stumbled across the safe house. *Bad news.*

The deputy continued, "The owner wants to thank you and maybe give you a reward. Let me tell you where the house is."

He gave directions, starting with "It's not far from where that Arapaho Indian guy lived. I think his name was Red Fire. Yeah, that's it. Red Fire. Turn off the main road at Clover Creek."

After he outlined a couple more twists and turns, he ended the call by saying, "I'll wait here until you arrive. Hurry."

Jack rose and crossed the cavern to stand beside her. Dusky light slid across her stricken face. She whispered, "Danny was warning me. When we were growing up, 'Red Fire' was our code for trouble."

"Even though he made the call, he was telling you to stay away."

"Rojas has him." Her voice quavered. "We can't leave him with that bastard."

The deputy's probability for survival was slim. Neither Rojas nor the feds could afford to release a lawman who would testify against them. Jack knew that the smart move was to drive away and try not to think about what was happening to Caitlyn's friend. It was more important for him to get to that trial and testify.

But Jack wasn't made that way. He couldn't leave someone else to die in his place. "Give me the phone."

"What are you going to do?"

"I'm going to save your friend."

He hit the callback button and waited. With each ring, Jack's hopes sank lower. Danny could already be dead.

The voice that finally answered was unfamiliar. "I'm expecting you."

"I'll be there." As soon as the words left his mouth, Jack knew that he'd done hostage negotiations before. The first step was to give the hostage takers what they wanted. Then demand proof of life. "I need to speak with Danny."

"He's tied up." The cryptic comment was followed by cold laughter. "All tied up."

"If I don't talk to him, you won't see me again. Not until we meet in court."

"Hold on." There were sounds of shuffling and a couple of thuds. Then Danny came on the phone. "It's me. Danny Laurence."

Jack asked, "Have you been harmed?"

"Where's Caitlyn?"

She spoke up. "I'm here, Danny. Are you all right?"

"I'm fine," he said. "The only way we're going to get through this is to do what they say."

Jack assumed that Rojas had threatened Danny's family and friends. He must have told Danny that if he caused trouble, his loved ones would suffer. "I can arrange protection for—"

"No." Danny was adamant. "The less they know, the better."

Jack agreed. He had a new respect for the deputy, who was willing to sacrifice himself to keep others safe.

The other voice came on the phone. "You'd be wise to listen to Danny. Contact no one else."

"Understood."

"Come to the house. You know where it is. And bring the girl."

To do as he said would be suicide. "I want a different meeting place. Neutral ground."

"You have no right to make demands."

"I'm the one you want," Jack said. "I assume I'm talking to Gregorio Rojas. Am I right?"

"Continue."

"If you don't get your hands on me, I'll testify at that trial in Chicago. And your brother will go to jail for the rest of his life. You want me. And the only way you'll get me is if you agree to a meet."

There was a long, very long, pause. "Where?"

"I'll call you back in fifteen minutes with the location. Bring Danny. If he's hurt, the deal is off."

Jack disconnected the call and turned off the phone. As he strapped on the tool belt that had been modified to a holster, he turned to Caitlyn. "How long will it take to get to your house?"

"If we move fast, fifteen minutes. What are we going to do?"

"I need for you to think of a meeting place for the hostage exchange. Somewhere secluded."

He climbed through the slit in the rocks and reached back to help her. The sun had dipped behind the mountains, and the forests were filled with shadow. Though Jack would have preferred waiting for at least an hour when it would be pitch-dark, he knew they didn't have that option. They needed to strike quickly. He started a mental clock, ticking down fifteen minutes until the next phone call.

Rojas had the advantage of superior manpower and weapons. Jack's edge was his mobility and his instincts. And Caitlyn. If Jack had been alone in the forest, he would have wasted precious moments figuring out where he was. She knew the way through the trees and back to her cabin. She leapt from rock to rock. In unobstructed stretches, they ran full out. They were at the long slope leading down to her house within ten minutes.

At the edge of the trees, he crouched beside her. "Good job."

She accepted his compliment with a nod. "I don't see any light from my cabin. Do you think Rojas left a man there?"

His henchmen weren't clever enough to leave the lights turned off. The federal marshals were another story. They'd know better than to betray their position by making themselves at home.

He figured that the marshals would want to distance themselves from the hostage situation as much as possible. They probably weren't at the safe house with Rojas, which left them free to search.

Thinking back to his time in custody, Jack remembered three marshals. Two of them, including the guy with the Texas twang, had been on horseback at the cave. Where was the third man? Hiding in Caitlyn's cabin? In the barn?

"How do we do this?" she asked.

"Give me the car keys."

"I'm driving," she said. "I know my way around this area and you don't. It's logical for me to be behind the wheel."

Logical, but not safe. He didn't want her to be part of the action, but leaving her alone and unguarded in the forest was equally dangerous. "What if you freeze up again?"

"I won't. Not while Danny's life is in danger. I know what's at stake."

There wasn't time to argue, and she was right about knowing the territory. "We'll slip down the hill, run to your car and get in. If we're fired upon, keep your head low and drive fast."

She nodded. "It's been fifteen minutes. You should call

them back. The best meeting place I can think of is the old cemetery by Sterling Creek. It's a half mile down a road that nobody ever uses."

"Don't need directions." He took out the phone. "They won't agree to our location anyway."

"How do you know?"

"Apparently, I've done stuff like this before. I'm sure that Rojas will want the advantage of choosing the location."

His phone call took less than a minute. As he predicted, Rojas refused to come to the cemetery and insisted that they use a deserted ranch house. Jack ended the call by saying, "That's too far from where we are. I'll get back to you in ten minutes."

"Wait," she said. "You need to tell them more. They'll hurt Danny."

"Not yet they won't." He shoved her phone into his pocket. "Follow me down the slope. If the third marshal is in your house, he might start shooting. That's your signal to run back to the cave and stay there."

"What about—"

"No more talking."

He started down the hill, keeping to the shadows as much as possible. A twig snapped under his boot. There was no way to muffle the sound of their footsteps. He compensated by moving swiftly. If they got to the car before the marshal had time to pinpoint their location and react, there was a good chance that they could get away clean.

He dove into the passenger seat. Caitlyn was behind the wheel of her dark green SUV. She cranked the key in the ignition and they drove away from her cabin.

No shots were fired. There was no sign of pursuit.

Instead of being relieved, Jack's suspicions were aroused. The marshals were up to something. He was damn sure that Rojas used a threat to Danny's family to get him to cooperate, and he was equally certain that the three traitorous marshals wouldn't allow a bloodbath. If the feds had any hope of protecting their butts, they had to turn the tide in their direction. They needed to look like heroes.

Jack expected the marshals to throw him under the bus.

In the meantime, he and Caitlyn had to get Danny away from Rojas. She was doing her best, driving like a Grand Prix master on the narrow, graded road.

"New car?" he asked. The interior still had the fresh-from-the-showroom smell.

"I'm leasing for a year." Her eyes riveted to the road ahead. "She handles well for a clunky SUV."

"She?"

"All my vehicles are female," she said. "This one is kind of sedate. I'm calling her Ms. Peacock because she's green."

He figured that Ms. Peacock had all the bells and whistles, including GPS mapping and a locator. She wasn't the best car to use for a getaway. "How long until we get to the safe house?"

"At normal speed, twenty minutes. I can do it in fifteen."

"Make it eight," he said.

She shot him a quick glance and juiced the accelerator. "You got it."

When he made the next phone call, his goal was to keep Rojas on the line for as long as possible while they made their approach. Timing was essential to the success of his plan.

Jack had no intention of meeting Rojas at an alternate location. He wanted to be in position for an attack when they were leaving the safe house and not expecting to see him.

After he and Rojas bickered back and forth, Jack said,

"I'll agree to a meeting at the place you named. It's going to take us forty-five minutes to get there, but Caitlyn knows where it is."

"Forty-five minutes, then."

"And I've got a couple of conditions," Jack said. "First of all, you can't harm Danny. I need your word of honor that you won't touch him."

"Done." Rojas was terse.

He was lying. Rojas had as much honor as a snake. Jack lied back to him. "I trust you, Gregorio. We can handle this hostage exchange without bloodshed. Here's how it's going to work."

Speaking slowly, Jack rambled through a complicated plan to trade himself for Danny, while Caitlyn careened around a wide curve. They passed the entry gate for the Circle L Ranch and a fenced meadow populated with a herd of cattle. The road narrowed slightly and went through a series of hairpin turns before opening up into a straight line. They were nearing the intersection with a main road.

He talked to Rojas about being set free on a plane to Costa Rica. "And you'll never hear from me again."

"Yes, yes. Whatever you want."

"Well, then. We have an agreement," Jack said. "I'll see you in about forty-five minutes."

He disconnected the call and turned to Caitlyn. "How far are we from the safe house?"

"Within a mile."

"Nice job, Speed Racer."

"You should see me in a Hummer."

This woman had been to war. She knew how to handle herself when she wasn't disabled by fear. "Cut your head-lights. Get as close as you can without turning into the driveway."

She nodded. "What do we do when we get there?"

"You park the car and stay with it. I'll get close and grab Danny. We'll run back to you."

When she turned off the headlights, she had to slow her frantic speed; there wasn't enough daylight to see the road clearly. "What if something goes wrong?"

"It won't."

Not if he could help it.

Chapter Ten

After her mad race on the twisting gravel roads, Caitlyn was dizzy with emotion. Excited by the speed. Angry about Danny's capture. Grateful that she'd made it to the safe house without careening into a tree or spinning off a hairpin turn into a ditch. Apprehensive about what might happen next. Adrenaline surged through her veins. Her skin prickled with enough electricity to power a small village.

With fingers clenched on the steering wheel, she eased her green SUV into a hidden spot behind a stand of pine trees and killed the engine. Jack had told her to wait. She was unarmed; there was nothing she could do to help rescue Danny.

While embedded with the troops, she'd been in this position before. Watching as the soldiers prepared for a mission. Hearing the determination in their voices. Knowing that some of them would not come back.

But she wasn't an observer anymore. *This is my mission. My friend is in danger.* It would have been reassuring to have a combat helmet and ballistic vest to gird for warfare. Not that the clothing or the weaponry made a difference. Being battle-ready was a state of mind that came from training and experience that she didn't have. Though she'd been to war, she was a civilian.

If saving Danny had depended on writing a thought-provoking essay, Caitlyn would have been helpful. But in this situation? Jack knew better than she did.

She fidgeted in the driver's seat. From where she was parked, she couldn't even see the house. She needed to move. If she didn't take action, the tension building inside her would explode. After turning off the light that automatically came on when the door opened, she quietly unfastened the latch and crept from the vehicle. She approached the barbed-wire fence surrounding the property.

The waning moon hung low in the night sky, but there was enough starlight to see Jack as he darted through the tall brush toward the low, flat ranch house. He stayed parallel to the one-lane asphalt driveway that was roughly the length of a city block.

At the house, Rojas and his men made no attempt to conceal their presence. In addition to light pouring through the front and side windows, the porch was lit. To the right of the house was the horse barn and corral. The black SUV that had earlier visited her house was parked outside. And two other sedans, probably rentals. How many men were inside?

She paced along the fence line, then returned to her SUV, then back to the fence. Squinting hard, she saw Jack as he disappeared into the shadows near the house. He moved with stealth and confidence. In the natural order of things, she figured Jack was a predator. A dangerous man. The only reason he kept himself hidden was to surprise his prey.

But how could he possibly take on Rojas and his men with nothing more than a tool belt and two bullets? These men were killers, violent and sadistic. She'd read the news stories about the cartel crimes in Mexico. They were as brutal as the Afghani warlord she'd interviewed. Her mind flashed terrifying images. Memories. She had seen the mutilated corpses. *Stop! I can't go there. I can't let myself slip into fear.*

Amnesia would have been a relief. Jack was lucky to have his past erased, but she wouldn't have wished for the same fate. Not all her memories were bad; she'd had a happy childhood. There were many proud moments she never wanted to forget, like the first time she'd seen her byline in print and the thrill of tracking down a story. And Christmas morning. And her sixteenth birthday. And falling in love. Closing her eyes, she forced herself to remember a wonderful time.

Sunset on a beach. Palm trees swayed in the breeze. She held hands with a tall, handsome man as they walked at the water's edge. The cool water lapped at her bare ankles. She looked up at him and saw...

Jack! Shirtless and muscular, the scars on his torso were landmarks to the past he'd forgotten. His grin teased her as he leaned closer. Before they kissed, she opened her eyes.

The night surrounded her. She wanted Jack's embrace. To be honest, she wanted more intimacy than a simple kiss. If they got out of this alive, she would make love to him. Together, they'd create a memory—a moment of passion that was destined to never be repeated.

His destiny was set. After he testified, he'd disappear into the witness protection program. Even if that hadn't been the case, she really didn't see herself in a long-term relationship with a former member of the Santoro family.

She tucked a hank of hair behind her ear and stared toward the house. Why were they taking so long? They had to leave soon to get to the meeting place.

She wished Jack had explained what he was going to do, but she couldn't blame him for not outlining his plan. There hadn't been time to discuss options. And he really couldn't count on her for backup. Not after she'd frozen when fired upon. *That wouldn't happen again. It couldn't.*

Though she trembled, she felt no fear. Anger dominated her mind—white-hot anger. Tension set fire to her rage. She wanted to yell, not whimper.

Consciously, she fed the flame. She despised Rojas and his men, hated the way they victimized Danny and threatened his family. Their cruelty outraged her. She wanted justice and retribution for every criminal act the cartel had committed.

Her anger ran deep. There had been times—while she observed the troops—when she had wondered if she was capable of killing another human being. At this moment, she felt like she could.

The front door to the house opened, and she heard voices. A man stepped onto the porch. He was too far away for her to tell much about him, but she didn't think she'd seen him before. Had Rojas called in reinforcements?

From her vantage point outside the barbed wire, Caitlyn mentally took the measure of the distance between her SUV and the front door to the house. It was over a hundred yards, maybe closer to two hundred. Jack had told her to wait until he rescued Danny and they ran to the car. That plan wouldn't work if Danny wasn't capable of running.

She needed to bring her SUV closer.

FROM THE EDGE OF THE house, Jack watched a young man with a buzz cut saunter across the yard between the front door and the vehicles. His path led past the place where Jack was hiding, but Buzz Cut didn't notice him. This guy was oblivious. He flipped car keys into the air and caught them. His casual manner indicated that he wasn't a decision-maker but somebody who obeyed orders. Rojas must have sent Buzz Cut to bring the car around to the front door.

Using implements from the tool belt, Jack armed himself. The claw hammer was in his right hand. A screwdriver in the left. Though Buzz Cut carried a gun in a shoulder holster, Jack's weapons were also lethal. Not many men survived a hammer blow to the skull. Not that he intended to kill this guy. Not unless he had to.

A memory flashed in his brain.

Keeping a half-block distance, he tailed the man with fiery red hair. The bastard walked with his chest out and his arms swinging as though he was king of the world.

Pure hatred churned in Jack's gut. In his pocket his hand held a serrated-edge switchblade, illegal in this state. With one quick slash, he could sever the redheaded man's carotid artery. Within four minutes, the man would bleed out.

There were too many witnesses on the street. The timing wasn't right. Revenge would have to wait.

Jack shook his head to erase the memory. The past would have to wait; he needed to be one hundred percent focused on the present.

From quick glances through the windows of the house, he had counted seven men, including Rojas and the big guy named Drew, who was nursing his injured leg. He couldn't tell if any of these men were the federal marshals, but he didn't think so.

Danny was slumped over in a chair with his wrists tied to the arms. The black hood that covered his head counted as a positive sign. Rojas was making sure that the deputy wouldn't see too much.

Jack figured that Rojas and his crew would leave soon so they could get to the meeting place first and set up an ambush. They wouldn't be expecting an attack here. Since there were seven plus Danny, they'd need two cars.

When Buzz Cut pointed the automatic lock opener at the black SUV, Jack decided to make his first move. He could eliminate Buzz Cut and take his weapon without anyone being the wiser. Stepping out of the shadows, he sprinted toward the SUV.

By the time Buzz Cut realized that he wasn't alone and turned around, Jack was on top of him, looking into his eyes, seeing his disbelief and surprise. With the hammer tilted sideways, he swung carefully. The glancing blow was enough to knock Buzz Cut unconscious but not hard enough to shatter his skull. He'd live.

Grabbing the gun from the holster, he hauled the young man into the shadows beside the horse barn and returned to the black SUV. Jack slid behind the wheel and drove to the front door, where he left the engine running while he slid out the passenger-side door and waited on the opposite side of the car.

Two other men lumbered from the house. Both were stocky and muscular. They were gorillas, not the kind of guys you'd want to meet in a dark alley. Walking toward the other car—a dark sedan—they argued.

One of them was limping. He grabbed the other man's wrist and growled, "Give me the keys. I'll drive."

"You're injured. You should sit back and shut up."

"Don't tell me what to do."

The uninjured man shook off the other's grasp and took a couple of quick steps away from him.

Jack hoped these two would drive away before Rojas emerged from the house with Danny. If they left, he had two fewer adversaries to worry about.

"Hey!" The man with the limp rushed forward. The

effort of ignoring his pain showed in his clenched jaw. "I'm driving. You'll get lost."

"How can I get lost? We're supposed to follow the SUV."

That wasn't what Jack wanted to hear. With these two armed men in the car behind the SUV, he couldn't pull Danny away from his captors without getting both of them shot.

The threat from these two had to be eliminated, but quietly. If Jack fired a gun, he'd alert Rojas to his presence. That wouldn't be good for Danny.

It took a minimum exertion of stealth to approach the twosome as they fought over the car keys. They were so engrossed in their petty griping that Jack could have announced himself with a coronet fanfare and they wouldn't have noticed.

He aimed for the uninjured man first. A quick blow from the hammer took him down.

The second man reacted. He went for his gun. *Dumb move.*

Jack didn't think he'd been trained in martial arts, but he had experience in street fighting. Striking fast was key. While the other man reached for his gun, closed his fingers around the grip and drew the weapon, Jack made a single move—a backhanded slash with the screwdriver. The edge tore a deep gash. The gorilla gasped, looked down at the blood oozing from his gut. Jack finished him off with a roundhouse right to the jaw.

In a matter of seconds, both men lay unconscious at his feet. Jack took the car keys they'd been arguing about and threw them into the weeds.

Three down, four to go. One of the remaining men was Drew Kelso, the guy who would be slowed down by his leg injury. Another was Rojas who probably wasn't accustomed to doing his own dirty work. That left two armed thugs.

Jack holstered his hammer and screwdriver in the tool belt. His work as Mister Fix-it was over. For this portion of the rescue, he needed firepower. He gripped one of the semiautomatic handguns and ran toward the SUV that still had the engine running.

He resumed his position at the front of the SUV and crouched between the headlights. The bad thing about street fighting was that you couldn't plan ahead. Winning the fight was all about instinct and reaction. His only goal was to get Danny away from here unharmed.

Looking up the road, he tried to see where Caitlyn had parked her car. The outline was barely visible through a stand of trees. It wasn't going to be easy to get Danny all the way up that driveway, but he didn't want Caitlyn to come closer. He wanted her to stay safe, untouched. When he was done here, he wanted to be able to look into her clear blue eyes and assure her that the world wasn't a terrible place. Sometimes, the good guys came out on top.

The last group appeared in the doorway of the safe house. One man escorted Danny, holding his arm and shoving him forward. The black hood still covered Danny's head, and his wrists were handcuffed in front of him. He stumbled, and his escort yanked him upright.

Kelso and Rojas had not yet appeared.

Another man went to open the back door of the SUV.

Jack made his move. Using the butt of the gun, he smacked the guy holding Danny on the head. The guy staggered a step forward, leaning against the car. His legs folded.

"Danny," Jack whispered, "I'm on your side. Don't resist."

With one hand he yanked the hood off the deputy's head. With the other he pulled him out of the line of fire.

The guy who had been opening the car door grabbed for his holster. He was out of reach; Jack had to shoot. At this point-blank range, he'd blow a hole six inches wide in the guy's gut.

Though the automatic handgun was unfamiliar, Jack aimed for the thug's weapon and squeezed off a single shot. The thug's gun went flying. He screamed in pain and clutched his hand to his chest. Then he took off running.

Rojas and Kelso came onto the porch. They looked surprised by the chaos in the yard. These men weren't accustomed to being hunted. They considered themselves to be the attackers, the predators at the top of the food chain. Not this time.

Rojas stared into his face. "You. Nick Racine."

The name stopped him short. Echoes of memory surged inside him. An angry voice, his father, yelled the name. A woman whispered it in soft, sultry tones. A teacher took roll call. *Racine, Racine, Racine.*

"No." That wasn't him. He unleashed a spray of bullets toward the porch. Too late.

His few seconds of hesitation cost him dearly. It had been just enough time for Kelso and Rojas to retreat into the house.

Though Jack cursed himself for his lapse, he wasn't entirely sure that he would have shot them. It was his duty to take them into custody. Death was too easy for these bastards; they deserved a life sentence in a small, gray cell. *His duty?* What the hell was he thinking?

He pulled Danny around to the opposite side of the car. If he could maneuver them into the vehicle, he might be able to drive away. As he reached for the door handle, a burst of gunfire exploded from inside the house. Bullets pinged against the black SUV. A window shattered. Using this vehicle wasn't a good option. It was directly in the line of fire. There had to be another way.

He looked at Danny. His face was battered and swollen. His eyes seemed unfocused. When he leaned against the car, he slid to the ground. His cuffed hands fell into his lap.

"Danny, can you hear me?"

He nodded slowly.

"Do you think you can run?"

He raised his hand to wipe the blood from his split lip. "I'll do whatever it takes."

His fighting spirit was admirable. But was he physically capable of moving fast? If Jack was alone, he could have easily escaped, but he couldn't make a dash across the open meadow while dragging an injured man. Peering around the front end of the car, he returned fire. Should have killed Rojas and Kelso when he had the chance. Shouldn't have held back.

He and Danny were trapped, pinned down.

He turned his head and saw Caitlyn's green SUV zooming down the driveway. She was driving in reverse, coming to their rescue.

For once in his life, he wasn't alone. He had Caitlyn for a partner, and she was one hell of a good woman.

Chapter Eleven

Driving backward down a long driveway wasn't easy. Caitlyn slipped off the asphalt and heard the slap of brush against the side of her SUV. Her tires skittered on the loose gravel at the edge of the drive.

The bursts of gunfire rattled inside her brain, but she didn't succumb to a paralyzed PTSD flashback. When she'd been standing at the barbed-wire fence and had seen Jack and Danny pinned down by gunfire, she knew she had to rescue them. Nothing else mattered.

Looking over her shoulder, she saw the headlights of the black SUV. There was plenty of time to hit her brakes, but she decided to use Ms. Peacock as a battering ram, putting the other vehicle out of commission.

Her rear end smacked the front grille of the black SUV with a satisfying crash that jolted her back against the seat. Good thing she'd buckled up. Bullets snapped against her car. The rear windows splintered. Ducking low in her seat, she should have been terrified, but her focus was on the rescue. *Please, God, let them get away unharmed. Don't let anything happen to...*

The back door to her SUV swung open. Danny crawled inside. He'd been beaten. His face was red as raw meat. She'd never been so glad to see him.

"Caitlyn, I didn't mean for you to come after me. When

I gave you the 'Red Fire' signal, I thought you'd call the sheriff and—"

"Shut up, Danny."

Looking over her shoulder, she saw Jack take aim and blast the tires of the black SUV before he dove in beside Danny. As soon as his door closed, she slipped into Drive and took off. At the turn to the main road, the tail end of her SUV fishtailed, but she maintained control. Ms. Peacock was doing a fine job. Caitlyn might have to change her name to something less ladylike and more daring. Maybe she should be the Green Hornet.

Jack reached between the seats and rested his hand on her shoulder. His fingers tightened in a gentle squeeze. "Thanks."

"You told me not to move, but when I saw you and Danny trapped, I had to help you."

"You did exactly the right thing, babe."

Usually when a man called her "babe" or "honey" or "sweetheart," she snapped at him. "Babe" sounded sexy when Jack said it. "Where are we going?"

From the backseat, Danny said, "Circle L. We were supposed to go there for dinner, Sandra and me. I've got to make sure she's okay. And Heather, too."

"It's going to be okay," Jack said calmly. "Let's see if we can get those cuffs off."

"Not important." Danny's voice was hoarse with urgency. "I have to see them. You don't understand."

"Sure, I do," Jack said. "Rojas threatened you. He told you that your wife and sister would be harmed if you didn't cooperate. Is that right?"

"Yes."

"I expect that he went into brutal details because that's the kind of man he is. Sadistic bastard." Though Jack kept his tone low and controlled, she heard the steely echo of his anger. "Those look like they might be your own cuffs. Got a key?"

"There's an extra key in my wallet. Back pocket."

Keeping her eyes on the road, Caitlyn said, "We can telephone Heather if you want."

"Good idea," Jack said. "We won't be bothered by Rojas for a little while. His big, black SUV isn't going anywhere. Why don't you pull over, Caitlyn. You can take care of Danny, and I'll drive."

She guided the car to a stop on the shoulder. When she turned in her seat, she saw that Jack had removed the tool belt and was unlocking Danny's cuffs. She took out her cell phone and hit the speed dial for the Circle L Ranch. Heather answered in a brisk, no-nonsense tone.

"It's Caitlyn. Are you all right?"

"Sure am."

"And Sandra? Is she there?"

"I'm fine. Sandra's fine. I picked up your tethered horses, and they're fine." Her voice dropped. "What's going on? What kind of trouble have you gotten yourself into?"

Caitlyn was satisfied. If Heather had been in danger, she would have found a way to tell her. "There's somebody here who wants to talk to you."

She passed the phone to Danny. His hand was shaking so much that he could barely hold it. "I love you, sis. I don't tell you enough. But I do." He gasped out a sob. "Put my wife on the phone."

Giving Danny some privacy, Caitlyn left the car and circled around to the back. She winced as she observed the amount of damage she'd done. One fender and the tail-light were smashed. The rear door to her SUV was beyond repair. Three windows were broken, and there were bullet holes along the driver's side. Explaining this incident to her insurance company wasn't going to be easy.

Jack stepped around the other side of the car and stood facing her. His hand slid down her arm in a caress, and he took the car keys from her. "If anything happens to me, there's something I want you to know."

"What do you mean?" As far as she was concerned, they were out of danger. Almost. "Nothing is going to happen to you."

His mouth curved in that teasing grin that made her want to kiss him. "Just in case."

"Damn it, Jack. Do you always have to look on the dark side?"

"Like I told you before, I always plan for the worst."

Reaching up, she stroked the rough stubble on his jaw. The light from the waning moon and the stars outlined the rugged planes of his face. "I couldn't tell exactly what you did at the safe house, but from what I saw, you were amazing. You caused enough concussions to keep a brain specialist busy for weeks."

"Assuming those guys had functional brains."

One thing she had observed didn't make sense. "It looked like you had the drop on Rojas. But you didn't shoot."

"Not my job," he said.

As far as she knew, he'd been an enforcer for the Santoro family. In that line of work, she was fairly sure that his duties included murder. When she thought about it, she realized that Jack hadn't killed anyone. Not at the safe house. Not at her cabin. "I'd like to know more about this job of yours."

"So would I." He tapped the side of his head. "Amnesia."

"Convenient."

"Not really."

His large hand slipped around her neck, and he pulled her closer. His lips were warm against hers. As she leaned toward him, the tips of her breasts grazed his chest. A shiver of awareness washed through her, leaving a tingling sensation.

When they kissed, she was hungry for more. Especially now. She knew her time with Jack was limited. Her torso pressed firmly against him. Her arms encircled him.

"Caitlyn," Danny bellowed from inside the car.

She tore herself away from Jack's embrace. As guilty as a teenager caught in the act, she put a polite distance between them. "I guess we have places to go."

"Here's what I want you to know," he said. "You're going to be all right."

Why was he telling her this? She cocked her head to one side. "Explain."

"You have doubts about yourself and your career. That's why you're living in the mountains like a hermit."

Though his characterization irked her, she didn't deny it. "Go on."

"You're scared. But you don't have to be. You're tough, Caitlyn. You're strong enough to take whatever life throws at you. If we had more time together, I'd—"

"Caitlyn," Danny called again. "We need to get going."

Jack shrugged. "I believe in you. Whatever happens, you're going to be fine."

As he walked past her on his way to the driver's seat, he patted her butt. Again, this wasn't a gesture she would usually accept without complaint, but she said nothing.

His reassurance was shockingly perceptive. It didn't seem fair that a man who was so good-looking and capable would also be wise.

In spite of the time she'd spent alone—time that was supposed to be for reflection and renewal—she hadn't made the connection between her PTSD fear and her doubts about her career. She'd been afraid of just about everything. Until now.

When she'd realized that Jack and Danny needed her, she'd been able to overcome her fear and do what had to be done. *I'm going to be all right.*

She was damaged but not broken. Her life would mend. All the energy she'd poured into fixing up the cabin could be turned into something she was actually good at.

In her heart, she'd always known what she was meant to do. She was a journalist, a seeker of truth. Losing her assignment in the Middle East didn't negate her skill or her talent. There were plenty of other stories to write…starting with Jack. He had a story she was itching to write.

As she settled into the backseat next to Danny, she asked Jack, "Do you need directions to the Circle L?"

"I remember the way."

Of course he would. He did everything well. When she turned her attention to Danny, her mood darkened. She was accustomed to seeing her old friend as a cool, confident leader—the most popular guy in the county, the local hero. Being held hostage had devastated him, and she feared that these wounds went deeper than the bruises on his face. His shoulders slumped. His uniform was stained with blood, torn and disheveled. The acrid smell of sweat clung to him.

Gently, she took his hand. Instead of offering false reassurances, she said the only positive thing she could think of. "We're almost at the Circle L. You'll be with your wife soon."

"I called the sheriff," he said. "He'll arrange for body-guards for Sandra and Heather until that sick bastard is in custody."

From the front seat, Jack said, "Arresting Rojas will be dangerous."

"You don't have to tell me." With an effort, Danny lifted his head and looked toward the front seat. "You're the man they're looking for, aren't you? The witness."

"That's right," Caitlyn informed him. "He's also the guy who saved your butt."

"And I thank you for that," Danny said. "I didn't think I'd get away in one piece. Thought I was a dead man."

She didn't like seeing him this way. She missed his natural arrogance. "I wish there was something I could do for you. I don't have any first-aid stuff in the car."

"It's all right." He exhaled slowly and spoke to the back of Jack's head. "You did a good job negotiating. I only heard one side, but you convinced them to do what you wanted."

"I had an advantage," Jack said. "I knew Rojas would lie. He'd try to set up a meet where he could get there first and set up an ambush. I just had to stall him long enough so that I could beat him to the punch."

"What's your name?" Danny asked.

Caitlyn answered, "You can call him Jack."

"As in Jack Dalton?" Danny turned toward her. "I thought we established that Jack Dalton was in jail sleeping off a drunk and disorderly."

There was no simple way to explain how she'd gotten involved with Jack and how he had amnesia. "Just call him Jack for now."

Danny sank back against the seat and closed his eyes. His lips barely moved as he spoke. "You were always good at getting yourself into trouble, Caitlyn. Remember? And you thought you were so smart. A regular Little Miss Know-It-All."

"I don't just think I'm smart," she said. "I really am."

"Not always."

He seemed to be implying that she'd made a mistake. "Is there something you need to tell me?"

He spoke in a barely audible whisper. "How well do you know Jack?"

"Well enough to trust him with my life. Why do you ask?"

"There were eight men at the house, not including me. One of them was a federal marshal. He was dead." Danny looked down at his hands. "I knew he was a lawman because they pinned his badge to his forehead. He was... mutilated."

She glanced toward the front seat. Jack had worried about the whereabouts of the third marshal. Apparently, he wasn't in on the scheme with Rojas and the other two. And he had paid the ultimate price. "I'm sorry."

"How about you, Jack?" Danny's tone turned hostile. "Are you sorry about the marshal's death?"

"Stop it, Danny." What was wrong with him? She reached forward and tapped Jack on the shoulder. "We're here. This is the turn for the Circle L."

He drove through the open gate toward a well-lit, two-story ranch house that was painted white with slate-gray trim. A tall, thick cottonwood tree stood as high as the roof. Though there were no children at the Circle L, a tire swing hung from one of the branches.

The ranch looked like a peaceful sanctuary, but Caitlyn had the sense that something wasn't right. "Danny, what's going on?"

"There are my girls." The hint of a smile touched his lips as he gazed toward the wraparound porch where Heather stood with her arms braced against the railing. Beside her was a delicate-looking blonde who had to be Sandra. "They're safe. That's all that matters."

Jack pulled up close to the porch and parked. As soon

as he turned off the engine, two men emerged from the shadows. They moved quickly and with purpose, flanking the vehicle. The one who stood at the driver's side window pointed a rifle at Jack's head.

"U.S. marshal," he said with an unmistakably Texan twang. "I'm taking you into custody."

Chapter Twelve

If the marshals got their way, Jack would be cuffed and carted off, never to be seen again. Caitlyn refused to let that happen.

Her experience as a reporter in the world's hot spots had taught her to talk her way around just about anything. She'd been the first journalist to wrangle an interview with an aging Afghani warlord who fought with the mujahideen. She'd interviewed politicians and generals, even faced a serial killer on death row. Argument was her battlefield. Words were her weapons.

She bolted from the car and launched her verbal attack at the two marshals. Though she spoke with authority, she wasn't sure exactly what she'd said—something along the lines of legal and jurisdictional issues. "Danny was first deputy on the scene, which means he has custody. The Douglas County sheriff is responsible for this man."

Still holding his rifle on Jack, the Texan drawled, "What in hell are you yapping about?"

"He's ours," she said.

Brandishing the handcuffs she'd removed from Danny's wrists only moments ago, she opened the driver-side door and leaned inside. She whispered, "Let me handle this."

Staring straight ahead, Jack sat with both hands gripping the steering wheel. He turned his head and met her gaze. A bond of trust stretched between them. He believed in her; he'd told her so. It was time for her to justify his confidence.

As she snapped a cuff on his right wrist, he muttered under his breath, "You'd better be right about this."

"You should know by now. I'm almost always right."

"Little Miss Know-It-All."

When he stepped out of the car, she fastened the other cuff. Though she considered pressing the key into his palm so he could escape, she decided against it. Jack unchained was a force of nature, and she preferred a little finesse. The fewer bodies he left in his wake, the better.

Whirling, she faced the marshal from Texas. "Lower your weapon."

Danny—the big, fat traitor—was out of the car and appeared to be gathering his strength to object, but his wife, Heather and a couple of ranch hands swarmed around him, determined to help him whether or not he wanted to be helped.

One of the ranch hands bumped the rifle, and Heather snapped at the marshal, "You heard Caitlyn. Put down your weapon before you accidentally shoot yourself in the foot."

The Texan scowled but did as she said. His partner stalked around to their side of the car and spoke up. "Thanks for your help, folks. We've got it. This man is in our custody."

"Where's your warrant?" Caitlyn demanded.

"Don't need one." The gray-haired marshal produced his wallet and showed her his five-point star badge and his marshal credentials.

Caitlyn inspected his documents. "You're Marshal Steven Patterson."

"Correct." His jaw was speckled with bristly white

stubble, and his gray eyes were red-rimmed with exhaustion. "I'd appreciate if you'd step aside and let us do our job."

"Is this man a criminal?"

"No."

"Then why are you taking him?"

"He's a witness," Patterson said.

"A protected witness?"

"Correct."

"Pointing a rifle in his face doesn't seem like the best way to keep your witness safe," she said. "Maybe he doesn't want your so-called protection."

"He's in our custody. That's all you need to know."

Caitlyn nudged Heather's arm. "Does that sound right to you?"

Heather drew herself up to her full height. In her boots, she was nearly as tall as Jack, and she towered over Patterson. She hooked her thumb in her belt, right next to her revolver.

Caitlyn noticed that all the ranch hands were armed; they must have heard that there was danger, and they all watched Heather for their cues. She said, "Nobody does anything until my brother is taken care of. Sandra, you get Danny inside and call the doc."

Danny's petite blonde wife didn't need instruction; she was focused one hundred percent on her husband. Her devotion touched Caitlyn, and she would have been happy that Danny had found the perfect mate if she hadn't wanted to kill him for leading them into this trap.

Patterson spoke to Heather, "Looks like you have everything under control, ma'am. We'll be going now."

"Hold on," she said. "The Circle L is *my* ranch. *My* property. We do things *my* way. On *my* schedule."

"What are you saying?"

"I want you to answer Caitlyn's questions," Heather said.

"I don't answer to you." Patterson's polite veneer was worn thin. "I'm a federal officer, and your ranch isn't some kind of sovereign nation."

He couldn't have picked a worse argument, and Caitlyn was glad to see him digging his own grave. In this part of the world, respect for ownership of the land was as deeply engrained as the brands on the cattle. "Marshal Patterson, I can tell that you haven't spent much time in the West." To his partner, she said, "Explain it to him, Tex. Tell him how we feel about our land."

"The name's Bryant," said the younger marshal. "And I promise you, Miss Heather, we ain't here to cause trouble."

"I'll be the judge of that." Heather watched Sandra and the ranch hands escort her brother into the house, then she swung back toward Caitlyn. "What were you saying?"

"According to Marshal Patterson, he can take a witness into custody whether he wants to be protected or not. Now, that doesn't seem fair, especially since Patterson is a U.S. Marshal. The *U* and the *S* stand for *us,* as in you and me. He works for us. And I'm pretty sure I wouldn't want to be dragged off without my permission."

"She's got a point," Heather said.

"And I've got a job," Patterson said.

Caitlyn pulled out her cell phone. "Before you proceed, I need to make sure I have the facts right. I want to verify with the director of the Marshals Service or the attorney general."

"You can't."

"Oh, I think I can. I'm a journalist for a national news service." A little white lie since she wasn't actually employed at the moment. Using her cell, she snapped a photo of Patterson and his partner. "As a reporter, it's my job to raise holy hell if this situation isn't handled properly. Will you call the director? Or should I?"

Bryant asked his partner, "Can she do that?"

"Damn right I can."

Jack spoke up. "I'd advise you to listen to her."

"Why's that?"

"She might look like a Barbie doll, but this woman is G.I. Jane. She was embedded with the troops. Just came back from a war zone."

Patterson regarded her with a little more respect and a lot more loathing. "Is that so?"

"She knows people," Jack said. "Important people. The kind of people who could end the careers of a couple of marshals who screwed up."

"Bad luck for you," she said to Patterson. "I'm guessing that you're close to retirement. It would be a shame to lose your pension."

Two police vehicles careened down the driveway and parked, effectively blocking the exit. Four deputies rushed toward them, firing questions about what had happened to Danny and who was responsible. The confusion rose to the edge of chaos.

"Enough," Patterson said loudly. "All of you. Back off."

Frustration turned his complexion an unhealthy shade of brick red. He grasped Jack's upper arm—a move that Caitlyn saw as a huge mistake. The muscles in Jack's shoulders bunched as though he was preparing to throw off Patterson's hand. Even unarmed and in cuffs, he was capable of annihilating the two marshals. He might even be able to defeat the deputies, grab a vehicle and run.

But she didn't like the odds. There were too many guns. Too many nervous trigger fingers.

"Marshal Patterson," she said, "I have a suggestion."

He was desperate enough to listen. "Go on."

"You and your partner could step into the house. I'm sure Heather would let you use her office. And you could contact your superior officer for further instructions. When you produce verification that you have jurisdictional custody of this witness, we'll all be satisfied."

"Fine," he said, "but we're taking this man with us into the den while we make our phone calls."

It wasn't exactly the outcome Caitlyn had hoped for. The marshals weren't going to give up easily, and she'd have to come up with another ruse to get Jack away from them. But she'd bought some time. And nobody had gotten killed.

EVER SINCE DANNY MENTIONED the marshal who had been murdered and mutilated, Jack had been remembering details of what had happened to him at the safe house when Rojas came after him. How many times had he asked himself about the third marshal? At a deep, subconscious level, he had sensed the importance of the third man.

His name, Jack clearly remembered, was Hank Perry. His age, forty-two. He stood five feet ten inches. Brown hair and eyes. He was divorced, and his oldest son had just graduated from high school.

Hank Perry was dead. He'd given his life to protect Jack. Somehow, Jack would make sure that Perry's ultimate sacrifice would not be in vain. Somehow, he had to escape and make it back to Chicago for the trial.

Sitting on the floor in the den, he rested his back against a wall of bookshelves with his cuffed wrists in his lap. No doubt the two marshals in the room with him would have liked to hogtie him and pull a hood over his head, but they had to treat him humanely or Caitlyn would raise a stink.

Though he kept his face expressionless, Jack smiled inside when he thought of how she'd leapt to his defense. In spite of her dirty clothes and tangled blond hair, she'd transformed into a person of stature. With gravitas equal to Lady Justice herself, Caitlyn had created a wall of obstacles. Using wild-eyed logic and aggressive questions, she'd backed the marshals into a corner.

With grim satisfaction, he was glad that he'd taken a moment before they got to the ranch to tell her how he felt about her. Life experience had shaken her determination, but she'd made a full recovery. They made a good team. With her mouth and his muscle, they could have done great things together.

He looked over at Patterson, who slouched in the swivel chair behind the desk. He'd been on his cell phone for the past fifteen minutes. His side of the conversation was a lame explanation of how he and Bryant had been attacked, lost their witness and had their colleague murdered by Rojas.

Patterson admitted, over and over, that they'd made a mistake in not calling for backup. His excuse was that he feared a showdown with Rojas would give the cartel gang a reason to commit wholesale murder in this peaceful Colorado mountain community.

While he talked on his phone, Patterson juggled the SIG Sauer P-226 that he'd confiscated along with all the other weapons Jack had taken from Rojas. The SIG had belonged to Perry. Watching Patterson play with that honorable man's gun made Jack's blood boil.

The tall Texan marshal with the hundred-mile stare sauntered across the den and stood in front of Jack. With the toe of his cowboy boot, he nudged Jack's foot. "You're kind of quiet."

Brilliant observation, genius. Since they'd entered the den, Jack hadn't said a word. He'd been too consumed with memories of the midnight assault on the safe house. His mind echoed with the blast of semiautomatic gunfire and Perry's shout of warning. In the dark, he hadn't been able to identify the men who came after them. And he couldn't exactly recall how he'd gotten his head wound. But he'd seen Perry take a bullet and stagger back to his feet. With his last breath, he'd fought.

All of Patterson's talk about "doing his job" turned Jack's stomach. Patterson didn't have a clue about the real responsibility of being a U.S. marshal. He was a coward. A traitor.

Bryant squatted down to Jack's level. "We didn't get much chance to talk when you were at the safe house. I'm low man on the totem pole, so my assignment was to patrol outdoors."

Except for when Rojas showed up. Jack didn't remember seeing Patterson or Bryant during the attack. Their plan had probably been to leave him alone and unguarded.

Bryant continued, "Is all the stuff they say about you true? About the legendary Nick Racine?"

There was that name again. Racine, Nick Racine. Rojas had shouted it out, distracting him. If that was his real name, he ought to remember, but he couldn't make the connection. "What have you heard?"

"That you killed twelve men using nothing more than your belt buckle and your bare hands."

Though Jack was sure that hadn't happened, he nodded. If he impressed Bryant, he might convince the young man to take his side against Patterson. "What else?"

"You survived for a month in the desert with no food or water."

That was legendary, all right. "I had a good teacher, a wise old man who lived in Arizona. I owe it to him to pass on this knowledge. You could learn."

"Me?" Bryant shook his head. "I've never exactly been at the top of the class."

"It's not book learning. It's instinct."

"I got instincts." His brow lowered as he concentrated. "Seems like a damn shame to kill you, but we can't have you telling the truth to the Marshals Service."

In a low voice, Jack said, "It wasn't your fault. You were just following orders. It was Patterson who told Rojas the location of the safe house, wasn't it?"

"That's right. The old man arranged for the money, told me all we had to do was leave the house for an hour. Rojas was supposed to swoop in, grab you and take off. Slick and easy."

"Except for Perry," Jack said.

"Oh man, that was a big mistake. Rojas promised that Perry wasn't going to get hurt."

Yeah, sure, and then the Easter Bunny would leave them all pretty-colored eggs. Bryant was young, but he wasn't naive enough to trust a man like Rojas. At some point, the marshal had made a deliberate decision to turn his head and look the other way. "What was supposed to happen to me?"

"Guess I didn't think that far ahead."

Thinking wasn't Bryant's strong suit. "You can make up for your mistake. I'll take care of it."

"You're trying to trick me. That's part of the legend, too. You can change your identity like a shape-shifter."

"I'm not lying."

"I still don't believe you. The way Patterson tells it,

you've gone rogue. You know what that means? Being a rogue?"

Jack said nothing. The question was too ridiculous to answer. Though Bryant was a moron, he knew enough to follow orders from Patterson. A dangerous combination—stupidity and loyalty.

"One time," Bryant said, "I saw a television show about rogue elephants in Africa. My gal likes to watch that educational stuff. Anyway, there was this big, old elephant with giant tusks. We got a forty-six-inch flatscreen, and I'm telling you, that elephant was big. You might even say he was legendary. Like you."

"I'm an elephant?"

"A rogue," Bryant said. "The safari guy said the only way to handle a rogue was to kill him before he killed you."

I'm a dead man.

Chapter Thirteen

In the front room of the ranch house, Caitlyn positioned herself so she could keep an eye on the closed door to the den. Her mind raced as she tried to come up with a plan. Though she wanted to believe that the marshals wouldn't dare hurt Jack while he was in their custody, she knew better. They couldn't let him live. He had witnessed their treachery.

She could insist on accompanying them while they took Jack, but that might mean they'd kill her, too.

Looking down at the cell phone in her hand, she willed it to ring. She'd left a message for her former lover in Chicago, but she hadn't talked to him in years and didn't know if he was still employed at the newspaper. Her stateside contacts had dried up after she'd been stationed in the Middle East for so long. The only highly placed individuals she could call for a favor were in the military, and they couldn't help with this problem. If Patterson got the go-ahead from his superior officer, there wasn't much she could do to stop him from taking Jack.

When Heather handed her a steaming mug of coffee, Caitlyn grinned at her friend and said, "Thanks for taking my side."

"I didn't like those marshals when they showed up here and said they were supposed to protect us. Everybody who works at the Circle L has at least one gun. We take care of ourselves."

Considering the viciousness of Rojas and his men, Caitlyn was glad it hadn't come to a showdown. "Your instincts are right about the marshals. They're working with the bad guys."

"Fill me in."

Caitlyn glanced around at the other people in the room—ranch hands and a couple of deputies who were making phone calls. Since she didn't want to broadcast her story, she spoke in a quiet tone. "Jack is a federal witness who's supposed to testify on Tuesday in Chicago. He was in protective custody at a safe house that was attacked last night. He escaped, riding the gray mare that showed up on my doorstep. Here's the important thing, those marshals were supposed to be guarding him, but they stepped aside and let the bad guys go after him."

"Not all of them." Danny limped into the room, leaning on his pretty little wife for support. "One of the marshals died a heroic death in the line of duty."

Though he'd changed into a fresh shirt and his face was cleaned up, he still looked like hell. Caitlyn didn't feel sorry for him; Danny had betrayed them. "You knew the marshals were waiting here for Jack."

"They came here to protect my family."

"How did they know?" she demanded. "If they weren't working with Rojas, how did they know your family was in danger?"

"They were keeping an eye on the safe house," Danny said, defending them. "They must have seen what happened to me."

"And yet, they did nothing to rescue you. They didn't contact the sheriff, didn't call for backup. What kind of lawmen operate like that?"

"If they'd called for an assault on the safe house, I'd be dead right now."

His wife shuddered. "Don't say that."

"I'm okay, Sandra." He patted her arm. "There's nothing to worry about."

"You should be resting until the doc gets here. Let me take you upstairs to bed."

"Not until this is settled."

Her lips pulled into a tight, disapproving line, but she said nothing else. Caitlyn sympathized with her dilemma. It wasn't easy to love a stubborn man who wouldn't let anyone fight his battles for him. A man like Jack? Though she couldn't compare her relationship with Jack to a marriage or even to being in love, she cared about him. How could she not care? He'd saved her life. She thought of how he'd rescued her when she froze and his quiet heroics when at the safe house. He was a one-man strike force. But that wasn't why she cared so much. He'd seen inside her. He brought out the best in her. And, oh my, the man knew how to kiss.

She glared at Danny. "You don't know the whole story, but I'm not saying another word until you sit down. You look like you're about to collapse."

"She's right." Sandra gave her a grateful nod. "Let's all get settled and figure this out."

While Sandra made her husband comfortable in a leather armchair near the fireplace, Caitlyn perched on the edge of a rocking chair beside him. In as calm a tone as she could manage, she said, "You've got to admit that the actions of those two marshals were questionable. They had a whole day to track down Rojas and his men. What the hell were they doing?"

"Their job," Danny said. "They were tracking down their runaway witness."

At the cave, they'd come close. "They almost found us."

"Hold on." Heather held up her hand, signaling a halt. "It sounds like you and Jack were hiding from the marshals. Why would you do that?"

"We were on the run." When Caitlyn thought back, the afternoon seemed like a lifetime ago. "Rojas and his men showed up at my cabin. Because the gray horse came to my place, they must have figured that Jack had also been there. When they showed up, I was in the barn. They had guns. They were yelling. I've never been so scared in my life."

A residual wave of fear washed through her as she remembered turning to stone. "Jack had been watching my house. He rescued me. We took off on horseback."

"It's a damn good thing he was there," Heather said, "or else you'd be as beat up as my brother."

"We were hiding in that cavern that's not far from my cabin—the one with the water that runs all the way through it. Those two marshals nearly found us. I didn't see them, but I recognized the Texas accent."

"What did they say?" Heather asked.

She was tempted to lie and tell them that the marshals talked about murdering her and Jack, but she needed to stay on the high road. "Nothing incriminating."

"You should have spoken up," Danny said. "If you'd turned Jack in, this whole thing would have been over."

"Why are you so dead set against him?" Her anger flared. "He's a good man."

"He's a witness in a mob crime, probably a criminal himself who agreed to testify in exchange for immunity. I said it before, Caitlyn, and I'll say it again. You don't know anything about this guy."

Unable to sit still, she rose from the rocking chair so

quickly that it almost overturned. "I haven't finished telling what happened. If you don't mind, I'd like to continue."

"Go right ahead."

"While Jack and I were hiding, we got a message from Danny that told us he'd been captured by Rojas and was being held at the safe house. Jack didn't hesitate. Not for one minute. He knew he had to get Danny out of there."

Sandra's eyes widened. "Jack saved Danny?"

"If it weren't for Jack, you'd be a dead man. Right, Danny?"

He nodded slowly. "Right."

"I don't understand," Sandra said. "This man risked his life for you, and you're willing to sit back and watch while he gets dragged off in handcuffs."

"You're not seeing the big picture," he said.

"What's bigger than saving your life? Oh, Danny, you're not thinking straight."

He shifted in the big leather chair. "As far as I'm concerned, Jack could be working with Rojas. He might be responsible for the death of that marshal."

Caitlyn scoffed. "That's crazy."

"Yeah? Well, explain this for me. Jack had the drop on Rojas and that other guy. He could have pulled the trigger and taken them out. Why didn't he shoot?"

She didn't have a logical response. "I don't know."

"Because he's part of this scheme," Danny said. "He let Rojas get away. On purpose."

"Or maybe Jack isn't a murderer. Maybe he didn't want to shoot a man in the back."

"I'm sure he's got a smooth-talking answer," Danny said. "He's slick enough to convince you that he's some kind of hero, but I don't believe him. I'll take the word of a federal marshal over that of a criminal turned witness."

"Even when he saved you," Heather said, as she rose

from her chair and stood beside Caitlyn. "I hate to say this because you're my brother, but Danny, you're a jerk. And just about as perceptive as a fence post."

He frowned and looked toward his wife.

Sandra arched an eyebrow. "I'm with Heather on this. Caitlyn, what do you need?"

She was glad for these two votes of confidence. Before this was over, she'd need all the allies she could get. "I don't object to Jack being taken into protective custody. He wants to testify and break up the Rojas cartel. It's important to him. But I don't want those two marshals to be alone with him. They can't be trusted."

The front door swung open and Bob Woodley marched inside. He wasn't even pretending to be a docile, law-abiding citizen. In his right hand, he held his hunting rifle. In spite of his age, he emanated vitality and energy. His clothes were as disheveled as if he'd just gotten out of bed. His thick, white hair looked like he'd combed it with an eggbeater. As soon as he spotted Caitlyn, he charged toward her and pulled her into a bone-crunching hug.

"I'm sorry," he said. "I brought those bastards to your house. I put you in danger."

"You didn't know," she said.

"If anything had happened to you, I'd never forgive myself. Your mother would never forgive me."

"I'm fine." She separated from his ferocious hug and smiled up at him. "How did you hear about what happened?"

"Being an elected official, I have an inside track. Half the lawmen in Colorado—state patrol, SWAT teams, cops and deputies—are involved in a manhunt, looking for Rojas. I assume he's the fellow who told me his name was Reynolds."

"He lied to you, lied to everybody."

Danny struggled to get out of his chair. "Everybody else is mobilized. I should—"

"Sit down," Sandra said. "You've done enough."

Woodley took a look at him. "What the hell happened to your face?"

"Long story," he said. "Tell me what else is going on."

"I don't know much. As soon as I heard Caitlyn was in trouble, I jumped in my Ford Fairlane and raced over here." He turned back to her. "You're not hurt, are you?"

"I'm worried. Something terrible is about to happen, and I can't stop it."

Woodley drew himself up. "Tell me how I can help."

"That goes for me, too," Heather said. "I don't want to see the man who saved my brother's life get into any more trouble."

"All of you," Danny said, "stop it. You need to back off and let the marshals do their job. That's the law."

Caitlyn confronted him. "Sometimes, the law isn't right. Jack saved you. The marshals were willing to let you die."

"But I'm an officer of the law."

"That means you're sworn to enforce justice," she said, "even if it means stepping outside the law."

He winced. The bruises on his face were a crude reminder of what he'd suffered at the hands of Rojas. His gaze rested on his sister, then on his wife. "I wanted to keep you both safe."

"I know," Sandra said. She rested her small hand gently on his cheek. "Now, we have to do the right thing."

When they looked to her for direction, Caitlyn felt warm inside. Her heart expanded. These people were her friends, as loyal to her as the troops in combat.

The beginnings of a plan tickled the inside of her head. "There might be something we can do."

NEGOTIATING WITH BRYANT or Patterson was futile. Jack's only option was to fight. He had the vague outline of a plan. He'd wait until they left the Circle L Ranch; no point in having anyone else hurt in the crossfire. He'd go after Bryant first. Though the younger marshal wasn't quick-witted, his reflexes were good. Then he'd take out Patterson. Vague, extremely vague. This version of planning fell mostly into the category of wishful thinking.

Though Jack could hear people coming and going outside the door to the den, this room was quiet, except for Bryant's tuneless humming of a country-western song and Patterson's urgent phone conversations.

The old man was kidding himself if he thought he'd get out of this mess with his job intact. Another marshal had been brutally murdered, and that kind of error wouldn't be excused with a slap on the wrist. Jack wondered how much Rojas had paid for their treachery; he hoped it wasn't nearly enough to make up for their lost pensions.

Wearily, Patterson stood behind the desk. In the past half hour, he'd aged ten years. His jowls sagged and his eyes sunk deep in their sockets. He concluded his conversation with a crisp "Yes, sir." When he turned toward Bryant, a cold smile twisted his thin, bloodless lips. "They bought it."

Eager as a puppy, Bryant bounded toward the desk. "Are you telling me that we ain't going to get blamed for Perry being killed?"

"We'll be fine," Patterson said, "as long as you stick to the story. All you have to say is that we were asleep at the safe house, and Perry was on watch. Rojas killed him and went after Jack. Before we had time to react, it was over."

"Got it." Bryant nodded, easily satisfied. "What do we do right now?"

"We have our orders." He held his cell phone so Jack could see. "I've got a couple of emailed verifications from on high. That ought to keep your girlfriend happy."

"She's not my girlfriend," Jack said. No way did he want any repercussions to bounce back on Caitlyn. "She's just a woman who happened to be in the wrong place at the wrong time."

"But she's a reporter, and that means trouble. Not that she'll get any answers after we're gone. Everything about this case is going to turn top secret."

Jack thought he was seriously underestimating Caitlyn's abilities but said nothing. He wanted Patterson to think he was getting away clean.

Bryant asked, "What are our orders?"

"We go to a private airfield not far from here. A chopper picks us up and flies us to Colorado Springs. From there, we get a flight to Chicago."

Jack didn't like the sound of these orders. A short drive didn't give him much time to act. "How do you rate a private chopper?"

"Since Rojas is still on the loose, our situation is considered eminently dangerous." There was a flash of anger in his dulled eyes. "But you won't be riding on that chopper. Rojas is my excuse for you to be dead before we even get to the airfield."

There was a knock on the door. Danny stepped inside. Though he moved stiffly, he looked like he was well on the way to recovery. "Marshal Patterson, we have a problem."

"Now what?"

"There's an FBI agent on his way to talk to you."

"FBI," Bryant yelped.

"Our local congressman, Bob Woodley, showed up, and he's pretty peeved. He called an FBI agent he's worked with. I'm afraid if you don't humor Woodley, he'll be on the phone to the governor."

"Let him." Patterson waved his cell phone. "I have authorization to take this man into custody."

"Great," Danny said. "All you need to do is talk to Woodley. It'll only take a minute. He wants to see both of you. I'll keep an eye on your witness."

As soon as Patterson and Bryant left the room, Danny went to the window and yanked it open. "Get the hell out of here."

"Why are you doing this?" Jack asked.

"Let's just say this makes us even."

He didn't waste another second wondering why Danny had a change of heart. Jack knew the answer. Caitlyn.

Chapter Fourteen

Caitlyn was impressed with Jack's agility as he slipped through the den window into the shrubs at the side of the house. His cuffed wrists didn't hamper his movements in the least.

Without speaking, she motioned to him. As soon as he reached her side, she whispered, "Duck down and stay low. We're going to weave through these cars."

He glanced over his shoulder. "I'd rather run for open terrain. I can make it to the barn."

"No time to explain. We do it my way."

She'd already arranged with Heather to lay down a couple of false trails. Moments ago, Heather had instructed two of the ranch hands to saddle up and ride to the far pasture to check on the couple hundred head of cattle grazing in that area. Another guy was driving one of the four-wheelers toward the south end of the ranch. Caitlyn figured the marshals would be distracted by those tracks while she and Jack got away.

He followed as she crept around the eight or nine vehicles that were parked helter-skelter at the front door of the Circle L ranch house. She moved stealthily, being careful not to attract attention from the ranch hands who had gathered near the barn or the two deputies on the porch. Though she couldn't make out the words in specific conversations, she heard tension in their voices. By now, everyone was aware of the threat from Rojas.

When she got to Woodley's huge, finned, turquoise-and-cream-colored 1957 Ford Fairlane, she unlocked the trunk and pointed to the inside.

He shot her a look that was half anger and half disbelief. Then he glanced around. With all these people, he couldn't run without being seen. Grumbling, he climbed inside.

She joined him and pulled the trunk closed. The dark covered them as tightly as shrink wrap. The air smelled of gas, grease and grit. Even though this space was big for a car trunk, they were jammed together. Her legs twined with his. She couldn't find a good place to put her arms without embracing him.

"The cuffs," he said.

She dug in her jeans pocket for the key. After a bit of clumsy groping, she used the flashlight function on her cell phone so she could see well enough to unlock the cuffs.

As soon as he was free, he caught hold of her hand and turned the cell phone light so he could see her. "You combed your hair," he said, "and changed your clothes."

"Thanks for noticing."

"You look nice in blue," he whispered.

"What is this? A first date?"

Before he turned the light off, she caught a glimpse of his sexy grin. Being this close to Jack was already having a sensual effect on her. She tucked her arms over her breasts so she wouldn't be rubbing against his chest.

His upper arm draped around her with his hand resting on the small of her back. He asked, "How is Danny going to explain my escape?"

"By the time the marshals get back to the den, Danny will be upstairs in bed with his wife standing guard over him. None of the local guys are going to give him a hard time. They all think he's a hero."

Keeping her voice low, she told him about the decoy trails they'd set out for the marshals to follow. "Assuming that they're able to track in the dark. Patterson doesn't strike me as somebody who knows his way around the outdoors, but I'll bet the Texan has done his share of hunting."

"That's possible," Jack said. "There has to be something Bryant is good at."

The voices from the ranch house took on a note of urgency. There were sounds of footsteps hustling and doors being slammed. She guessed that the marshals had discovered Jack's escape. The arm he'd wrapped around her tightened protectively. She knew that they needed to be silent.

With her eyes closed, she pressed her face into the crook of his neck. His musky scent teased her nostrils. After a day on the run, he definitely didn't smell like cologne. But she didn't mind the earthy odor; it was masculine and somehow attractive. Heat radiated from his pores. His chest rose and fell as he breathed, and even that action was sexy. If she relaxed and allowed her body to melt into his, she knew she'd be overwhelmed.

Mentally, she distanced herself from him. More than once, she'd asked herself why she was so invested in Jack's rescue. The big reason was utterly apparent. He was a good man, trying to do the right thing, and he didn't deserve to be threatened, especially not by the men who were assigned to protect him. She had to fight for Jack because it was the right thing to do. Her motivations were based on truth, justice and the American way.

And it didn't hurt that he was hot. Being close to him set off a fiery chemistry that was anything but high-minded.

She didn't want to lose him, didn't want this feeling of passion to dissipate into nothingness.

Trying to get comfortable, she wriggled her legs, and he reacted with a twitch. They needed to be careful. If the Ford Fairlane started bouncing, they'd be found for sure.

The voices came closer. She thought she heard Patterson shouting angry orders. Car doors creaked open and slammed shut, but she didn't hear anyone driving away. Were they searching the cars? Someone bumped into the fender of the Fairlane, and she caught her breath to keep from making noise.

Until now, she'd been too busy planning and thinking to acknowledge the undercurrent of fear that started earlier today. If they were found, the consequences would be disastrous. She never should have gotten all these other people involved. Danny could lose his job for helping Jack escape. There might be legal charges against Heather and Woodley. As for Jack? If the marshals took him, they'd kill him. She trembled. *What have I done?*

Jack whispered in her ear, "Scared?"

Though he couldn't see her in the dark, she nodded.

"Think of something else," he said. "Something good."

That was a childish solution, like whistling in a graveyard to show the ghosts you weren't afraid. Tension squeezed her lungs. She felt a scream rising in the back of her throat.

"You have some good memories." His voice was one step up from silence. "Think of your childhood."

She remembered a summer afternoon. She was sixteen and had just gotten her driver's license. Her mom asked her to deliver a basket of muffins to Mr. Woodley's house.

Determined not to have an accident, she drove very carefully past the Circle L and went to Mr. Woodley's house. He sat on a rocker on the front porch, waiting for her. Most of her parents' friends ignored her or regarded

*her with the sort of suspicion and disdain adults reserved
for teenagers. Mr. Woodley was different—a high school
English teacher who actually enjoyed his students.*

*He accepted the muffins and told her to thank her mom.
"Now let's get to the real reason you came to visit."*

*He escorted her to the computer in his spare bedroom.
While they were staying at the cabin, her parents banned
all use of electronics, especially the internet. Her brother
and she were supposed to spend the summer appreciat-
ing nature, but she had more on her mind than gathering
pinecones and wading in creeks.*

*A few days before, she had been at the Circle L when
a mare birthed her foal. She needed to write about the
experience. While she waited for the computer to boot
up, she pulled a small spiral notebook from her back
pocket. The pages were densely scribbled with notes, which
she held up for Mr. Woodley to see. "I interviewed the
veterinarian."*

"That will give some depth to your story."

*"And I want to talk to the ranch hands so I can get an
idea of what life is going to hold for the baby horse."*

*"I thought you had the makings of a poet, but I see I
was wrong." Mr. Woodley placed his hand on her shoulder.
"Someday, you're going to be a fine journalist."*

Her memory soothed the panic that had threatened to
overwhelm her. Her breathing settled into a regular pattern.
Caitlyn was a long way from calm, but she wasn't about to
explode.

When she felt someone yanking on the door handle of
the Fairlane, she was jerked back to the present. Whoever
had been tugging let go with a string of curses.

Woodley's voice boomed from nearby. "Be careful, Patterson. This is a classic vehicle."

"Unlock it." Patterson's voice was terse.

"Sure thing," Woodley said. "But nobody's in there. I always keep my car locked. It's a habit."

She heard the door open. The car rocked, and she assumed that Patterson had climbed inside to look into the backseat. Silently, she prayed that he'd move on. Their hiding place in the trunk seemed as obvious as a wrapped birthday present with a big red bow.

Patterson growled, "You've caused me a lot of trouble, old man."

"Let's talk it over with my friend from the FBI. He ought to be here any minute."

"I don't have time to waste with the FBI." He raised his voice. "Bryant, I'm over here."

In a breathless rush, the Texan said, "I was in the barn. Think we got a trail to follow. There's a couple of horses gone from their stalls."

"I should have known," Patterson muttered. "He took off on horseback. Again."

A moment passed. The sounds of the searchers became more distant. The door of the Ford Fairlane opened. The car jostled as someone got behind the steering wheel. The engine started. As the car went in reverse, she heard Mr. Woodley say, "On our way. Over the river and through the woods."

They'd pulled it off. A clean getaway.

HIDING IN THE TRUNK of a car wasn't the most manly way to escape, but Jack didn't mind. The ancient suspension system in the old Ford bounced Caitlyn against him with every bump they hit, and there were a lot of bumps on the graded gravel roads. They probably hadn't traveled a mile before her clenched arms loosened up, and she accidentally smacked him with the handcuffs she still held.

"Give me those," he said.

"Can't see where you are. I'll stick them in the pocket of this lovely blue jacket that's probably going to be filthy by the time I get out of the trunk."

"That'd be a shame." He hadn't been lying when he told her she looked pretty.

After one huge jolt, she started to giggle. Her unbridled laughter was as bright as the inside of the trunk was dark. Her legs tangled with his, accidentally rubbing against his thighs and groin. They were bumping apart and grinding together. It was like making love in a blender.

On a relatively smooth stretch of road, he asked, "Do you mind telling me where we're going?"

"I considered riding all the way to Denver," she said. "But there's too much going on in this area. The manhunt for Rojas is massive. The police have heavy-duty surveillance and roadblocks. The car could be stopped and searched."

And he didn't dare turn himself over to anyone in law enforcement. No matter what they thought, they'd be obliged to take him into custody and turn him over to Patterson. "I don't expect the cops are going to be happy about my escape from the Circle L."

She bumped against his chest. "Probably not."

"You never answered my question."

"Do you really want to know where we're going?" she teased. "Wouldn't you rather sit back and let me take care of every little thing?"

He had to admit that she'd done a good job of springing him from Patterson's custody. She was a problem solver, smart and competent. But he liked being the one in charge. "Tell me."

"Or else? How are you going to make me talk?"

He knew what he'd like to do. With her body rubbing up

against him in many inappropriate places, there was one predominant thought in his mind. He held her tight.

"Here's what I'll do to you, babe. First, I'm going to kiss you until your lips are numb. Then I'm going to take off that blue jacket and unbutton your shirt. And I'm going to grab you here." He lowered his hand and squeezed her butt. "You're going to be putty. You'll tell me everything I want to know."

"Bob Woodley's house," she peeped. "That's where we're headed."

"Woodley? The guy who owns this car?" If the Ford Fairlane was any indication, he didn't think Woodley's house would be safe. People who lived in the past tended to be less than vigilant when it came to the present.

"He told me that he was robbed last year, and he put in a state-of-the-art security system."

Jack doubted that good old Bob Woodley could guarantee their safety, but he needed a place to rest, recuperate and eat something more substantial than energy bars. Since last night, he'd caught only a few hours' sleep in the cavern. His body still ached with old bruises. Whenever he recalled the wound on the back of his head, it answered him with a quiet throb.

The car stopped and the engine went quiet. He heard the sound of a mechanical garage door closing.

The trunk opened. After being in darkness, the overhead bulb in the two-car garage glared like a klieg light. Untangling himself from Caitlyn took a moment and unleashed another burst of giggles from her.

Finally, Jack was on his feet. The first thing he noticed was that the second car in the garage was a Land Rover that couldn't have been more than two or three years old—a sensible vehicle for someone who lived in the mountains. A tool bench at the back of the garage displayed a neat array of power tools. Apparently, the old man had an organized side to his personality. Caitlyn had spoken fondly of Woodley. A retired English teacher. A friend of her parents.

He faced the rangy, white-haired stranger who had played a pivotal role in his rescue. Though there weren't sufficient words to thank him, Jack said, "I appreciate what you've done."

Woodley assessed him with a stern gaze. "You're the fellow who caused all this trouble."

Jack held out his hand. "Call me Jack."

"That's not your real name." With a firm grip, Woodley shook his hand. "I don't cotton to men who hide behind aliases. Let's use your real name. Nick Racine."

Chapter Fifteen

Jack wasn't often caught off guard. His natural wariness kept him on his toes, ready to react to any threat. The name Nick Racine was dangerous. As soon as Woodley spoke it, Jack thought of plausible excuses for the alias. Deception was second nature to him, but he couldn't look this good man in the eye and lie to him. More important, Jack wanted—no, needed—to be truthful with Caitlyn.

She eyed him suspiciously then focused on Woodley. "Where did you hear that name?"

"From my friend in the FBI. He's one of my former students, and he doesn't have any reason to lie to me."

"What did he say?"

"He spoke to the marshal on the phone." Woodley scowled. "By the way, that Patterson fellow is rude and unpleasant. I try to see the best in people, but that guy was shifty."

"Agreed," Caitlyn said briskly. "And then?"

"My young FBI friend warned me that there wasn't much he could do to stop the marshals. That was when he mentioned the name Nick Racine." He stared hard at Jack. "I thought it strange because Caitlyn called you something else."

When she turned her gaze on Jack, she'd switched into her journalist persona. Her eyes were clear. Her attitude, cool. She was nothing like the soft woman who had been giggling in the trunk of the Ford Fairlane and rubbing up against him. "Have you ever heard the name Nick Racine before?"

He didn't connect with that identity and he sure as hell didn't believe the stories Bryant had been spouting about his supposedly legendary deeds. If he truly was a one-man strike force, shouldn't he be able to remember? "Bryant and Patterson said I was Nick Racine."

"I thought you were Tony Perez."

So did I. He shrugged. There wasn't anything he could say to clarify his identity.

"We need to look into this." She pivoted and marched toward the side door in the garage. "I'll need to use the computer."

"Hold on," Woodley said. "Who's Tony Perez? Why in blazes doesn't this man know his own name?"

She came back and stood before him. "The important thing for you to know is that this man—I'm going to call him Jack—is a decent human being. He risked his life to rescue Danny, and he saved me from a gang of men with guns." She took both of Woodley's hands in hers. "I trust Jack. And I'm asking you to do the same."

The way he looked at Caitlyn reminded Jack of an affectionate uncle with his fair-haired niece. The old man was proud of her accomplishments. "You've grown up to be quite a woman. I always knew you'd turn out okay."

"You were one of the first people who believed in me. You encouraged me to be a journalist."

"It's not hard to pick out a diamond in a bowl of sand." He gave her a wink and turned to Jack. "All right, young man. If Caitlyn vouches for you, I've got to accept you. With all your fake names."

"Thank you, sir."

"Now," she said, "lead me to the computer."

Woodley circled around the car and went to the door. "Are you two hungry?"

"Starved," Caitlyn said. "You know what I really want? When you used to come over to our cabin and play Scrabble with Mom and Dad, you always made grilled cheese sandwiches and tomato soup for me and my brother. Comfort food."

"Coming right up," he said, "but I don't want you two in the kitchen with me. There are too many lights, too many windows and too many people looking for you."

Jack appreciated Woodley's caution. Rojas was still at large. And Patterson might decide to come here after he was done with his wild goose chase. Jack followed Caitlyn and Woodley through the door that led directly into the house.

Woodley said, "I don't want to turn on any lights."

Again, Jack approved. Moonlight through the windows provided enough illumination to find their way through a living room and down a hallway. In a small bedroom, Woodley turned on the overhead light.

The windows were covered with shades and curtains. The decor was a mixture of antique and high-tech. A laptop computer rested on a carved oak, rolltop desk with a matching office chair. Wooden bookshelves held the eclectic collection of an avid reader, ranging from poetry to electronics manuals. A patchwork quilt covered the double bed with a curlicue brass frame. One corner was devoted to surveillance and security.

"Here's where you'll be sleeping, Jack." The old man went to the security equipment and flipped a couple of switches. "These four infrared screens show the outdoor views of my property. The garage, front door, northern side and western. The back of the house butts up to a hillside and is inaccessible. I've activated the motion sensors at a twenty-yard perimeter around the house and the burglar alarm in case anybody jiggles the door or busts a window."

In the unformed memories of his past, Jack knew he'd seen similar security arrangements. "This is a sophisticated system. Did you install it yourself?"

"It's overkill," Woodley admitted. "When I got robbed, I was so ticked off that I set this place up as a fortress, mostly because I enjoyed fiddling around with the electronics."

"He's always been that way," Caitlyn said. She'd already positioned herself at the desk where she opened the laptop. "If he hadn't been an English teacher, Mr. Woodley would have been a mechanic."

"And a damn good one—good enough to keep my 1957 Ford Fairlane in running condition."

Jack liked the old guy—a man who could work with his hands and with his mind. "I'm impressed."

"And you're going to be even more excited by my grilled cheese sandwiches. Before I head out to the kitchen, there's one more thing I need to show you." He stepped into the hallway and pointed at a closed door. "This is going to be Caitlyn's bedroom. Understand?"

"Yes, sir." Jack had been hoping they'd have to sleep in the same room, preferably in the same bed. No such luck.

He closed the door behind Woodley and went to the rolltop desk, where Caitlyn sat hunched over the computer. Her fingers skipped across the keyboard as she started her identity search. "Should I look for Nicholas Racine or Nick?"

"Neither. I'm not Nick Racine."

"Other people seem to think you are. We need to research the possibilities."

Buried deep in the back of his mind was something akin to dread; he didn't want to be Nick Racine. Uncovering that identity would cause no end of pain. "I have a better idea. Look up Tony Perez."

In a couple of minutes, she'd accessed a site that showed his mug shot. His hair was longer, as were his sideburns, and he had a soul patch on his chin.

"That's you," Caitlyn said. "Love the facial hair."

He massaged the spot between his lower lip and his chin that was now rough with stubble. "That settles it. We know my real identity."

"Do you remember being Tony Perez?"

He had a crystal clear memory of watching Mark Santoro die and of being shot. "I remember some things."

She pointed to the computer screen. "This is your address in Chicago. Tell me about the place where you lived."

Her voice was firm and demanding. Bossy, in fact. And he wasn't inclined to take orders. "Are you interviewing me?"

"I'm looking for answers, yes."

"What's the point? We know Rojas wants to kill me to keep me from testifying. He paid off the marshals, and they need me dead so they can keep their jobs. Those are the facts. My name isn't going to change them."

She rose from the desk chair and faced him. Curiosity shone in her eyes. The color of her jacket emphasized the deep blue of her irises. "Don't you want to know who you are?"

"I like being Jack Dalton." A man without a past had no regrets.

"Please cooperate."

"Are you asking because you care or because you're a reporter?"

"I'll admit that you're a damn good story. And I suppose I could say that I care about you." With her thumb and index finger she measured an inch. "Maybe this much."

"Not much incentive."

She rolled her eyes. "Has anyone ever told you that you're a giant pain in the butt?"

"I'd like to answer that question but, damn…" He shot her a grin. "I just don't remember."

"Tell me about the place where you lived in Chicago," she repeated.

He tore his gaze away from her and paced as though moving around would jog his memory. "It was a one-bedroom apartment in an older building with an ancient elevator. I was on the third floor." A picture took shape in his mind. "Brown sofa. Television. Wood table full of clutter. I had a king-size bed. I like big beds."

"Did you have a girlfriend to share that bed?"

In his mind, he saw a woman with long hair and too much eye makeup. "A blonde. That's my type. Blondes with long legs. Kind of like you."

"Lucky me," she said. "Keep talking."

"The woman in Chicago wasn't anything special. We dated." And she had spent a few hours in his king-size bed. "She was no big deal."

"Where did you live before that?"

In the corner of the room, he stared at the surveillance screens that surrounded the house. In infrared view, the trunks of pine trees were ghostly shadows. "There isn't time for us to work backward through my rental history. What do you really want to know?"

"I've never interviewed someone with amnesia. I'm trying to find the key that makes you remember."

"Tony Perez. I grew up in southern California." His biography flashed before him as clearly and neatly as though it had been written out on a sheet of paper. He filled in details about growing up in foster care and never knowing his parents. He'd gotten in trouble as a kid for stealing cars and shoplifting. "I lived in Arizona for a while. How am I doing?"

"Considering that you started from zero, I'm surprised. You remember a lot."

He had details. He could visualize his driver's license and recite his Social Security number. But none of it seemed real. His identity as Tony Perez seemed like something he'd seen in a movie, but he wasn't making it up. "Remembering isn't the kind of relief I thought it would be."

"How did you make a living?"

He recited a string of menial jobs. "Then I hooked up with Santoro. I collected his debts."

"An enforcer," she said. "That makes sense. I've seen you in action, and you can be very intimidating."

"I'm not a thug." He didn't want her to think of him that way. "Getting people to do what you want is more about attitude than actual violence. I developed a reputation. People were scared of me. That threat was enough."

"There had to be a reason why they were afraid. What was your reputation based on?"

"Word of mouth and a couple of well-placed lies."

He went to the bed, propped the dark blue pillows against the headboard and took off his boots so he wouldn't get the patchwork quilt dirty. Then he leaned back against the pillows with his legs stretched out straight in front of him. For the first time today, he allowed himself to relax. God, he was tired.

Caitlyn perched on the edge of the bed beside his legs, positioning herself so she wasn't touching him. "I'm interested in how you set yourself up as a dangerous person."

"First you've got to build a reputation. Other people

have to say you're tough. In Chicago, I used a snitch and a couple of cops. The stories they told made me sound like a cold-blooded sadist."

"Cops? How did you get them to lie for you?"

"Give them something they want. A bribe. A promise. A gift. Just like Rojas got Patterson to work for him."

"Then what?" she asked.

"You need to prove yourself. I picked the biggest, toughest guy in the gang and took him down. I didn't kill him or do any permanent damage, but I hurt him enough that he knew I could have killed him. In a way, he owed me his life."

"Keep your enemies close." She regarded him thoughtfully. "This is beginning to sound like Sun Tzu, *The Art of War.*"

"All warfare is deception," he quoted.

"Your life as Tony Perez sounds complicated. Why would you go through such an elaborate setup?"

A good question. "I was in a new town. I needed to get close to power. That's what I do." He laced his fingers behind his head and leaned back. Exhaustion tugged at his eyelids.

"Okay, you established your reputation and you proved yourself," she said. "What next?"

"I needed an ally. Somebody who had my back. That was Mark Santoro. When I first met him, I was using him. But he became a friend."

Santoro wasn't a saint. Pretty much the opposite. He was a head man in a drug-running crime family, but he was loyal to his crew and strong-willed. He had a family—twin girls who would grow up without their father.

"You still grieve for him," she said.

"His death was unnecessary and pointless," he said. "I

should have seen the attack coming, should have known what Rojas was planning."

"How could you know?"

"It was my job."

"Protecting your boss?" she asked.

Though he nodded, he knew there was something more. Only a few hours ago, Greg Rojas looked him in the eye and called him Nick Racine. Jack had been so startled that he lost his chance to shoot in spite of his need for revenge. He wanted Rojas to suffer for the part he'd played in the death of Mark Santoro and for... There was another name, another person.

An intense rage exploded behind his eyelids in a blinding fireball. Someone else had been murdered. He had to remember. Until he knew that name, his soul was empty. His life had no meaning.

There was a reason he had played this complicated charade with Mark Santoro.

"Jack?" He heard Caitlyn calling him back to reality. "Jack, are you all right?"

He had to find the answers, and he knew where to start. "We need more information on Nick Racine."

Chapter Sixteen

Near midnight, Jack lay on his back and stared up at the ceiling above the bed. His body floated in a sea of exhaustion, but his mind wouldn't succumb to sleep. The surveillance screens in the corner cast an eerie, gray light across the flat surface. His memories took shape.

He saw the number eight on the scuffed beige door of the motel room. The night was heavy, dark and cold. The red-haired man unlocked door number eight and walked inside carrying a black gym bag.

Jack blinked. He knew what came next, knew he should close his eyes, but he couldn't stop himself from staring as the scene played out. He watched himself.

He parked a block away and crept toward a clump of leafless shrubs at the edge of the motel parking lot. There, he waited impatiently with his Beretta M9 automatic. This wasn't murder; it was an execution for a man who lived outside the law. His name was Eric Deaver. He'd done unspeakable things.

The curtains in room number eight didn't close all the way. Through the gap, he saw the flicker from a television screen. Was Eric Deaver lying on the bed? Laughing at lame jokes from late-night talk-show hosts?

The door flung open. Red-haired Deaver was silhou-

*etted in the frame. He gripped guns with both hands. He
bellowed, "I know you're here."*

*One shot. One bullet. In the center of his forehead. It
was over. Justice was served.*

Still caught up in his memory, Jack heard the knob on
his bedroom door click. He bolted from the bed, ready to
fight to the death.

CAITLYN PAUSED WITH her hand on the doorknob. Entering Jack's bedroom might be a really foolish move. She
shifted her weight, and the floorboards creaked. Maybe she
should trot back to her bedroom and put on more clothes.
Not that the oversize T-shirt and terry-cloth bathrobe she'd
borrowed from Woodley counted as a seductive negligee,
but she didn't want Jack to get the wrong idea.

I'm not going to have sex with him. She'd known Jack
for only a day. From the little he'd told her about his past,
he was a scary guy. And there was absolutely no chance of
any future relationship. She didn't want him to think that
appearing at his bedroom door was some kind of booty
call. There would be no lovemaking. She did, however,
intend to sleep in the same room as him.

If she left him alone, she was certain that he wouldn't
be here in the morning. He'd made it clear that he didn't
want to work with a partner because of the unknown, the
intensity, the danger, blah, blah, blah. She wasn't going to
be shuffled aside. If he was going to run, she'd be at his
side. He was her story, and she intended to follow him to
the conclusion.

Twisting the knob, she opened the door and poked her
head inside. Before she had a chance to whisper his name,
he'd grabbed her around the throat. His arm was steel.
She couldn't move, couldn't breathe, felt herself losing
consciousness.

When he suddenly released his grip, she fell to the floor, gasping.

"Never," he said, "never sneak up on me like that."

She coughed. "What was I supposed to do?"

"Knock."

Though he was right and she really didn't expect an apology, he could have at least helped her to her feet. Instead, he went to the security corner and stared at the screens. Unspeaking, he kept his back toward her. Hostility rolled off from his wide, muscular shoulders in waves.

She stood, turned on the overhead light and padded to his bed where she sat on the edge. She adjusted her bathrobe to cover her breasts. As extra protection, she was still wearing her sports bra. "I'm sorry I couldn't find anything about Nick Racine on the internet."

"Not your fault," he muttered.

She'd tried. As a journalist, she'd learned how to use the computer to track down leads, and she'd employed every bit of her skill to locate information on Nick Racine. She'd hopscotched through databases, scanned websites and probed blogs. Though she'd found plenty of people named Nick Racine, none fit his description. "The identity should have showed up somewhere. In a credit file or bank record or work history. It's almost like Nick Racine was erased."

"It's possible," he said without turning around.

Glaring at his backside, she got distracted by the snug fit of his black jersey boxer shorts. His legs were long, muscular and masculine, with just the right amount of black hair. His bare feet and long toes looked oddly vulnerable.

She tucked her own feet—in sensible white cotton socks—up under her. "We need to make plans for tomorrow. I'm sure Mr. Woodley won't kick us out, but the marshals are going to be canvassing the area."

"I'll be gone before first light."

She noticed that he hadn't included her in his plans. "I'm coming with you."

He pivoted and came toward her. The fact that he wasn't wearing a lot of clothing made him seem bigger and more intimidating. Stubble outlined his jaw. His black eyebrows pulled down in an angry scowl. "There's no reason for you to be in danger."

"I was embedded with the troops. I can handle it."

"This is different," he said. "Use Woodley's contact at the FBI. Put yourself in his protection until Rojas is under lock and key."

An hour ago, Woodley had gotten an update on the police activity. The safe house had been secured and four men arrested after a shoot-out. Rojas and two of his men had escaped. "What if he isn't caught?"

"That means he's out of the country, and you'll never see him again."

"What are you going to do?"

His chin lifted. "It's better if you don't know."

She wasn't ready to let go. There were too many unanswered questions. "I'll decide what's best for me."

There was something different about him, but she couldn't exactly put her finger on it. A heaviness? A dark, brooding anger? He said, "This isn't your fight."

"Earlier, you asked if I was interested in you because you're a good story. Well, you're right. You're on the run, a witness in a gangland murder and a victim of unscrupulous federal officers. And let's not forget the amnesia angle. Jack, if I can get inside your head and write your story, I could be looking at a Pulitzer."

"You want inside my head?"

"That's right," she said.

"You're not going to like what you find." He lowered

himself into the desk chair and leaned forward, his elbows resting on his knees. The focus in his green eyes was painfully sharp. "I killed a man."

A murder confession? That wasn't what she wanted to hear. She held herself tightly under control, refusing to flinch. "Are you sure? What did you remember?"

"I saw the bullet pierce his skull, saw the light go out in his eyes. And I was glad to execute the bastard. I felt no guilt, no regret."

This memory wasn't consistent with what she'd seen of Jack. In dealing with the men at the safe house, he hadn't opened fire and gunned them down. His behavior was logical and precise; he didn't act like a killer. "Who was he?"

"I know his name," he said, "but I don't know why I needed to end his life. I believe the reason is tied to Rojas."

"Why?"

Though he was looking right at her, his gaze was distant. "I keep replaying that moment when I had the drop on Rojas and didn't shoot. It wasn't an ethical concern that kept me from pulling the trigger. I could have winged him without killing him."

From what she'd seen, he was a good marksman and his reflexes were lightning fast. No doubt he could have disabled Rojas and Kelso with surgical precision. "Why didn't you shoot?"

"He yelled out the name Nick Racine, as though he recognized me. And something clicked inside my head. Everything was clear. The confusion and sorrow and rage I'd been carrying around for years vanished in a puff of smoke. I knew. Knew the answer."

His voice had fallen to a hush. If she hadn't already been intrigued by him, this moment would have captured her interest. What had become clear to him? What truth had he learned? She dared not speak and break the profound silence.

"Gregorio Rojas is the answer," he said, "but I don't know the question. I need to figure it out."

"You seem to be remembering more pieces of your past all the time. If you're patient, it'll come to you."

He shook his head. "I was on this quest long before I lost my memory. It's the reason I went to work for Santoro, the reason I agreed to testify. Somehow, all of what's happened ties together."

She had to get to the bottom of this. Never in her career had she been issued such a clear challenge. "Where should we start?"

He rose from the chair, took her hand and pulled her to her feet. With gallantry unbefitting a man dressed only in jockey shorts and a T-shirt, he escorted her to the door. "Go back to bed. We both need our sleep."

"Promise you won't leave without me."

"I won't lie to you." For a moment, the hint of a smile touched his mouth and she thought he was going to kiss her, but he turned and went to his bed. As he stretched out on the sheets, he said, "Good night, Caitlyn."

Trying to get rid of me? It's not that easy, Jack. She went to the bed and leaned over him, close enough to kiss but not touching. "I'm glad you won't lie to me."

"I owe you that much."

"Actually, quite a bit more." She reached into the pocket of her bathrobe and took out the handcuffs. In one swift click, she fastened one around his right wrist and the other around her left. "You won't be going anywhere without me."

His gaze went to the steel cuffs, then to her face. His

sexy grin spread slowly. "If you wanted to sleep with me, all you had to do was ask."

"We're only going to sleep." It took an effort to hold on to that resolution while she was this close to him, but she was determined.

"I don't believe you." His voice was warm, intimate, seductive. "If you wanted to keep me here, you could have handcuffed me to this fancy brass bed frame."

"As if you couldn't pick the lock? No way. Hooking us together is the only way I can be sure where you are."

She showed him the key to the cuffs. Then she stuck her hand inside her bathrobe and T-shirt, tucking the key safely into her sports bra.

"Do you really think that's going to stop me?"

"I know you won't hurt me."

"You're right, babe." He caught hold of her right arm and pulled her down on top on him. "This won't hurt a bit."

The bathrobe tangled around her legs as she struggled to get away from him, and she was reminded of how their bodies bounced against each other during that crazy ride in the trunk of the Ford Fairlane. There was no way to avoid touching him. She knew this would happen. How could she not know? What had she been thinking?

The answer was obvious. Maybe, just maybe, she didn't want to escape. Maybe she'd come to him hoping that he'd make love to her. The magnetism between them was undeniable. Why shouldn't she relent?

"No," she said, speaking as much to herself as to him. "This is what you want."

He undid the tie on the bathrobe and pushed it out of the way. He was on top of her. Through the thin fabric of her T-shirt, she felt his body heat, and the warmth tempted her. She felt herself melting.

His face was inches away from hers. If she kissed him,

she knew this battle would be over. She wouldn't be able to stop herself.

She twisted her head on the pillow so she was looking away from him, staring at the wall beside the bed. Through clenched teeth, she said, "Stop it. I mean now."

He rolled off her. They were lying beside each other with their cuffed wrists in the middle.

"Can't blame me for getting the wrong idea," he said. "When a woman comes into your bedroom in the middle of the night with a set of handcuffs—"

"I know what this looks like." Excitement made her voice shaky; she couldn't stop her heart from throbbing. "I'm using the handcuffs for professional reasons."

"And what profession might that be?"

"I'm a reporter, and you're a story. If I want to get my career in order, I need to show that I can be an effective investigative journalist. You understand what I'm saying, I know you do. You're the one who told me I was going to be okay, that all I needed was to believe in myself."

"That wasn't much of a deduction," he said. "Anybody who's met you knows you're smart enough to accomplish great things."

"But I was scared. Paralyzed. I didn't believe in myself."

She'd hidden at her cabin like a hermit. When her position in the Middle East was cut, she knew it wasn't because she was doing a bad job. The decision was based on budgets and revenue. Still, she couldn't help feeling that she'd failed. Not anymore.

Jack's story had all the hooks that readers love, from involvement with a crime family to being on the run to corruption within the marshals. Not to mention his mysterious past. His story was worth a whole book or a miniseries, and she'd be the one to write it. She'd be damned if she would miss a single minute.

"You're right, Caitlyn. I believe in you."

His surprising moments of sensitivity made it even harder to resist him. "If we're going to get a good night's sleep, we should turn off the lights."

She climbed out of the bed, pulling him behind her with the handcuffs. She hit the light switch, and the bedroom faded into the half darkness. The glow from the surveillance screens lit their way back to the bed.

Finding a comfortable position with their hands cuffed together wasn't easy. They both ended up on their sides, facing each other. In the dim light, she saw that his eyes were closed. His lashes were long, thick and black. Any woman would kill for eyelashes like that. But there was nothing feminine about his face. Not with the stubble that outlined his sexy mouth. Not with his strong cheekbones and jaw.

Sleep was the furthest thing from her mind. She asked, "Do we have a plan for tomorrow?"

"No particular plan, just a couple of ideas. I figured I'd stick around this area. Do some investigating."

"Shouldn't you be focused on escape?"

"There's still three days before the trial. I want to use that time."

"How did you plan on getting around?"

"Woodley has a nice little ATV in a shed behind the garage and I—"

"You can't steal his four-wheeler," she said firmly. "After the risk he took for you, how could you even think of hijacking his property?"

His eyelids opened. "Woodley and I already talked about it. He gave me the keys."

"Well, good." She shouldn't have accused him. No

matter what had happened in his past, Jack was far too loyal to betray the people who treated him right. "I can ride on the back of the ATV. You'll be glad you brought me along. I can guide you through the backcountry."

For a long moment, he gazed at her. A deep sense of yearning urged her toward him. She wanted to touch him, to glide into his embrace. Physically, he was everything she wanted in a man—tall, lean and muscular. She even liked the scars she knew were under his T-shirt.

"Tell me the reason," he said, "that we can't make love."

"I don't know who you are—Tony or Nick or someone else altogether."

"You know me as Jack."

She certainly did. He was the stranger who showed up on her doorstep, the man who saved her life and believed in her. "It's only been a day."

"A matter of timing."

Though she didn't have silly rules, such as not kissing on the first date, she didn't want to rush into lovemaking. Intimacy was a risk she wasn't ready to take. "Timing is important."

"Tomorrow," he said, "we'll have known each other twice as long. That should be enough."

She closed her eyes and pretended to sleep.

Chapter Seventeen

Though the curtains and shades over the bedroom windows blocked out the light, Jack sensed that it was close to dawn. His inner alarm clock, which he considered more accurate than a Swiss timepiece, told him that he'd been in bed for five hours. He lifted his head from the pillow and craned his neck to see the digital clock on the desk. Four forty-seven. Time to get moving.

In spite of the handcuffs, he'd slept well. The cozy presence of a woman in his bed reminded him of what normal life was all about. Her scent, the little kitten sounds she made in her sleep and the way her body occasionally rubbed against him made him feel alive. He looked over at Caitlyn. His eyes had become accustomed to the dim light from the surveillance screens, and he could see fairly well. Her bathrobe was open and her long T-shirt had hiked up, giving him an unfettered view of her long, firm legs. One knee was bent, and her toes pointed like a ballerina midleap. Her free arm arched above her head. For a slender woman, she took up a lot of space. He grinned. *Bed hog.*

Leaning over her, he studied the delicate angles of her face from the sweep of her eyebrows to the tip of her chin. Her straight blond hair fell in wisps across her cheeks. Her lips parted slightly, and her breathing was slow and steady. She was still asleep.

Her need to follow him and get his whole story was understandable, and he appreciated her dedication to her career. But he'd rather work alone. If he could unfasten the handcuff and slip away before she missed him, that would be all for the best. The trick would be to retrieve the key from her bra without waking her up.

He lightly touched the bare skin below her collarbone. Her breathing didn't change. Beneath her shapeless T-shirt, her chest rose and fell in a steady pattern.

Slowly, slowly, he moved his fingertips toward the valley between her breasts. He'd been in custody since he was shot, hadn't been anywhere near a woman for five months. Her skin was soft and warm, enticing him. He wanted to touch her all over, to taste her mouth, her throat, the tips of her breasts. He wanted her legs wrapped around him. Her arms, clinging to him. Her idea of waiting for a specific number of hours or days or weeks before making love was ridiculous. They were consenting adults, obviously attracted to each other. Why the hell shouldn't they seize the moment?

Under her T-shirt, he felt the edge of her sports bra. Just a little lower…

Her eyelids snapped open. "Are you trying to cop a feel or grab the key?"

"Both."

"How about neither?" She pushed his hand away. "Go back to sleep."

"It's time to go. Unless you want to watch me pee, you should unlock the cuffs."

"Ew. I'm not following you into the bathroom." As she fished the key from her bra, she glanced at the clock. "It's not even five o'clock."

"You could stay here and sleep in."

"Not an option," she said. "But this is really, really early. Do we have to leave now?"

"I promised Woodley I'd be gone before he got out of bed. If the police come knocking, he can honestly say that he has no idea where I went."

"Fine." She unlocked the cuffs and rubbed the red circle on her wrist. "I get the bathroom first."

"Hurry."

"Less than five minutes," she promised.

"Don't turn on any lights," he warned. Though Woodley's security system hadn't sounded an alert, it didn't hurt to be careful. *Always plan for the worst-case scenario.* The marshals could be staking out the house.

Jack doubted that Rojas was still in the area. A wealthy man like him was able to pay for an arranged escape. He probably had a private chopper on call.

After her allotted five minutes, Caitlyn peeked in to tell him she was done, and he took his turn. Though he would have liked to shave, he followed his own warning and kept the lights in the bathroom off. Back in his bedroom, he dressed in a fresh T-shirt and jeans provided by Woodley. The old man had also given Jack a lightweight canvas jacket in khaki. The keys to the ATV were in the front pocket.

Caitlyn joined him. She'd yanked her hair into a ponytail and thrown on the clothes she'd worn last night. The blue jacket was grungy from being in the car trunk, but she still looked fresh and awake.

Together, they went down the hallway, pretending that they hadn't made enough noise to wake their host. Jack hoped Woodley's taste in all-terrain vehicles didn't mirror his love of vintage cars.

Circling the house, they entered the shed behind the garage, closed the door and turned on the light. The two-person ATV wasn't brand-new but probably less than ten years old. The dents and scratches on the frame indicated that Woodley had ridden this four-wheeler hard, but Jack trusted the man who liked mechanics to keep all his vehicles in good running order. A blue helmet rested on the well-worn front seat. The lid on the storage container behind the second seat was propped open, and Caitlyn looked inside.

"This is so sweet," she said. "He packed a sleeping bag, a canteen and some food for you."

"Woodley's a good man."

She started searching thought the other outdoor gear in the shed. "He didn't know I'd be coming along. We need to find another sleeping bag and helmet. Maybe a tent in case we need to set up camp."

"We're not going on a field trip."

"Which brings up an important question," she said. "Where exactly are we going?"

The best way for him to figure out why he'd executed the red-haired man was to learn more about Nick Racine. The name still didn't resonate with him. He had hoped the hours of sleep might heal the holes in his memory, but no such luck. He needed to investigate.

Since Patterson and Bryant had identified him as Racine when he was in their custody, Jack thought he might find clues at the place where they'd held him. "We're going back to the safe house."

She found a second blue helmet which she plopped on her head. "But it's a crime scene. Mr. Woodley said the police had their shoot-out with the Rojas men there. Won't the area be closed off?"

"We'll see."

She stuffed a second sleeping bag into the carrier and closed the lid. "Have you ever driven an ATV before?"

"Oh, yeah."

During the time he spent in the desert with his mentor, they used dune buggies to get around. This ATV—with its solid frame and seriously heavy-duty tires—was the muscular big brother of those dune buggies. Jack was looking forward to riding over the hillsides. Pushing hard, he wheeled the ATV out of the shed and locked the door behind him.

"Don't forget your helmet," she said.

"Colorado doesn't have a helmet law."

"Humor me." She shoved the helmet into his hands. "We're in enough danger without getting into a crash and busting our heads open."

Helmet in place, he climbed onto the seat. Caitlyn mounted behind him. Her arms weren't wrapped around him like they'd be on a dirt bike, but she was close enough to lean forward and tap the back of his helmet.

He turned his head. "What was that for?"

"Just excited," she said. "Let her rip."

He turned the key in the ignition. The engine roared as he drove away, threading his way through the tree trunks, heading uphill and away from the road. In the thin light before the dawn, he couldn't see clearly and had to move at a slow pace through the forest. It was difficult to gauge distances, and he added a couple more dents to the frame of the ATV.

At the crest of the ridge above Woodley's house, she flicked her fingers against his helmet and said, "You should go east. That's to your right. And head downhill."

He might have guessed as much, but he was glad to have her confirmation. The ATV rumbled along a narrow path, louder than a Harley. This vehicle wasn't made for stealth; they'd have to park a distance away from the safe house and approach on foot.

As they meandered through the trees, the rising sun

painted the sky in tones of pale pink and yellow, streaked with the long wisps of cirrus clouds. The dawn light gave form to the rising hills and dark forests.

When they came to a meadow, the wide-open space beckoned to him. After picking his way cautiously, he wanted to go fast. He gunned the engine and floored it. They were flying, careening over the uneven terrain with the fresh wind whipping around them. He felt free. Behind him, Caitlyn yelped and laughed in sheer exhilaration.

At the far side of the meadow, she tapped his helmet again. "Jack, you need to stop."

He pulled onto a flat space and killed the engine.

Immediately, she jumped off the back seat and took off her helmet. She winced and rubbed at her tailbone. "Ow, ow, ow."

"Are you okay?"

"Going over those ruts, I really whacked my bottom." She stretched and groaned and stretched again. "I'm fine. It's nothing a good massage won't fix."

"I'd volunteer for that job."

"I bet you would."

The light of a new day glimmered in her blond hair, and she beamed a smile. The combination of nature's awesome beauty and Caitlyn's lively energy delighted him. His blood was still rushing with the sensation of speed. He was… happy.

He dropped his gaze, knowing that he'd felt this way before. As Nick or Tony or Jack or whoever the hell he was, he had experienced happiness. A dangerous emotion often followed by despair. "How far are we from the safe house?"

She approached him. "What's wrong?"

"I want to get there before it's too late."

"We're not far," she said. "I can't give you exact coordinates, but the safe house and Mr. Woodley's place are both to the east of Pinedale. From the top of that ridge, we ought to be able to get our bearings."

After she got back onto the ATV, he headed toward the high point. His skill in maneuvering had improved to the extent that he only ran over one small shrub on the way.

She tapped his helmet. "Park here."

He turned off the engine, dismounted and took off the helmet. "You've got to stop flicking my helmet."

She shrugged. "I used to do that with one of my drivers in the Middle East. We were covered in protective gear, and tapping his helmet was the best way to get his attention."

"I don't like it." He hiked uphill to the edge of the cliff. A long view spread before him. To the south, he saw the main road and the turnoff to the safe house. Surrounding trees blocked his view of the house itself.

Standing beside him, Caitlyn bragged, "Am I good or what?"

Without her knowledge of the area, he could have been wandering these mountains for hours. "You have an impressive sense of direction."

"I used to ride over here to visit Mr. Woodley and then go exploring. Never once did I get lost."

That dangerous happiness lingered inside him, and he realized that she was a big part of that feeling. Though she could be irritating and aggressive, she challenged him in a good way. He wanted to pull her into his arms for a hug. Instead, he teased, "You have the instincts of a bloodhound."

"Are you calling me a dog?"

"I'm saying that it's no wonder you turned out to be a reporter. You always find your way."

She leaned her back against a boulder and folded her arms below her breasts. "Getting close to the safe house is going to be a problem. We can't muffle the engine noise. And it's getting lighter by the minute."

Though it couldn't have been much past five-thirty, the sun was rising fast. "If anybody's at the safe house, we'll turn back. If not, the noise won't matter."

"I can't believe the police left the place abandoned," she said. "Don't they need to process the crime scene?"

"Real life isn't like the movies. In most cases, there isn't a crack team of CSI investigators on hand. I'd expect the local law enforcement to be occupied with their manhunt. The search for Rojas."

"And for you." She pushed herself away from the boulder and came closer to him. "I've been thinking. Would it be so bad to turn yourself in?"

"I'm not going anywhere with the marshals."

"You don't have to," she said. "After the sheriff has taken a look at the safe house, Patterson and Bryant won't have much credibility. No matter what their excuse, it's obvious that they fouled up royally."

"True."

"Anybody would understand why you refused to be in their custody."

"True again."

Her gaze searched his face. "If you turn yourself in, you'll be taken to Chicago and sequestered before the trial. After that, you'll probably be in the witness protection program. I might not see you again."

He couldn't resist her any longer. His arm slipped around her waist, and he pulled her against him. "If you want to find me, you will."

"But there are rules."

"Since when did the rules stand in your way?"

She was a fighter, doing what she thought was right in

spite of conventions and restrictions. She'd arranged to spring him from the custody of the marshals.

Her head tilted back. Her lips parted. He kissed her long and hard. They needed to be on the move. Didn't have a moment to spare. Still, he took his time, savoring this moment when her body melted against him. He wanted to make love to her in the soft light of dawn, and he could feel her yearning. She wanted it, too.

He murmured, "Have we known each other long enough?"

"Not yet." She exhaled a sigh. "Soon."

They were meant to be together. He knew it.

some of the windows and the mail.../...
enough.

Chapter Eighteen

Jack saw only one vehicle outside the safe house: the black SUV with the demolished front end and the flat tires. Since there was no reason for the police to conceal their presence, he assumed no one was here guarding the place. Still, he used caution, parking about a hundred yards away in a forested area and camouflaging their ATV with loose brush.

As they approached the house, Caitlyn said, "They didn't even put up yellow crime scene tape. This doesn't seem right."

"I'm guessing the sheriff has his hands full." Last night, local law enforcement had taken five dangerous men into custody, dealt with the death of U.S. Marshal Hank Perry and started a manhunt. There would be jurisdictional considerations. Not to mention dealing with the media. "I expect they'll call in CSI's from Denver or even from the FBI."

"But shouldn't a deputy be here to make sure people like us don't come in and mess up the scene?"

He didn't sense a trap, but he'd been wrong before. "Let's not question our good luck. We'll get in and out ASAP."

The front door was locked, but enough of the windows had been shot out that it wasn't a problem to shove one open and climb inside. In spite of the devastation caused by last night's firefight, Jack recognized the front room and the adjoining kitchen with pine paneling on two of the walls. He remembered sitting at the table, playing penny-ante poker with the marshals; he had suspected Patterson of cheating.

In the middle of the hallway, he went into the room where he'd been sleeping and turned on the overhead light. Shutters were closed and locked over the only window. The simple furnishings included a single bed, dresser and desk.

"Charming," Caitlyn said sarcastically. "This looks like a pine-paneled prison cell."

"The Marshals Service doesn't use interior decorators. The idea is to keep the witness safe. That's why the windows are shuttered."

"It wouldn't hurt to hang a couple of pictures or stick a ficus in the corner." She went to the desk and pulled open the middle drawer. "What are we looking for?"

"I'd like to find my wallet." He rifled through the dresser. His T-shirts and clothing were bland and familiar, nothing special. "I didn't have time to grab anything when we were under assault."

She held up a paperback book. "Science fiction?"

"I like androids. And don't bother reading anything into that."

"But it's so accurate," she said. "It totally makes sense that you'd be attracted to a human-looking creature with super-abilities and no real emotions."

He had emotions, plenty of them. They pressed at the edge of his peripheral vision like certain blindness. When he had slept in this room, his name was Nick Racine. Pieces of that identity were drawing together, threatening to overwhelm him. "It was a mistake to come here."

"What are you remembering?"

Too much. Not enough. "We should go."

She stepped in front of the door, blocking his retreat. "You can't run away from this. Sooner or later, you'll have to quit using the name of some poor guy who wanted to be my handyman."

She was right, damn it. "Where do I start?"

"With something you remember. Tell me what happened when you were attacked. It was close to midnight, right?"

"Yes." He didn't want to remember.

"You were in bed," she said.

"That's right." He pivoted and went to the unmade bed. In the paneling above the headboard, he spotted six bullet holes in a close pattern, probably fired from a semi-automatic.

"What did you hear?" she asked.

"I was asleep. A noise woke me. The sound of a door slamming or a distant shout. I didn't know exactly what it was, but I got up, pulled on my pants and flannel shirt. Stuck my feet into my boots. Then all hell broke loose. I heard gunfire."

"Did someone come into the room?"

"The door crashed open. Perry shoved me down on the floor. Everything happened fast." The vision inside his head was chaos. Bullets flying. The flash of a knife blade. A burst of pain. "Perry was shot, but he got back up. We made it to the door at the end of the hallway. We were outside. Fighting for our lives."

"What about Patterson and Bryant?"

"Didn't see them. Perry must have told me they deserted us because I was mad." A sudden realization occurred to him. "I didn't have my gun, didn't have time to get my gun."

"Why is that important?" she asked.

He looked down into her bright blue eyes. "You're good at this interviewing stuff."

"It's kind of my job, Jack. And don't change the subject. Why is your gun important?"

"For one thing, I wasn't supposed to be armed. That's not the way witness protection works."

"I don't suppose it is," she said.

"If I hadn't been trying to hide my weapon, I would have slept with the gun beside the bed. Within easy reach." A mistake he'd never make again. "My response would have been faster. Perry wouldn't have died."

He crossed the room. The closet door was open. Hanging inside were a couple of shirts, a jacket and the charcoal-gray suit he intended to wear at the trial. He closed the door, knelt and pulled at the edge of the paneling near the floor. A foot-long section came off in his hand. He had created a cache inside the wall. Inside was a gray flannel bag.

"Very cool," she said. "Those are some serious precautions you took."

He opened the drawstring on the bag, reached inside and removed the Beretta M9. This gun belonged to Nick Racine; it carried a lot of memories. The grip felt like shaking hands with an old friend. His identity was coming back to him.

Something else was in the bag. Through the cloth, he felt a round object that was probably about an inch in diameter. He shook the bag, and it fell onto the floor by his feet. The gleam of silver caught his gaze.

"An earring," Caitlyn said.

Holding the post between his thumb and forefinger, he lifted the earring to eye level. Delicate threads wove a weblike pattern inside the circle. A dream catcher.

He sat on the floor, holding his gun in one hand and the silver earring in the other. Memory overpowered him.

He saw her from afar—lovely as an oasis in the rugged desert terrain. She stood in the open doorway of an adobe house. Her thick, black hair fell in loose curls to her shoulders. When he parked his car and got out, she ran to greet him. The closer she came, the more beautiful she was. Her dark eyes lit from the inside.

She threw herself into his arms. "Oh, Nick. I missed you so much."

He loved this woman. Elena. His wife.

A sob caught in the back of his throat, and he swallowed his sorrow. Oceans of tears wouldn't bring her back. He stared at the earring. "She didn't like jewelry. Rings got in the way when she was working with clay. Necklaces were too fancy. But she wore these earrings. Do you know the legend behind the dream catcher?"

In a quiet voice, Caitlyn said, "The web allows good dreams to filter through and stops the nightmares."

"I gave her these earrings so she'd sleep easy when I wasn't around to protect her." He remembered the silver dream catcher glimmering against her shining black hair. "Nothing could keep her safe. When I found her body, she was wearing only one of these earrings."

It had been his hope to bury her with the earrings, and he'd searched long and hard for the mate to this one. He'd gone through her closet, checked the box of jewelry she never wore, had felt along every inch of floor in the house, and he'd come up empty-handed.

Someone had taken the earring. The murderer.

But the red-haired man didn't have it.

With a sigh, he continued, "I lost them both. My wife and her father, my mentor. It was almost four years ago. I blamed myself for not being there, but Elena wasn't killed because of me. She was staying with her father, and he had enemies."

"Did Rojas kill them?" she asked.

"Someone hired the red-haired man. I wasn't sure who and I needed to know. That's why I created the identity of Tony Perez. Through Santoro, I thought I'd get close enough to the Rojas brothers to find out who was responsible." But he'd failed. The old familiar emptiness spread through him. He didn't care if he lived or died. "That's the life story of Nick Racine."

An identity he never wished to resume.

CAITLYN KNELT BESIDE HIM on the floor with her hands in her lap, itching to reach out to him and hold him. She was there for him, supporting him. If he wanted to talk, she'd listen. If he needed to cry, her shoulder was ready and waiting.

But he didn't reach out. His gaze averted, he withdrew into himself.

She'd seen this reaction from others. No stranger to tragedy, she had experienced the aftermath of violent death while embedded with the troops. Everyone dealt with the pain of sudden loss in their own way, and his grief was deep, intense, almost unimaginable. His wife had been murdered. At the same time, he'd lost his mentor—a man who not only taught him but was his father-in-law.

No wonder Jack had retreated into amnesia. It must have been a relief to shed the burden of being Nick Racine.

He stared at the dream catcher earring. The delicate silver strands contrasted with his rough hands. What was he thinking? What memories haunted him?

From outside, she heard the grating of tires on the gravel driveway. Someone was approaching the safe house.

Though she thought this might be a good time for him to turn himself in, that wasn't her decision to make.

Softly, she spoke his name. "Nick?"

He didn't seem to hear her.

"Nick, there's a car coming."

Immobile, he continued to stare at the memento from his dead wife.

More loudly, she said, "Jack."

He looked at her as though he was seeing her for the first time. He pressed the dream catcher against his lips and slipped it into his pocket. Slowly, he rose to his feet. "We'll see who it is before we decide what to do."

He directed her down the hallway to the rear door, unfastened the lock and stepped outside. She followed as he rounded the house and stopped. From this vantage point, they could see the front of the house.

Jack peeked around the edge. Under his breath, he cursed.

Caitlyn looked past his shoulder and saw Bryant and Patterson emerge from their vehicle. Until now, she and Jack had been riding on a wave of good luck. They'd escaped from the ranch and hidden at Woodley's without anyone coming after them. Apparently, that positive trend had reversed. The two marshals were the last people she wanted to meet.

"What should we do?" She looked to Jack for an answer, but he'd sunk back into a daze of sorrow. He leaned against the wall of the house, staring blankly into the distance.

This apathy didn't work for her. They were in trouble, and she needed for him to be sharp and focused. She needed for him to be Jack.

Bryant took off his cowboy hat and dragged his hand through his hair. "I still don't get it. Why the hell did you make such a big stink about this place being our jurisdiction?"

"Because it is." Patterson dragged his feet. The older man's exhaustion was evident. "This safe house belongs to the U.S. Marshals Service. Besides, I need to keep the CSI's away. When they start prowling around, they'll find clues."

"They're going to figure out what we did, especially when the men they've got in custody start talking."

"Rojas's men? They won't talk. They're too afraid of their boss to make a peep."

"It's over. We ain't going to get out of this." The tall Texan leaned against the side of the vehicle. "I don't want to go to prison, man. I say we make a run for it."

"There's another option."

She watched as Patterson opened the back door of the vehicle and reached inside. Jack had roused himself enough to observe, and she was glad that he'd decided to pay attention.

When Patterson emerged from the car, he held an automatic gun in his hand.

"It's the SIG Sauer," Jack whispered. "Perry's gun."

Jack had also been using that gun. He'd spent all but two bullets defending her when Rojas and his men came after her at her house.

Patterson rounded the front of the car and raised the gun, aiming at the center of Bryant's chest. "Sorry, kid."

The tall Texan turned toward his partner. His back was to them as he held up both hands. "What are you doing?"

"Don't worry. I'm not going to kill you."

"Kill me? What?"

"My God, you're dumb." She saw disgust in Patterson's weary face. "I'm so damned tired of having to explain every tiny detail to you. This is simple. I need to convince our supervisor that Nick Racine went off the rails and is dangerous."

"By shooting me?"

"I'll tell them that Nick shot you," Patterson said. "This gun is proof. Nick used it. When ballistics compares bullets, it proves that he's dangerous."

"Don't do it," Bryant pleaded. "We can go on the run. Rojas will protect us. He'll give us more money and—"

"Shut up," Patterson snapped. "I'm not going into hiding. I have a family. I have a pension. I'm not giving those things up."

Quietly, Jack said, "Patterson can't trust the kid to keep his mouth shut. He's going to kill him."

Apparently, Bryant had come to the same conclusion. He reached for the gun on his belt.

Jack stepped clear of the house, took aim and fired.

His marksmanship was nothing short of amazing. His bullet hit Patterson's arm. He clutched at the wound near his shoulder and staggered backward. The SIG fell from his hand.

Bryant reacted. He whirled, gun in hand, and faced Jack.

"Drop it," Jack said.

The Texan looked back at the partner who had intended to kill him. Then at Jack. Caitlyn could almost see the wheels turning inside his head as he made his decision. *The wrong decision.*

He fired at Jack.

She heard the bullet smack into the house just above her head.

Jack returned fire. Two shots. Two hits.

The Texan fell to the dirt.

Chapter Nineteen

There was a lot of blood, but both marshals were still moving. Not dead. Caitlyn wondered why she wasn't shrinking into the shadows at the side of the house, paralyzed by terror, and then she realized that she wasn't afraid; she trusted Jack to protect her.

Patterson lurched backward and braced himself against the car. With his good arm, he reached across his body toward the gun on his hip.

"Don't try it," Jack warned. "You make one more move, and my next bullet goes through the center of your forehead."

The gray-haired marshal dropped his arm. His left hand was bloody from the wound on his right arm. His dark windbreaker with U.S. Marshal stenciled across the back was slick with gore.

On the ground, Bryant struggled to sit up. His face contorted in pain, and he was groaning, almost sobbing. In his beige jacket, his injuries were more obvious. One of Jack's bullets had ripped through his right shoulder. He'd also been shot in the right thigh. His gun was out of his reach, and he seemed to be suffering too much to go after it.

Caitlyn asked, "What are you going to do with them?"

"First, I'll make sure they're completely disarmed. They're both wearing ankle holsters and probably have a

couple of other weapons stashed. Next, I'll get rid of their
cell phones."

"Will you kill them?"

"Not unless it's necessary," he said. "I want you to go
back to the ATV and wait for me."

Her natural curiosity told her to stay and observe. She
wanted to see how Jack got these men to give up their
weapons and to hear what they said to each other. By leaving, she'd be walking out before the story was finished.

But she was well aware that she and Jack had no backup.
This situation wasn't like anything she'd encountered in
the Middle East. Replacement troops weren't going to be
riding over the hill to help them out. The smartest thing she
could do was to follow Jack's orders. "I'll be waiting."

She jogged around the house and the barn to the forest
where they'd hidden the four-wheeler. Was Jack going to
finish what he'd started? With her out of the way, would he
kill the marshals? She remembered what he'd told her about
executing the man who'd murdered his wife. In her frame
of reference, an execution meant killing in cold blood. In
his identity as Nick Racine, he was a murderer.

But Jack wasn't. Though he didn't hesitate to use physical violence, he hadn't killed anyone. He'd said it wasn't
his job. Had he been talking about an occupation? Clearly,
he had training in marksmanship, and his hand-to-hand
combat skills were finely honed.

At the ATV, she pulled away the brush that camouflaged
the vehicle. There was a lot she didn't know about Nick
Racine. A lot she needed to find out.

Right now, there was a more pressing issue. By shooting the marshals, Jack had—ironically—given credence to
Patterson's plan to discredit him. When the marshals were
rescued, they would accuse Jack of ambushing them. Every

law-enforcement person involved in the search for Rojas would shift their focus toward Jack. And toward her.

There was no way they could turn themselves in with any guarantee of safety. Not unless she could negotiate the terms with someone she trusted, someone like Danny or Mr. Woodley. She wished she'd kept up with her contacts stateside. At one time, she'd known people in high places. There were still a few. A plan began to form in her mind.

She saw Jack running toward her. Since she hadn't heard any other gunfire, she assumed he hadn't shot Patterson and Bryant. There wasn't any blood on his clothes, so he hadn't knifed them. She might have thought less of him if he'd murdered the marshals, even though they were despicable men who deserved punishment.

He climbed onto the front seat of the ATV. "Let's roll."

"I know exactly which way to go."

Their first challenge would be to get across the main highway without being seen. Since it was early on a Sunday, there wouldn't be much traffic, but law enforcement would be watching the roads. Leaning forward and shouting over the noise of the engine, she directed him to a ridge overlooking a section of road that wasn't fenced. "Stop here."

He killed the engine. "Use your cell phone. Call 911 and get an ambulance out to the safe house."

"Are you sure?"

"I don't like those two morons, but they're still marshals. They must have done something useful in their lives."

As far as she was concerned, that was an awfully generous assumption. Still, she made the call and turned off her phone.

To Jack she said, "You could have killed them."

"That's not who I am."

"Nick Racine?"

He pulled off his helmet and turned in his seat. She studied his face, searching for the terrible sadness that consumed him when he held the silver dream catcher. His expression was grim and as unreadable as granite.

"I've committed murder," he said, "but I'm not a killer. If there's another way, that's the path I'll chose."

"Why?"

"Death is permanent. If you make a mistake, there's no chance for a do-over."

She knew they needed to get moving. There wasn't time for him to answer all the questions that boiled inside her brain. "I want to know about Nick Racine."

Like the sun coming out from behind a cloud, the sexy grin slid onto his face. "Call me Jack."

She answered with a smile of her own. "As if you were born in the moment you walked up to my cabin?"

"Something like that."

What an amazing fantasy! Yesterday morning, the only thought in her mind had been repairing the roof on her barn. She certainly hadn't been thinking about a mate, but if she had imagined the perfect man, he'd be strong, handsome and capable. He'd be complex and interesting. He'd be sexy. He'd be…Jack.

Her heart gave a hard thump against her rib cage. There was no denying her attraction to him. Did it really matter who he was or what he'd done? Fate had dropped him into her life. She was meant to be with him.

She picked up her helmet. "We need to get across the road without anybody seeing us."

"Hang on."

He turned the key in the ignition and maneuvered down the hill. This stretch of road was relatively straight, with good visibility in either direction. There were no other vehicles in sight. The ATV bounced over a ditch, onto the shoulder and across the pavement. It seemed that they'd made it safely across this hurdle, but she wanted to be sure.

"Go into the trees and stop," she said.

He followed her instructions and parked again. He must have been following her line of thinking because he quickly dismounted and moved to a position where he could see the road which was a couple of hundred yards from where they were standing. His gaze scanned from left to right. "We're not being followed."

A beat-up Dodge truck rumbled along the road, traveling a lot faster than the limit. She saw nothing suspicious about his speed; people who lived in the mountains treated the posted limits as guidelines rather than laws.

She heard the wail of an emergency vehicle. As they watched, an ambulance raced past. It was followed by an SUV with the sheriff's logo on the door. In just a few minutes, Patterson would be spewing his lies to the local officers.

"We're in big trouble," she murmured.

His arm encircled her waist. With the thumb of his other hand, he lifted her chin so she was looking up at him. "This might be the right time for you to turn yourself in. After Patterson tells the cops how I went berserk and shot them both, the search is going to get intense. Dangerous."

"I'm pretty sure he's going to implicate me in his lies." She slipped her arm around him. Their bodies had become accustomed to each other; they fit together perfectly. "Besides, you need me. I have a plan that's nothing short of brilliant."

"Brilliant, huh?"

When he combed his fingers through her hair, she realized that her ponytail had come undone. She shook her head. "I must look awful. Do I have helmet hair?"

"Tell me about this plan."

"The way I figure, being taken into custody isn't really the problem. You want to make it to the trial to testify."

"Correct." He kissed the center of her forehead.

"We need to find someone in authority who can facilitate the process and get you to court." Though his kiss distracted her, she kept talking. "I actually do have a contact I can call upon. Someone who knows me and trusts me."

"Who?"

"He's a full-bird colonel, and he's stationed at the Air Force Academy. Once we're on the base, we're under the jurisdiction of the military. Nobody else can touch us, neither the police nor the marshals."

Jack pulled his head back and looked at her with a combination of surprise and appreciation that made her feel warm inside. "How did you get to be so smart?"

"You have your talents," she said, "and I have mine."

"And what makes you think he won't throw us into the brig?"

"He's a fair man," she said. "He'll at least listen to what I have to say. We spent enough time together in the Middle East for him to know that I'm trustworthy."

"Let's contact him and put an end to this. Give him a call on your cell phone."

"I can't really do that. Technically, he doesn't have jurisdiction if we're not on the base. We have to go there. But the Academy isn't that far, only about forty-five miles."

"So all we have to do is make it across forty-five miles through rugged mountain terrain. On a four-wheeler. With deputies, cops, the Marshals Service and the FBI looking for us."

"And possibly Rojas," she said.

He snugged her tightly against him. "Piece of cake."

His kiss was quick and urgent. There wasn't time for

a delicate building of passion; they needed to put miles between themselves and the search parties.

They took their places on the four-wheeler, and he asked, "Any instructions?"

"Keep going in a southeastern direction. Avoid the roads, the fences and cabins."

Turning invisible would have been a handy trick, but neither she nor Jack was magical. To find their way through the mountains, they would have to rely on her sense of direction and her memory.

During the summers when her family stayed at the cabin, she and her brother had taken daylong horse rides to Colorado Springs. Mostly, they'd followed marked trails and roads—an option that she and Jack didn't have. Still, she figured that she wasn't plunging into an altogether unfamiliar wilderness.

Instead of going deeper into the forested area, Jack drove at the edge of the trees, putting distance between them and the safe house. Their route was parallel to a barbed-wire fence with a rugged dirt path beside it. Other four-wheelers probably used that path. Following it would have allowed them to go faster, but she didn't want to risk running into anyone else.

When the distance between the trees and the fence narrowed, Jack veered into the trees. Their progress was slow and bumpy. This vehicle wasn't built for comfort or for long-distance travel. Her already-bruised tailbone ached.

After what seemed like an eternity, Jack found a space without cabins or road and came to a stop. She immediately hopped off, stretched and walked stiffly.

Jack looked up toward the sun. "It's getting close to noon. Do you any idea where we are?"

"My butt is in hell," she muttered. "All I can say for sure is that we're in the front range of the Rockies."

"A while back, I spotted a road sign. It said something about Roxborough State Park and Sedalia."

"Great," she muttered.

"We've been headed south and mostly east."

"I know."

She'd been pointing him that way. Their route would have been easier if they'd followed South Platte River Road, but she knew there would be fishermen—witnesses who might feel compelled to report a noisy ATV that was scaring the trout.

Jack went to a storage container behind the second seat and opened the lid. "You said Woodley packed some food."

Dear, sweet Mr. Woodley. She hoped he wouldn't be fooled by Patterson's lies, wouldn't think the worst of her. Sooner or later, he'd probably contact her parents. She shuddered to think of what they'd say. Mom hadn't been at all happy when she'd taken the assignment in the Middle East. Now Caitlyn was on the run with a desperate fugitive.

She took out her cell phone. "I should give Mr. Woodley a call."

"Don't turn it on."

She paused with the phone in her hand, watching as he held the quart-size canteen to his lips and took a long glug. He wiped his mouth with the back of his hand and said, "Even if your phone is supposedly untraceable, we can't take a chance. It's likely the FBI is involved in the manhunt. They might have equipment to track the signal."

Morosely, she shoved the phone back into her pocket. "I suppose using the GPS function to get our bearings is out of the question."

He held out a sandwich. "Eat something. It'll make your butt feel better."

Though his logic left a lot to be desired, she took the

food. Her mouth was so dry that she nearly choked, but the ham-and-cheese sandwich tasted good. A hot cup of coffee would have been heaven, but she settled for water.

Jack ate his sandwich in a couple of giant bites and started digging through their supplies. "There are a couple of oranges and bananas. And a whole box of energy bars. What is it with you mountain people and granola?"

"Easy to carry and yummy to eat. Give me one."

After taking in food and water, she felt immeasurably better—nearly human, in fact. When Jack suggested hiking to the top of the rise to get their bearings, she was ready. Any activity that didn't involve sitting sounded good.

Her muscles stretched as she hiked. She swung her arms and wiggled her hips. Walking the rest of the way to the Air Force Academy seemed preferable to more hours on the back of the ATV.

She joined Jack on the rocky crest devoid of trees. The wind brushed through the tangles in her hair, which undoubtedly resembled a bird's nest, but she didn't care. An incredible panorama filled her vision and gave her strength. In the distance, she saw Pike's Peak, capped with snow.

Energizing her body seemed to help her brain. As she gazed across the rugged landscape, she knew where they were and where they should be headed. She pointed. "We go that way."

"Any particular reason why?"

"The best place to hide is in plain sight," she said. "We're close to the Rampart Range Recreational Area. It's full of trails that are sanctioned for ATVs. With our helmets, we'll blend in with the other off-roaders."

He didn't answer immediately. Preoccupied, he stared into the sky. "I see a chopper."

"And there will be a lot more planes and gliders and

such as we get closer to the Academy. It's nothing to worry about."

"You're probably right." He shrugged but still looked worried. "I like your plan. If we're on a trail, we can move faster."

"Okay," she said. "Let's hit the road, Jack."

He raised an eyebrow. "How long have you been waiting to say that?"

"Hours."

Not all of her thinking was about escape. Sometimes, they just needed a chuckle.

Chapter Twenty

Though Jack made several more rest stops in the afternoon, the constant vibration of the four-wheeler was getting to him. Navigating this machine through the wilderness was like crashing through a maze on a bucking bronco.

When they found the groomed trails of the Rampart Range Recreational Area, the ride was a hundred times smoother. In comparison to open terrain, these trails were like cruising on polished marble. Finally, they were getting somewhere. Approaching the last step in their journey.

As soon as he was taken into custody by Caitlyn's colonel, he'd be swept into the system and transported to Chicago to testify. His time with her would be over. Sure, they'd promise to see each other again after the trial. They'd make plans. Maybe even meet for coffee. But she'd be charging back into her career. And he'd likely be in witness protection.

He didn't want to lose her.

Other ATVs and dirt bikes buzzed along the trails around them, careening around sharp turns and flying over bumps in the road. Woodley's four-wheeler was more utilitarian than recreational, not designed for stunts. Their top speed was about forty or forty-five, and Jack was moving considerably slower.

A skinny teenager in a flame helmet zipped past them and shouted, "Step on it, Grandpa."

"I'll step on you," he muttered. He cranked the accelerator. Then he backed off. This was no time for a motocross race.

At a fork in the trail, he stopped at a carved wooden marker with arrows pointing the way to different trails. Behind him, Caitlyn was quick to choose. "Left," she said. "It's a camping area."

He didn't much care for organized campsites; having other people around ruined the experience. "What if we have to register? Neither of us have wallets or IDs."

"We don't have to stay there," she said. "But we can fill our water bottle. And maybe there's a bathroom. Oh, God, I'd love to find a bathroom. Even an outhouse."

A half mile down the trail was a large camping area with several separate sites, two of which were occupied by other ATV riders. Their campfires tinted the air with pungent smoke. His concern about registering was unfounded. There wasn't a ranger station, just a couple of restrooms in a small house designed to look like a log cabin. He parked behind the restrooms and watched as Caitlyn went inside.

He stood for a minute and waited before he decided it wasn't necessary to stand guard. If anyone had been following them, they'd have made their move long before now. He glanced around the area. *Were they safe?* More than once, he'd seen choppers swooping like giant dragonflies across the skies. *Aerial surveillance?* It was possible. But the helicopters hadn't come closer or hovered above them.

He took his helmet with him as he strolled through the groomed area surrounded by a thick forest of lodgepole pine and Douglas fir. This land had been untouched by wildfires, and the foliage grew in robust clumps. A narrow creek trickled beyond the edge of the campground. He stood beside it and listened to the sound of rippling water mingled with the distant voices of the other campers.

The late afternoon sunlight reflected on the water as it rushed to join with a wider river or a lake or, perhaps, to flow all the way to the Gulf of Mexico. Everything had a destination. Every person had a future, even a man with no past.

He used to be Nick Racine. Not anymore. Though the full picture of his past was hazy, he vividly remembered the soul-deep devastation after Elena's murder. The single earring in his pocket reminded him of broken dreams—a future he'd lost. Tragedy had consumed him. Then rage. Then he'd embarked on the quest for revenge that turned him into a murderer.

When amnesia wiped the slate clean, he was freed from his past. He didn't know what fate had directed him to Caitlyn's cabin, but he was grateful. She had refused to give up on him. She'd believed in him. Literally, she knew Jack Dalton better than anyone else.

She came up beside him. "I found a brochure in a box at the bathroom. There's a trail map."

The squiggly lines marking the trails resembled a tangle of yarn, but he zoomed in on the important part. "Here's where we come out. Woodland Park."

"From there, it's a straight shot to the back entrance to the Air Force Academy," she said. "We're close. But it's late. I think we should stop for the night."

It wasn't necessary to stop. Their vehicle had headlights, and Jack knew he could push his endurance and reach the Academy tonight. But he was in favor of camping tonight; he didn't want his time with her to end. He pointed to a location on the map. "We'll camp here."

She squinted to read the tiny name beside the dot. "Devil's Spike? The code says there's no bathroom or water."

"It's not far from here. Looks like a couple of squiggly miles up the road we're on."

"Why can't we stay right here?"

"Witnesses," he said.

He turned on his heel and walked back to the four-wheeler. His reason for choosing the most remote location on the map was simple: he wanted to be alone, completely alone, with her.

Grumbling, she climbed onto the back of the ATV. In less than fifteen minutes, they'd climbed a zigzag trail to the Devil's Spike area. Each campsite consisted of a cleared space, a table and a fire ring. Each was separated from the others by trees and rocks. All were deserted. It was Sunday night, not a time when many people were camping.

While Caitlyn climbed onto the top of the wood picnic table and sat with her feet on the bench, he took the sleeping bags from the storage container. Since they didn't have a tent or any other gear, setting up camp was simply a matter of spreading the bags on the flattest part of the clearing.

He took the freshly filled water bottle and joined her on the table. Devil's Spike was higher than the other campground. From this vantage point, they overlooked rolling hills covered with trees and dotted with jagged rock formations—one of which was probably supposed to be the Spike. In the west, the sun had begun to set, coloring the sky a brilliant magenta and gilding the underbellies of clouds with molten gold.

For a change, Caitlyn was quiet. And so was he.

After spending the entire day with the roar of the ATV motor, the stillness of the mountains was a relief. The wind was cool enough to be refreshing without making him shiver.

He gazed toward her. The glow of the sunset touched her cheekbones and picked out strands of gold in her hair. He'd told her several times that she was smart, tough and brave, but he'd forgotten the most important thing. She was a beautiful woman.

She exhaled a sigh and stretched, rotating her shoulders and turning her head from side to side.

"Sore?" he asked.

"From my toes to the top of my head. My butt is killing me."

"I've got a cure." He brushed the twigs and pine cones from the surface of the table. "Lie down. I'll give you a massage."

She hesitated for a nanosecond before stripping off her jacket, which she folded into a makeshift pillow. She lay down on her stomach on the table. "Be gentle," she said. "I'm not a big fan of the deep tissue stuff."

He started by lightly kneading the tense muscles of her shoulders and neck. The fabric of her T-shirt bunched under his fingers. "You really should be nude."

"If I was naked on this table, I'd come away with a belly full of splinters."

He stroked lower on her back. He could count her ribs, but her body was soft and feminine, with a slim waist and a sensual flare of her hips. *Really beautiful.* He needed to tell her.

When he returned to her shoulders, she gave a soft moan—the kind of sound that lovers made. For several minutes, he continued to massage, and her moans got deeper and more sensual. "Oh, Jack. That's amazing."

He agreed. It felt pretty damned good to him, too.

As he rubbed near her tailbone, she tensed. "Be careful, that hurts."

"Let me take a look."

Before she could object, he reached around to unbutton her jeans. He slid the denim down her hips. A patch of black and blue colored the milky skin above her bottom.

She grumbled, "Are you staring at my butt?"

"You've got a nice little bruise back here."

"Really?" She twisted her torso, trying to look over her shoulder. "Where?"

"Without a mirror, you aren't going to be able to see it."

"Are you sure it's bruised?"

"How does this feel?" With two fingers, he pressed against bruise.

"Hurts," she said. "What should I do about it?"

"I could kiss it and make it better."

She rolled onto her back and looked up at him. Her eyes were the purest blue he'd ever seen. Now was the time to give her his sincere compliments about her beauty, but he found himself tongue-tied. What the hell was wrong with him? He wasn't inexperienced with women, but this felt like his first time.

"There's something," he blurted, "something I need to say."

Her eyebrows pulled down. "What is it?"

He couldn't blame her for being worried. Every time she turned around, he threw some giant revelation at her. She probably though he was going to confess to the crime of the century. "It's nothing bad."

"Okay," she said hesitantly.

"I wanted you to know that I appreciate you." *Real smooth, Jack.*

"And I appreciate you, too."

They sounded less intimate than coworkers discussing a business project. He took a breath and started over. "I like the way your hair slips out of the ponytail and falls across your cheek. And the way you squint when you're thinking. And the little gasping noise you make when you laugh."

"I don't snort," she said.

"You catch your breath, as though laughter surprises you. It's a happy sound." Feeling more confident, he glided his hand along her arm. "I like the proportion of your shoulders and your hips. And your long legs. What I'm trying to say is that you're beautiful, Caitlyn."

She reached up and touched his cheek. "Last night, I didn't think we'd known each other long enough to make love."

"And now?"

"It's time."

That was all he needed to hear. He kissed the smile from her lips.

FINALLY! HE WAS KISSING HER. Caitlyn clung to him. His massage had lit her fuse, and she was certain that she'd explode into a million pieces if they didn't make love now, right now.

She expected Jack to show his passion with the same skill he showed in every other physical activity, but he had seemed unsure of himself. His clumsiness was endearing, but not what she was looking for. She wanted him to sweep her off her feet.

As he deepened the kiss, she felt his attitude change. He went from boyish to manly. Dominating and powerful, he took charge. With a surge of strength, he yanked her off the picnic table.

"You're so damn beautiful," he said.

"So are you."

"Men aren't."

"You are."

He carried her across the clearing. She knew he wouldn't stumble or drop her; she trusted him. In his arms, she felt completely safe.

His step was sure as he bent his legs and lowered her onto the smooth fabric of the sleeping bag on the ground. Not exactly a feather bed, but she was accustomed to sleeping in rough conditions.

Impatient, she tried to pull him down on top of her, but he sat back on his heels. Twilight wrapped around him. His eyes glistened as he consumed her with a gaze. Then he went to her feet and removed her shoes and socks.

She looked down the length of her body, watching him as he stroked her instep and pressed on her toes. Another massage. Incredible! Most men required hours of pleading before they'd rub your feet. A burst of sensual tremors slithered up her legs, rising from her bare feet to her groin. She exhaled a low moan of sheer pleasure.

He moved up her body to her already unfastened jeans. His hand slid inside her waistband. Her thighs spread, welcoming his touch. Quivering in anticipation, she arched her back, inadvertently putting pressure on her bruised tailbone. Pain shot through her. "Ouch."

He stopped what he was doing and stretched out beside her. "Does it hurt?"

"Yes, but I don't want to stop."

"There's only one thing to do." He held her tightly and flipped onto his back. The move was so unexpected that she gasped. She loved the way he manhandled her.

"I get it," she said. "I have to be on top."

She liked this plan. As they undressed each other, she felt like she had some control. She decided the moment when their bare flesh would make contact. Lying naked on top of him, she reveled in the head-to-toe sensation. The cool mountain breeze that flowed down her spine contrasted the heat generated by their joined bodies.

Even though Jack was on the bottom, he remained the aggressor. He directed her with gentle shifts in position and not-so-subtle touches. Her thighs spread. As she straddled him, he moved her hips up and down, rubbing hard.

They were both breathless when he said, "You know I don't have a condom."

"I'm on the pill." Though she craved him, she hesitated. In his life as Racine and as Perez the mob enforcer, he'd been exposed to a lot of bad things. "Do you have any issues I should know about?"

"I'm clean. Haven't made love since I was in the hospital."

Her fingers ran along the edge of the scar on his torso. "You were Tony Perez when you were shot."

"A lifetime ago."

When he pulled her against his body, she knew that one night with him wasn't enough. She couldn't imagine a lifetime without Jack.

Chapter Twenty-One

Caitlyn had been right to assume that Jack would be a great lover. He knew all the right moves and some unusual twists that had surprised and delighted her. Their first bout of lovemaking had been fierce and hungry. The second time was more about gentleness and finesse.

On her side, she curled up inside the sleeping bags they'd zipped together. No other campers had chosen Devil's Spike, and she was glad for the privacy as she watched Jack—naked except for his boots—as he started a fire in the rock-lined pit.

Though she was enjoying the show, she said, "We don't really need a fire. We don't have anything to cook."

Crouched in the darkness, he coaxed the flames. "It's a primal thing. Like a caveman."

His long, lean body was far too sculpted to be that of a primitive man. She'd told him that he was beautiful, and she'd meant it. He reminded her of a perfect sculpture.

"We don't need the fire for warmth," she said. The early summer night was chilly, but the thermal sleeping bag would keep them warm enough.

He stepped away from the pit and looked down on the tiny dancing flames. "Call it ambience. Or protection from bears. Every campsite needs a fire."

When he crawled into the sleeping bag beside her, his

skin was cold. It took a couple minute of giggling and wrestling for them both to get comfortable. They ended up in a spooning position, facing the fire with his arms snuggled around her.

Turning her head, she looked up through the tracery of pine boughs into a brilliant, starry night. She should have been perfectly content, but the wheels in the back of her mind had started turning. She was thinking about tomorrow. Turning to the colonel for help was the right thing to do, and she was sure he'd get Jack where he needed to be for the trial. And then what would happen?

As a journalist, she could use her press credentials to stay in touch with him until she'd written her story. But she couldn't violate the rules of witness protection to be with him unless she was willing to give up her own identity and disappear. She couldn't do that, couldn't sever her ties with her family and friends. The most important thing she'd learned from this experience was the value of friendship. She and Jack never would have escaped if it hadn't been for Heather, Danny and Mr. Woodley.

"After you testify," she said, "do you have to go into the WitSec program?"

"I was wondering how long it would take."

"How long what would take?"

He nuzzled her ear. "Until you started asking questions again."

"I don't want to say goodbye to you tomorrow." They had forged a bond, made a connection unlike anything she'd ever known. She might actually be falling in love with him. "We need to spend more time together."

"I wonder how much money I have."

"What?" She wriggled around until she was facing him. "What are you thinking?"

"When I was Nick Racine, I wonder if I was rich or poor or somewhere in between."

They hadn't had much luck researching his finances or his identity on the computer. "I couldn't find Nick Racine in any of the usual credit databases. Online, you don't exist."

"Which brings up a couple of possibilities," he said. "I might be someone who lived completely off the grid. Or I might have a numbered Swiss bank account."

"Those are the choices? Either you were a criminal or a mogul?"

"I vote for mogul. Then I wouldn't have to worry about WitSec. I'd buy an island in the tropics with a waterfall, and we could live there, eating coconuts and mangos."

"Not the best location for a reporter," she said.

"You'd adjust, and I'd buy you a newspaper of your own. *The Caitlyn Daily News.*" With the firelight glimmering in his tousled black hair, he was disconcertingly gorgeous.

"Unfortunately, we don't know if you're a crook or a billionaire. We need more information. Seems like we're back to the beginning. We need to know more about your past."

"Blank," he said. "Not being able to remember isn't entirely due to amnesia. I consciously erased Nick Racine. Couldn't live with the tragedy. Or with the way I handled my revenge."

She was tired and hungry. Having him naked beside her made her want to spend the rest of the night making love. But this was important; the future depended on it. "Let's try to figure out the easy stuff. Like your occupation."

"Nothing comes to mind."

With the tip of her finger, she traced the jagged scar from his bullet wound. Other injuries had left their marks on his body. Obviously, he'd lived a physically active, dangerous life. "I think we can rule out Sunday school teacher and peace activist."

"I could be a peace activist," he protested. "I have a gentle side. I like flowers."

"Flowers, huh?" She supposed that any memory was good. "What kind of flowers?"

"Orchids." His sexy grin slid into place. "That's a good sign, right? Orchids are expensive."

He was the furthest thing from a hothouse flower that she could imagine. "Let's go with your skills. What kind of work requires you to be a marksman? Why would you be trained in hand-to-hand combat?"

"The military," he said, "but that doesn't fit. I have no memory of basic training or being on a base, can't imagine myself in a uniform. Besides, you checked military data and didn't find a record of Nick Racine."

Some jobs in the military weren't part of the records. He could have been trained in a special operation—the kind that didn't leave a paper trail. Or he could have been working for an outside organization. "You might be a mercenary."

"Maybe."

She'd never interviewed a mercenary but had met a few. They were cruel, emotionless men with cold eyes and even colder hearts. "You have the skills but not the temperament. If you were a mercenary, you would have slit the throats of Rojas's men at the safe house."

"That's not how I roll." He caressed the line of her throat. "I'm a lover, not a fighter."

She caught his hand. "You're both."

"There's no point in figuring out my past. Tomorrow, when I turn myself in, the federal prosecutors in charge of the trial in Chicago will fill in the blanks. I'm sure they have a fat dossier on Nick Racine and Tony Perez." He raised their hands to his lips and brushed a kiss on her knuckles. "On Tuesday, I'll testify."

She hated this neat, logical package. "What about me? What happens to us?"

"I won't let you go." Though he spoke softly, his voice rang with determination. "Before I met you and became Jack Dalton, I didn't give a damn about my future. I was empty. Didn't care if I lived or died. You changed that."

She'd never been anyone's reason for living. Unexpected tears welled up behind her eyelids. "What next?"

"The possibilities are endless, babe."

A tear slipped down her cheek, and he kissed it away. She never wanted him to leave. She wouldn't say goodbye to him. No matter what.

THE NEXT MORNING, Jack studied the trail map to find the most direct route to Woodland Park. The ATV was running low on fuel, and he didn't want their plan to be derailed by something as mundane as running out of gas.

His focus was clear. He wanted to get this thing over with so he could start his new life. No longer consumed by his past, he was ready for the future.

Caitlyn sat gingerly on the backseat of the four-wheeler. "Know what I want?"

He draped an arm around her shoulder and gave her a quick but thorough kiss. "Some of this?"

She glided her hand down his chest and tugged on the waistband of his jeans. With a grin, she released the fabric and patted his gut. "I really, really want steak and eggs. A medium-rare T-bone. And hash browns."

"When we get to the Academy, I'm sure your colonel friend can arrange it."

"I'm starved." She put on her helmet. "I burned off a lot of calories last night."

"It was a good workout." Their lovemaking hadn't been overly athletic but it had been sustained. He couldn't get enough of her, and he was pretty sure that feeling went both ways. "A lot more fun than when I was training for the triathlon."

She whipped her helmet off and stared at him. "You were in a triathlon?"

He remembered swimming, biking and running with the sun blistering down on his head and shoulders. "My goal was to finish in the top twenty."

"Did you?"

"Sixteenth."

"This is a positive sign, Jack. Your memories are falling back into place."

He wasn't sure how much he wanted to remember. The triathlon had been a proud achievement, but he couldn't help thinking that something in his past would come between them. "It's good to know I don't have permanent brain damage."

When he mounted the ATV and drove away from their campsite, the fuel gauge dipped into the reserve tank. How many more miles did they have before it died? Caitlyn had told him that Woodland Park was only ten miles from the Academy, but she'd been iffy on distances.

The trails were clearly marked, and it didn't take long to find the main road—the most direct route. Barely two lanes, the graded dirt had the reddish color of sandstone. There wasn't much traffic, but the vehicles varied from dirt bikes and ATVs to regular two-wheel drive cars. When a slick, cherry-red, top-down Jeep Wrangler passed them, he watched with envy. The Jeep was a nice ride that made sense on this scenic road. In contrast, Woodley's utilitarian ATV was like driving a lawn mower; it would be virtually useless in a chase.

Being around other vehicles reminded him that they weren't on a pleasure outing. He and Caitlyn were still the center of a manhunt. Last night, he'd felt safer. Nobody could have tracked their bizarre cross-country route from Pinedale.

Today was different. On this road, they weren't hidden by forest. They could be picked out in aerial surveillance. Patterson had talked about hitching a ride on a helicopter. What if that chopper stayed around? What if the marshals had an eye in the sky?

The dirt road snaked along the side of a mountain. Every twisting turn revealed another panorama. At a high point, he pulled onto the shoulder and stopped.

"Something wrong?" Caitlyn asked.

"Not yet."

He walked to the edge of the cliff. In the distance was Pike's Peak, glistening in the morning sunshine. A ribbon of road twisted through the trees below them.

"Nobody can recognize us in our helmets," she said.

It was in his nature to plan for the worst possible outcome. If they were pursued, the dramatic views on a high road without a guardrail would turn into a death trap. Too easily, they could be forced over the edge.

A dark SUV whipped along the road below them. The driver was going too fast, kicking up swirls of dust when he skidded onto the shoulder. "What does that car make you think of?"

"The black SUV," she said. "Rojas."

Gregorio Rojas was wealthy enough to pay for his own aerial surveillance. One of those choppers or gliders had been looking for them, and Rojas himself had come to finish the job.

He climbed onto the ATV and maneuvered if off the road where he hid behind a fat boulder. He and Caitlyn removed their helmets and waited. His Beretta was in his hand.

The SUV zoomed past their hiding place. Its dark-tinted windows made it impossible to see who was inside, but the passengers in this car weren't taking the time to enjoy the mountain scenery.

"They're going too fast," Caitlyn said. "If they meet anybody on this narrow road, they're going to scare the hell out of them."

"Or force them off the road," he said. "And the people they want to meet are us."

"How did they find us?"

"By now the sheriff has probably figured out how we escaped from the ranch. They'll know we took Woodley's four-wheeler. Aerial surveillance will be looking for a two-seat ATV ridden by people in bright blue helmets."

"But how does Rojas know?"

"Patterson." The marshal would have told his lies about how Jack attacked them and shot them. Patterson would still be in the law enforcement loop. "He's feeding information to Rojas."

Any doubt Jack might have had about who was in the SUV vanished when the car came roaring back down the road in the opposite direction. Rojas was searching for them, pinpointing their position. And he wasn't known for leaving survivors.

Chapter Twenty-Two

Jack knew he'd been in similar situations when he was on the run. Memories flashed: hiding in a dry ravine waiting for the sun to set, being chased across a rooftop in San Diego, jumping from an overpass onto a ledge.

In each memory he was alone. The only life he'd risked was his own. He refused to put Caitlyn in danger.

"We can't outrun them in the four-wheeler," he said.

"Do we keep going on foot?"

"Not safe. They'll be armed with sniper rifles. As soon as they spot us, we're dead."

She took out her cell phone. "We need reinforcements. I'm calling the colonel at the Academy."

"What are you going to tell him?"

"The truth," she said. "I'm in danger, and I need his help."

It couldn't hurt to have backup on the way, but Jack needed to do something now. He had to level the playing field. That meant disabling the SUV. Shooting the tires with a handgun was nearly impossible, even for him. But he had to try.

As they watched from their hiding place, the SUV drove past again, moving more slowly this time. At the wide end of the road where he'd pulled off, they turned and went back up the hill and disappeared behind a curve.

"I want you to stay hidden," he said. "If anything happens to me, run."

"Forget it. I'm not leaving you."

He gazed into her clear blue eyes. She'd come a long way from being the woman who froze in terror, but she didn't have his experience or skill. "They're not after you. Rojas wants me dead so I can't testify against his brother."

"But we're a team." Her chin jutted stubbornly. "There's got to be something I can do to help."

"Survive," he said. "That's what I ask of you, Caitlyn. I need for you to get through this in one piece."

"Without you?"

There were worse things than death.

"I lost my wife," he said. "If anything happened to you, I might as well hang it up. I couldn't live with the pain, can't bear to lose another woman I love."

CAITLYN HEARD THE WORDS, but it took a moment for them to sink in. *He loved her.*

She'd been telling herself that she was with him because he was a good story, but she'd violated the cardinal rule of journalism by getting involved with her subject. Involved? Wasn't that a mild way of describing their mind-blowing sex last night? She gave up the pretense. When it came to Jack, she wasn't objective.

"I love you, too."

His sexy grin mesmerized her. "This is going to work out, babe. You stay hidden. Stay safe."

He turned away from her and grabbed his helmet. In a crouch, he dodged through the trees and rocks.

She still held her cell phone, but she couldn't make the call until she knew what Jack was doing. Being careful to stay where she couldn't be seen from the road, she moved to a position beside a tall boulder. Peering through the trunks of trees, she caught a glimpse of his khaki jacket before he ducked behind a shrub at the edge of the cliff where the road made a sharp, hairpin curve.

She saw the SUV coming down the hill toward him.

Many of the people she'd interviewed over the years had told her that the moments before a disaster were so intense that everything happened in slow motion. She'd never experienced that sensation until now. The SUV with dark-tinted windows seemed to be creeping forward an inch at a time.

As she watched, Jack rose from his hiding place. On the edge of the cliff, he stood straight and tall. A gust of wind blew his jacket open. She thought she could see his jaw clench as he raised his gun and sighted down the barrel.

The windows on the SUV descended. A man leaned from the passenger seat. Rojas himself? He had a gun.

A scream crawled up the back of her throat, and she pressed her hands over her mouth to keep from making a noise. *Oh, God. Jack, what are you doing?*

The SUV lurched forward, coming at Jack.

The driver would be forced to turn. If he tried to hit Jack, the car would fly over the edge of the cliff.

She heard two gunshots.

The windshield cracked, but the car kept coming.

The front grille was only a few feet away from Jack. He fired again and again with both hands bracing his gun.

He dived out of the way as the big vehicle swerved into a turn. It was sideways on the corner of the road when the front tire slipped over the loose gravel on the shoulder. Off balance, the car flipped onto its side as it plummeted over the edge.

"Jack." She screamed his name. "Jack, are you all right?"

She couldn't see him.

CLINGING TO THE TRUNK of a scraggly little pine to keep from sliding down the steep incline, Jack ducked his head to avoid the flying shards of rock. A few feet from him, the SUV crashed down the cliff on its side. The drop was close to vertical for about sixty feet. Then the vehicle smashed into an outcropping of rock. Forward momentum flipped the SUV onto the roof, and it slid. The terrain leveled out, but the SUV kept going until it plowed into two tall pine trees.

The upper branches of the trees trembled. Dirt churned in the air. In the aftermath, there was silence, swirling dust and the stink of gasoline.

With his Beretta in his hand, Jack climbed down the craggy rocks toward the SUV that had come to rest upside down.

Nothing moved. The roof was caved in but not flattened. Rojas could have survived. Even if he was injured, he'd shoot to kill.

Keeping his distance, Jack watched and waited.

"Jack!"

Looking up, he saw Caitlyn standing at the top of the cliff. She looked like an angel—a very worried angel.

Waving, he called to her. "I'm all right. Stay where you are."

But she was already climbing over the ledge.

An arm thrust through the open passenger window of the SUV. Rojas clawed his way forward until he was half-way out. One side of his face was raw and bloody. His right arm twisted at an unnatural angle. "Help me."

"Throw out your guns," Jack said.

"Get me out of here. Before the damn car explodes."

"Where's your driver?"

"Dead. His neck broke. Dead." Rojas dragged himself forward an inch at a time. His hips were through the window. "I know it's you. Nick Racine. You son of a bitch."

Jack approached, keeping his Beretta aimed at Rojas, not taking any chances. A wounded man could be dangerous; he had nothing to lose.

Rojas hauled himself free of the car. His left leg, like his arm, was in bad shape. Breathing hard, he rolled onto his back. His face screwed into a knot, fighting the pain.

As far as Jack could tell, he was unarmed.

Caitlyn was all the way down the hill. Not taking his eyes off his enemy, Jack said to her, "Don't come any closer."

"Ambulance," Rojas said. "Get me an ambulance."

"I have my phone," she said.

"Make the 911 call." Jack stood over the injured man. "Make one false move, and I'll shoot."

Rojas glared up with pure hatred in his dark eyes. Deep abrasions had shredded the right side of his face. "You wanted to ruin my family. You and the other damned feds."

What other feds? "Who?"

"DEA."

That was the answer that had eluded him. Three little letters: DEA. In his mind he saw his badge and his official identification papers. He was a DEA agent, an officer of the law. Huge chunks of memory fell into place.

"Bastard." Rojas turned his head and spat. "You sent my brother to jail. You tried to destroy me."

"That's what happens when you're running a drug cartel. You get caught."

With his good hand, Rojas reached into his jacket pocket.

Jack tensed, ready to shoot.

Rojas withdrew a fist. He held his arm toward Jack and opened his hand. "I still win."

In his bloody hand he held a delicate silver dream catcher, the mate of the one Jack had found at the safe house. That earring was as good as a confession. Rojas was responsible for Elena's murder; he had hired the hit man.

Jack stood and aimed his gun at the center of Rojas's chest. If any man deserved killing, it was him. "Why?"

"Her papa was my enemy." His eyelids closed. "Didn't know she was your woman. But I'm glad."

"Rot in hell." He could have pulled the trigger, but it would be more painful for Rojas to survive. He took the earring from the unconscious man's hand, turned his back and walked toward Caitlyn.

She ran to him and threw herself into his arms. "Never do anything like that again. Never."

"I can't make that promise."

She stepped back. Her eyes filled with questions, but she said, "We'd better hurry. I called for an ambulance. That means the police will be here any minute."

"We don't have to run anymore. I remembered. Everything." He took a breath, accepting his identity. "I'm a DEA agent. Most of my work is undercover. I was taught by Elena's father, based in Arizona."

"DEA?" She cocked her head to one side. "You're an undercover agent?"

"That's why I don't have a presence on the internet. I have to keep my identity hidden. It's also how I knew how to turn myself into Tony Perez."

"It's also how you became Jack Dalton."

He didn't want her to think that she was nothing more than another project. "I haven't lied to you. Okay, I did at first when I claimed somebody else's identity. But after that I've told you as much of the truth as I could remember."

"It fits," she said. "When the marshals nearly found us in the cave, they said something about backup. Why didn't you call the DEA for backup?"

"If it hadn't been for the amnesia, I could have contacted my superiors. We wouldn't have gone through all this. Listen, Caitlyn, I'm sorry for scaring the hell out of you. Sorry I put you in danger. Sorry I dragged your friends into this mess. But there's a silver lining."

She gazed past his shoulder to the wreckage of the SUV. "There is?"

He took her hand. "I fell in love with you."

Her lips pinched together. "Is that Jack Dalton talking? Or Nick Racine?"

"Does it matter? They're all me."

Her eyes grew brighter. "Does this mean you won't have to go into witness protection after you testify?"

"If I remember correctly, the agreement I made with the federal prosecutors has me testifying in closed court as Tony Perez. After the trial, Tony disappears. And I go back to my life."

"We can be together?"

"That's right." He caught hold of her hand and pulled her into an easy embrace. "We're together. Until you get sick of me."

"Not going to happen." She rested her head on his chest. "No way can I leave you before I have my Pulitzer-winning story written. It just keeps getting better and better. I start out with the story of a federal witness on the run, and then you turn out to be an undercover agent with amnesia."

His heart sank. This was going to be an obstacle. "You can't write this story."

NO MATTER HOW MANY times he explained it to her, Caitlyn still didn't understand. In the hangar of the small airport where they were waiting for the private jet that would take Jack to Chicago, she paced back and forth in front of him.

"What if I don't use your real name or any of your aliases?"

"You'd still be in danger." He shifted on the worn leather sofa that was pushed up against the metal wall of the hangar. "People who have a problem with me—cartels like Rojas—would know they could find me through you."

She flung herself onto the sofa beside him. Though she would have preferred having this conversation in private, he had two marshals and another DEA agent keeping an eye on him. They stood in a clump by the open door of the hangar. All of them wore sunglasses. All of them were armed.

Her time with Jack was limited. The plane had already landed and was taxiing toward the hangar.

"What happens," she asked, "when we're together and somebody wants to know what you do for a living?"

"Tell them I'm a Sunday school teacher. Or an independently wealthy mogul."

"Even my friends?"

"Especially your friends."

"I hate this." Her life as a journalist was based on ferreting out the truth. How could she live a lie?

He leaned forward, resting his elbows on his knees. "There is a solution. You could have your story published under someone else's name."

"Then who's going to pick up my Pulitzer?"

The main purpose of writing this story was to reestablish herself as an investigative reporter. If she gave the writing credit to someone else, she'd be back to zero. "I have a better idea. You could quit your job."

He shook his head. "I'm pretty good at what I do."

"So am I."

She'd never anticipated this kind of impasse. Before she got involved with Jack, her main project was fixing the roof on the barn. She'd been thinking about giving up her career. It was his belief in her that reminded her how much she loved being a journalist. She couldn't turn her back on a story like this.

The DEA agent approached them. "Time to go."

"Give me a minute," Jack said.

They both stood, and she looked up at him. "You know, I could just write the story, anyway."

"That's your choice."

Her decision was clear. She could be with him and live a lie. Or she could write her story and say goodbye. "I want both."

He rested his hands on her shoulders and gave her a quick kiss. "I hope I'll see you when the trial is over."

As she watched him walk away, her vision blurred with tears. Love wasn't supposed to be this hard.

Chapter Twenty-Three

Nick Racine, aka Tony Perez, was under close protection for the two-week duration of the Rojas trial in Chicago. No phone calls. No emails. No meetings. If he'd insisted, he could have made some kind of arrangement to contact Caitlyn, but he wanted to give her space.

He missed her. It wasn't the same kind of devastating pain he'd felt after Elena's murder. Caitlyn's absence was a gnawing ache that grew sharper with every hour they were apart. There was so much he wanted to tell her, so many things he'd learned about himself.

His childhood was something he never wanted to clearly remember. An alcoholic father. A mother who deserted him. And years in foster care. The only positive was that he'd learned how to fight at an early age.

His financial situation didn't elevate him to mogul status, but he was well-set. He didn't own property, but he did have a numbered Swiss bank account in a different name.

There were dozens of identities he'd used, but the only person he wanted to be was Jack Dalton, the man who was loved by Caitlyn Morris.

At the Federal Courthouse in Chicago, he waited in the hallway outside the courtroom where the trail had taken place. The jury had finished their deliberations.

As a witness, he wasn't allowed inside the room where

he could see the look on Tom Rojas's face, but he wanted to know the verdict as soon as it was announced. Gregorio Rojas hadn't survived the car crash. If his brother was found guilty, the cartel was dead. Jack's revenge was complete.

Mentally, he corrected himself. Nick Racine had lived for revenge and allowed his grief to poison his life. As Jack, he had much more to live for. The future was within his grasp. He just had to make Caitlyn see things his way.

He sensed her presence and turned his head. There she was, striding confidently down the hallway toward him. Her newly trimmed blond hair fell to her shoulders in a smooth curtain. The skirt on her white linen suit was short enough to be interesting. Her high heels were red.

He stood to meet her, and when she stopped a few feet away from him, he was itching to yank her into his arms, to mess up her coiffed hair and kiss the lipstick off her mouth.

With a grin, he said, "You clean up good."

"So do you." She reached toward him and glided her fingers along the lapel of his jacket. "A designer suit."

"It turns out that I've got good taste."

"I knew that. After all, you like me."

Having her this close was driving him crazy. She was everything he wanted. "The way I feel about you goes a lot deeper than liking."

The door to the courtroom swung open. They were about to hear what the jury had decided. This was the moment Jack had been waiting for, the reason he'd taken the Tony Perez identity, the culmination of his revenge.

A woman stepped into the hall. "He's guilty."

Jack should have felt elation, but all he could do was stare into Caitlyn's blue eyes and hope. "It's over. I'm a free man."

She placed a newspaper in his hand. "The front-page article is about corruption in the U.S. Marshals Service. Patterson and Bryant don't come off well."

They were already in jail, and he hoped they would stay there for a long time. Jack glanced at the article, then back at her. "I guess you made your decision."

"I did." With a manicured fingernail she pointed to the byline. "That's my friend. There's no mention of you or me in the article. I'm just an unnamed source."

"You chose me."

"I chose both," she said. "As a matter of fact, I sold a four-part series to a magazine based on something I learned about when I was with you. Amnesia."

"Is the story about what happened?"

"Not everything is about you, big guy." She grinned. "I've been interviewing shrinks and experts. There's a guy who lost his memory for thirteen years, started a new life and got married. Then he woke up one day and remembered who he was. And a woman who—"

"Little Miss Know-It-All."

"I had to write about it," she said. "Because of you. Because you're unforgettable."

He pulled her into his arms and kissed her. The reality of holding her was better than his memories.

No matter what it took, he would never let her go.

* * * * *

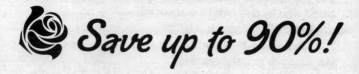